"I am Slippery Jim diGriz— THE STAINLESS STEEL RAT

"There aren't many like me in the Universe. I can switch personalities and faces in a flash—rob any bank in any star system, no matter if the guards are robot, human, or *other*—con a space captain out of his ship— start a war or stop one, whichever pays the most.

"I'm so slippery that when the cops finally caught up with me, there was only one thing they could do.

"They made me a cop . . ."

Berkley books by Harry Harrison

THE ADVENTURES OF THE STAINLESS STEEL RAT

THE DEATHWORLD TRILOGY

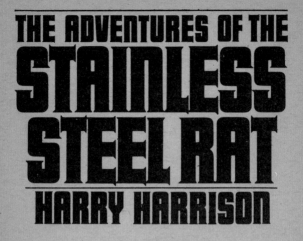

THE ADVENTURES OF THE STAINLESS STEEL RAT

HARRY HARRISON

BERKLEY BOOKS, NEW YORK

THE ADVENTURES OF THE STAINLESS STEEL RAT

A Berkley Book / published by arrangement with
the author

PRINTING HISTORY
Berkley edition / August 1978
Sixth printing / April 1982

CONTENTS

The Stainless Steel Rat   1

The Stainless Steel Rat's Revenge   127

The Stainless Steel Rat Saves the World   277

For Hans Stefan Santesson

THE ADVENTURES OF THE STAINLESS STEEL RAT

The Stainless Steel Rat

1

WHEN THE OFFICE door opened suddenly I knew the game was up. It had been a money-maker—but it was all over. As the cop walked in I sat back in the chair and put on a happy grin. He had the same somber expression and heavy foot that they all have—and the same lack of humor. I almost knew to the word what he was going to say before he uttered a syllable.

"James Bolivar diGriz I arrest you on the charge—"

I was waiting for the word *charge*, I thought it made a nice touch that way. As he said it I pressed the button that set off the charge of black powder in the ceiling, the crossbeam buckled and the three-ton safe dropped through right on the top of the cop's head. He squashed very nicely, thank you. The cloud of plaster dust settled and all I could see of him was one hand, slightly crumpled. It twitched a bit and the index finger pointed at me accusingly. His voice was a little muffled by the safe and sounded a bit annoyed. In fact he repeated himself a bit.

". . . On the charge of illegal entry, theft, forgery—"

He ran on like that for a while, it was an impressive list but I had heard it all before. I didn't let it interfere with my stuffing all the money from the desk drawers into my suitcase. The list ended with a new charge and I would swear on a stack of thousand credit notes *that* high that there was a hurt tone in his voice.

"In addition the charge of assaulting a police robot will be added to your record. This was foolish since my brain and larynx are armored and in my midsection—"

"That I know well, George, but your little two-way radio is in the top of your pointed head and I don't want you reporting to your friends just yet."

One good kick knocked the escape panel out of the wall and gave access to the steps to the basement. As I skirted the rubble on the floor the robot's fingers snapped out at my leg, but I had been waiting for that and they closed about two inches short. I have been followed by enough police robots to know by now how indestructible they are. You can blow them up or knock them down and they

3

keep coming after you; dragging themselves by one good finger and spouting saccharine morality all the while. That's what this one was doing. Give up my life of crime and pay my debt to society and such. I could still hear his voice echoing down the stairwell as I reached the basement.

Every second was timed now. I had about three minutes before they would be on my tail, and it would take me exactly one minute and eight seconds to get clear of the building. That wasn't much of a lead and I would need all of it. Another kick panel opened out into the label-removing room. None of the robots looked up as I moved down the aisle—I would have been surprised if they had. They were all low-grade M types, short on brains and good only for simple, repetitive work. That was why I hired them. They had no curiosity as to why they were taking the labels off the filled cans of azote fruits, or what was at the other end of the moving belt that brought the cans through the wall. They didn't even look up when I unlocked the Door That Was Never Unlocked that led through the wall. I left it open behind me as I had no more secrets now.

Keeping next to the rumbling belt, I stepped through the jagged hole I had chopped in the wall of the government warehouse. I had installed the belt too, this and the hole were the illegal acts that I had to do myself. Another locked door opened into the warehouse. The automatic fork-lift truck was busily piling cans onto the belt and digging fresh ones out of the ceiling-high piles. This fork-lift had hardly enough brains to be called a robot, it just followed taped directions to load the cans. I stepped around it and dog-trotted down the aisle. Behind me the sounds of my illegal activity died away. It gave me a warm feeling to still hear it going full blast like that.

It *had* been one of the nicest little rackets I had ever managed. For a small capital outlay I had rented the warehouse that backed on the government warehouse. A simple hole in the wall and I had access to the entire stock of stored goods, long-term supplies that I knew would be untouched for months or years in a warehouse this size. Untouched, that is, until I came along.

After the hole had been made and the belt installed it was just a matter of business. I hired the robots to remove the old labels and substitute the colorful ones I had printed. Then I marketed my goods in a strictly legal fashion. My stock was the best and due to my imaginative operation my costs were very low. I could afford to undersell my competitors and still make a handsome profit. The local wholesalers had been quick to sense a bargain and I had orders for months ahead. It *had* been a good operation—and could have gone on for quite a while.

I stifled that train of thought before it started. One lesson that has to be remembered in my line of business is that when an operation is over it is OVER! The temptation to stay just one more day or to cash just one more check can be almost overwhelming, ah, how well I know. I also know that it is also the best way to get better acquainted with the police.

> *Turn your back and walk away—*
> *And live to graft another day.*

That's my motto and it's a good one. I got where I am because I stuck to it.

And daydreams aren't part of getting away from the police.

I pushed all thoughts from my mind as I reached the end of the aisle. The entire area outside must have been swarming with cops by this time and I had to move fast and make no mistakes. A fast look right and left. Nobody in sight. Two steps ahead and press the elevator button. I had put a meter on this back elevator and it showed that the thing was used once a month on the average.

It arrived in about three seconds, empty, and I jumped in, thumbing the roof button at the same time. The ride seemed to go on forever, but that was just subjective. By the record it was exactly fourteen seconds. This was the most dangerous part of the trip. I tightened up as the elevator slowed. My .75 caliber recoilless was in my hand, that would take care of one cop, but no more.

The door shuffled open and I relaxed. Nothing. They must have the entire area covered on the ground so they hadn't bothered to put cops on the roof.

In the open air now I could hear the sirens fot the first time—a wonderful sound. They must have had half of the entire police force out from the amount of noise they were making. I accepted it as any artist accepts tribute.

The board was behind the elevator shaft where I had left it. A little weather-stained but still strong. A few seconds to carry it to the edge of the parapet and reach it across to the next building.

Gently, this was the one dangerous spot where speed didn't count. Carefully into the end of the board, the suitcase held against my chest to keep my center of gravity over the board. One step at a time. A thousand-foot drop to the ground. If you don't look down you can't fall . . .

Over. Time for speed. The board behind the parapet, if they didn't see it at first my trail would be covered for a while at least. Ten fast steps and there was the door to the stairwell. It opened easily—and it better have—I had put enough oil on the hinges. Once inside I threw the bolt and took a long, deep breath. I wasn't out of it yet, but the worst part where I ran the most risk was past. Two uninterrupted minutes here and they would never find James Bolivar, alias "Slippery Jim", diGriz.

The stairwell at the roof was a musty, badly lit cubicle that was never visited. I had checked it carefully a week before for phono and optic bugs and it had been clear. The dust looked undisturbed, except for my own footprints. I had to take a chance that it hadn't been bugged since then. The calculated risk must be accepted in this business.

Good-by James diGriz, weight ninety-eight kilos, age about forty-five, thick in the middle and heavy in the jowls, a typical business man whose picture graces the police files of a thousand planets—also his fingerprints. They went first. When you wear them they feel like a second skin, a touch of solvent though and they peel off like a pair of transparent gloves.

All my clothes next—and then the girdle in reverse—that lovely paunch that straps around my belly and holds twenty kilos of lead mixed with thermite. A quick wipe from the bottle of bleach and my hair was its natural shade of brown, the eyebrows, too. The nose plugs and cheek pads hurt coming out, but that only lasts a second. Then the blue-eyed contact lenses. This process leaves me mother-naked and I always feel as if I have been born again. In a sense it is true, I had become a new man, twenty kilos lighter, ten years younger and with a completely different description. The large suitcase held a complete change of clothes and a pair of dark-rimmed glasses that replaced the contact lenses. All the loose money fitted neatly into a brief case.

When I straightened up I really felt as if ten years had been stripped from me. I was so used to wearing that weight that I never noticed it—until it was gone. Put a real spring in my step.

The thermite would take care of all the evidence. I kicked it all into a heap and triggered the fuse. It caught with a roar and bottles, clothes, bag, shoes, weights, et al, burned with a cheerful glare. The police would find a charred spot on the cement and microanalysis might get them a few molecules off the walls, but that was all they would get. The glare of the burning thermite threw jumping shadows around me as I walked down three flights to the one hundred twelfth floor.

Luck was still with me, there was no one on the floor when I opened the door. One minute later the express elevator let me and a handful of other business types out into the lobby.

Only one door was open to the street and a portable TV camera was trained on it. No attempt was being made to stop people from going in and out of the building, most of them didn't even notice the camera and the little group of cops around it. I walked towards it at an even pace. Strong nerves count for a lot in this business.

For one instant I was square in the field of that cold, glass eye, then I was past. Nothing happened so I knew I was clear. That camera must have fed directly to the main computer at police headquarters, if my description had been close enough to the one they had on file those robots would have been notified and I would have been pinned before I had taken a step. You can't outmove a computer-robot combination, not when they move and react in micro-seconds—but you can outthink them. I had done it again.

A cab took me about ten blocks away. I waited until it was out of sight then took another one. It wasn't until I was in the third cab that I felt safe enough to go to the space terminal. The sounds of sirens were growing fainter and fainter behind me and only an occasional police car tore by in the opposite direction.

They were sure making a big fuss over a little larceny, but that's the way it goes on these overcivilized worlds. Crime is such a rarity now that the police really get carried away when they run across some. In a way I can't blame them, giving out traffic tickets must be an awful dull job. I really believe they ought to thank me for putting a little excitement in their otherwise dull lives.

2

IT WAS A nice ride to the spaceport being located, of course, far out of town. I had time to lean back and watch the scenery and gather my thoughts. Even time to be a little philosophical. For one thing I could enjoy a good cigar again, I smoked only cigarettes in my other personality and never violated that personality, even in strictest privacy. The cigars were still fresh in the pocket humidor where I had put them six months ago. I sucked a long mouthful and blew the smoke out at the flashing scenery. It was good to be off the job, just about as good as being on it. I could never make my mind up which period I enjoyed more—I guess they are both right at the time.

My life is so different from that of the overwhelming majority of people in our society that I doubt if I could even explain it to them. They exist in a fat, rich union of worlds that have almost forgotten the meaning of the word crime. There are few malcontents and even fewer that are socially maladjusted. The few of these that are born, in spite of centuries of genetic control, are caught early and the aberration quickly adjusted. Some don't show their weakness until they are adults, they are the ones who try their hand at petty crime—burglary, shoplifting or such. They get away with it for a week or two or a month or two, depending on the degree of their native intelligence. But sure as atomic decay—and just as pre-destined—the police reach out and pull them in.

That is almost the full extent of crime in our organized, dandified society. Ninety-nine per cent of it, let's say. It is that last and vital one per cent that keeps the police departments in business. That one per cent is me, and a handful of men scattered around the galaxy. Theoretically we can't exist, and if we do exist we can't operate—but we do. We are the rats in the wainscoting of society—we operate outside of their barriers and outside of their rules. Society had more rats when the rules were looser, just as the old wooden buildings had more rats than the concrete buildings that came later. But they still had rats. Now that society is all ferroconcrete and stainless steel there are fewer gaps between the joints, and it takes a smart rat to find them. A stainless steel rat is right at home in this environment.

It is a proud and lonely thing to be a stainless steel rat—and it is the greatest experience in the galaxy if you can get away with it. The sociological experts can't seem to agree why we exist, some even doubt that we do. The most widely accepted theory says that we are victims of delayed psychological disturbance that shows no evidence in childhood when it can be detected and corrected and only appears later in life. I have naturally given a lot of thought to the topic and I don't hold with that idea at all.

A few years back I wrote a small book on the subject—under a nom de plume of course—that was rather well received. My theory is that the aberration is a philosophical one, not a psychological one. At a certain stage the realization strikes through that one must either live outside of society's bonds or die of absolute boredom. There is no future or freedom in the circumscribed life and the only other life is complete rejection of the rules. There is no longer room for the soldier of fortune or the gentleman adventurer who can live both within and outside of society. Today it is all or nothing. To save my own sanity I chose the nothing.

The cab just reached the spaceport as I hit on this negative line of thought and I was glad to abandon it. Loneliness is the thing to fear in this business, that and self-pity can destroy you if they get the upper hand. Action has always helped me, the elation of danger and escape always clears my mind. When I paid the cab I short-changed the driver right under his nose, palming one of the credit notes in the act of handing it to him. He was blind as a riveted bulkhead, his gullibility had me humming with delight. The tip I gave him more than made up the loss since I only do this sort of petty business to break the monotony.

There was a robot clerk behind the ticket window, he had that extra third eye in the center of his forehead that meant a camera. It clicked slightly as I purchased a ticket, recording my face and destination. A normal precaution on the part of the police, I would have been surprised if it hadn't happened. My destination was intersystem so I doubted if the picture would appear any place except in the files. I wasn't making an interstellar hop this time, as I usually did after a big job, it wasn't necessary. After a job a single world or a small system is too small for more work, but Beta Cygnus has a system of almost twenty planets all with terrafied weather. This planet, III, was too hot now, but the rest of the system was wide open. There was a lot of commercial rivalry within the system and I knew their police departments didn't co-operate too well. They would pay the price for that. My ticket was for Moriy, number XVIII, a large and mostly agricultural planet.

There were a number of little stores at the spaceport. I shopped them carefully and outfitted a new suitcase with a complete wardrobe and traveling essentials. The tailor was saved for last. He ran up a couple of traveling suits and a formal kilt for me and I took them into the fitting booth. Strictly by accident I managed to hang one of the suits over the optic bug on the wall and made undressing sounds with my feet while I doctored the ticket I had just bought. The other end of my cigar cutter was a punch; with it I altered the keyed holes that indicated my destination. I was now going to planet X, not XVIII, and I had lost almost two hundred credits with the alteration. That's the secret of ticket and order changing. Don't raise the face value—there is too good a chance that this will be noticed. If you lower the value and lose money on the deal, even if it is caught, people will be sure it is a mistake on the machine's part. There is never the shadow of a doubt, since why should anyone change a ticket to lose money?

Before the police could be suspicious I had the suit off the bug and tried it on, taking my time. Almost everything was ready now, I had about an hour to kill before the ship left. I spent the time wisely by going to an automatic cleaner and having all my new clothes cleaned and pressed. Nothing interests a customs man more than a suitcase full of unworn clothes.

Customs was a snap and when the ship was about half full I boarded her and took a seat near the hostess. I flirted with her until she walked away, having classified me in the category of MALE, BRASH, ANNOYING. An old girl who had the seat next to mine also had me filed in the same drawer and was looking out of the window with obvious ice on her shoulder. I dozed off happily since there is one thing better than not being noticed and that is being noticed and filed into a category. Your description gets mixed up with every other guy in the file and that is the end of it.

When I woke up we were almost to planet X, I half dozed in the chair until we touched down, then smoked a cigar while my bag cleared customs. My locked brief case of money raised no suspicions since I had foresightedly forged papers six months ago with my occupation listed as *bank messenger*. Interplanet credit was almost nonexistent in this system, so the customs men were used to seeing a lot of cash go back and forth.

Almost by habit I confused the trail a little more and ended up in the large manufacturing city of Brouggh over one thousand kilometers from the point where I had landed. Using an entirely new set of identification papers I registered at a quiet hotel in the suburbs.

Usually after a big job like this I rest up for a month or two; this was one time though I didn't feel like a rest. While I was making small purchases around town to rebuild the personality of James diGriz, I was also keeping my eyes open for new business opportunities. The very first day I was out I saw what looked like a natural—and each day it looked better and better.

One of the main reasons I have stayed out of the arms of the law for as long as I have, is that I have never repeated myself. I have dreamed up some of the sweetest little rackets, run them off once, then stayed away from them forever after. About the only thing they had in common was the fact that they all made money. About the only thing I hadn't hit to date was out and out armed robbery. It was time for a change and it looked like that was it.

While I was rebuilding the paunchy personality of Slippery Jim I was making plans for the operation. Just about the time the finger-print gloves were ready the entire business was planned. It was simple like all good operations should be, the less details there are, the less things there are that can go wrong.

I was going to hold up Moraio's, the largest retail store in the city. Every evening at exactly the same time, an armored car took the day's receipts to the bank. It was a tempting prize—a gigantic sum in untraceable small bills. The only real problem as far as I was concerned was how one man could handle the sheer bulk and weight of all that money. When I had an answer to that the entire operation was ready.

All the preparations were, of course, made only in my mind until the personality of James diGriz was again ready. The day I slipped that weighted belly back on, I felt I was back in uniform. I lit my first cigarette almost with satisfaction, then went to work. A day or two for some purchases and a few simple thefts and I was ready. I scheduled the following afternoon for the job.

A large tractor-truck that I had bought was the key to the operation—along with some necessary alterations I had made to the interior. I parked the truck in an "L" shaped alley about a half mile from Moraio's. The truck almost completely blocked the alley but that wasn't important since it was used only in the early morning. It was a leisurely stroll back to the department store, I reached it at almost the same moment that the armored truck pulled up. I leaned against the wall of the gigantic building while the guards carried out the money. My money.

To someone of little imagination I suppose it would have been an awe-inspiring sight. At least five armed guards standing around the entrance, two more inside the truck as well as the driver and his assistant. As an added precaution there were three monocycles purring next to the curb. They would go with the truck as protection on the road. Oh, very impressive. I had to stifle a grin behind my cigarette when I thought about what was going to happen to those elaborate precautions.

I had been counting the handtrucks of money as they rolled out of the door. There were always fifteen, no more, no less; this practice made it easy for me to know the exact time to begin. Just as fourteen was being loaded into the armored truck, load number fifteen appeared in the store entrance. The truck driver had been counting the way I had, he stepped down from the cab and moved to the door in the rear in order to lock it when loading was finished.

We synchronized perfectly as we strolled by each other. At the moment he reached the rear door I reached the cab. Quietly and smoothly I climbed up into it and slammed the door behind me. The assistant had just enough time to open his mouth and pop his eyes when I placed an anesthetic bomb on his lap; he slumped in an instant. I was, of course, wearing the correct filter plugs in my nostrils. As I started the motor with my left hand, I threw a larger bomb through the connecting window to the rear with my right. There were some reassuring thumps as the guards there dropped over the bags of change.

This entire process hadn't taken six seconds. The guards on the steps were just waking up to the fact that something was wrong. I gave them a cheerful wave through the window and gunned the armored truck away from the curb. One of them tried to run and throw himself through the open rear door but he was a little too late. It all had happened so fast that not one of them had thought to shoot, I had been sure there would be a *few* bullets. The sedentary life on these planets does slow the reflexes.

The monocycle drivers caught on a lot faster, they were after me before the truck had gone a hundred feet. I slowed down until they had caught up, then stamped on the accelerator, keeping just enough speed so they couldn't pass me.

Their sirens were screaming of course and they had their guns working; it was just as I had planned. We tore down the street like jet racers and the traffic melted away before us. They didn't have time to think and realize that *they* were making sure the road was clear for my escape. The situation was very humorous and I'm afraid I chuckled out loud as I tooled the truck around the tight corners.

Of course the alarm had been turned in and the road blocks must have been forming up ahead—but that half mile went by fast at the speed we were doing. It was a matter of seconds before I saw the alley mouth ahead. I turned the truck into it, at the same time pressing the button on my pocket short wave.

Along the entire length of the alley my smoke bombs ignited. They were, of course, home made, as was all my equipment, nevertheless they produced an adequately dense cloud in that narrow alley. I pulled the truck a bit to the right until the fenders scraped the wall and only slightly reduced my speed, this way I could steer by touch. The monocycle drivers of course couldn't do this and had the choice of stopping or rushing headlong into the darkness. I hope they made the right decision and none of them were hurt.

The same radio impulse that triggered the bombs was supposed to have opened the rear door of the trailer truck up ahead and dropped the ramp. It had worked fine when I had tested it, I could only hope now that it did the same in practice. I tried to estimate the distance I had gone in the alley by timing my speed, but I was a little off. The front wheels of the truck hit the ramp with a destructive crash and the armored truck bounced rather than rolled into the interior of the larger van. I was jarred around a bit and had just enough sense left to jam on the brakes before I plowed right through into the cab.

Smoke from the bombs made a black midnight of everything, that and my shaken-up brains almost ruined the entire operation. Valuable seconds went by while I leaned against the truck wall trying to get oriented. I don't know how long it took, when I finally did stumble back to the rear door I could hear the guards' voices calling back and forth through the smoke. They heard the bent ramp creak as I lifted it so I threw two gas bombs out to quiet them down.

The smoke was starting to thin as I climbed up to the cab of the tractor and gunned it into life. A few feet down the alley and I broke through into sunlight. The alley mouth opened out into a main street a few feet ahead and I saw two police cars tear by. When the truck reached the street I stopped and took careful note of all witnesses. None of them showed any interest in the truck or the alley. Apparently all the commotion was still at the other end of the alley. I poured power into the engine and rolled out into the street, away from the store I had just robbed.

Of course I only went a few blocks in that direction then turned down a side street. At the next corner I turned again and headed back towards Moraio's, the scene of my recent crime. The cool air coming in the window soon had me feeling better, I actually whistled a bit as I threaded the big truck through the service roads.

It would have been fine to go up the highway in front of Moraio's, and see all the excitement, but that would have been only asking for trouble. Time was still important. I had carefully laid out a route that avoided all congested traffic and this was what I followed. It was only a matter of minutes before I was pulling into the loading area in the back of the big store. There was a certain amount of excitement here but it was lost in the normal bustle of commerce. Here and there a knot of truck drivers or shipping foremen were exchanging views on the robbery, since robots don't gossip the normal work was going on. The men were, of course, so excited that no attention was paid to my truck when I pulled into the parking line next to the other vans. I killed the engine and settled back with a satisfied sigh.

The first part was complete. The second part of the operation was just as important though. I dug into my paunch for the kit that I always take on the job—for such an emergency as this. Normally, I don't believe in stimulants, but I ws still groggy from the banging around. Two cc's of Linoten in my ante cubital cleared that up quickly enough. The spring was back in my step when I went into the back of the van.

The driver's assistant and the guards were still out and would stay that way for at least ten hours. I arranged them in a neat row in the front of the truck where they wouldn't be in my way, and went to work.

The armored car almost filled the body of the trailer as I knew it would; therefore I had fastened the boxes to the walls. They were fine, strong shipping boxes with Moraio's printed all over them. It had been a minor theft from their warehouse that should go unnoticed. I pulled the boxes down and folded them for packing, I was soon sweating and had to take my shirt off as I packed the money bundles into the boxes.

It took almost two hours to stuff and seal the boxes with tape. Every ten minutes or so I would check through the peephole in the door; only the normal activities were going on. The police undoubtedly had the entire town sealed and were tearing it apart building by building looking for the truck. I was fairly sure that the last place they would think of looking was the rear of the robbed store.

The warehouse that had provided the boxes had also provided a supply of shipping forms. I fixed one of these on each box, addressed to different pick-up addresses and marked paid of course, and was ready to finish the operation.

It was almost dark by this time, however I knew that the shipping department would be busy most of the night. The engine caught on the first revolution and I pulled out of the parking rank and backed slowly up to the platform. There was a relatively quiet area where the shipping dock met the receiving dock, I stopped the trailer as close to the dividing line as I could. I didn't open the rear door until all the workmen were faced in a different direction. Even the stupidest of them would have been interested in why a truck was unloading the firm's own boxes. As I piled them up on the platform I threw a tarp over them, it only took a few minutes. Only when the truck gates were closed and locked did I pull off the tarp and sit down on the boxes for a smoke.

It wasn't a long wait. Before the cigarette was finished a robot from the shipping department passed close enough for me to call him.

"Over there. The M-19 that was loading these burned out a brakeband, you better see that they're taken care of."

His eyes glowed with the light of duty. Some of these higher M types take their job very seriously. I had to step back quickly as the fork lifts and M-trucks appeared out of the doors behind me. There was a scurry of loading and sorting and my haul vanished down the platform. I lighted another cigarette and watched for a while as the boxes were coded and stamped and loaded on the outgoing trucks and local belts.

All that was left for me now was the disposing of the truck on some side street and changing personalities.

As I was getting into the truck I realized for the first time that something was wrong. I, of course, had been keeping an eye on the gate—but not watching it closely enough. Trucks had been going in and out. Now the realization hit me like a hammer blow over the solar plexus. They were the same trucks going both ways. A large, red cross-country job was just pulling out. I heard the echo of its exhaust roar down the street—then die away to an idling grumble. When it roared up again it didn't go away, instead the truck came in through the second gate. There were police cars waiting outside that wall. Waiting for me.

3

FOR THE FIRST time in my career I felt the sharp fear of the hunted man. This was the first time I had ever had the police on my trail when I wasn't expecting them. The money was lost, that much was certain, but I was no longer concerned with that. It was me they were after now.

Think first, then act. I was safe enough for the moment. They were, of course, moving in on me, going slowly as they had no idea of where I was in the giant loading yard. How had they found me? *That* was the important point. The local police are used to an almost crimeless world, they couldn't have found my trail this quickly. In fact, I hadn't left a trail. Whoever had set the trap here had done it with logic and reason.

Unbidden the words jumped into my mind.

The Special Corps.

Nothing was ever printed about it, only a thousand whispered words heard on a thousand worlds around the galaxy. The Special Corps, the branch of the League that took care of the troubles that individual planets couldn't solve. The Corps was supposed to have finished off the remnants of Haskell's Raiders after the peace, of putting the illegal T & Z Traders out of business, of finally catching Inskipp. And now they were after me.

They were out there waiting for me to make a break. They were thinking of all the ways out just as I was—and they were blocking them. I had to think fast and I had to think right.

Only two ways out. Through the gates or through the store. The gates were too well covered to make a break, in the store there would be other exits. It had to be that way. Even as I made the conclusion I knew that other minds had made it too, that men were moving in to cover those doors. That thought brought fear—and made me angry as well. The very idea that someone could outthink me was odious. They could try all right—but I would give them a run for their money. I still had a few tricks left.

First, a little misdirection. I started the truck, left it in low gear and aimed it at the gate. When it was going straight I locked the steering wheel with the friction clamp and dropped out the far side of the cab and strolled back to the warehouse. Once inside I moved faster. Behind me I heard some shots, a heavy crump, and a lot of shouting. That was more like it.

The night locks were connected on the doors that led to the store proper. An old-fashioned alarm that I could disconnect in a few moments. My pick-locks opened the door and I gave it a quick kick with my foot and turned away. There were no alarm bells, but I knew that somewhere in the building an indicator showed that the door was opened. As fast as I could run I went to the last door on the opposite side of the building. This time I made sure the alarm was disconnected before I went through the door. I locked it behind me.

It is the hardest job in the world to run and be quiet at the same time. My lungs were burning before I reached the employees' entrance. A few times I saw flashlights ahead and had to double down different aisles, it was mostly luck that I made it without being spotted. There were two men in uniform standing in front of the door I wanted to go out of. Keeping as close to the wall as I could, I made it to within twenty feet of them before I threw the gas grenade. For one second I was sure that they had gas masks on and I had reached the end of the road—then they slumped down. One of them was blocking the door, I rolled him aside and slid it open a few inches.

The searchlight couldn't have been more than thirty feet from the door; when it flashed on the light was more pain than glare. I dropped the instant it came on and the slugs from the machine pistol ate a line of glaring holes across the door. My ears were numb from the roar of the exploding slugs and I could just make out the thud of running footsteps. My own .75 was in my hand and I put an entire clip of slugs through the door, aiming high so I wouldn't hurt anyone. It would not stop them, but it should slow them down.

They returned the fire, must have been a whole squad out there. Pieces of plastic flew out of the back wall and slugs screamed down the corridor. It was good cover, I knew there was nobody coming up behind me. Keeping as flat as I could I crawled in the opposite direction, out of the line of fire. I turned two corners before I was far enough from the guns to risk standing up. My knees were shaky and great blobs of color kept fogging my vision. The searchlight had done a good job, I could barely see at all in the dim light.

I kept moving slowly, trying to get as far away from the gunfire as possible. The squad outside had fired as soon as I had opened the door, that meant standing orders to shoot at anyone who tried to leave the building. A nice trap. The cops inside would keep looking until they found me. If I tried to leave I would be blasted. I was beginning to feel very much like a trapped rat.

Every light in the store came on and I stopped, frozen. I was near the wall of a large farm-goods showroom. Across the room from me were three soldiers. We spotted each other at the same time, I dived for the door with bullets slapping all around me. The military was in it too, they sure must have wanted me bad. A bank of elevators was on the other side of the door—and stairs leading up. I hit the elevator in one bounce and punched the sub-basement button, and just got out ahead of the closing doors. The stairs were back towards the approaching soldiers, I felt like I was running right into their guns. I must have made the turn into the stairs a split second ahead of their arrival. Up the stairs and around the first landing before they were even with the bottom. Luck was still on my side. They hadn't seen me and were sure I had gone down. I sagged against the wall, listening to the shouts and whistle blowing as they turned the hunt towards the basement.

There was one smart one in the bunch. While the others were all following the phony trail I heard him start slowly up the stairs. I didn't have any gas grenades left, all I could do was climb up ahead of him, trying to do it without making a sound.

He came on slowly and steadily and I stayed ahead of him. We went up four flights that way, me in my stockinged feet with my shoes around my neck, his heavy boots behind me making a dull rasping on the metal stairs.

As I started up the fifth flight I stopped, my foot halfway up a step.

Someone else was coming down, someone wearing the same kind of military boots. I found the door to the hall, opened it behind me and slipped through. There was a long hall in front of me lined with offices of some kind. I began to run the length of it, trying to reach a turning before the door behind me could open and those exploding slugs tear me in half. The hall seemed endless and I suddenly realized I would never reach the end in time.

I was a rat looking for a hole—and there was none. The doors were locked, all of them, I tried each as I came to it, knowing I would never make it. That stairwell door was opening behind me and the gun was coming up. I didn't dare turn and look but I could feel it. When the door opened under my hand I fell through before I realized what had happened. I locked it behind me and leaned against it in the darkness, panting like a spent animal. Then the light came on and I saw the man sitting behind the desk, smiling at me.

There is a limit to the amount of shock the human body can absorb. I'd had mine. I didn't care if he shot me or offered a cigarette—I had reached the end of my line. He did neither. He offered me a cigar instead.

"Have one of these, diGriz, I believe they're your brand."

The body is a slave of habit. Even with death a few inches away it will respond to established custom. My fingers moved of their own volition and took the cigar, my lips clenched it and my lungs sucked it into life. And all the time my eyes watched the man behind the desk waiting for death to reach out.

It must have shown. He waved towards a chair and carefully kept both hands in sight on top of the desk. I still had my gun, it was trained on him.

"Sit down diGriz and put that cannon away. If I wanted to kill you, I could have done it a lot easier than herding you into this room." His eyebrows moved up in surprise when he saw the expression on my face. "Don't tell me you thought it was an accident that you ended up here?"

I had, up until that moment, and the lack of intelligent reasoning on my part brought on a wave of shame that snapped me back to reality. I had been outwitted and outfought, the least I could do was surrender graciously. I threw the gun on the desk and dropped into the offered chair. He swept the pistol neatly into a drawer and relaxed a bit himself.

"Had me worried there for a minute, the way you stood there rolling your eyes and waving this piece of field artillery around."

"Who are you?"

He smiled at the abruptness of my tone. "Well, it doesn't matter who I am. What does matter is the organization that I represent."

"The Corps?"

"Exactly. The Special Corps. You didn't think I was the local police, did you? They have orders to shoot you on sight. It was only after I told them how to find you that they let the Corps come along on the job. I have some of my men in the building, they're the ones who herded you up here. The rest are all locals with itchy trigger fingers."

It wasn't very flattering but it was true. I had been pushed around like a class M robot, with every move charted in advance. The old boy behind the desk—for the first time I realized he was about sixty-five—really had my number. The game was over.

"All right Mr. Detective, you have me so there is no sense in gloating. What's next on the program? Psychological reorientation, lobotomy—or just plain firing squad?"

"None of those, I'm afraid. I am here to offer you a job on the Corps."

The whole thing was so ludicrous that I almost fell out of the chair laughing. Me. James diGriz, the interplanet thief working as a policeman. It was just too funny. He sat patiently, waiting until I was through.

"I will admit it has its ludicrous side—but only at first glance. If you stop to think, you will have to admit that who is better qualified to catch a thief than another thief?"

There was more than a little truth in that, but I wasn't buying my freedom by turning stool pigeon.

"An interesting offer, but I'm not getting out of this by playing the rat. There is even a code among thieves, you know."

That made him angry. He was bigger than he looked sitting down and the fist he shook in my face was as large as a shoe.

"What kind of stupidity do you call that? It sounds like a line out of a TV thriller. You've never met another crook in your whole life and you know it! And if you did you would cheerfully turn him in if you could make a profit on the deal. The entire essence of your life is individualism—that and the excitement of doing what others can't do. Well that's over now, and you better start admitting it to yourself. You can no longer be the interplanet playboy you used to be—but you *can* do a job that will require every bit of your special talents and abilities. Have you ever killed a man?"

His change of pace caught me off guard, I stumbled out an answer.

"No . . . not that I know of."

"Well you haven't, if that will make you sleep any better at night. You're not a homicidal, I checked that on your record before I came out after you. That is why I know you will join the Corps and get a great deal of pleasure out of going after the *other* kind of criminal who is sick, not just socially protesting. The man who can kill and enjoy it."

He was too convincing, he had all the answers. I had only one more argument and I threw it in with the air of a last ditch defense.

"What about the Corps, if they ever find out you are hiring half-reformed criminals to do your dirty work we will both be shot at dawn.''

This time it was his turn to laugh. I could see nothing funny so I ignored him until he was finished.

''In the first place my boy, *I* am the Corps—at least the man at the top—and what do you think *my* name is? Harold Peters Inskipp, that's what it is!''

''Not the Inskipp that—''

''The same. Inskipp the Uncatchable. The man who looted the Pharsydion II in mid-flight and pulled all those other deals I'm sure you read about in your misspent youth. I was recruited just the way you were.''

He had me on the ropes and knew it. He moved in for the kill.

''And who do you think the rest of our agents are? I don't mean the bright-eyed grads of our technical schools, like the ones on my squad downstairs. I mean the full agents. The men who plan the operations, do the preliminary fieldwork and see that everything comes off smoothly. They're crooks. All crooks. The better they were on their own, the better a job they do for the Corps. It's a great, big, brawling universe and you would be surprised at some of the problems that come up. The only men we can recruit to do the job are the ones who have already succeeded at it.

''Are you on?''

It had happened too fast and I hadn't had time to think. I would probably go on arguing for an hour. But way down in the back of my mind the decision had been made. I was going to do it, I couldn't say no.

I was losing something, and I hoped I wouldn't miss it. No matter what freedom I had working with an organization, I would still be working with other people. The old carefree, sole responsibility days were over. I was joining the ranks of society again.

There was the beginning of a warm feeling at the thought. It would at least be the end of loneliness. Friendship would make up for what I had lost.

4

I HAVE NEVER been more wrong.

The people I met were dull to the point of extinction. They treated me like just another cog going around with the rest of the wheels. I was coggy all right, and kept wondering how I had ever gotten into this mess. Not really wondering, since the memory was still quite vivid. I was carried along with the rest of the gears, their teeth sunk into mine.

We ended up on a planetoid, that much was obvious. But I hadn't the dimmest idea of what planets we were near or even what solar system we were in. Everything was highly secret and hush-hush, as this place was obviously the super-secret headquarters and main base of the Corps School too.

This part I liked. It was the only thing that kept me from cracking out. Dull as the cubes were who taught the courses, the material was something I could really sink my teeth into and shake. I began to see how crude my operations had been. With the gadgetry and techniques I soaked up I could be ten times the crook I had been before. Pushing the thought firmly away helped for a while, but it had a way of sneaking back and whispering nastily in my ear during periods of depression and gloom.

Things went from dull to dead. Half my time was spent working at the files, learning about the numberless successes and few failures of the Corps. I contemplated cracking out, yet at the same time couldn't help but wonder if this wasn't part of a testing period—to see if I had enough sticktoitiveness to last. I swallowed my temper, muffled my yawns, and took a careful look around. If I couldn't crack out—I could crack *in*. There had to be something I could do to terminate this term of penal servitude.

It wasn't easy—but I found it. By the time I tracked everything down it was well into sleep period. But that was all right. In some ways it even made it more interesting.

When it comes to picking locks and cracking safes I admit to no master. The door to Inskipp's private quarters had an old-fashioned tumbler drum that was easier to pick than my teeth. I must have gone through that door without breaking step. Quiet as I was though, Inskipp still heard me. The light came on and there he was sitting up in bed pointing a .75 caliber recoilless at my sternum.

"You should have more brains than that, diGriz," he snarled. "Creeping into my room at night! You could have been shot."

"No I couldn't," I told him, as he stowed the cannon back under his pillow. "A man with a curiosity bump as big as yours will always talk first and shoot later. And besides—none of this pussy-footing around in the dark would be necessary if your screen was open and I could have got a call through."

Inskipp yawned and poured himself a glass of water from the dispenser unit above the bed. "Just because I head the Special Corps, doesn't mean that I *am* the Special Corps," he said moistly while he drained the glass. "I have to sleep sometime. My screen is open only for emergency calls, not for every agent who needs his hand held."

"Meaning I am in the hand-holding category?" I asked with as much sweetness as I could.

"Put yourself in any category you damn well please," he grumbled as he slumped down in the bed. "And also put yourself out into the hall and see me tomorrow during working hours."

He was at my mercy, really. He wanted sleep so much. And he was going to be wide awake so very soon.

"Do you know what this is?" I asked him, poking a large glossy pic under his long broken nose. One eye opened slowly.

"Big warship of some kind, looks like Empire lines. Now for the last time—go away!" he said.

"A very good guess for this late at night," I told him cheerily. "It is a late Empire battleship of the Warlord class. Undoubtedly one of the most truly efficient engines of destruction ever manufactured. Over a half mile of defensive screens and armament that could probably turn any fleet existent today into fine radioactive ash—"

"Except for the fact that the last one was broken up for scrap over a thousand years ago," he mumbled.

I leaned over and put my lips close to his ear. So there would be no chance of misunderstanding. Speaking softly but clearly.

"True, true," I said. "But wouldn't you be just a *little* bit interested if I was to tell you that one is being built today?"

Oh, it was beautiful to watch. The covers went one way and Inskipp went the other. In a single unfolding, concerted motion he left the horizontal and recumbent and stood tensely vertical against the wall. Examining the pic of the battleship under the light. He apparently did not believe in pajama bottoms and it hurt me to see the goose bumps rising on those thin shanks. But if the legs were thin, the voice was more than full enough to make up for the difference.

"Talk, blast you diGriz—*talk!*" he roared. "What is this nonsense about a battleship? Who's building it?"

I had my nail file and was touching up a cuticle, holding it out for inspection before I said anything. From the corner of my eye I could see him getting purple about the face—but he kept quiet. I savored my small moment of power.

"Put diGriz in charge of the record room for a while, you said, that way he can learn the ropes. Burrowing around in century-old, dusty files will be just the thing for a free spirit like Slippery Jim diGriz. Teach him discipline. Show him what the Corps stands for. At the same time it will get the records in shape. They have been needing reorganization for quite a while."

Inskipp opened his mouth, made a choking noise, then closed it. He undoubtedly realized that any interruption would only lengthen my explanation, not shorten it. I smiled and nodded at his decision, then continued.

"So you thought you had me safely out of the way. Breaking my spirit under the guise of 'giving me a little background in the Corps' activities.' In this sense your plan failed. Something else happened instead. I nosed through the files and found them most interesting. Particularly the C & M setup—the Categorizer and Memory. That building full of machinery that takes in and digests news and reports from all the planets in the galaxy, indexes it to every category it can possibly relate, then files it. Great machine to work with. I had it digging out spaceship info for me, something I have always been interested in—"

"You should be," Inskipp interrupted rudely. "You've stolen enough of them in your time."

I gave him a hurt look and went on—slowly. "I won't bore you with all the details, since you seem impatient, but eventually I turned up this plan." He had it out of my fingers before it cleared my wallet.

"What are you getting at?" he mumbled as he ran his eyes over the blueprints. "This is an ordinary heavy-cargo and passenger job. It's no more a Warlord battleship than I am."

It is hard to curl your lips with contempt and talk at the same time, but I succeeded. "Of course. You don't expect them to file warship plans with the League Registry, do you? But, as I said, I know more than a little bit about ships. It seemed to me this thing was just too big for the use intended. Enough old ships are fuel-wasters, you don't have to build new ones to do that. This started me thinking and I punched for a complete list of ships that size that had been constructed in the past. You can imagine my surprise when, after three minutes of groaning, the C & M only produced six. One was built for self-sustaining colony attempt at the second galaxy. For all we know she is still on the way. The other five were all D-class colonizers, built during the Expansion when large populations were moved. Too big to be practical now.

"I was still teased, as I had no idea what a ship this large could be used for. So I removed the time interlock on the C & M and let it pick around through the entire history of space to see if it could find a comparison. It sure did. Right at the Golden Age of Empire expansion, the giant Warlord battleship. The machine even found a blueprint for me."

Inskipp grabbed again and began comparing the two prints. I leaned over his shoulder and pointed out the interesting parts.

"Notice—if the engine room specs are changed slightly to include this cargo hold, there is plenty of room for the brutes needed. This superstructure—obviously just tacked onto the plans—gets thrown away and turrets take its place. The hulls are identical. A change here, a shift there, and the stodgy freighter becomes the fast battlewagon. These changes could be made during construction, then plans filed. By the time anyone in the League found out what was being built the ship would be finished and launched. Of course, this could all be coincidence—the plans of a newly built ship agreeing to six places with those of a ship built a thousand years ago. But if you think so, I will give you hundred-to-one odds you are wrong, any size bet you name."

I wasn't winning any sucker bets that night. Inskipp had led just as crooked a youth as I had, and needed no help in smelling a fishy deal. While he pulled on his clothes he shot questions at me.

"And the name of the peace-loving planet that is building this bad-memory from the past?"

"Cittanuvo. Second planet of a B star in Corona Borealis. No other colonized planets in the system."

"Never heard of it," Inskipp said as we took the private drop chute to his office. "Which may be a good or a bad sign. Wouldn't be the first time trouble came from some out-of-the-way spot I never even knew existed."

With the automatic disregard for others of the truly dedicated, he pressed the scramble button on his desk. Very quickly sleepy-eyed clerks and assistants were bringing files and records. We went through them together.

Modesty prevented me from speaking first, but I had a very short wait before Inskipp reached the same conclusion I had. He hurled a folder the length of the room and scowled out at the harsh dawn light.

"The more I look at this thing," he said, "the fishier it gets. This planet seems to have no possible motive or use for a battleship. But they are building one—*that* I will swear on a stack of one thousand credit notes as high as this building. Yet what will they do with it when they have it built? They have an expanding culture, no unemployment, a surplus of heavy metals and ready markets for all they produce. No hereditary enemies, feuds or the like. If it wasn't for this battleship thing, I would call them an ideal League planet. I have to know more about them."

"I've already called the spaceport—in your name of course," I told him. "Ordered a fast courier ship. I'll leave within the hour."

"Aren't you getting a little ahead of yourself, diGriz," he said. Voice chill as the icecap. "I still give the orders and I'll tell you when you're ready for an independent command."

I was sweetness and light because a lot depended on his decision. "Just trying to help, chief, get things ready in case you wanted more info. And this isn't really an operation, just a reconnaissance. I can do that as well as any of the experienced operators. And it may give me the experience I need, so that some day, I, too, will be qualified to join the ranks . . ."

"All right," he said. "Stop shoveling it on while I can still breathe. Get out there. Find out what is happening. Then get back. Nothing else—and that's an order."

By the way he said it, I knew he thought there was little chance of its happening that way. And he was right.

5

A QUICK STOP at supply and record sections gave me everything I needed. The sun was barely clear of the horizon when the silver barb of my ship lifted in the gray field, then blasted into space.

The trip took only a few days, more than enough time to memorize everything I needed to know about Cittanuvo. And the more I knew the less I could understand their need for a battleship. It didn't fit. Cittanuvo was a secondary settlement out of the Cellini system, and I had run into these settlements before. They were all united in a loose alliance and bickered a lot among themselves, but never came to blows. If anything, they shared a universal abhorrence of war.

Yet they were secretly building a battleship.

Since I was only chasing my tail with this line of thought, I put it out of my mind and worked on some tri-di chess problems. This filled the time until Cittanuvo blinked into the bow screen.

One of my most effective mottoes has always been, "Secrecy can be an obviousity." What the magicians call misdirection. Let people notice what is hidden. This was why I landed at midday, on the largest field on the planet, after a very showy approach. I was already dressed for my role, and out of the ship before the landing braces stopped vibrating. Buckling the fur cape around my shoulders with the platinum clasp, I stamped down the ramp. The sturdy little M-3 robot rumbled after me with my bags. Heading directly towards the main gate, I ignored the scurry of activity around the customs building. Only when a uniformed under-official of some kind ran over to me, did I give the field any attention.

Before he could talk I did, foot in the door and stay on top.

"Beautiful planet you have here. Delightful climate! Ideal spot for a country home. Friendly people, always willing to help strangers and all that I imagine. That's what I like. Makes me feel grateful. Very pleased to meet you. I am the Grand Duke Sant' Angelo." I shook his hand enthusiastically at this point and let a one hundred credit note slip into his palm.

"Now," I added, "I wonder if you would ask the customs agents

27

to look at my bags here. Don't want to waste time, do we? The ship is open, they can check that whenever they please.''

My manner, clothes, jewelry, the easy way I passed money around and the luxurious sheen of my bags, could mean only one thing. There was little that was worth smuggling into or out of Cittanuvo. Certainly nothing a rich man would be interested in. The official murmured something with a smile, spoke a few words into his phone, and the job was done.

A small wave of customs men hung stickers on my luggage, peeked into one or two for conformity's sake, and waved me through. I shook hands all around—a rustling handclasp of course—then was on my way. A cab was summoned, a hotel suggested. I nodded agreement and settled back while the robot loaded the bags about me.

The ship was completely clean. Everything I might need for the job was in my luggage. Some of it quite lethal and explosive, and very embarrassing if it were discovered in my bags. In the safety of my hotel suite I made a change of clothes and personality. After the robot had checked the rooms for bugs.

And very nice gadgets too, these Corps robots. It looked and acted like a moron M-3 all the time. It was anything but. The brain was as good as any other robot brain I have known, plus the fact that the chunky body was crammed with devices and machines of varying use. It chugged slowly around the room, moving my bags and laying out my kit. And all the time following a careful route that covered every inch of the suite. When it had finished it stopped and called the all-clear.

''All rooms checked. Results negative except for one optic bug in that wall.''

''Should you be pointing like that?'' I asked the robot. ''Might make people suspicious, you know.''

''Impossible,'' the robot said with mechanical surety. ''I brushed against it and it is now unserviceable.''

With this assurance I pulled off my flashy clothes and slipped into the midnight black dress uniform of an admiral in the League Grand Fleet. It came complete with decorations, gold bullion, and all the necessary documents. I thought it a little showy myself, but it was just the thing to make the right impression on Cittanuvo. Like many other planets, this one was uniform-conscious. Delivery boys, street cleaners, clerks—all had to have characteristic uniforms.

Much prestige attached to them, and my black dress outfit should rate as high as any uniform in the galaxy.

A long cloak would conceal the uniform while I left the hotel, but the gold-encrusted helmet and a brief case of papers were a problem. I had never explored all the possibilities of the pseudo M-3 robot, perhaps it could be of help.

"You there, short and chunky," I called. "Do you have any concealed compartments or drawers built into your steel hide? If so, let's see."

For a second I thought the robot had exploded. The thing had more drawers in it than a battery of cash registers. Big, small, flat, thin, they shot out on all sides. One held a gun and two more were stuffed with grenades; the rest were empty. I put the hat in one, the brief case in another and snapped my fingers. The drawers slid shut and its metal hide was as smooth as ever.

I pulled on a fancy sports cap, buckled the cape up tight, and was ready to go. The luggage was all boobytrapped and could defend itself. Guns, gas, poison needles, the usual sort of thing. In the last resort it would blow itself up. The M-3 went down by a freight elevator. I used a back stairs and we met in the street.

Since it was still daylight I didn't take a heli, but rented a groundcar instead. We had a leisurely drive out into the country and reached President Ferraro's house after dark.

As befitted the top official of a rich planet, the place was a mansion. But the security precautions were ludicrous to say the least. I took myself and a three hundred fifty kilo robot through the guards and alarms without causing the slightest stir. President Ferraro, a bachelor, was eating his dinner. This gave me enough undisturbed time to search his study.

There was absolutely nothing. Nothing to do with wars or battleships that is. If I had been interested in blackmail I had enough evidence in my hand to support me for life. I was looking for something bigger than political corruption, however.

When Ferraro rolled into his study after dinner the room was dark. I heard him murmur something about the servants and fumble for the switch. Before he found it, the robot closed the door and turned on the lights. I sat behind his desk, all his personal papers before me—weighted down with a pistol—and as fierce a scowl as I could raise smeared across my face. Before he got over the shock I snapped an order at him.

"Come over here and sit down, *quick!*"

The robot hustled him across the room at the same time, so he had
no choice except to obey. When he saw the papers on the desk his
eyes bulged and he just gurgled a little. Before he could recover I
threw a thick folder in front of him.

"I am Admiral Thar, League Grand Fleet. These are my credentials. You had better check them." Since they were as good as any
real admiral's I didn't worry in the slightest. Ferraro went through
them as carefully as he could in his rattled state, even checking the
seals under UV. It gave him time to regain a bit of control and he
used it to bluster.

"What do you mean by entering my private quarters and bur-
glaring—"

"You're in very bad trouble," I said in as gloomy a voice as I
could muster.

Ferraro's tanned face went a dirty gray at my words. I pressed the
advantage.

"I am arresting you for conspiracy, extortion, theft, and whatever other charges develop after a careful review of these documents.
Seize him." This last order was directed at the robot who was well
briefed in its role. It rumbled forward and locked its hand around
Ferraro's wrist, handcuff style. He barely noticed.

"I can explain," he said desperately. "Everything can be explained. There is no need to make such charges. I don't know what
papers you have there, so I wouldn't attempt to say they are all
forgeries. I have many enemies you know. If the League knew the
difficulties faced on a backward planet like this . . ."

"That will be entirely enough," I snapped, cutting him off with a
wave of my hand. "All those questions will be answered by a court
at the proper time. There is only one question I want an answer to
now. Why are you building that battleship?"

The man was a great actor. His eyes opened wide, his jaw
dropped, he sank back into the chair as if he had been tapped lightly
with a hammer. When he managed to speak the words were completely unnecessary; he had already registered every evidence of
injured innocence.

"What battleship?" he gasped.

"The Warlord class battleship that is being built at the Cenerentola Spaceyards. Disguised behind these blueprints." I threw them
across the desk to him, and pointed to the one corner. "Those are
your initials there, authorizing construction."

Ferraro still had the baffled act going as he fumbled with the papers, examined the initials and such. I gave him plenty of time. He finally put them down, shaking his head.

"I know nothing about any battleship. These are the plans for a new cargo liner. Those are my initials, I recall putting them there."

I phrased my question carefully, as I had him right where I wanted him now. "You deny any knowledge of the Warlord battleship that is being built from these modified plans."

"These are the plans for an ordinary passenger-freighter, that is all I know."

His words had the simple innocence of a young child's. Was he ever caught. I sat back with a relaxed sigh and lit a cigar.

"Wouldn't you be interested in knowing something about that robot who is holding you," I said. He looked down, as if aware for the first time that the robot had been holding him by the wrist during the interview. "That is no ordinary robot. It has a number of interesting devices built into its fingertips. Thermocouples, galvanometers, things like that. While you talked it registered your skin temperature, blood pressure, amount of perspiration and such. In other words it is an efficient and fast working lie detector. We will now hear all about your lies."

Ferraro pulled away from the robot's hand as if it had been a poisonous snake. I blew a relaxed smoke ring. "Report," I said to the robot. "Has this man told any lies?"

"Many," the robot said. "Exactly seventy-four per cent of all statements he made were false."

"Very good," I nodded, throwing the last lock on my trap. "That means he knows all about this battleship."

"The subject has no knowledge of the battleship," the robot said coldly. "All of his statements concerning the construction of this ship were true."

Now it was my turn for the gaping and eye-popping act while Ferraro pulled himself together. He had no idea I wasn't interested in his other hanky-panky, but could tell I had had a low blow. It took an effort, but I managed to get my mind back into gear and consider the evidence.

If President Ferraro didn't know about the battleship, he must have been taken in by the cover-up job. But if he wasn't responsible—who was? Some militaristic clique that meant to overthrow him and take power? I didn't know enough about the planet, so I enlisted Ferraro on my side.

This was easy—even without the threat of exposure of the documents I had found in his files. Using their disclosure as a prod I could have made him jump through hoops. It wasn't necessary. As soon as I showed him the different blueprints and explained the possibilities he understood. If anything, he was more eager than I was to find out who was using his administration as a cat's-paw. By silent agreement the documents were forgotten.

We agreed that the next logical step would be the Cenerentola Spaceyards. He had some idea of sniffing around quietly first, trying to get a line to his political opponents. I gave him to understand that the League, and the League Navy in particular, wanted to stop the construction of the battleship. After that he could play his politics. With this point understood he called his car and squadron of guards and we made a parade to the shipyards. It was a four-hour drive and we made plans on the way down.

The spaceyard manager was named Rocca, and he was happily asleep when we arrived. But not for long. The parade of uniforms and guns in the middle of the night had him frightened into a state where he could hardly walk. I imagine he was as full of petty larceny as Ferraro. No innocent man could have looked so terror stricken. Taking advantage of the situation, I latched my motorized lie detector onto him and began snapping the questions.

Even before I had all the answers I began to get the drift of things. They were a little frightening, too. The manager of the spaceyard that was building the ship had no idea of its true nature.

Anyone with less self-esteem than myself—or who had led a more honest early life—might have doubted his own reasoning at that moment. I didn't. The ship on the ways *still* resembled a warship to six places. And knowing human nature the way I do, that was too much of a coincidence to expect. Occam's razor always points the way. If there are two choices to take, take the simpler. In this case I chose the natural acquisitive instinct of man as opposed to blind chance and accident. Nevertheless I put the theory to the test.

Looking over the original blueprints again, the big superstructure hit my eye. In order to turn the ship into a warship that would have to be one of the first things to go.

"Rocca!" I barked, in what I hoped was authentic old space-dog manner. "Look at these plans, at this space-going front porch here. Is it still being built onto the ship?"

He shook his head at once and said, "No, the plans were changed. We had to fit in some kind of new meteor-repelling gear for operating in the planetary debris belt."

I flipped through my case and drew out a plan. "Does your new gear look anything like this?'' I asked, throwing it across the table to him.

He rubbed his jaw while he looked at it. "Well," he said hesitatingly, "I don't want to say for certain. After all, these details aren't in my department, I'm just responsible for final assembly, not unit work. But this surely looks like the thing they installed. Big thing. Lots of power leads—"

It was a battleship all right, no doubt of that now. I was mentally reaching around to pat myself on the back when the meaning of his words sank in.

"Installed!" I shouted. "Did you say installed?"

Rocca collapsed away from my roar and gnawed his nails. "Yes—" he said, "not too long ago. I remember there was some trouble . . ."

"And what else?" I interrupted him. Cold moisture was beginning to collect along my spine now. "The drives, controls—are they in, too?"

"Why, yes," he said. "How did you know? The normal scheduling was changed around, causing a great deal of unnecessary trouble."

The cold sweat was now a running river of fear. I was beginning to have the feeling that I had been missing the boat all along the line. The original estimated date of completion was nearly a year away. But there was no real reason why that couldn't be changed, too.

"Cars! Guns!" I bellowed. "To the spaceyard. If that ship is anywhere near completion, we are in big, *big* trouble!"

All the bored guards had a great time with the sirens, lights, accelerators on the floor and that sort of thing. We blasted a screaming hole through the night right to the spaceyard and through the gate.

It didn't make any difference, we were still too late. A uniformed watchman frantically waved to us and the whole convoy jerked to a stop.

The ship was gone.

Rocca couldn't believe it, neither could the president. They wandered up and down the empty ways where it had been built. I just crunched down in the back of the car, chewing my cigar to pieces and cursing myself for being a fool.

I had missed the obvious fact, being carried away by the thought of a planetary government building a warship. The government was involved for sure—but only as a pawn. No little planet-bound political mind could have dreamed up as big a scheme as this. I smelled a rat—a stainless steel one. Someone who operated the way I had done before my conversion.

Now that the rodent was well out of the bag I knew just where to look, and had a pretty good idea of what I would find. Rocca, the spaceyard manager, had staggered back and was pulling at his hair, cursing and crying at the same time. President Ferraro had his gun out and was staring at it grimly. It was hard to tell if he was thinking of murder or suicide. I didn't care which. All he had to worry about was the next election, when the voters and the political competition would carve him up for losing the ship. My troubles were a little bigger.

I had to find the battleship before it blasted its way across the galaxy.

"Rocca!" I shouted. "Get into the car. I want to see your records—*all* of your records—and I want to see them right now."

He climbed wearily in and had directed the driver before he fully realized what was happening. Blinking at the sickly light of dawn brought him slowly back to reality.

"But admiral . . . the hour! Everyone will be asleep . . ."

I just growled, but it was enough. Rocca caught the idea from my expression and grabbed the car phone. The office doors were open when we got there.

Normally I curse the paper tangles of bureaucracy, but this was one time when I blessed them all. These people had it down to a fine science. Not a rivet fell, but that its fall was noted—in quintupli-cate. And later followed up with a memo, *rivet, wastage, query*. The facts I needed were all neatly tucked away in their paper catacombs. All I had to do was sniff them out. I didn't try to look for first causes, this would have taken too long. Instead I concentrated my attention on the recent modifications, like the gun turret, that would quickly give me a trail to the guilty parties.

Once the clerks understood what I had in mind they hurled themselves into their work, urged on by the fires of patriotism and the burning voices of their superiors. All I had to do was suggest a line of search and the relevant documents would begin appearing at once.

Bit by bit a pattern started to emerge. A delicate webwork of forgery, bribery, chicanery and falsehood. It could only have been conceived by a mind as brilliantly crooked as my own. I chewed my lip with jealousy. Like all great ideas, this one was basically simple.

A party or parties unknown had neatly warped the ship construction program to their own ends. Undoubtedly they had started the program for the giant transport, that would have to be checked later. And once the program was underway, it had been guided with a skill that bordered on genius. Orders were originated in many places, passed on, changed and shuffled. I painfully traced each one to its source. Many times the source was a forgery. Some changes seemed to be unexplainable, until I noticed the officers in question had a temporary secretary while their normal assistants were ill. All the girls had had food poisoning, a regular epidemic it seemed. Each of them in turn had been replaced by the same girl. She stayed just long enough in each position to see that the battleship plan moved forward one more notch.

This girl was obviously the assistant to the Mastermind who originated the scheme. He sat in the center of the plot, like a spider on its web pulling the strings that set things into motion. My first thought that a gang was involved proved wrong. All my secondary suspects turned out to be simple forgeries, not individuals. In the few cases where forgery wasn't adequate, my mysterious X had apparently hired himself to do the job. X himself had the permanent job of Assistant Engineering Designer. One by one the untangled threads ran to this office. He also had a secretary whose "illnesses" coincided with her employment in other offices.

When I straightened up from my desk the ache in my back stabbed like a hot wire. I swallowed a painkiller and looked around at my drooping, sack-eyed assistants who had shared the sleepless seventy-two hour task. They sat or slumped against the furniture, waiting for my conclusions. Even President Ferraro was there, his hair looking scraggly where he had pulled out handfuls.

"You've found them, the criminal ring?" he asked, his fingers groping over his scalp for a fresh hold.

"I have found them, yes," I said hoarsely. "But not a criminal ring. An inspired master criminal—who apparently has more executive ability in one ear lobe than all your bribe-bloated bureaucrats—and his female assistant. They pulled the entire job by themselves. His name, or undoubtedly pseudoname, is Pepe Nero. The girl is called Angelina . . ."

"Arrest them at once! Guards . . . guards—" Ferraro's voice died away as he ran out of the room. I talked to his vanishing back.

"That is just what we intend to do, but it's a little difficult at the moment since they are the ones who not only built the battleship, but undoubtedly stole it as well. It was fully automated so no crew is necessary."

"What do you plan to do?" one of the clerks asked.

"I shall do nothing," I told him, with the snapped precision of an old space veteran. "The League fleet is already closing in on the renegades and you will be informed of the capture. Thank you for your assistance."

6

I THREW THEM as snappy a salute as I could muster and they filed out. Staring gloomily at their backs I envied for one moment their simple faith in the League Navy. When in reality the vengeful fleet was just as imaginary as my admiral's rating. This was still a job for the Corps. Inskipp would have to be given the latest information at once. I had sent him a psigram about the theft, but there was no answer as yet. Maybe the identity of the thieves would stir some response out of him.

My message was in code, but it could be quickly broken if someone wanted to try hard enough. I took it to the message center myself. The psiman was in his transparent cubicle and I locked myself in with him. His eyes were unfocused as he spoke softly into a mike, pulling in a message from somewhere across the galaxy. Outside the rushing transcribers copied, coded and filed messages, but no sound penetrated the insulated wall. I waited until his attention clicked back into the room, and handed him the sheets of paper.

"League Central 14—rush," I told him.

He raised his eyebrows, but didn't ask any questions. Establishing contact only took a few seconds, as they had an entire battery of psimen for their communications. He read the code words carefully, shaping them with his mouth but not speaking aloud, the power of his thoughts carrying across the light-years of distance. As soon as he was finished I took back the sheet, tore it up and pocketed the pieces.

I had my answer back quickly enough, Inskipp must have been hovering around waiting for my message. The mike was turned off to the transcribers outside, and I took the code groups down in shorthand myself.

". . . xybb dfil fdno, and if you don't—don't come back!"

The message broke into clear at the end and the psiman smiled as he spoke the words. I broke the point off my stylus and growled at him not to repeat *any* of this message, as it was classified, and I would personally see him shot if he did. That got rid of the smile, but didn't make me feel any better.

The decoded message turned out not to be as bad as I had imagined. Until further notice I was in charge of tracking and capturing the stolen battleship. I could call on the League for any aid I needed. I would keep my identity as an admiral for the rest of the job. I was to keep him informed of progress. Only those ominous last words in clear kept my happiness from being complete.

I had been handed my long-awaited assignment. But translated into simple terms my orders were to get the battleship, or it would be my neck. Never a word about my efforts in uncovering the plot in the first place. This is a heartless world we live in.

This moment of self-pity relaxed me and I immediately went to bed. Since my main job now was waiting, I could wait just as well asleep.

And waiting was all I could do. Of course there were secondary tasks, such as ordering a Naval cruiser for my own use, and digging for more information on the thieves, but these really were secondary to my main purpose. Which was waiting for bad news. There was no place I could go that would be better situated for the chase than Cittanuvo. The missing ship could have gone in any direction. With each passing minute the sphere of probable locations grew larger by the power of the squared cube. I kept the on-watch crew of the cruiser at duty stations and confined the rest within a one hundred yard radius of the ship.

There was little more information on Pepe and Angelina, they had covered their tracks well. Their backgrounds were unknown, though the fact they both talked with a slight accent suggested an off-world origin. There was one dim picture of Pepe, chubby but looking too grim to be a happy fat boy. There was no picture of the girl. I shuffled the meager findings, controlled my impatience, and kept the ship's psiman busy pulling in all the reports of any kind of trouble in space. The navigator and I plotted their locations in his tank, comparing the positions in relation to the growing sphere that enclosed all the possible locations of the stolen ship. Some of the disasters and apparent accidents hit inside this area, but further investigation proved them all to have natural causes.

I had left standing orders that all reports falling inside the danger area were to be brought to me at any time. The messenger woke me from a deep sleep, turning on the light and handing me the slip of paper. I blinked myself awake, read the first two lines, and pressed the *action station* alarm over my bunk. I'll say this, the Navy boys know their business. When the sirens screamed, the crew secured ship and blasted off before I had finished reading the report. As soon as my eyeballs unsquashed back into focus I read it through, then once more carefully from the beginning.

It looked like the one we had been waiting for. There were no witnesses to the tragedy, but a number of monitor stations had picked up the discharge static of a large energy weapon being fired. Triangulation had led investigators to the spot where they found a freighter, *Ogget's Dream*, with a hole punched through it as big as a railroad tunnel. The freighter's cargo of plutonium was gone.

I read *Pepe* in every line of the message. Since he was flying an undermanned battleship, he had used it in the most efficient way possible. If he attempted to negotiate or threaten another ship, the element of chance would be introduced. So he had simply roared up to the unsuspecting freighter and blasted her with the monster guns his battleship packed. All eighteen men aboard had been killed instantly. The thieves were also murderers.

I was under pressure now to act. And under a greater pressure not to make any mistakes. Roly-poly Pepe had shown himself to be a ruthless killer. He knew what he wanted—then reached out and took it. Destroying anyone who stood in his way. More people would die before this was over, it was up to me to keep that number as small as possible.

Ideally I should have rushed out the fleet with guns blazing and dragged him to justice. Very nice, and I wished it could be done that way. Except where was he? A battleship may be gigantic on some terms of reference, but in the immensity of the galaxy it is microscopically infinitesimal. As long as it stayed out of the regular lanes of commerce, and clear of detector stations and planets, it would never be found.

Then how *could* I find it—and having found it, catch it? When the infernal thing was more than a match for any ship it might meet. That was my problem. It had kept me awake nights and talking to myself days, since there was no easy answer.

I had to construct a solution, slowly and carefully. Since I couldn't be sure where Pepe was going to be next, I had to make him go where I wanted him to.

There were some things in my favor. The most important was the fact I had forced him to make his play before he was absolutely ready. It wasn't chance that he had left the same day I arrived on Cittanuvo. Any plan as elaborate as his certainly included warning of approaching danger. The drive on the battleship, as well as controls and primary armament had been installed weeks before I showed up. Much of the subsidiary work remained to be done when the ship had left. One witness of the theft had graphically described the power lines and cables dangling from the ship's locks when she lifted.

My arrival had forced Pepe off balance. Now I had to keep pushing until he fell. This meant I had to think as he did, fall into his plan, think ahead—then trap him. Set a thief to catch a thief. A great theory, only I felt uncomfortably on the spot when I tried to put it into practice.

A drink helped, as did a cigar. Puffing on it, staring at the smooth bulkhead, relaxed me a bit. After all—there aren't that many things you can do with a battleship. You can't run a big con, blow safes or make burmedex with it. It is hell-on-jets for space piracy, but that's about all.

"Great, great—but why a battleship?"

I was talking to myself, normally a bad sign, but right now I didn't care. The mood of space piracy had seized me and I had been going along fine. Until this glaring inconsistency jumped out and hit me square in the eye.

Why a battleship? Why all the trouble and years of work to get a ship that two people could just barely manage? With a tenth of the effort Pepe could have had a cruiser that would have suited his purposes just as well.

Just as good for space piracy, that is—but not for *his* purposes. He had wanted a battleship, and he had gotten himself a battleship. Which meant he had more in mind than simple piracy. What? It was obvious that Pepe was a monomaniac, an egomaniac, and as psychotic as a shorted computer. Some day the mystery of how he had slipped through the screen of official testing would have to be investigated. That wasn't my concern now. He still had to be caught.

A plan was beginning to take shape in my head, but I didn't rush it. First I had to be sure that I knew him well. Any man that can con an entire world into building a battleship for him—then steal it from them—is not going to stop there. The ship would need a crew, a base for refueling and a mission.

Fuel had been taken care of first, the gutted hull of *Ogget's Dream* was silent witness to that. There were countless planets that could be used as a base. Getting a crew would be more difficult in these peaceful times, although I could think of a few answers to that one, too. Raid the mental hospitals and jails. Do that often enough and you would have a crew that would make any pirate chief proud. Though piracy was, of course, too mean an ambition to ascribe to this boy. Did he want to rule a whole planet—or maybe an entire system? Or more? I shuddered a bit as the thought hit me. Was there really anything that could stop a plan like this once it got rolling ? During the Kingly Wars any number of types with a couple of ships and less brains than Pepe had set up just this kind of empire. They were all pulled down in the end, since their success depended on one-man rule. But the price that had to be paid first!

This was the plan and I felt in my bones that I was right. I might be wrong on some of the minor details, they weren't important. I knew the general outline of the idea, just as when I bumped into a mark I knew how much he could be taken for, and just how to do it. There are natural laws in crime as in every other field of human endeavor. I *knew* this was it.

"Get the Communications Officer in here at once," I shouted at the intercom. "Also a couple of clerks with transcribers. And fast—this is a matter of life or death!" This last had a hollow ring, and I realized my enthusiasm had carried me out of character. I buttoned my collar, straightened my ribbons and squared my shoulders. By the time they knocked on the door I was all admiral again.

Acting on my orders the ship dropped out of warpdrive so our psiman could get through to the other operators. Captain Steng grumbled as we floated there with the engines silent, wasting precious days, while half his crew was involved in getting out what appeared to be insane instructions. My plan was beyond his understanding. Which is, of course, why he is a captain and I'm an admiral, even a temporary one.

Following my orders, the navigator again constructed a sphere of speculation in his tank. The surface of the sphere contacted all the star systems a day's flight ahead of the maximum flight of the stolen battleship. There weren't too many of these at first and the psiman could handle them all, calling each in turn and sending news releases to the Naval Public Relations officers there. As the sphere kept growing he started to drop behind, steadily losing ground. By this time I had a general release prepared, along with directions for use and follow-up, which he sent to Central 14. The battery of psimen there contacted the individual planets and all we had to do was keep adding to the list of planets.

The release and follow-ups all harped on one theme. I expanded on it, waxed enthusiastic, condemned it, and worked it into an interview. I wrote as many variations as I could, so it could be slipped into as many different formats as possible. In one form or another I wanted the basic information in every magazine, newspaper and journal inside that expanding sphere.

"What in the devil does this nonsense *mean*?" Captain Steng asked peevishly. He had long since given up the entire operation as a futile one, and spent most of the time in his cabin worrying about the effect of it on his service record. Boredom or curiosity had driven him out, and he was reading one of my releases with horror.

"Billionaire to found own world . . . space yacht filled with luxuries to last a hundred years," the captain's face grew red as he flipped through the stack of notes. "What connection does this tripe have with catching those murderers?"

When we were alone he was anything but courteous to me, having assured himself by not-too-subtle questioning that I was a spurious admiral. There was no doubt I was still in charge, but our relationship was anything but formal.

"This tripe and nonsense," I told him, "is the bait that will snag our fish. A trap for Pepe and his partner in crime."

"Who is this mysterious billionaire?"

"Me," I said. "I've always wanted to be rich."

"But this ship, the space yacht, where is it?"

"Being built now in the naval shipyard at Udrydde. We're almost ready to go there now, soon as this batch of instructions goes out."

Captain Steng dropped the releases onto the table, then carefully wiped his hands off to remove any possible infection. He was trying to be fair and considerate of my views, and not succeeding in the slightest.

"It doesn't make sense," he growled. "How can you be sure this killer will ever read one of these things. And if he does—why should he be interested? It looks to me as if you are wasting time while he slips through your fingers. The alarm should be out and every ship notified. The Navy alerted and patrols set on all lanes—"

"Which he could easily avoid by going around, or better yet not even bother about, since he can lick any ship we have. That's not the answer," I told him. "This Pepe is smart and as tricky as a fixed gambling machine. That's his strength—and his weakness as well. Characters like that never think it possible for someone else to outthink them. Which is what *I'm* going to do."

"Modest, aren't you," Steng said.

"I try not to be," I told him. "False modesty is the refuge of the incompetent. I'm going to catch this thug and I'll tell you how I'll do it. He's going to hit again soon, and wherever he hits there will be some kind of a periodical with my plant in it. Whatever else he is after, he is going to take all of the magazines and papers he can find. Partly to satisfy his own ego, but mostly to keep track of the things he is interested in. Such as ship sailings.''

''You're just guessing—you don't know all this.''

His automatic assumption of my incompetence was beginning to get me annoyed. I bridled my temper and tried one last time.

''Yes, I'm guessing—an informed guess—but I do know some facts as well. *Ogget's Dream* was cleaned out of all reading matter, that was one of the first things I checked. We can't stop the battleship from attacking again, but we can see to it that the time after that she sails into a trap.''

''I don't know,'' the captain said, ''it sounds to me like . . .''

I never heard what it sounded like, which is all right since he was getting under my skin and I might have been tempted to pull my pseudo-rank. The alarm sirens cut his sentence off and we footraced to the communications room.

Captain Steng won by a nose, it was his ship and he knew all the shortcuts. The psiman was holding out a transcription, but he summed it up in one sentence. He looked at me while he talked and his face was hard and cold.

''They hit again, knocked out a Navy supply satellite, thirty-four men dead.''

''If your plan doesn't work, *admiral*,'' the captain whispered hoarsely in my ear, ''I'll personally see that you're flayed alive!''

''If my plan doesn't work, *captain*—there won't be enough of my skin left to pick up with a tweezer. Now if you please, I'd like to get to Udrydde and board my ship as soon as possible.''

The easy-going hatred and contempt of all my associates had annoyed me, thrown me off balance. I was thinking with anger now, not with logic. Forcing a bit of control, I ordered my thoughts, checking off a mental list.

''Belay that last command,'' I shouted, getting back into my old space-dog mood. ''Get a call through first and find out if any of our plants were picked up during the raid.''

While the psiman unfocused his eyes and mumbled under his breath I riffled some papers, relaxed and cool. The ratings and officers waited tensely, and made some slight attempt to conceal their hatred of me. It took about ten minutes to get an answer.

"Affirmative," the psiman said. "A store ship docked there twenty hours before the attack. Among other things, it left newspapers containing the article."

"Very good," I said calmly. "Send a general order to suspend all future activity with the planted releases. Send it by psimen only, no mention on any other Naval signaling equipment, there's a good chance now it might be 'overheard.'"

I strolled out slowly, in command of the situation. Keeping my face turned away so they couldn't see the cold sweat.

It was a fast run to Udrydde where my billionaire's yacht, the *Eldorado*, was waiting. The dockyard commander showed me the ship, and made a noble effort to control his curiosity. I took a sadistic revenge on the Navy by not telling him a word about my mission. After checking out the controls and special apparatus with the technicians, I cleared the ship. There was a tape in the automatic navigator that would put me on the course mentioned in all the articles, just a press of a button and I would be on my way. I pressed the button.

It was a beautiful ship, and the dockyard had been lavish with their attention to detail. From bow to rear tubes she was plated in pure gold. There are other metals with a higher albedo, but none that give a richer effect. All the fittings, inside and out, were either machine-turned or plated. All this work could not have been done in the time allotted, the Navy must have adapted a luxury yacht to my needs.

Everything was ready. Either Pepe would make his move—or I would sail on to my billionaire's paradise planet. If that happened, it would be best if I stayed there.

Now that I was in space, past the point of no return, all the doubts that I had dismissed fought for attention. The plan that had seemed so clear and logical now began to look like a patched and crazy makeshift.

"Hold on there, sailor," I said to myself. Using my best admiral's voice. "Nothing has changed. It's still the best and *only* plan possible under the circumstances."

Was it? Could I be sure that Pepe, flying his mountain of a ship and eating Navy rations, would be interested in some of the comforts and luxuries of life? Or if the luxuries didn't catch his eye, would he be interested in the planetary homesteading gear? I had loaded the cards with all the things he might want, and planted the information where he could get it. He had the bait now—but would he grab the hook?

I couldn't tell. And I could work myself into a neurotic state if I kept running through the worry cycle. It took an effort to concentrate on anything else, but it had to be made. The next four days passed very slowly.

7

WHEN THE ALARM blew off, all I felt was an intense sensation of relief. I might be dead and blasted to dust in the next few minutes, but that didn't seem to make much difference.

Pepe had swallowed the bait. There was only one ship in the galaxy that could knock back a blip that big at such a distance. It was closing fast, using the raw energy of the battleship engines for a headlong approach. My ship bucked a bit as the tug-beams locked on at maximum distance. The radio bleeped at me for attention at the same time. I waited as long as I dared, then flipped it on. The voice boomed out.

". . . That you are under the guns of a warship! Don't attempt to run, signal, take evasive action, or in any other way . . ."

"Who are you—and what the devil do you want?" I spluttered into the mike. I had my scanner on, so they could see me, but my own screen stayed dark. They weren't sending any picture. In a way it made my act easier, I just played to an unseen audience. They could see the rich cut of my clothes, the luxurious cabin behind me. Of course they couldn't see my hands.

"It doesn't matter who we are," the radio boomed again. "Just obey orders if you care to live. Stay away from the controls until we have tied on, then do exactly as I say."

There were two distant clangs as magnetic grapples hit the hull. A little later the ship lurched, drawn home against the battleship. I let my eyes roll in fear, looking around for a way to escape—and taking a peek at the outside scanners. The yacht was flush against the space-filling bulk of the other ship. I pressed the button that sent the torch-wielding robot on his way.

"Now let me tell you something," I snapped into the mike, wiping away the worried billionaire expression. "First I'll repeat your own warning—obey orders if you want to live. I'll show you why—"

When I threw the big switch a carefully worked out sequence took place. First, of course, the hull was magnetized and the bombs fused. A light blinked as the scanner in the cabin turned off, and the one in the generator room came on. I checked the monitor screen to make sure, then started into the spacesuit. It had to be done fast, at the same time it was necessary to talk naturally. They must still think of me as sitting in the control room.

"That's the ship's generators you're looking at," I said. "Ninety-eight per cent of their output is now feeding into coils that make an electromagnet of this ship's hull. You will find it very hard to separate us. And I would advise you not to try."

The suit was on, and I kept the running chatter up through the mike in the helmet, relaying to the ship's transmitter. The scene in the monitor receiver changed.

"You are now looking at a hydrogen bomb that is primed and aware of the magnetic field holding our ships together. It will, of course, go off if you try to pull away." I grabbed up the monitor receiver and ran toward the air lock.

"This is a different bomb now," I said, keeping one eye on the screen and the other on the slowly opening outer door. "This one has receptors on the hull. If you attempt to destroy any part of this ship, or even gain entry to it, this one will detonate."

I was in space now, leaping across to the gigantic wall of the other ship.

"What do you want?" These were the first words Pepe had spoken since his first threats.

"I want to talk to you, arrange a deal. Something that would be profitable for both of us. But let me first show you the rest of the bombs, so you won't get any strange ideas about co-operating."

Of course I *had* to show him the rest of the bombs, there was no getting out of it. The scanners in the ship were following a planned program. I made light talk about all my massive armament that would carry us both to perdition, while I climbed through the hole in the battleship's hull. There was no armor or warning devices at this spot, it had been chosen carefully from the blueprints.

"Yeah, yeah . . . I take your word for it, you're a flying bomb. So stop with this roving reporter bit and tell me what you have in mind."

This time I didn't answer him, because I was running and panting like a dog, and had the mike turned off. Just ahead, if the blueprints were right, was the door to the control room. Pepe should be there.

I stepped through, gun out, and pointed it at the back of his head. Angelina stood next to him, looking at the screen.

"The game's over," I said. "Stand up slowly and keep your hands in sight."

"What do you mean," he said angrily, looking at the screen in front of him. The girl caught wise first. She spun around and pointed.

"He's *here!*"

They both stared, gaped at me, caught off guard and completely unprepared.

"You're under arrest, crime-king," I told him. "And your girl friend."

Angelina rolled her eyes up and slid slowly to the floor. Real or faked, I didn't care. I kept the gun on Pepe's pudgy form while he picked her up and carried her to an acceleration couch against the wall.

"What . . . what will happen now?" He quavered the question. His pouchy jaws shook and I swear there were tears in his eyes. I was not impressed by his acting since I could clearly remember the dead men floating in space. He stumbled over to a chair, half dropping into it.

"Will they do anything to me?" Angelina asked. Her eyes were open now.

"I have no idea of what will happen to you," I told her truthfully. "That is up to the courts to decide."

"But he *made* me do all those things," she wailed. She was young, dark and beautiful, the tears did nothing to spoil this.

Pepe dropped his face into his hands and his shoulders shook. I flicked the gun his way and snapped at him.

"Sit up, Pepe. I find it very hard to believe that you are crying. There are some Naval ships on the way now, the automatic alarm was triggered about a minute ago. I'm sure they'll be glad to see the man who . . ."

"Don't let them take me, please!" Angelina was on her feet now, her back pressed to the wall. "They'll put me in prison, do things to my mind!" She shrunk away as she spoke, stumbling along the wall. I looked back at Pepe, not wanting to have my eyes off him for an instant.

"There's nothing I can do," I told her. I glanced her way and a small door was swinging open and she was gone.

"Don't try to run," I shouted after her, "it can't do any good!"

Pepe made a strangling noise and I looked back to him quickly. He was sitting up now and his face was dry of tears. In fact he was laughing, not crying.

"So she caught you too, Mr. Wise-cop, poor little Angelina with the soft eyes." He broke down again, shaking with laughter.

"What do you mean," I growled.

"Don't you catch yet? The story she told you was true—except she twisted it around a bit. The whole plan, building the battleship, then stealing it, was *hers*. She pulled me into it, played me like an accordion. I fell in love with her, hating myself and happy at the same time. Well—I'm glad now it's over. At least I gave her a chance to get away, I owe her that much. Though I thought I would explode when she went into that innocence act!"

The cold feeling was now a ball of ice that threatened to paralyze me. "You're lying," I said hoarsely, and even I didn't believe it.

"Sorry. That's the way it is. Your brain-boys will pick my skull to pieces and find out the truth anyway. There's no point in lying now."

"We'll search the ship, she can't hide for long."

"She won't have to," Pepe said. "There's a fast scout we picked up, stowed in one of the holds. That must be it leaving now." We could feel the vibration, distantly through the floor.

"The Navy will get her," I told him, with far more conviction than I felt.

"Maybe," he said, suddenly slumped and tired, no longer laughing. "Maybe they will. But I gave her her chance. It is all over for me now, but she knows that I loved her to the end." He bared his teeth in sudden pain. "Not that she will care in the slightest."

I kept the gun on him and neither of us moved while the Navy ships pulled up and their boots stamped outside. I had captured my battleship and the raids were over. And I couldn't be blamed if the girl had slipped away. If she evaded the Navy ships, that was their fault, not mine.

I had my victory all right.

Bit I wasn't too happy about it. I had a premonition that I wasn't finished with Angelina yet.

8

LIFE WOULD HAVE been much sweeter if my uneasy hunch hadn't proven to be true. You can't blame the Navy for being taken in by Angelina—they were neither the first nor the last to underestimate the mind that lay behind those melting eyes. And I try not to blame myself either. After my first mistake in letting Angelina slip out I tried not to make a second. I wasn't completely convinced yet that Pepe was telling the truth about her. The entire story might be a complicated lie to confuse and throw me off guard. I have a very suspicious mind. Playing it safe, I kept the muzzle of my gun aimed exactly between his eyes with my fingers resting lightly on the trigger. I kept it there until a squad of space marines thundered in and took over. As soon as they put the grab on Pepe I sent out an all-ships alarm about Angelina, with a special take-all-precautions priority. Even before all the ships had acknowledged receipt her scout rocket was sighted on the detector screen.

I sighed with a great deal of relief. If she did turn out to be the brains of the operation I didn't want her slipping away. She, Pepe and the battleship made a nice package to turn over to Inskipp. There was no chance of her escaping now, with ships closing in on her from every direction. They were experienced at this sort of thing and it was only a matter of time before they had her. Turning over the battleship to the navy, I went back to the luxury yacht and tapped the stores for a large glass of Scotch whisky (that had never been within twenty lightyears of Earth) and a long cigar. Sitting comfortably in front of the screen I monitored the chase.

Angelina wriggled painfully on the hook, making high-G turns to avoid capture. She'd be black and blue from head to foot after some of those 15-G accelerations. It was all for nothing because in the end they still caught her in a tractor web and closed in. All the thrashing around had just gained her a little time. None of us realized how important this time really was until the boarding party cracked into the ship.

It was empty of course.

Fully ten days went by before we pieced together what had really happened. It was ruthless and ugly, and even if the psych docs hadn't assured me that Pepe had told the truth, I would have recognized the manner in which the escape was carried out. Angelina was one step ahead of us all the way. When she had escaped from the battleship in the scout rocket she had made no attempt to flee. Instead she must have gone at full blast to the nearest navy ship, a twelve-man pocket cruiser. They of course had no idea what had really happened aboard the battleship, as I hadn't put out the general alarm yet. I should have done that as soon as she had escaped. If I had, twelve good men might still be alive. We'll never know what story she told them, but it was obvious they weren't on their guard. Probably something about being a prisoner and escaping during the fighting. In any case she took the ship. Five of the men were dead of gas poisoning the others shot. We discovered this when the cruiser was later found drifting and inert, parsecs away. After capturing the cruiser she had set the controls on the scout ship for evasion tactics and launched it. While we were all merrily chasing it she simply let her ship drop behind the chase and vanished from the fleet. Her trail blurs there, though it is obvious she must have captured another ship. What this ship was, and where she went in it, was a complete mystery.

Back in Corps headquarters I found myself trying to explain this all to Inskipp. He had a cold eye and hardened manner and I found myself trying to justify my actions.

"You can't win them all," I said. "I brought home your battleship and Pepe—may his personality rest in peace now that it has been erased. Angelina tricked me and got away, I'll admit that. But she did a much better job of fooling the boys in the navy!"

"Why so much venom?" Inskipp asked in an arid voice. "No one's accusing you of dereliction of duty. You sound like a man with a guilty conscience. You did a good job. A fine job. A great job . . . for a first assignment. . . ."

"You're doing it again!" I howled. "Prodding my conscience to see how soft it is. Like keeping *him* around." I pointed to Pepe Nero who was sitting near us in the restaurant eating slowly, mumbling to himself with vacant-eyed dullness. His old personality had been stripped from his mind and a new one implanted. Only the body remained of the old Pepe who had loved Angelina and stolen a battleship.

"The psychs are working on a new theory of body-personality," Inskipp said blandly, "so why not keep him around here under observation? If any of his criminal tendencies should develop in the new personality we'll be in a wonderful spot to recruit him for the Corps. Does he bother you?''

"Not him," I snorted. "After the massacres he pulled for his psychotic girlfriend you could grind him into hamburger for all I care. But he does remind me that she is still out there somewhere. Free and planning new mischief. I want to go after her.''

"Well you're not," Inskipp said. "You've asked me before and I have refused before. The topic is now closed.''

"But I could . . .''

"You could *what?*" He gave me a nasty chuckle. "Every law officer in the galaxy has a pic of her and there is a continual search going on. How could you possibly do more than they are already doing?''

"I couldn't, I guess," I grumbled. "So the hell with it, as you say." I pushed my plate away and stood and stretched as naturally as I could. "I'm going to get a large jug of liquid refreshment and go to my quarters and nurse my sorrows.''

"You do that. And forget Angelina. Come to my office at 0900 hours tomorrow and you better be sober.''

"Slavedriver," I moaned, going out the door and turning down the hall towards the residence wing. As soon as I was out of sight I took a side ramp that led to the spaceport.

That's one lesson I had already learned from Angelina. When you have a plan put it into action instantly. Don't let it lie around and get stale and have other people start thinking about it themselves. I was putting myself up against the shrewdest man in the business right now, and the thought alone was enough to make me sweat. I was going against Inskipp's direct orders, walking out on him and the Corps. Not really walking out, since I only wanted to finish the job I had started for them. But I was obviously the only one who would look at it that way.

There were tools, gadgets and a good deal of money in my quarters that would come in very handy on this job. I would just have to do without them. When Inskipp started to think about my sudden conversion to his point of view I wanted to be well away in space.

A mechanic with a drag-robot was pulling an agent's ship into place on the launching ramp. I stamped over and used my official voice.

"Is that my ship?''

"No, sir—it's for Full Agent Nielsen, there he is coming up now.''

"Check with control central, will you? It's going to be rush no matter how we handle it."

"New job, Jimmy?" Ove asked as he came up. I nodded and watched the mechanic until he vanished around the corner.

"Same old business," I said. "And how's your tennis game coming?" I asked, lifting my hand with an imaginary racket.

"Getting better all the time," he said, turning his head to look at his ship.

"I'll teach you a new stroke," I said, bringing my hand down sharply and catching him on the side of the neck with the straightened edge. He folded without a sound and I lowered him gently to the deck and dragged him out of sight behind a row of lubrication drums. I gently pried the box with the course tapes from his limp fingers.

Before the mechanic could return I was in the ship and had the lock sealed. I fed the course tape into the controls and punched the tower combination for clearance. There was a subjective century of waiting, during which eternal period of time I produced a fine beading of sweat all over my head. Then the green light came on.

Step one and still in the clear. As soon as the launching acceleration stopped I was out of the chair and attacking the control panel with the screwdriver ready in my hand. There was always a remote control unit here so that any Corps ship could be flown from a distance. I had discovered it on my first flight in one of these ships since I have always maintained that there is a positive value to being nosey. I disconnected the input and output leads, then dived for the engine room.

Perhaps I am too suspicious or have too low an opinion of mankind. Or of Inskipp, who had his own rules on most subjects. Someone more trusting than I would have ignored the radio controlled suicide bomb built into the engine. This could be used to scuttle the ship in case of capture. I didn't think they would use it on me except as a last resort. Nevertheless I still wanted it disconnected.

The bomb was an integral part of the engine mounting, a solid block of bermedex built into the casing. The lid dropped off easily enough and inside there was a maze of circuits all leading to a fuse screwed into the thick metal. It had a big hex-head on it and I scraped my knuckles trying to get a wrench around it and turn it in the close quarters. With a last grate of bruised flesh and knuckle bones I twisted it free. It hung down from its wire leads, a nerve drawn from a deadly tooth.

Then it exploded with a loud bang and a cloud of black smoke.

With most unnatural calm I looked from the cloud of dispersing smoke back to the black hole in the bermedex charge. This would have turned the ship and its contents into a fine dust.

"Inskipp," I said, but my throat was dry and my voice cracked and I had to start again. "Inskipp, I get your message. You thought you were giving me my discharge. Accept instead my resignation from the Special Corps."

9

MY MOST OVERWHELMING feeling was one of relief. I was on my own again and responsible to no man. I actually hummed a bit as I dropped the ship out of warpdrive long enough to slip in a course tape chosen at random from the file. There would be no chance of an intercept this way and I could cut a tape for a new course once I was well clear of the headquarters station.

A course to where? I wasn't sure yet. That would require a bit of research, though there was no doubt about what I would be doing. Looking for Angelina. At first thought it seemed a little stupid to be taking on a job the Corps had refused me. It was still their job. On second thought I realized that it had nothing to do with the Corps now. Angy had pulled a fast one on me, pinned on the prize-chump medal. That is something that you just don't do to Slippery Jim diGriz. Call it ego if you like. But ego is the only thing that keeps a man in my profession operating. Remove that and you have removed everything. I had no real idea of what I would do with her when I found her. Probably turn her over to the police, since people like her gave the business a bad name. Better to worry about cooking the fish after I had caught it.

A plan was necessary, so I prepared all the plan producing ingredients. For one terrible moment I thought there were no cigars in the ship. Then the service unit groaned and produced a box from some dark corner of the deep freeze. Not the recommended way to store cigars, but much better than having none at all. Nielsen always favored a rare brand of potent akvavit and I had no objections to drinking it. Feet up, throat lubricated and cigar smoking, I put the thinkbox to work on the project.

To begin with, I had to put myself in Angelina's place at the time of her escape. I would like to have gone back physically to the scene, but I'm not that thick. There was guaranteed to be a trigger-happy navy ship or two sitting there. However this is the kind of problem they build computers to solve, so I fed in the coordinates of the space action where it all had happened. There was no need for notes on this—those figures were scratched inside my forehead in letters of fire. The computer had a large memory store and a high speed scan. It hummed happily when I asked for the stars nearest to the given position. In under thirteen seconds it flipped through its catalogs, counted on its fingers and rang its little computation-finished bell for me. I copied off the numbers of the first dozen stars, then pressed the cancel when I saw the distances were getting too great to be relevant anymore.

Now I must think like Angelina. I had to be hunted, hurried, a murderess with twelve fresh corpses of my own manufacture piled around me. In every direction rode the enemy. She would have the same list, ground out by the computer on the stolen cruiser. Now—where to? Tension and speed. Get going somewhere. Somewhere away from here. A glance at the list and the answer seemed obvious. The two nearest stars were in the same quadrant of the sky, within fifteen degrees of each other. They were roughly equidistant. What was more important was the fact that star number three was in a different sector of the sky and twice as far away.

That was the way to go, toward the first two stars. It was the sort of decision that can be made in a hurry and still be sound. Head toward suns and worlds and the lanes where other ships could be found. The cruiser would have to be gotten rid of before any planets were approached—the faster the better since every ship in the galaxy would be looking for it. Them meet another ship—ship X—and capture it. Abandon the cruiser and . . . do what?

My tenuous line of logic was ready to snap at this point so I strengthened it with some akvavit and a fresh cigar. With my eyes half closed in reverie I tried to rebuild the flight. Capture the ship and—head for a planet. As long as she was alone in space Angelina was in constant danger. A planetfall and a change of personality were called for. When I looked up those two target stars in the catalog the planetary choice was obvious. A barbaric sounding place named Freibur.

There were a half dozen other settled planets around the two suns, but all eliminated themselves easily. Either too lightly settled, so that a stranger would be easily spotted, or organized and integrated so well that it would be impossible to be around long without some notice being taken. Freibur shared none of these difficulties. It had been in the league for less than two hundred years, and would be in a happily chaotic state. A mixture of the old and new, pre-contact culture and post-contact civilization. The perfect place for her to slip into quietly, and lose herself until she could appear with a fresh identity.

Reaching this conclusion produced a double glow of satisfaction. This was more than a mental exercise in survival since I was now roughly in the same place Angelina had been. The incident with the scuttling charge was a strong indication of the value the Corps put on their ships—and the low value they placed on deserters. Freibur was a place that would suit me perfectly. I retired happily with a slight buzz on and a scorched mouth from the dehydrated cigars.

When I dragged myself back to consciousness it was time to drop out of warpspace and plot a new course. Except there was one thing I had to do first. A lot of the little facts I knew had *not* been picked up in the Corps. One fact—normally of interest only to warpdrive technicians—concerns the curious propagation of radiation in warpspace. Radio waves in particular. They just don't go anyplace. If you broadcast on one frequency you get a strong return signal on all frequencies, as if the radio waves had been squeezed out thin and bounced right back. Normally of no interest, this exotic phenomena is just the thing to find out if your ship is bugged. I put nothing beyond the Special Corps, and bugging their own ships seemed a logical precaution. A concealed radio, transmitting on a narrow band, would lead them right to me wherever I went. This I had to find out before getting near any planets.

There was a squeal and a growl from the speaker and I cursed my former employers. But before I wasted my time looking for a transmitter I ought to be sure one was there. Whatever was producing the signal seemed too weak to be picked up at any distance. Some quick work with a few sheets of shielding showed that my mysterious signal was nothing more than leaking radiation from the receiver itself. After it was shielded the ether was quiet. I enjoyed a sigh of justified satisfaction and dropped out of warp.

Once I had a course plotted the trip wasn't a long one. I took the opportunity to scrounge through the ship's equipment and put together a kit for future use. The elaborate make-up and appearance-alteration machinery begged to be used, and of course I did. Re-building the working-personality of Slippery Jim was a positive pleasure. As the nose plugs and cheek pads slipped into place and the dye seeped into my hair I sighed and relaxed with happiness, an old war horse getting back on the job.

Then I scowled, growled at myself in the mirror and began to remove the disguise as carefully as I had assumed it. It has always been axiomatic with me that there is no relaxation in this line of business, and anything done by rote usually leads to disaster. Inskipp knew my old working personality only too well and they would surely be looking for me under that description as well as my normal one. The second time around I took a little more care with the disguise and built up an entirely different appearance. A simple one—with facial and hair changes—that would be easily maintained. The more elaborate a job of make-up is the more time it takes to keep it accurate. Freibur was a big question-mark so far and I didn't want to be loaded with any extra responsibilities like this. I wanted to go in relaxed, sniff around and see if I could pick up Angelina's trail.

There were still two subjective days left in warpdrive and I put these to good use making some simple gadgetry that might come in handy. Pinhead grenades, tie-clasp pistols, ring-drills—the usual thing. I only brushed away the scraps and cleaned the shop up when the ship signaled the end of the trip.

The only city on Freibur with a ground controlled spaceport was at Freiburbad, which was situated on the shore of an immense lake, the only sizeable body of fresh water on the planet. Looking at the sunlight glinting from it I had the sudden desire for a swim. This urge must have been the genesis of my idea to drown the stolen ship. Leave it at the bottom of a deep spot in the lake and it would always be handy if needed.

I made planetfall over a jagged mountain range and picked up not as much as a beep on the radar. Coming in over the lake after dark I detected navigation radar from the spaceport, but my ship wouldn't get too far inshore. A rainstorm—cut through with hail—shortened visibility and removed my earlier bathing desire. There was a deep underwater channel not too far from shore and I touched down above it while I put my kit together. It would be foolish to carry too much, but some of the Corps gear was too valuable to leave behind. Sealing it in a waterproof cover I strapped it to my spacesuit and opened the air lock. Rain and darkness washed over me as I struck out for the unseen shore. I imagined rather than heard the gurgle behind me as the ship sank gently to the bottom.

Swimming in a spacesuit is about as easy to manage as making love in free fall. I churned my way to shore in a state of near exhaustion. After crawling out of the suit I had a great deal of pleasure watching it burn to a cinder under the heat of three thermite bombs. I particularly enjoyed kicking the resultant hissing slag into the lake. The rain hammered down and washed all traces of the burning away. Apparently even the fierce light of the thermite had gone unobserved in the downpour. Huddling under a waterproof sheet I waited damply and miserably for dawn.

Sometime during the night I dozed off without meaning to because it was already light when I woke up. Something was very wrong, and before I could remember what had woken me the voice called again.

"Going to Freiburbad? Of course, where else is there to go? I'm going there myself. Got a boat. Old boat but a good boat. Beats walking . . ."

The voice went on and on, but I wasn't listening. I was cursing myself for being caught unaware by this joker with the long-playing voice. He was riding in a small boat just off shore; the thing was low in the water with bales and bundles, and the man's head stuck above the top of everything. While his jaw kept moving I had a chance to look at him and draw my sleep-sodden wits together. He had a wild and bristly beard that stuck out in all directions, and tiny dark eyes hidden under the most decrepit hat I had ever seen. Some of my startled panic ebbed away. If this oddball wasn't a plant, the accidental meeting might be turned to my benefit.

When mattress-face stopped to drag in a long overdue breath I accepted his offer and reached for the gunwale of the boat and drew it closer. I picked up my bundle—getting my hand on my gunbutt as I did it—and jumped in. There didn't seem to be any need for caution. Zug—that was his name, I plucked it out of the flowing stream of his monologue—bent over an outboard motor clamped to the stern and coaxed it to life. It was a tired looking atomic heat-exchanger, simple but efficient. No moving parts, it simply sucked in cold lake water, heated it to a boil and shot it out through an underwater jet. Made almost no sound while running, which was how the rig had slid up without wakening me.

Everything about Zug seemed normal—I still wasn't completely convinced and kept the gun close to my hand—but if it was normal I had hit a piece of luck. His cataract of words washed over me and I began to understand why. Apparently he was a hunter, bringing his pelts to market after months of solitude and silence. The sight of a human face had induced a sort of verbal diarrhea which I made no attempt to stop. He was answering a lot of questions for me.

One thing that had been a worry were my clothes. I had finally decided to wear a one-piece ship suit, done in neutral gray. You see this kind of outfit, with minor variations, on planets right across the galaxy. It had passed unnoticed by Zug, which wasn't really saying much since he was anything but a clothes fancier. He must have made his jacket himself out of the local fur. It was purplish-black and must have been very fine before the grease and twigs had been rubbed in. His pants were made of machine-woven cloth and his boots were the same as mine, of eternene plastic. If he was allowed to walk around loose in this outfit, mine would surely never be noticed.

What I could see of Zug's equipment bore out the impression gained from his clothes. The old and new mixed together. A world like Freibur, not too long in the League, would be expected to be like that. The electrostatic rifle leaning against a bundle of steel bolts for the crossbow made a typical picture. Undoubtedly the Voice of The Wilderness here could use both weapons with equal facility. I settled down on the soft bundles and enjoyed the voyage and the visual pleasures of the misty dawn, bathed continually in a flow of words.

We reached Freiburbad before noon. Zug had more of an ambition to talk than to be talked to, and a few vague remarks of mine about going to the city satisfied him. He greatly enjoyed the food concentrates from my pack and reciprocated by producing a flask of some noxious home brew he had distilled in his mountain retreat. The taste was indescribably awful and left the mouth feeling as if it had been rasped by steel wool soaked in sulphuric acid. But the first few drinks numbed and after that we enjoyed the trip—until we tied up at a fish-smelling dock outside the city. We almost swamped the boat getting out of it, which we thought hysterically funny, and which will give you some indication of our mental state at the time. I walked into the city proper and sat in a park until my head cleared.

The old and the new pressed shoulders here, plastic fronted buildings wedged in between brick and plaster. Steel, glass, wood and stone all mixed with complete indifference. The people were the same, dressed in a strange mixture of types and styles. I took more notice of them than they did of me. A newsrobot was the only thing that singled me out for attention. It blatted its dull offerings in my ear and waved a board with the printed headlines until I bought a paper to get rid of it. League currency was in circulation here, as well as local money, and the robot made no protest when I slipped a credit in its chest slot, though it did give me change in Freibur *gilden*—undoubtedly at a ruinous rate of exchange. At least that's the way I would have done it if I were programming the thing.

All of the news was unimportant and trivial—the advertisements were of much more interest. Looking through the big hotels I compared their offered pleasures and prices.

It was this that set me to trembling and sweating with terror. How quickly we lose the ingrained habits of a lifetime. After a month on the side of law and order I was acting like an honest man!

"You're a criminal," I muttered through clenched teeth, and spat on a NO SPITTING sign. "You hate the law and live happily without it. You are a law unto yourself, and the most honest man in the galaxy. You can't break any rules since you make them up yourself and change them whenever you see fit."

All of this was true, and I hated myself for forgetting it. That little period of honesty in the Corps was working like a blight to destroy all of my best anti-social tendencies.

"Think dirty!" I cried aloud, startling a girl who was walking by on the path. I leered to prove that she had heard correctly and she hurried quickly away. That was better. I left myself at the same time, in the opposite direction, looking for an opportunity to do bad. I had to reestablish my identity before I could even consider finding Angelina.

Opportunity was easy to find. Within ten minutes I had spotted my target. I had all the equipment I might need in my sack. What I would use for the job I stowed in my pockets and waist wallet, then checked my bag in a public locker.

Everything about the First Bank of Freibur begged to be cracked. It had three entrances, four guards and was busily crowded. Four human guards! No bank in existence would pay all those salaries if they had electronic protection. It was an effort not to hum with happiness as I stood in line for one of the *human* clerks. Fully automated banks aren't hard to rob, they just require different techniques. This mixture of man and machine was the easiest of all.

"Change a League ten-star for gilden," I said, slapping the shiny coin on the counter before him.

"Yessir," the cashier said, only glancing at the coin and feeding it into the accounting machine next to him. His fingers had already set up the amount for me in gilden, even before the *currency valid* signal blinked on. My money rattled down into the cup before me and I counted it slowly. This was done mechanically, because my mind was really on the ten credit coin now rolling and clinking down inside the machine's innards. When I was sure it had finished its trip and landed in the vault I pressed the button on my wrist transmitter.

It was beautiful, that was the only word for it. The kind of thing that leaves a warm glow lodged in the memory, that produces a twinge of happiness for years after whenever it is nudged. That little ten credit coin had taken hours to construct and every minute was worth it. I had sliced it in half, hollowed it out, loaded it with lead back to its original weight, built in a tiny radio receiver, a fuse and a charge of burmedex, which now went off with an incredibly satisfactory explosion. A grinding thump deep in the bank's entrails was followed by a tremendous amount of clanking and banging. The rear wall—containing the vault—split open and disgorged a torrent of money and smoke. Some last effort of the expiring accounting machine gave me an unexpected dividend. The money dispensers at every cashier's station burst into frantic life. A torrent of large and small coins poured out on the startled customers who quickly mastered their surprise and began grabbing. Their moment of pleasure was brief because the same radio cue had set off the smoke and gas bombs I had thoughtfully dropped in all the wastebaskets. Unnoticed in the excitement, I threw a few more gas bombs in with the cashiers. This gas is an effective mixture of my own concoction, a sinister brew of regurgitants and lachrymatories. Its effect was instantaneous and powerful. (There were of course no children in the bank, since I don't believe in being cruel to those too young to protect themselves.) Within seconds the clients and employees found themselves unable to see, and too preoccupied to take any notice of me.

As the gas rolled towards me I lowered my head and slipped the goggles over my eyes. When I looked up I was the only person in the bank that was able to see. I was of course careful to breathe through the filter plugs in my nose, so I could enjoy the continued digestion of my last meal. My teller had vanished from sight and I did a neat dive through the opening, sliding across the counter on my stomach.

After this it was just a matter of pick and choose, there was certainly no shortage of money rolling around loose. I ignored the small stuff and went to the source, the riven vault out of which poured a golden torrent. Within two minutes I had filled the bag I had brought and was ready to leave. The smoke near the doors was thinning a bit, but a few more grenades took care of that.

Everything was working perfectly and under control, except for one fool of a guard who was making a nuisance of himself. His tiny brain realized dimly that something wrong was going on, so he was staggering in circles firing his gun. It was a wonder he hadn't hit anyone yet. I took the gun away and hit him on the head with it.

The smoke was densest near the doors, making it impossible to see out. It was just as impossible of course to see in, so no one in the street had any real idea of what had happened. They of course knew *something* was wrong; two policemen had rushed in with guns drawn . . . but were now as helpless as the rest. I organized the relief of the sufferers then, and began pulling and guiding them to the door. When I had enough of a crowd collected I joined them and we all crawled out into the street together. I put the goggles in my pocket and kept my eyes closed until I had groped clear of the gas. Some worthy citizens helped me and I thanked them, tears streaming down my face from the fringes of the gas, and went my way.

That's how easy it is. That's how easy it always is if you plan ahead and don't take foolish risks. My morale was high and the blood sang in my veins. Life was deliciously crooked and worth living again. Finding Angelina's trail now would be simplicity itself. There was nothing I couldn't do.

Staying on the crest of this emotional wave, I rented a room in a spacemen's hotel near the port, cleaned up and strode forth to enjoy the pleasures of life. There were many rough-and-ready joints in the area and I made the rounds. I had a steak in one and a drink apiece in each of the others. If Angelina had come to Freibur she would surely have passed—at least briefly—through this area. The trail would be here, I felt that in my bones. Crooked bones once again, and sympathetic to her own lawlessness.

"Howsabout buying a girl a drink," the tart said spiritlessly, and I shook my head no with the same lack of interest. The hostesses, pallid creatures of the night, were coming out as the evening progressed. I was getting a good share of propositions since I had taken care to look like a spaceman on leave, always a good source of revenue for these women. This one was the latest of a number who had approached me. A little better looking than most, at least better constructed. I watched her walking away with interest that bordered on admiration. Her skirt was short, tight and slashed high up on the sides. High heels lent a rotating motion to this producing a most effective result. She reached the bar and turned to survey the room, and I couldn't help but appreciate the rest of her. Her blouse was made of thin strips of shimmering fabric, joined together only at the tops and bottoms. They separated to reveal enticing slices of creamy skin whenever she moved, and I'm sure had the desired effect on masculine libidos.

My eyes finally reached her face—a long trip since I had started the survey at her ankles—and she was quite attractive. Almost familiar. . . .

Exactly at this instant my heart gave a grinding thud in my chest and I grew rigid in my chair. It seemed impossible—yet it had to be true.

She was Angelina.

10

HER HAIR HAD been bleached and there were some simple and obvious changes in her features. They had been altered just enough so it would be impossible to identify her from a photograph or a description. She could never be recognized.

Except by me, that is. I had seen her in the stolen battleship and I had talked to her. And the nice part was I could identify her and she would have no idea of who I was. She had seen me only briefly—in a spacesuit with a tinted faceplate—and I'm sure had plenty of other things to think about at the time.

This was the climax of the most successful day of my life. The fetid air of the dive was like wine in my nostrils. I relaxed and savored every last drop of irony in the situation. You had to give the girl credit, though. She had adopted a perfect cover. I myself had never imagined she would stay here, and I thought I had weighed all of the possibilities. Because she had taken a good bit of the stolen cash with her, I had never considered she would be living like a penniless tramp. The girl had guts, you had to give her credit. She had adopted an almost perfect disguise and blended neatly into the background. If only she wasn't so damned kill-happy—what a team we would make!

My heart gave the second grinding thump of the evening when I realized the dead-end trail down which my emotions were leading me. Angelina was disaster to anyone she came near. Inside that lovely head squatted a highly intelligent but strangely warped brain. For my own sake I would be better off thinking about the corpses she had piled up, not about her figure. There was only one thing to be done. Get her away from here and turn her over to the Corps. I didn't even consider how I felt about the Corps—or how they felt about me. This was an entirely different affair that had to be done neatly and with dispatch before I changed my mind.

I joined her at the bar and ordered two double shots of the local battery acid. Being careful, I deepened my voice and changed my accent and manner of speaking. Angelina had heard enough of my voice to identify it easily—that was the one thing I had to be aware of.

"Drink up, doll," I said raising my drink and leering at her. "Then we go up to your place. You got a place don't you?"

"I gotta place you gotta League ten-spot in hard change?"

"Of course," I grumbled, feigning insult. "You think I'm buying this bilge-juice on the arm?"

"I ain't no cafeteria pay-on-your-way-out," she said with a bored lack of interest that was magnificent. "Pay now and then we go."

When I flipped the ten credits her way she speared it neatly out of the air, weighed it, bit it, and vanished it inside her belt. I looked on with frank admiration, which she would mistake for carnal interest, but was in reality appreciation of the faultless manner with which she played her role. Only when she turned away did I make myself remember that this was business not pleasure, and I had a stern duty to perform. My resolution was wavering and I screwed it tight again with a memory of corpses floating in space. Draining my glass I followed her marvelous rotation out of the bar and down a noisome alley.

The dark decrepitude of the narrow passage jarred my reflexes awake. Angelina played her part well, but I doubted if she bedded down with all the space tramps who hit this port. There was a good chance that she had a confederate around who had a strong right arm with a heavy object clutched tightly in his hand. Or perhaps I'm naturally suspicious. My hand was on the gun in my pocket but I didn't need to use it. We treaded across another street and turned into a hallway. She went first and we didn't talk. No one came near us or even bothered to notice us. When she unlocked her room I relaxed a bit. It was small and tawdry, but offered no possible hiding place for an accomplice. Angelina went straight to the bed and I checked the door to see if it really was locked. It was.

When I turned around she was pointing a .75 caliber recoilless automatic at me, so big and ugly that she had to hold it in both tiny hands.

"What the hell is the racket?" I blustered, fighting back the sick sensation that I had missed an important clue someplace along the line. My hand was still on the gun in my pocket but trying to draw it would be instant suicide.

"I'm going to kill you without ever even knowing your name," she said sweetly, with a cute smile that showed even white teeth. "But you have this coming for ruining my battleship operation."

Still she didn't fire, but her grin widened until it was almost a laugh. She was enjoying the uncontrolled expressions on my face as

I recognized the fact that I had been out-thought all the way along the line. That the trapper was the trappee. That she had me exactly precisely where she wanted me and there wasn't a single bloody damn thing I could do about it.

Angelina finally had to laugh out loud, a laugh clear and charming as a silver bell, as she watched me reach these sickening conclusions one after another. She was an artist to her fingertips and waited just long enough for me to understand everything. Then, at the exact and ultimate moment of my maximum realization and despair she pulled the trigger.

Not once, but over and over again.

Four tearing, thundering bullets of pain directly into my heart. And a final slug directly between my eyes.

11

IT WASN'T REALLY consciousness, but a sort of ruddy, pain-filled blur. A gut-gripping nausea fought with the pain, but the pain won easily. Part of the trouble was that my eyes were closed, yet opening them was incredibly difficult. I finally managed it and could make out a face swimming in a blur above me.

"What happened?" the blur asked.

"I was going to ask you the same thing . . ." I said, and stopped, surprised at how weak and bubbly my voice was. Something brushed across my lips and I saw a red-stained pad as it went away.

After I blinked some sight back into my eyes, blur-face turned out to be a youngish man dressed in white. A doctor I suppose, and I was aware of motion; we must be driving in an ambulance.

"Who shot you?" the doctor asked. "Someone reported the shots and you'll pleased to know we got there just in the old nick of time. You've lost a lot of blood—some of which I've replaced—have multiple fractures of the radius and ulna, an extensive bullet wound in your forearm, a further wound in your right temple, possible fracture of the skull, extremely probable fractures in your ribs and the possibility of internal injuries. Someone got a grudge against you? Who?"

Who? My darling Angelina, that's who. Temptress, sorceress, murderess, that's who tried to kill me. I remembered now. The wide black muzzle of the gun looking big enough to park a spaceship in. The fire blasting out of it, the slugs hammering into me, and the pain as my expensive, guaranteed, bulletproof underwear soaked up the impact of the bullets, spreading it across the entire front of my body. I remembered the hope that this would satisfy her and the despair of hope as the muzzle of that reeking gun lifted to my face.

I remembered the last instant of regret as I put my arms before my face and threw myself sideways in a vain attempt at escape.

The funny thing is that escape attempt had worked. The bullet that had smashed my forearm must have been deflected enough by the bone to carom off my skull, instead of catching it point blank and drilling on through. All this had produced satisfactory quantities of blood and an immobile body on the floor. That had caused Angelina's mistake, her only one. The boom of the gun in that tiny room, my apparent corpse, the blood, it must have all rattled the female side of her, at least a bit. She had to leave fast before the shots were investigated and she had not taken that extra bit of time to make sure.

"Lie down," the doctor said. "I'll give you an injection that will knock you out for a week if you don't lie down!"

Only when he said this did I realize I was half sitting up in the stretcher and chuckling a particularly dirty laugh. I let myself be pushed down easily, since my chest was drenched in pain whenever I moved.

Right at that moment my mind began ticking over plans for making the most of the situation. Ignoring the pain as well as I could I looked around the ambulance, looking for a way to capitalize on the bit of luck that had kept me still alive while she thought I was dead.

We pulled up at the hospital then, and there was nothing much I could do in the ambulance except steal the stylus and official forms from the rack above my head. My right arm was still good, though it hurt like fire whenever I moved. A robot snapped the wheels down on my stretcher, latched onto it and wheeled it inside. As it went by the doctor he slipped some papers into a holder near my head and waved good-by to me. I gave him back a gallant smile as I trundled into the butcher shop.

As soon as he was out of sight I pulled out the papers and scanned them quickly. Here lay my opportunity if I had enough time to grab it. There was the doctor's report—in quadruplicate. Until these forms were fed into the machinery I didn't exist. I was in a statistical limbo out of which I would be born into the hospital. Stillborn if I had my way. I pushed my pillow off onto the corridor floor and the robot stopped. He paid no attention to my writing and didn't seem to mind stopping two more times to rescue the pillow, giving me time to finish my forgery.

This Doctor Mcvbklz—at least that's what his signature reads like—had a lot to learn about signing papers. He had left acres of clear space between the last line of the report and his signature. I filled this with a very passable imitation of his handwriting. *Massive internal hemorrhage, shock* . . . I wrote, *died en route*. This

sounded official enough. I quickly added *All attempts resuscitation
failed*. I had a moment of doubt about spelling this jaw breaker, but
since Dr. Mcvbklz thought there were two P's in *multiple* he could
be expected to muff this one too. This last line made sure there
wouldn't be any hanky-panky with needles and electric prods to jazz
some life back into the corpse. We turned out of the corridor just as I
slipped the forms back into their slot and lay back trying to look
dead.

"Here's a D.O.A., Svend," someone called out, rustling the
papers behind my head. I heard the robot rolling away, untroubled
by the fact that his writing, pillow-shedding patient was suddenly
dead. This lack of curiosity is what I like about robots. I tried to
think dead thoughts and hoped the right expression was showing on
my face. Something jerked at my left foot and my boot and sock
were pulled off. A hand grabbed my foot.

"How tragic," this sympathetic soul said, "he's still warm.
Maybe we should put him on the table and get the revival team
down." What a nosey, mealy-mouthed, interfering sod he was.

"Nah," the voice of a wiser and cooler head said from across the
room. "They tried the works in the ambulance. Slide him in the
box."

A terrifying pain lanced through my foot and I almost gave the
whole show away. Only the fiercest control enabled me to lie
unmoving while this clown grimly tightened the wire around my big
toe. There was a tag hanging from the wire and I heartily wished the
same tag was hung from his ear secured by the same throttling wire.
Pain from the toe washed up and joined the ache in my chest, head
and arm, and I fought for corpselike rigidity as the stretcher trundled
along.

Somewhere behind me a heavy door opened and a wave of frigid
air struck my skin. I allowed myself a quick look through my lashes.
If the corpses in this chop shop were stashed into individual freezers
I was about to be suddenly restored to life. I could think of a lot more
pleasant ways of dying than in an ice box with the door handle on the
outside. Lady Luck was still galloping along at my shoulder because
my toe-amputator was dragging me, stretcher and all, into a good-
sized room. There were slabs on all sides and a number of dearly
departed had already arrived before me.

With no attempt at gentleness I was slid onto a freezing surface.
Footsteps went away from me across the room, the door closed
heavily and the lights went out.

My morale hit bottom at this moment. I had been through a lot for one day, and was thoroughly battered, bruised, contused and concussed. Being locked in a black room full of corpses had an unusually depressing effect on me. In spite of the pain in my chest and the tag trailing from my toe, I managed to slide off the slab and hobble to the door. Panic grew as I lost my direction, easing off only when I walked square into the wall. My fingers found a switch and the lights came back on. And of course my moral fiber stiffened at the same moment.

The door was perfectly designed, I couldn't have done better myself, with no window and a handle on the inside. There was even a bolt so that it could be locked from this side, though for what hideous reason I couldn't possibly imagine. It gave me some needed privacy though, so I slipped it into place.

Although the room was full, no one was paying any attention to me. The first thing I did was unwind the wire and massage some life back into my numb toe. On the yellow tag were the large black letters D.O.A. and a handwritten number, the same one that had been on the form I had altered. This was too good an opportunity to miss. I took the tag off the toe of the most badly battered male corpse and substituted mine. His tag I pocketed, then spent a merry few minutes changing around all the other tags. During this process I took a right shoe from the corpse with the biggest feet and jammed my frozen left foot into it. All the tags were hung from the left big toe and I loudly cursed such needless precision. My chest was bare where my shipsuit and bulletproof cover had been cut away. One of my silent friends had a warm shirt he didn't need, so I borrowed that too.

Don't think for a second that all this was easy. I was staggering and mumbling to myself while I did it. When it was finished I slapped off the light and cracked the door of the freezer. The air from the hall felt like a furnace. There wasn't a soul in sight so I closed the vault and staggered over to the nearest door. It was to a storeroom and the only thing there that I could use was a chair. I sat in this as long as I dared, then went looking again. The next door was locked but the third one opened to a dark room where I could hear someone breathing evenly in his sleep. This was more like it.

Whoever this sacktime artist was, he surely knew his sleeping trade. I rifled the room and fumbled with the clothes I found and put them on clumsily—yet he never heard a sound. Which was probably the best thing for him because I was in a skull-fracturing humor. The novelty of this little affair had worn off and all I could think about was the pain. There was a hat too, so I put this on and checked out. I saw people at a distance, but no one was watching when I pushed open an emergency exit and found myself back on the rain-drenched streets of Freiburbad.

12

THAT NIGHT AND the next few days are hazy in the memory for obvious reasons. It was a risk to go back to my room, but a calculated one. The chances were good that Angelina didn't know of its existence or, even if she had found out, that she wouldn't have done anything about it. I was dead and she had no further interest in me. This appeared to be true, because I wasn't bothered after I was in the room. I had the management send up some food and at least two bottles of liquor a day so it would look like I was on an extended and solitary bender. The rotgut went down the drain and I picked a bit at the food while my body slowly recovered. I kept my aching flesh drenched in antibiotics and loaded with pain-killers, and counted myself lucky.

On the third morning I felt weak but almost human. My arm in the cast throbbed when I moved it, the black and blue marks on my chest were turning gorgeous shades of violet and gold, but my headache was almost gone. It was time to plan for the future. I sipped some of the liquor I had been using to flush out the plumbing and called down for the newspapers of the past three days. The ancient delivery tube wheezed and disgorged them onto the table. Going through them carefully, I was pleased to discover that my plan had worked much better than should have been expected.

The day after my murder there had been items in every paper about it, grubbed from the hospital records by the slothful news-hounds who hadn't even bothered to glance at the corpse. That was all. Nothing later about Big Hospital Scandal in Missing Corpse or Suit Brought Because That's Not Uncle Frim In The Coffin. If my jiggery-pokery in the frozen meat locker had been uncovered, it was being kept a hospital family secret and heads were rolling in private.

Angelina, my sharpshooting sweetheart, must then think of me as securely dead, a victim of her own murderous trigger finger. Nothing could be better. As soon as I was able to I would be getting back on her trail again, the job of tracking her made immensely simpler by her believing me to be a whisp of greasy smoke in the local crematorium. There was plenty of time now to plan this thing and plan it right. No more funny business about who was hunting whom. I was going to get as much pleasure out of arresting Angelina as she had derived from blasting away at me with her portable artillery.

It was a humiliating but true fact that she had outmaneuvered me all the way down the line. She had stolen the battleship from under my nose, torn a wide swath through galactic shipping, then escaped neatly right under my gun. What made the situation most embarrassing was that she had set a trap for me—when I thought I was hunting her. Hindsight is a great revealer of obviousities and this one was painfully clear now. While escaping from the captured battleship she had not been hysterical in the slightest. That role had been feigned. She had been studying me, every bit of my face that could be seen, every intonation of my voice. Hatred had seared my picture in her memory, and while escaping she must have considered constantly how I would be thinking when I followed her. At the safest and least obvious spot in her flight she had stopped—and waited. Knowing I would come and knowing that she would be more prepared for the encounter than I was. This was all past history. Now it was my turn to deal the cards.

All kinds of schemes and plans trotted through my head to be weighed and sampled. Top priority—before anything else was attempted—would be a complete physical change for me. This would be necessary if I wanted to catch up with Angelina. It was also required if I were to stay out of the long reach of the Corps. The fact had not been mentioned during my training, but I was fairly sure the only way one left the Special Corps was feet first. Though I was physically down and out there was nothing wrong with the old think box and I put it to use. Facts were needed, and I gave a small endowment to the city library in the form of rental fees. Fortunately there were filmcopies of all the local newspapers available, going back for years. I made the acquaintance of an extremely yellowish journal endearingly called "HOT NEWS!!" *Hot News!!* aimed at a popular readership—with a vocabulary I estimated at approximately three hundred words—who relished violence in its multiform aspects. Most of the time these were just copter accidents and such, with full color photos of course. But very often there were juicy muggings, sluggings and such which proved the quieting hand of galactic civilization still hadn't throttled Freibur completely. In among these exaggerated tales of violence lay the murky crime I was searching for.

Mankind has always been capricious in its lawmaking, inventing such intriguingly different terms as manslaughter, justified homicide and such, as if dead wasn't dead. Though fashions in both crime and sentencing come and go, there is one crime that will always bring universal detestation. That is the crime of being a bungling doctor. I have heard tell that certain savage tribes used to slaughter the physician if his patient died, a system that is not without merit. This singleminded loathing of the butchering quack is understandable. When ill, we deliver ourselves completely into the doctor's hands. We give a complete stranger the opportunity to toy with that which we value most. If this trust is violated there is naturally a hotness of temper among the witnesses or survivors.

Ordinary-citizen Vulff Sifternitz had formerly been the Highly Esteemed Doctor Sifternitz. *Hot News!* explained in overly lavish detail how he had mixed the life of Playboy and Surgeon until finally the knife in his twitching fingers had cut *that* instead of *this* and the life of a prominent politician had been shortened by a number of no doubt profitable years. We must give Vulff credit for the fact that he had made an attempt to sober up before going to work, so that it was D.T.'s not drunkenness that caused the fatal twitch. His license was removed and he must have been fined most of his savings since there were later references to his having been involved in more sordid medical affairs. Life had treated Vulff hard and dirty; he was just the man I was looking for. On my first rubber-legged trip out of my room I took the liberty of paying him a professional call.

To a person of my abilities tracking down a pseudolegal stranger in a foreign city on a far planet presents no problems. Just a matter of technique and I am rich in technique. When I hammered on the stained wooden door in the least-wholesome section of town I was ready to take the first step in my new plan.

"I have some business for you, Vulff," I told the bleary-eyed stewie who opened the door.

"Get the hell lost," he said and tried to close the door in my face. My carefully placed shoe prevented this and it took almost no effort at all to push in past him.

"I don't do any medical work," he mumbled, looking at my bandaged arm. "Not for police stoolies I don't, so get the hell lost."

"Your conversation is both dull and repetitious," I told him, because it was. "I am here to offer you a strictly legitimate business deal with value given for money received. The mere fact that it happens to be illegal should bother neither of us. Least of all you." I ignored his mumbled protests and looked into the next room.

"According to information of great reliability you live here in unmarried bliss with a girl named Zina. What I have to say is not for her undoubtedly shell-like ears. Where is she?"

"Out!" he shouted. "And you too, out!" He clutched a tall bottle by the neck and raised it threateningly.

"Would you like that?" I asked and dropped a thick wad of fresh bank notes on the table. "And that—and that—" I followed with two more bundles. The bottle slipped from his loose fingers and fell to the floor while his eyes bulged out further and further as if they were on pistons. I added a few more bundles to the pile until I had his undivided attention.

It really didn't take much discussion. Once he had assured himself that I really meant to go through with the proposition it was just a matter of settling the details. The money had an instantly sobering effect on him, and though he had a tendency to twitch and vibrate there was nothing wrong with his reasoning powers.

"Just one last problem," I said as I started to leave. "What about the worthy Zina—are you going to tell her about this?"

"You crazy?" Vulff asked with undisguised surprise.

"I suppose that means you won't tell her. Since only you and I are going to know about this operation, how are you going to explain your absence or where the money has come from?"

This was even more shocking to him. "Explain? To *her*? She isn't going to see either me or the money once I leave here. Which will be no more than ten minutes from now."

"I see," I said, and I did. I also thought it was rather uncharitable of him since the unlucky Zina had been supporting him by practicing a trade that most women shun. I made a mental note to see what could be done to even the score a little. In the future though. Right now I had to see to the dissolution of James Bolivar diGriz.

Sparing no expense I ordered all the surgical and operating room equipment that Vulff could suggest. Whenever possible I bought robot-controlled devices since he would be working alone. Everything was loaded in a heavy carrier rented for the occasion and we drove out to the house in the country together. Neither of us would trust the other out of his sight which was of course understandable. Financial payments were the hardest to arrange since the purehearted Dr. Vulff was sure I would bash in his skull and take back all of my money once the job was finished—never realizing of course that as long as there were banks I would never be broke. The safeguards were finally arranged to his satisfaction and we began our solitary and important business.

The house was lonely and self-contained, perched on the cliff above a far reach of the lake. What fresh food we needed was delivered once a week, along with the mail which consisted of drugs and other medical supplies. The operations began.

Modern surgical techniques being what they are there was of course no pain or shock. I was confined to bed and at times was loaded with so much sedation that days passed in a dreamy fog. Between two periods of radical surgery I took the precaution of seeing that a sleeping pill was included in Vulff's evening drink. This drink was of course non-alcoholic since his traveling this entire course mounted on the water wagon was one of the conditions of our agreement. Whenever he found it difficult I restored his resolution with a little more money. All this continence had his nerves on edge and I thought he would appreciate a good night's sleep. I also wanted to do a little investigating. When I was sure he was deeply under I picked the lock of his door and searched his room.

I suppose the gun was there as a matter of insurance, but you can never tell with these nervous types. My days of being a target were over if I had anything to say about it. The gun was a pocket model of a recoilless .50, neat and deadly. The mechanism worked fine and the cartridges still held all their deadly power, but there would be some difficulty in shooting the thing after I filed off the end of the firing pin.

Finding the camera was no shock since I have very little faith left in the basic wholesomeness of mankind. That I was his benefactor and financer wasn't enough for Vulff. He was lining up some blackmail just in case. There was plenty of exposed film, no doubt filled with studies of my unconscious face Before and After. I put all the film, including the unexposed rolls, under the x-ray machine for a nice long treatment and that settled that.

Vulff did a good job in the times when he wasn't moaning about the absence of spirituous beverages or nubile females. Bending and shortening my femurs altered my height and walk. Hands, face, skull, ears—all of these were changed permanently to build a new individual. Skillful use of the correct hormones caused a change in the pigment cells, darkening the natural color of my skin and hair, even altering the hair pattern itself. The last thing done, when Vulff's skill was at its peak, was a delicate touch on my vocal cords that deepened and roughened my speech.

When it was all finished Slippery Jim diGriz was dead and Hans Schmidt was born. Not a very inspired name I admit, but it was just designed to cover the period before I shed Vulff and began my important enterprise.

"Very good, very good indeed," I said, looking into the mirror and watching my fingers press a stranger's face.

"God, I could use a drink," Vulff gasped behind me, sitting on his already-packed bags. He had been hitting the medical alcohol the last few days, until I had spiked it with my favorite regurgitant, and he was nervously anxious to get back to some heavy drinking. "Give me the balance of the money that's due and let's get out of here!"

"Patience, doctor," I murmured and slipped him the packet of bills. He broke the bank wrapper and began to count them with quick, caressing touches of his fingers. "Waste of time doing that," I told him, but he kept right on. "I've taken the liberty of writing 'STOLEN' on each bill, with ink that will fluoresce when the bank puts it under the ultraviolet."

This stopped the counting all right, and drained him white at the same instant. I ought to warn him about the old ticker, that's the way he would pop off if he didn't watch out.

"What do you mean, stolen?" he choked after a bit.

"Well they were, you know. All of the money I paid you with was stolen." His face went even whiter and I was sure he would never reach fifty, not with circulation like that. "You shouldn't let it worry you. The other stuff was all in old bills. I've passed a lot of it without any trouble."

"But . . . *why*?" he finally squeezed out.

"Sensible question, doctor. I've sent the same amount—in untampered bills, of course—to your old friend Zina. I felt you owed her that much at least, after all she has done for you. Fair is fair you know."

He glared at me while I tossed all the machines, surgical supplies and such off the cliff. I was careful not to have my back to him when he was too close; other than this all the precautions had already been taken. When I glanced up by chance and saw that a covert smile had replaced the earlier expression, I knew it was time to reveal the rest of my arrangements.

"An air cab will be here in a few minutes; we'll leave together. I regret to inform you that there won't be enough time after we arrive in Freiburbad for you to seek out Zina and thrash her as planned, and get the money back." His guilty start proved that he was really an amateur at this sort of thing. I continued, hoping he would be grateful for this complete revelation of how to do things in an efficient criminal manner. "I've timed everything rather carefully from here on in. Today is a bit unusual in that there are two starships leaving the port within minutes of each other. I've booked a ticket on one for myself—here is your ticket on the other. I've paid in advance for it, though I don't expect you to thank me." He took the ticket with all the spirited interest of an old maid picking up a dead snake. "The need for speed—if you will pardon the rhyme—is urgent. A few minutes after your ship leaves an envelope will be delivered to the police describing your part in this operation."

Dear Doctor Vulff digested all this as we waited for the copter to arrive, and from his sickening expression I saw he could find no flaws in the arrangements. During the entire flight he huddled away from me in his chair and never said a word. Without a bon voyage or even a curse he made for his ship upon our arrival and I watched him board it. I of course merely went in the direction of mine and turned off before entering it. I had as much intention of leaving Freibur as I had of informing the police that an illegal operation had taken place. The last thing I wanted was attention. Both little lies had merely been devices to make sure that the alcoholic doctor went away and stayed away before he began his solitary journey to cirrhosis. There was no reason for me to leave, in fact every reason for me to stay.

Angelina was still on this planet, and I wanted no interference while I tracked her down.

Perhaps it was presumptuous of me to be so positive, yet I felt I knew Angelina very well by this time. Our crooked little minds rotated in many of the same cycles of dishonesty. Up to a certain point I felt I could predict her reactions with firm logic. Firstly—she would be very happy about my bloody destruction. She got the same big bang out of corpses that most girls get from new clothes. Thinking me dead would make following her that much easier. I knew she would take normal precautions against the police and other agents of the Corps. But they wouldn't know she was on Freibur—there was nothing to connect my death with her presence. Therefore she didn't have to run again, but could stay on this planet under a new cover and changed personality. That she would want to stay here I had very little doubt. Freibur was a planet that seemed designed for illegal operation. In my years of knocking around the known universe I had never before come up against a piece of fruit so ripe for plucking. A heady mixture of the old and the new. In the old, caste-ridden, feudalistic Freibur a stranger would have been instantly recognized and watched. On the modern League planets computers, mechanization, robots and an ever-vigilant police force left very little room for illegal operations. It was only when these two different cultures are mixed and merged that imaginative operations became really possible.

This planet was peaceful enough; you had to give the League societies experts credit for that much. Before they brought in the first antibiotic pill or punch-card computer, they saw to it that law and order were firmly instituted. Nevertheless the opportunities were still there if you knew where to look. Angelina knew where to look and so did I.

Except—after weeks of futile investigation—I finally faced the brutal fact that we were both looking for different things. I can't deny the time was spent pleasantly since I uncovered countless opportunities for fine jobs and lucrative capers. If it hadn't been for the pressure of finding Angelina I do believe I could have had the time of my life in this crook's paradise. This pleasure was denied me because the pressure to catch up with Angelina nagged at me constantly like an aching tooth.

Finding intuition wanting I tried mechanical means. Hiring the best computer available, I fed entire libraries into its memory circuits and set it countless problems. In the course of this kilowatt-consuming business I became an expert on the economy of Freibur, but in the end was no closer to finding Angelina than I had been when I started. She had a driving urge for power and control, but I had no idea in what way it would find its outlet. There were many economic solutions I turned up for grabbing the reins of Freibur society, but investigation showed that she was involved in none of these. The King—Villelm IX—seemed the obvious pressure point for actual physical control of the planet. A complete investigation of Vill, his family and close royal relatives, turned up some juicy scandal but no Angelina. I was stopped dead.

While drowning my sorrows in a bottle of distilled spirits the solution to this dilemma finally struck me. Admittedly I was sodden with drink at the time, yet the paralysis of my neural axons was undoubtedly the source of the idea. Any man that says he thinks better drunk than sober is a fool. But this was a different case altogether. I was feeling, not thinking, and my anger at her escape cracked the lid off my more civilized impulses. I choked a pillow to death imagining it was her neck and finally shouted, "Crazy, crazy, that's her trouble, all the way around the bend and dotty as polka-dots!" When I fell onto the bed everything swooped around and around in sickening circles and I mumbled, "Just plain crazy. I would have to be crazy myself to figure out which way she will jump next.'' With this my eyes closed and I fell asleep. While the words swam down through the alcohol-saturated layers until they reached a deeper level where a spark of rationality still dwelled.

When they hit bottom I was wide awake and sitting up in bed, struck dumb by the ghastly truth. I would require all the conviction I had—and a little more—to do it.

I would have to follow her down the path of insanity if I wanted to find her.

13

In the cold light of morning the idea didn't look any more attractive—or any less true. I could do it, or not do it, as I chose. There could be no doubting the wild tinge of insanity that colored Angelina's life. Every one of our contacts had been marked by a ruthless indifference to human life. She killed with coldness or with pleasure—as when she had shot me—but always with total disregard for people. I doubt if even she had any idea of how many murders she had committed in her lifetime. By her standards I was a rank amateur. I hadn't killed more than—that kind of violence was rarely necessary in my type of operation—surely no more than . . . none?

Well, well—old chicken-hearted revealed at last. Rough and tough diGriz the Killer who never killed! It was nothing to be ashamed of, quite the opposite in fact. I placed a value on human life, the one unchanging value in existence. Angelina valued herself and her desires, and nothing else. To follow her down the twisted path of her own making I would have to place myself in the same mental state that she lived in.

This is not as difficult as it sounds—at least in theory. I have had some experience with the psychotomimetic drugs and was well aware of their potency. Centuries of research have produced drugs that can simulate any mental condition in the user. Like to be paranoid for a day? Take a pill. You too can go around the bend, friend. It is a matter of record that people have actually tried these concoctions for kicks, but *that* bored with life I don't want to be. There would have to be a lot stronger reason before I would subject my delicate gray cells to this kind of jarring around. Like finding Angelina, for instance.

About the only good thing about these pixilation producers is the accepted fact that the effects are only temporary. When the drug wears off so do the hallucinations. I hoped. Nowhere in the texts I studied did they mention a devil's brew such as the one I was concocting. It was a laborious task hunting down all of Angelina's fascinating symptoms in the textbooks and trying to fit them to an inclusive psychotic pattern. I even called in some professional help to aid in analyzing her case, not mentioning, of course, to what use I intended to put the information. In the end I had a bottle of slightly smoky liquid and a taped recording of autohypnotic suggestions to play into my ears while the shot was taking effect. All that remained was screwing my courage to the sticking-place as they say in the classics. Not really all that remained—I wanted to take some precautions first. I rented a room in a cheap hotel and left orders not to be disturbed at any time. This was the first time I had ever tried this particular type of nonsense and since I had no idea of how foggy my memory would be I left a few notes around to remind me of the job. After a half day of this kind of preparation I realized I was making excuses.

"Well it's not easy to deliberately go insane," I told my rather pale reflection in the mirror. The reflection agreed but that didn't stop either of us from rolling up our sleeves and filling large hypodermic needles with murky madness.

"Here's looking at you," I said, and slipped the needle gently in the vein and slowly pushed the plunger home.

The results were anticlimactic to say the least. Outside of a ringing in my ears and a twinge of headache that quickly passed I felt nothing. I knew better than to go out though, so I read the newspaper for a while, until I felt tired. The whole thing seemed a little foolish and pretty much of a letdown. I went to sleep with the tape player whispering softly in my ears such ego-building epigrams as, "You are better than everyone else and you know it, and people who don't know it had better watch out," and "They are all fools and if you were in charge things would be different, and why *aren't* you in charge, it's easy enough."

Waking up was uncomfortable because of the pain in my ears where the earphones were still plugged in, my own stupid voice droning away at me. Nothing had changed and the whole futile experiment was a waste and waste makes me angry. The earphones broke in my hands and I felt better, felt much better still when I had stamped the tape player into a tangle of rubble.

My face rasped when I ran my hand over it; I had been days without a shave. Rubbing in the dip cream I looked into the mirror over the sink and an odd fact struck me for the first time. This new face fitted me a lot better than the old one. A fault of birth or the ugliness of my parents—whom I hated deeply, the only right thing they ever did was to produce me—had given me a face that didn't fit my personality. The new one was better, handsomer for one thing and a lot stronger. I should have thanked that fumble-finger quack Vulff for producing a masterpiece. I should have thanked him with a bullet. That would guarantee that no one would ever be able to trace me through him. It must have been a warm day and I was suffering a fever when I let him get safely away like that.

On the table was a piece of paper with a single word written on it, my own handwriting though I can't imagine why the hell I left it there. *Angelina* it said. Angelina, how I would love to get that tender white throat between my hands and squeeze until your eyeballs popped. Hah! I had to laugh at the thought, made a funny picture indeed. Yet I shouldn't be so flippant about it. Angelina was important. I was going to find her and nothing was going to stop me. She had made a fool of me and had tried to kill me. If anyone deserved to die it was her. It was an awful waste in some ways yet it had to be done. I shredded the note into fine pieces.

All at once the room was very oppressing and I wanted out. What made me doubly angry was the fact the key was missing. I remember taking it out, but had no idea where I had put it. The slob at the desk was slow at answering and I was tempted to tell him just what I thought of the service, but I refrained. There is only one permanent cure for these types. A spare key rattled into the basket of the pneumo and I let myself out. I needed some food and I needed some drink and most of all I needed a quiet place for some thought.

A nearby spot provided all three—after I had chased the hookers away. They were all dogs, and Angelina just playing a role had been better than this entire crowd lumped together. Angelina. She was on my mind tonight with a vengeance. The drinks warmed my gut and Angelina warmed my memory. To think that I had actually once considered turning her in or possibly killing her. What a waste! The only intelligent woman I had ever run across. And all woman—I'll never forget the way she walked in that dress. Once she had been tamed a bit—what a team we could make! This thought was so mentally aphrodisiac that my skin burned and I drained my glass at a single swallow.

Something had to be done; I had to find her. She would never have left a ripe plum of a planet like this one. A girl with her ambition could go right to the top here, nothing could stop her. And that's of course where she would be—eventually if not now. She must spend her life feeling damned because she was a woman, knowing she was better than the rest of the cruds around, then proving it to herself and them over and over again. My arrival would be the biggest favor Angelina could have. I didn't have to prove myself better than the hicks on this rubeified planet—just one look did that. When Angelina hooked up with me she could stop fighting, relax and take orders. The contest would be over for all time.

While I sat there something was nagging at me, some vital fact I had to remember—yet couldn't. For a second I fumbled with the memory before I realized what it was. The injection would be wearing off soon! I had to get back to the room, quickly. There had been some fear about the danger of this business, but I realized now that was just my earlier cowardice. This stuff was no more dangerous than aspirin. And at the same time it was the galaxy's greatest pick-up. New worlds of possibilities were opening up to me, my mind was clearer and my thoughts more logical. I wasn't going back to the old muddled-head stuff. At the bar I paid the bartender, my fingers tapping impatiently while he slothfully made change for me.

"A wiseguy?" I asked, loud enough for everyone in the joint to hear. "A customer is in a hurry so that's your chance to shortchange him. This is two gilden short." I held the money out in my palm and when he bent to count it I came up quick with the hand and let him have the whole thing right in the face, bills, coins, thumb and fingers. At the same time I told him—in a low voice so no one else could hear—just what I thought of him. Freibur slang is rich in insult and I used the best on him. I could have done more but I was in a hurry to get back to the hotel room, and teaching him a lesson would take time. When I turned to go I kept an eye behind me in a mirror across the room and it's a good thing I did. He pulled a length of pipe out from under the bar and raised it over my head. Of course I stood still to give him a nice target and not throw off his aim—only stepping aside as the arm came down, just moving enough to let the pipe skin by me.

It was no trick at all to grab the arm, keep it going down, and break the bone across the edge of the bar. The screams were heartwarming to say the least, and I only wish I had the time to stay and really give him something to scream about. There was just no time left.

"You saw him viciously attack me," I told the stunned customers as I headed for the door. Rough-and-tough had slumped down and was moaning out of sight somewhere behind the bar. "I'm going to call the police now—see that he doesn't leave." Of course he had as much intention of leaving as I had of calling the law. I was out the door long before any of them had made their minds up as to just what was going on.

Of course I couldn't run and draw any attention to myself.

Getting back to the hotel at a fast walk was the best I could do, but I was sweating all over from the tension. Inside the room the first thing I saw was the container on the table, with the needle wrapped in cloth beside it. My hands didn't shake, but they would have if I had let them. This was a very close thing.

Collapsed in a chair afterwards I held up the jar and saw that there was less than a millimeter of juice left. The very next thing on the agenda was the necessity of laying in a supply of the stuff. I could remember the formula clearly and would have no trouble rebuilding it. Of course there would be no drug suppliers open at this time of night, but that made things a lot easier. There is a law of history that says weapons were invented before money. In my suitcase was a recoilless .75 that could get me more of the galaxy's goods than all of the money in existence.

That was my mistake. Some nagging worry gnawed me then but I ignored it. The tension and then the relief after getting the shot had me all loosened up. On top of that was the need to hurry, the limited time I had to find what I needed and get it back to the hotel room. My thoughts were on the job and how best to do it as I unlocked the suitcase and reached for my gun lying right there on top of the clothes. At this point the thin voice in my memory was screaming inaudibly to me, but this only made me reach faster for the gun. Something was badly wrong and this was the thing that would fix it. As I grabbed the butt the memory broke through . . . just a little bit too slow.

Dropping the gun I dived for the door, too late by far. Behind me I heard a pop as the sleep-gas grenade I had put under the gun let go. Even as I fell forward into darkness I wondered how I could ever have possibly done such a stupid thing as that. . . .

14

COMING OUT OF the gas, my first feeling was one of regret. It is a truism that the workings of the mind are a source of constant astonishment. The effects of my devil's brew had worn off. There was nothing wrong with my memory, now that the posthypnotic blocks I had put on it had been removed. All too vividly I could recall the details of my interlude of madness. Though I sickened at the things I had thought and done, I simultaneously felt a twinge of regret that could not be abolished. There had been terrible freedom in standing so alone that even the lives of other men meant less than nothing. Undoubtedly a warped sensation, but still a tremendously attractive one. Like taking drugs. Even while detesting the thought I felt the desire for more of the same.

In spite of my twelve hours of forced sleep I was exhausted. It took all of my energy to drag over to the bed and collapse on it. Foresight had provided a bottle of stimulating spirits and I poured a glassful. Sipping at this I tried to put my mental house in order, not a very easy task. I have read many times about the cesspool of dark desires that lies in our subconscious minds, but this was the first time I had ever had mine stirred up. It was quite revealing to examine some of the things that had floated to the surface.

My attitude towards Angelina needed a good looking at. The most important fact I had to face was the strong attraction I felt for her. Love? Put any name to it you want—I suppose love will do as well as any, though this was no throbbing adolescent passion. I wasn't blind to her faults, in fact I rather detested them now that I knew her murderously amoral existence had an echo in my own mind. But logic and convictions have very little to do with emotions. Hating this side of her didn't remove the attraction of a personality so similar to my own. I echoed my psychotic self's attitude—what a team we might have made! This was of course impossible, but that didn't stop me from wanting it. Love and hate are reputed to be very close and in my case they were certainly rubbing shoulders. And the whole confused business wasn't helped in the slightest by the fact that Angelina was so damnably attractive. I took a long drag at my drink.

Finding her should be easy now. The carelessness with which I took this for granted was a little shocking. I had gained no new information while mentally aberrant. Just a great chunk of insight into the tortured grooves that my Angelina's mind trundled along. There could be no doubt that raw power was what she desired. This couldn't be obtained through influencing the king, I saw this now. Violence was the way, a power putsch, perhaps assassination, certainly revolution and turmoil of some kind. This had been the pattern in the bad old days on Freibur when sovereignty had been the prize of battle. Any of the nobility could be crowned, and whenever the old king's grip weakened it was a cue for a power struggle that would produce the new monarch. Of course that sort of thing had stopped as soon as the societics specialists from the League worked their little tricks.

The old days were on the way back—that was clear. Angelina was going to see this world bathed in blood and death to satisfy her own ambition. She was out there now—somewhere—grooming the man for the job. One of the counts, still very important in the semi-feudal economy, was having his ego inflated and guided by a new power behind the throne. This is the pattern Angelina had used before, and would be sure to use again. There could be no doubt.

Only one small factor was missing. Who was the man?

My dive into the depths of self-analysis had left a definitely unwholesome taste in my mouth that no amount of liquor could wash away. What I needed was a little touch of action to tone up my drooping nerve ends and accelerate my sluggish blood. Tracking down Angelina's front man would be just the charge my battery needed. Merely thinking about it helped, and it was with eagerness that I searched the newspaper for the Court News column. There was a Grand Ball just two days distant, the perfect cover for this operation.

For these two days I was kept busy on the many small tasks that put the polish of perfection on a job like this. Any boob can crash a party, in fact usually does, since that is all one seems to meet at this kind of affair. It takes a unique talent like mine to construct a cover personality that is unshakeable. Research supplied me with a homeland, a distant province poor in everything except a thick dialect that provided the base for most Freibur jokes. Because of these inherent handicaps the populace of Misteldross was noted for its pugnacity and general bullheadedness. There were minor nobility there who no one took much notice of, or kept any records about, enabling me to adopt the cover of Grav Bent Diebstall. The family name meant either bandit or tax-gatherer in the local dialect, which gives you an idea of the kind of economy they had had, as well as the source of the family title. A military tailor cut me a dress uniform and while I was being fitted I memorized great chunks of the family history to bore people with. I saw where I could be the life of any party.

Another thing I did was to send off a thick wad of money to the maimed bartender, who was now working with the handicap of having his arm in a cast. He really had short-changed me, but his suffering was entirely out of proportion to this minor crime. My anonymous gift was strictly conscience money and I felt much better after having done it.

A moonlight visit to the royal printers supplied an invitation to the party. My uniform fitted like a sausage skin, my boots gleamed enthusiastically and I was one of the first guests to arrive since the royal table had a tremendous reputation and work had increased my appetite. I crashed and clattered wonderfully when I bowed to the King—spurs and sword, they go all the way with the archaic nonsense on Freibur—and looked at him closely while he mumbled something inaudible. His eyes were glassy and unfocused and I realized there was some truth in the rumor that he always got stoned on his private bottle before coming to one of these affairs. Apparently he hated crowds and parties and much preferred to putter with his bugs—he was an amateur entomologist of no small talents. I passed on to the queen who was much more receptive. She was twenty years his junior and attractive in a handsomely inflated, bovine way. Rumor also had it that she was bored by his beetles and much preferred homo sapiens to lepidoptera. I tested this calumny by giving her hand an extra squeeze when I held it and queeny squeezed back with an expression of great interest. I moved on to the buffet.

While I ate, the guests continued to arrive. Watching them as they entered didn't interfere with my demolishing the food or sampling all of the wines. I had finished stoking up by the time the rest were just starting, so I could circulate among them. All of the women were subjected to my very close scrutiny, and most of them enjoyed it because, if I say so myself, with my new face and the fit of the uniform I cut a mean swath through the local types. I really wasn't expecting to run across Angelina's trail this easily, but there was always the chance. Only a few of the women even remotely resembled her, but it took only a few words each time to settle the fact that they were true-blue blue-blood and not my little interstellar killer. This task was made simpler by the fact that the Freibur beauties ran heavily towards the flesh, and Angelina was a neat and petite package. I went back to the bar.

"You have been given a Royal Command," an adenoidal voice said in my ear while fingers plucked at my sleeve. I turned and gave my best scowl to the character who still clutched the fabric.

"Let go the suit or I push your buck-toothed face the punch bowl in," I growled in my thickest Misteldrossian accent. He let go as if he had grabbed something hot and got all red and excited-looking. "That's better," I added, cutting off his next words. "Now—who wants to see me—the King?"

"Her majesty, the Queen," he managed to squeeze out between thin lips.

"That's good. I want to see her too. Show the way." I forged a way through the crowd while my new friend clattered behind, trying to pass me. I stopped before I reached the group around Queen Heida and let him get ahead all out of breath and sweating.

"Your majesty, this is the Baron—"

"Grav not Baron," I cut in with my hideously rich accent. "Grav Bent Diebstall from a poor provincial family, cheated centuries ago of our rightful title by thieving and jealous counts." I scowled straight at my guide as if he had been in the plot and he turned the flush on again.

"I don't recognize all of your honors, Grav Bent," the Queen said in her low voice that reminded me of pastures on a misty morn. She pointed to my manly chest, to the row of decorations I had purchased from a curio dealer just that morning.

"Galactic medals, your majesty. A younger son of the provincial nobility, his family impoverished by the greedy and corrupt, can find little opportunity to advance himself here on Freibur. That is why I took service offplanet and served for the best years of my youth in the Stellar Guard. These are for commonplace happenings such as battles, invasions and space boardings. But *this* is the one I can really take pride in—" I fingered through the jingling hardware until I came to an unsightly thing, all comets, novas and sparkling lights. "This is the Stellar Star, the most prized award in the Guards." I took it in my hand and gave it a long look. In fact I think it *was* a Guard decoration, given out for reenlisting or five years of K.P. or some such.

"It's beautiful," the Queen said. Her taste in medals was no better than her taste in clothes, but what can you expect on these backward planets.

"It is that," I agreed. "I don't enjoy describing the medal's history, but if it is a royal command . . . ?'' It was, and given very coyly indeed. I lied about my exploits for awhile and kept them all interested. There would be plenty of talk about me in the morning and I hoped some of it would trickle down to Angelina's ears, wherever she was hiding. Thinking of her took the edge off my fun, and I managed to excuse myself and go back to the bar.

I spent the rest of the evening talking up the wonders of my imaginary history to everyone I could nail. Most of them seemed to enjoy it, since the court was normally short on laughs. The only one who didn't seem to be getting a charge out of it was myself. Though the plan had seemed good at first, the more I became involved with it the slower it appeared. I might flutter around the fringe of these fantastically dull court circles for months without finding a lead to Angelina. The process had to be accelerated. There was one idea drifting in and out of my head, but it bordered on madness. If it misfired I would be either dead or barred from these noble circles forever. This last was a fate I could easily stand—but it wouldn't help me find my lovely quarry. However—if the plan did work it would shortcut all the other nonsense. I flipped a coin to decide, and of course won since I had palmed the coin before the toss. It was going to be action.

Before coming I had pocketed a few items that might come in handy during the course of the evening. One of them was a surefire introduction to the King in case I felt that getting nearer to him might be of some importance. I slipped this into an outer pocket, filled the largest glass I could find with sweet wine, and trundled through the cavernous rooms in search of my prey.

If King Villelm had been crocked when he arrived, he was now almost paralyzed. He must have had a steel bar sewn into the back of his white uniform jacket because I swear his own spine shouldn't have held him up. But he was still drinking and swaying back and forth, his head bobbing as though it were loosely attached. He had a crowd of old boys around him and they must have been swapping off-color stories because they gave me varying degrees of get-lost looks when I trundled up and snapped to attention. I was bigger than most of them and must have made a nice blob of color because I caught Villy's eye and the head slowly slewed around in my direction. One of his octogenarian cronies had met me earlier in the evening and was forced to make the introduction.

''A very great pleasure to meet your majesty,'' I droned with a bit of a drunken blur to my voice. Not that the King noticed, but some of the others did and scowled. ''I am by way of being a bit of an entomologist myself, if you will pardon the expression, hoping to follow in your royal footsteps. I am keen on this and feel that greater attention should be paid on Freibur, more respect given I should say, and more opportunity taken to utilize the advantageous aspects of the forminifera, lepidoptera and all the others. Heraldry, for instance, the flags might utilize the more visual aspects of insects . . ."

I babbled on like this for a while, the crowd getting impatient with the unwanted interruption. The King—who wasn't getting in more than one word in ten—got tired of nodding after a while and his attention began to wander. My voice thickened and blurred and I could see them wondering how to get rid of the drunk. When the first tentative hand reached out for my elbow I played my trump card.

"Because of your majesty's interest," I said, fumbling in my pocket, "I carefully kept this specimen, carrying it across the countless light years to reach its logical resting place, your highness's collection." Pulling out the flat plastic case, I held it under his nose. With an effort he blinked his watery eyes back into focus and let out a little gasp. The others crowded around and I gave them a few seconds to enjoy the thing.

Well it was a beautiful bug, I can't deny that. However it had not traveled across countless light years because I had just made it myself that morning. Most of the parts were assembled from other insects, with a few pieces of plastic thrown in where nature had let me down. Its body was as long as my hand, and it had three sets of wings, each set in a different color. There were a lot of legs underneath, pretty mismatched I'm afraid since they came from a dozen other insects and a lot of them got mashed or misplaced during construction. Some other nice touches like a massive stinger, three eyes, a corkscrew tail and such-like were not lost on my rapt audience. I had had the foresight to make the case of tinted plastic which blurred the contents nicely and hinted at rather than revealed them.

"But you must see it more closely, your highness," I said, snapping open the case while both of us swayed back and forth. This was a difficult juggling act as I had to hold the case in the same hand as my wine glass, leaving my other hand free to grasp the monstrosity. I plucked it out between thumb and forefinger and the King leaned close, the drink in his own glass slopping back and forth in his eagerness. I squeezed just a bit with my thumb and the bug popped forward in lively fashion and dived into the King's glass.

"Save it! Save it!" I cried, "A valuable specimen!" I plunged my fingers in after it and chased it around and around. Some of the drink slopped out staining Villelm's gilt-edged cuff. A gasp went up and angry voices sounded. Someone pulled hard at my shoulder.

"Leave off you title-stealing clots!" I shouted, and pulled away roughly from the grasp. The drowned insect flew out of my fingers and landed on the King's chest, from where it fell slowly to the floor, shedding wings, legs and other parts on the way. I must have used a very inferior glue. When I leaped to grab the dropping corpse the forgotten drink in my other hand splashed red and sticky onto the King's jacket. A howl of anger went up from the crowd.

I'll say this much for the King, he took it well. Stood there swaying like a tree in the storm, but offering no protest outside of mumbling, "I say . . . I say . . ." a few times. Not even when I rubbed the wine in with my handkerchief, treading on his toes by accident as the crowd behind pushed too close. One of them pulled hard at my arm, then let go when I shrugged. My arm struck against Villelm IX's noble chest and his royal upper plate popped out on the floor to add to the fun.

Fun it was too, once the old boys got cleared away. The younger nobility leaped to their majesty's defense and I showed them a thing or two about mix-it-up fighting that I had learned on a number of planets. They made up in energy what they lacked in technique and we had a really good go-around. Women screamed, strong men cursed and the King was half carried out of the fracas. After that things got dirty and I did too. I couldn't blame them, but that didn't stop me from giving just as good as I received.

My last memory is of a number of them holding me while another one hit me. I got him in the face with the shoe on my free leg, but they grabbed that too and his replacement turned off all the lights.

15

UNCIVILIZED AS MY behavior had been, the jailers persisted in treating me in a most civilized fashion. I grumbled about this and made their job as hard as possible. I hadn't voluntarily entered prison in order to win a popularity contest. Pulling all those gags on the poor old King had been a risk. *Lèse-majesté* is the sort of crime that is usually punishable by death. Happily the civilizing influences of the League had penetrated darkest Freibur, and the locals now fell over backwards to show me how law-abiding they were. I would have none of it. When they brought me a meal I ate it, then destroyed the dishes to show my contempt for this unlawful detention.

This was the bait. The bruises I had suffered would be a small enough price to pay if my attempt at publicity paid off in the right quarters. Without a doubt I was being discussed. A figure of shame, a traitor to my class. A violent man in a peaceful world, and a pugnacious, combative uncompromising one at that. In short I was all the things a good Freiburian detested, and the sort of a man Angelina should have a great deal of interest in.

In spite of its recent bloody past, Freibur was woefully short of roughneck manpower. Not at the very lowest levels of course; the portside drinkeries were stuffed with musclebound apes with pinhead brains. Angelina would be able to recruit all of those she needed. But strongarm squads alone wouldn't win her a victory. She needed allies and aid from the nobility, and from what I had seen this sort of talent was greatly lacking. In my indirect manner I had displayed all the traits she would be interested in, doing it in such a way that she wouldn't know the show had been arranged only for her. The trap was open, all she had to do was step into it.

Metal boomed as the turnkey rapped on the door. "You have visitors, Grav Diebstall," he said, opening the inner grill.

"Tell them to go to hell!" I shouted. "There's no one on this poxty planet I want to see."

Paying no attention to my request, he bowed in the governor of the prison and a pair of ancient types wearing black clothes and severe looks. I did the best I could to ignore them. They waited grimly until the guard had gone, then the skinniest opened a folder he was carrying and slowly drew out a sheet of paper with his fingertips.

"I will not sign a suicide note so you can butcher me in my sleep," I snarled at him. This rattled him a bit, but he tried to ignore it.

"That is an unfair suggestion," he intoned solemnly. "I am the Royal Attorney and would never condone such an action." All three of them nodded together as though they were pulled by one string, and the effect was so compulsive that I almost nodded myself.

"I will not commit suicide voluntarily," I said harshly to break the spell of agreement. "That is the last word that will be said on the subject."

The Royal Attorney had been around the courts long enough not to be thrown off his mark by this kind of obliquity. He coughed, rattled the paper, and got back to basics.

"There are a number of crimes you could be charged with young man," he droned, with an intensely gloomy expression draped on his face. I yawned, unimpressed. "I hope this will not have to be done," he went on, "since it would only cause harm to all concerned. The King himself does not wish to see this happen, and in fact has pressed upon me his earnest desire to have this affair ended quietly now. His desire for peace has prevailed upon us all, and I am here now to put his wish into action. If you will sign this apology, you will be placed aboard a starship leaving tonight. The matter will be ended."

"Trying to get rid of me to cover up your drunken brawls at the palace, hey?" I sneered. The Attorney's face purpled but he controlled his temper with a magnificent effort. If they threw me off the planet now everything was wasted.

"You are being insulting, sir!" he snorted. "You are not without blame in this matter, remember. I heartily recommend that you accept the King's leniency in this tragic affair and sign that apology." He handed the paper to me and I tore it to pieces.

"Apologize? Never!" I shouted at them. "I was merely defending my honor against your drunken louts and larcenous nobility, all descended from thieves who stole the titles rightly belonging to my family!"

They left then, and the prison governor was the only one young and sturdy enough for me to help on the way with the toe of my shoe in the appropriate spot. Everything was as it should be. The door

clanged shut behind them—on a rebellious, cantankerous, bellig-
erent son of the Freibur soil. I had arranged things perfectly to bring
me to the attention of Angelina. But unless she became interested in
me soon I stood a good chance of spending the rest of my days
behind these grim walls.

Waiting has always been bad for my nerves. I am a thinker during
moments of peace, but a man of action most of the time. It is one
thing to prepare a plan and leap boldly into it. It is another thing
altogether to sit around a grubby prison cell wondering if the plan
has worked or if there is a weak link in the chain of logic.

Should I crack out of this pokey? That shouldn't be hard to do,
but it had better be saved for a last resort. Once out I would have to
stay undercover and there would be no chance of her contacting me.
That was why I was gnawing my way through all my fingernails.
The next move was up to Angelina; all I could do was wait. I only
hoped that she would gather the right conclusions from all the
violent evidence I had supplied.

After a week I was stir-crazy. The Royal Attorney never came
back and there was no talk of a trial or sentencing. I had presented
them with an annoying problem, and they must have been scratching their heads feebly over it and hoping I would go away. I almost
did. Getting out of this backwoods jail would have been simplicity
itself. But I was waiting for a message from my deadly love. I toyed
with the possibilities of the things she might do. Perhaps arrange
pressure through the court to have me freed? Or smuggle in a file
and a note to see if I could break out on my own? This second
possibility appealed to me most and I shredded my bread every time
it arrived to see if anything had been baked into it. There was
nothing.

On the eighth day Angelina made her play, in the most forthright
manner of her own. It was night, but something unaccustomed
woke me up. Listening produced no answers, so I slipped over to the
barred opening in the door and saw a most attractive sight at the end
of the hall. The night guard was sprawled on the floor and a burly
masked figure dressed completely in black stood over him with a
cosh in one meaty hand. Another stranger, dressed like the first,
came up and they dragged the guard further along the hall towards
me. One of them rummaged in his waist wallet and produced a scrap
of red cloth that he put between the guard's limp fingers. Then they
turned towards my cell and I moved back out of sight, climbing
noiselessly into bed.

A key grated in the lock and the lights came on. I sat up blinking, giving a fine imitation of a man waking up.

"Who's there? What do you want?" I asked.

"Up quickly, and get dressed, Diebstall. You're getting out of here." This was the first thug I had seen, the blackjack still hanging from his hand. I sagged my jaw a bit, then leaped out of bed with my back to the wall.

"Assassins!" I hissed. "So that's vile King Villy's bright idea, is it? Going to put a rope around my neck and swear I hung myself? Well come on—but don't think it will be easy!"

"Don't be an idiot!" the man whispered. "And shut the big mouth. We're here to get you out. We're friends." Two more men, dressed the same way, pushed in behind him, and I had a glimpse of a fourth one in the hall.

"Friends!" I shouted. "Murderers is more like it! You'll pay dearly for this crime."

The fourth man, still in the hall, whispered something and they charged me. I wanted a better glimpse of the boss. He was a small man—if he *was* a man. His clothes were loose and bulky, and there was a stocking mask over his entire head. Angelina would be just about that tall. But before I could get a better look the thugs were on me. I kicked one in the stomach and ducked away. This was fighting barroom style and they had all the advantages. Without shoes or a weapon I didn't stand a chance, and they weren't afraid to use their coshes. I tried hard not to smile with victory as they worked me over.

Only reluctantly did I allow myself to be dragged to the place where I wanted to go.

16

BECAUSE THE POUNDING on the head had only made me groggy, one of them broke a sleep capsule under my nose and that was that for a while. So of course I had no idea of how far we had traveled or where on Freibur I was. They must have given me the antidote because the next thing I saw was a scrawny type with a hypodermic injector in his hand. He was peeling back my eyelid to look and I slapped his hand away.

"Going to torture me before you kill me, swine!" I said, remembering the role I had to play.

"Don't worry about that," a deep voice said behind me, "you are among friends. People who can understand your irritation with the present régime."

This voice wasn't much like Angelina's. Neither was the burly, sour-faced owner. The medic slid out and left us alone, and I wondered if the plan had slipped up somewhere. Iron-jaw with the beady eyes had a familiar look—I recognized him as one of the Freiburian nobility. I had memorized the lot and looking at his ugly face I dredged up a mnemonic. A midget painted bright red.

"Rdenrundt—The Count of Rdenrundt," I said, trying to remember what else I had read about him. "I might believe you were telling me the truth if you weren't his Highness's first cousin. I find it hard to consider that you would steal a man from the royal jail for your own purposes . . ."

"It's not important what you believe," he snapped angrily. He had a short fuse and it took him a moment to get his temper back under control. "Villelm may be my cousin—that doesn't mean I think he is the perfect ruler for our planet. You talked a lot about your claims to higher rank and the fact that you had been cheated. Did you mean that? Or are you just another parlor windbag? Think well before you answer—you may be committing yourself. There may be other people who feel as you do, that there is change in the wind."

Impulsive, enthusiastic, that was me. Loyal friend and deadly enemy and just solid guts when it came to a fight. Jumping forward I grabbed his hand and pumped it.

"If you are telling me the truth, then you have a man at your side who will go the whole course. If you are lying to me and this is some trick of the King's—well then, Count, be ready to fight!"

"No need to fight," he said, extracting his hand with some difficulty from my clutch. "Not between us at least. We have a difficult course ahead of us, and we must learn to rely upon each other." He cracked his knuckles and looked glumly out the window. "I sincerely hope that I will be able to rely on you. Freibur is a far different world from the one our ancestors ruled. The League has sapped the fight from our people. There are none I can really rely on."

"There's nothing wrong with the bunch who took me out of my cell. They seemed to do the job well enough."

"Muscle!" he spat, and pressed a button on the arm of his chair. "Thugs with heads of solid stone. I can hire all of those I need. What I need are men who can lead—help me to lead Freibur into its rightful future."

I didn't mention the man who led the muscle the previous night, the one who had stayed in the corridor. If Rdenrundt wasn't going to talk about Angelina I certainly couldn't bring up the topic. Since he wanted brain not brawn, I decided to give him a little.

"Did you dream up the torn piece of uniform left in the guard's hand in the prison? That was a good touch."

His eyes narrowed a bit when he turned to look at me. "You're quite observant, Bent," he said.

"A matter of training," I told him, trying to be both unassuming and positive at the same time. "There was this piece of red cloth with a button in the guard's hand, like something he had grabbed in a struggle. Yet all of the men I saw were dressed only in black. Perhaps a bit of misdirection. . . ."

"With each passing moment I'm getting happier that you have joined me," he said, and showed me all of his ragged teeth in an expression he must have thought was a grin. "The Old Duke's men wear red livery, as you undoubtedly know . . ."

"And the Old Duke is the strongest supporter of Villelm IX," I finished for him. "It wouldn't hurt in the slightest if he had a falling out with the King."

"Not the slightest," Rdenrundt echoed, and showed me all of his teeth again. I was beginning to dislike him intensely. If this was the front man Angelina had picked for her operation, then he was undoubtedly the best one for the job on the planet. But he was such a puffed-up crumb, with barely enough imagination to appreciate the ideas Angelina was feeding him. Yet I imagine he had the money and the title—and the ambition—which combination she had to have. Once more I wondered where she was.

Something came in through the door and I recoiled, thinking the war was on. It was only a robot, but it made such a hideous amount of hissing and clanking that I wondered what was wrong with it. The Count ordered the ghastly thing to wheel over the bar, as it turned away I saw what could have been a *chimney* projecting behind one shoulder. There was the distinct odor of coal smoke in the air.

"Does that robot burn *coal*—?" I gurgled.

"It goes," the Count said, pouring us out a pair of drinks. "It is a perfect example of what is wrong with the Freiburian economy under the gracious rule of Villelm the Incompetent. You don't see any robots like this in the capital!"

"I should hope not," I gasped, staring bug-eyed at the trickle of steam escaping from the thing, and the stains of rust and coal dust on its plates. "Of course I've been away a long time . . . things change . . ."

"They don't change fast enough! And don't act galactic-wise with me, Diebstall. I've been to Misteldross and seen how the rubes live. You have no robots at all—much less a contraption like this." He kicked at the thing in sullen anger and it staggered back a bit, valves clicking open as steam pumped into the leg pistons to straighten it up. "Two hundred years come next Grundlovsday we will have been in the League, milked dry and pacified by them—and for what? To provide luxuries for the King in Freiburbad. While out here we get a miserable consignment of a few robot brains and some control circuitry. We have to build the rest of the inefficient monsters ourselves. And out in the real sticks where you come from they think robot is a misspelling of a boat that goes with oars!"

He drained his glass and I made no attempt to explain to him the economics of galactic commerce, planetary prestige, or the multifold levels of intercommunication. This lost planet had been cut off from the mainstream of galactic culture for maybe a thousand years, until contact had been reestablished after the Breakdown. They were being eased back into the culture gradually, without any violent repercussions that might upset the process. Sure, a billion robots could be dumped here tomorrow. What good would that do the economy? It was certainly much better to bring in the control units and let the locals build the things for themselves. If they didn't like the final product they could improve the design instead of complaining.

The Count of course didn't see it this way. Angelina had done a nice job at playing upon his prejudices and desires. He was still glaring at the robot when he leaned forward and suddenly tapped a dial on the thing's side.

"Look at that!" he shouted. "Down to eighty pounds pressure! Next thing you know the thing will be falling on its face and burning the place down. Stoke, you idiot—*stoke!!*"

A couple of relays closed inside the contraption and the robot clanked and put the tray of glasses down. I took a very long drag on my drink and enjoyed the scene. Trundling over to the fireplace—at a slower pace now I'll admit—it opened a door in its stomach and flame belched out. Using the coal scoop in the pail it shoveled in a good portion of anthracite and banged the firedoor shut again. Rich black smoke boiled from its chimney. At least it was housebroken and didn't shake out its grate here.

"Outside, dammit, outside!" the Count shouted, coughing at the same time. The smoke was a little thick. I poured another drink and decided right then that I was going to like Rdenrundt.

I would have liked it a lot better if I could have found Angelina. This whole affair bore every sign of her light touch, yet she was nowhere in sight. I was shown to a room and met some of the officers on the Count's staff. One of them, Kurt, a youth of noble lineage but no money, showed me around the grounds. The place was a cross between a feudal keep and a small town, with a high wall cutting it off from the city proper. There appeared to be no obvious signs of the Count's plans, outside of the number of armed retainers who lounged about and practiced uninterestedly in the shooting ranges. It all looked too peaceful to be true—yet I had been brought here. That was no accident. I tried a little delicate questioning and Kurt was frank with his answers. Like a lot of the far-country gentry he bore a grudge against the central authorities, although he would of course never have gotten around to doing anything about it on his own. Somehow he had been recruited and was ready to go along with the plans, all of which were very vague to him. I doubt if he had ever seen a corpse. That he was telling me the truth about everything was obvious when I caught him in his first lie.

We had passed some women and bent a knee, and Kurt had volunteered the advice that they were the wives of two of the other officers.

"And you're married too?" I asked.

"No. Never had the time, I guess. Now I suppose it's too late, at least for awhile. When this whole business is over and life is a little more peaceful there'll be plenty of time to settle down.''

"How right," I agreed. "What about the Count? Is he married? I've been away so many years that it's hard to keep track of that kind of thing. Wives, children and such." Without being obvious I was watching him when I asked this, and he gave a little start.

"Well . . . yes, you might say. I mean the Count was married, but there was an accident, he's not married now . . ." His voice tapered away and he drew my attention to something else, happy to leave the topic.

Now if there is one thing that always marks Angelina's trail it is a corpse or two. It took no great amount of inspiration to connect her with the "accidental" death of the Count's wife. If the death had been natural Kurt would not have been afraid to talk about it. He didn't mention the topic again and I made no attempt to pump him. I had my lead. Angelina may not have been in sight—but her spoor was around me on all sides. It was just a matter of time now. As soon as I was able to, I would shake Kurt and hunt up the bullyboys who had spirited me out of the jail. Buy them a few drinks to assure them that there were no hard feelings about the beating they had given me. Then pump them adroitly about the man who had led them.

Angelina made her move first. One of the coal-burning robots came hissing and clanking around with a message. The Count would like to see me. I slicked my hair, tucked in my shirt and reported for duty.

I was pleased to see that the Count was a steady and solitary daytime drinker. In addition, there was very little tobacco in his cigarette; the sweet smoke filled the room. All this meant he was due for early dissolution, and I would not be numbered among his mourners. None of this showed in my expression or attitude of course. I was all flashing eye and hell-cracking attention.

"Is it action, sir? Is that why you sent for me?" I asked.

"Sit down, sit down," he mumbled, waving me towards a chair. "Relax. Want a cigarette?" He pushed the box towards me and I eyed the thin brown cylinders with distaste.

"Not today, sir. I'm laying off smoking for awhile. Sharpening up the old eye. Keeping the old trigger finger limber and ready for action."

The Count's mind was occupied elsewhere and I doubt if he heard a word I said. He chewed abstractedly at the inside of his cheek while he looked me up and down. A decision finally struggled up through his half-clotted brain.

"What do you know about the Radebrechen family?" he asked, which is about as exotic a question as I have ever had thrown at me.

"Absolutely nothing," I answered truthfully. "Should I?"

"No . . . no . . ." he answered vaguely, and went back to chewing his cheek. I was getting high just from breathing the air in the room and I wondered how he was feeling.

"Come with me," he said, pushing over his chair and almost falling on top of it. We plodded through a number of halls deeper into the building, until we came to a door, no different from the ones we had passed, except this one had a guard in front of it—a rough-looking brawny type with his arms casually crossed. Just casual enough to let his fingers hang over his pistol grip. He didn't budge when we came up.

"It's all right," the Duke of Rdenrundt said, with what I swear was a peevish tone. "He's with me."

"Gotta search him anyway," the guard said. "Orders."

More and more interesting. Who issued orders the Count couldn't change—in his own castle? As if I didn't know. And I recognized the guard's voice, he was one of the men who had taken me from my prison cell. He searched me quickly and efficiently, then stepped aside. The Count opened the door and I followed him in, trying not to tread on his heels.

One thing about reality—it is always so much superior to theory. I had every reason to believe that Angelina would be here, yet it was still a healthy shock to see her sitting at the table. A kind of electric charge in my spine tingled right up to the roots of my hair. This was a moment I had waited for for a very long time. It took a positive effort to relax and appear indifferent. At least as indifferent as any healthy young male is in front of an attractive package of femininity.

Of course this girl didn't resemble Angelina very much. Yet I still had no doubt. The face was changed as was the color of the hair. And though the face was a new one it still held the same sweet, angelic quality as the old. Her figure was much the way I remembered it, with perhaps a few slight improvements. Hers was a surface transformation, with no attempt at being as complete as the one I had had done to me.

"This is Grav Bent Diebstall," the count said, fixing his hot and smoky little eyes on her. "The man you wanted to see, Engela." So she was still an angel, though under a different name. That was a bad habit she should watch, only I wasn't going to tell her. A lot of people have been caught by taking an alias too similar to their old one.

"Why thank you, Cassitor," she said. Cassitor indeed! I'd look unhappy too if I had to go through life with a handle like Cassitor Rdenrundt. "It was very nice of you to bring Grav Bent here," she added in the same light and empty voice.

Cassi must have been expecting a warmer welcome because he stood first on one foot and then another and mumbled something which neither of us heard. But Angelina-Engela's welcome stayed at the same temperature, or perhaps dropped a degree or two as she shuffled some papers on the table in front of her. Even through his fog the Count caught on and went out mumbling something else under his breath that I was pretty sure was one of the shorter and more unwholesome words in the local dialect. We were alone.

"Why did you tell all those lies about being in the Stellar Guard," she asked in a quiet voice, apparently still busy at the papers. This was my cue to smile sardonically, and flick some imaginary dust from my sleeve.

"Well I certainly couldn't tell all those nice people what I've really been doing all these years I have been away, could I?" I responded with wide-eyed simplicity.

"What were you doing, Bent?" she asked and there wasn't a trace of any emotion in her voice.

"That's really my business, isn't it," I told her, matching toneless tone for tone. "And while we're asking questions, I would like to know who you are, and how come you seem to throw more weight around than the great Count Cassitor?" I'm good at playing this kind of guessing game. But Angy was just as good and dragged the conversation back to her own grounds.

"Since I am in the stronger position here, I think you'll find it wise to answer my questions. Don't be afraid of shocking me. You would be surprised at the things I know about."

No, Angelica love, I wouldn't be surprised at all. But I couldn't just tell all without a little resistance.."You're the one behind this revolution idea, aren't you," I said as a statement, not a question.

"Yes," she said, laying her cards on the table so she could see mine.

"Well if you must know then," I said, "I was smuggling. It is a very interesting occupation if you happen to know what to take where. For a number of years I found it was a most lucrative business. Finally though, a number of governments felt I was giving them unfair competition, since they were the only ones allowed to cheat the public. With the pressure on I returned to my sluggish native land for a period of rest.''

Angel-mine was buying no sealed packages and gave me an exhaustive cross-examination into my smuggling career that showed she had more than a passing knowledge of the field herself. I had of course no trouble answering her questions, since in my day I have turned many a megacredit in this illegal fashion. The only thing I was afraid of was making it too good, so I described a career of a successful but still young and not too professional operator. All the time I was talking I tried to live the role and believe everything I said. This was a crucial time when I must let drop no hints or mannerisms that might bring Slippery Jim diGriz to her mind. I had to be the local punk who had made good and was still on my way up in the universe.

Mind you—our talk was of course all most casual, and carried on in an atmosphere of passing drinks and lighting cigarettes all designed to relax me enough to make a few slips. I did of course, slipping in a lie or two about my successes that she would catch and credit to boyish enthusiasm. When the chit-chat slowed I tried a question of my own.

''Would you mind telling me what a local family named Radebrechen has to do with you?''

''What makes you ask?'' she said so calm and coolly.

''Your smiling friend Cassitor Rdenrundt asked me about them before we came here. I told him I knew nothing. What's their connection with you?''

''They want to kill me,''. she said.

''That would be a shame—and a waste,'' I told her with my best come-hither grin. She ignored it. ''What can I do about it?'' I asked, going back to business, since she didn't seem interested in my masculine attractions.

''I want you to be my bodyguard,'' she said, and when I smiled and opened my mouth to speak she went on, ''and please spare me any remarks about how it is a body you would like to guard. I get enough of that from Cassitor.''

''All I wanted to say was that I accepted the position,'' which was a big lie because I had had some such phrase in mind. It was hard to stay ahead of Angelina and I mustn't relax for an instant I reminded myself again. ''Just tell me about the people who are out to kill you.''

"It seems that Count Rdenrundt was married," Angelicious said, toying with her glass in a simple, girlish way. "His wife committed suicide in a very stupid and compromising manner. Her family—who are of course the Radebrechen—think I killed her, and want to revenge her supposed murder by killing me in turn. Apparently in this lost corner of Freibur the vendetta still has meaning, and this family of rich morons still subscribe to it."

All at once the picture was getting clearer. Count Rdenrundt—a born opportunist—aided his noble fortunes by marrying the daughter of this family. This must have worked well enough until Angelina came along. Then the extra wife was in the way, and ignorant of this charming local custom of revenge-killing, Angelina had removed a stumbling stone. Something had gone wrong—probably the Count had bungled, from the look of the man—and now the vendetta was on. And my Angel wanted me to interpose my frail flesh between her and the killers. Apparently she was finding this retarded planet more than she had bargained for. Now was the time for me to be bold.

"Wat it suicide?" I asked. "Or did you kill her?"

"Yes, I killed her," she said. The sparring was over and all our cards were on the table. The decision was up to me.

17

WELL WHAT ELSE was there to do? I hadn't come this far, getting myself shot, bashed on the head and well-stomped, just to arrest her. I mean I was going to arrest her, of course, but it was next to impossible in the center of the Count's stronghold. Besides that, I wanted to find out a bit more about the Count's proposed uprising, since this would certainly come within the jurisdiction of the Special Corps. If I was going to reenlist I had better bring along a few prizes to show my good intentions.

Anyway—I wasn't so sure I wanted to reenlist. It was a little hard to forget that scuttling charge they had tried to blow up under me. The whole thing wasn't so simple. There were a lot of things mixed up in this. One fact being that I enjoyed Angelina and most of the time I was with her I forgot about those bodies floating in space. They returned at night all right and chopped at my conscience, but I was always tired and went to sleep quickly before they could get through and bother me.

Life was a bed of roses, and I might as well enjoy it before the blossoms withered. Watching Angelady at work was a distinct pleasure, and if you stood my back to the wall and made me swear, I would be forced to admit that I learned a thing or two from her. Singlehandedly she was organizing a revolution on a peaceful planet—and it stood every chance of succeeding. In my small way I helped. The few times she mentioned a problem to me I had a ready answer and in all the cases she went along with my suggestions. Of course I had never toppled governments before, but there are basic laws in crime as in everything else, and it is just a matter of application. This didn't happen often. Most of the time during those first few weeks I was a plain bodyguard, keeping a wary eye out for assassins. This position had a certain ironical angle that appealed to me greatly.

However there was a serpent in our little Eden of Insurrection, and his name was Rdenrundt. I never heard much, but from a word caught here and there I began to see that the Count wasn't really cut out to be a revolutionary. The closer we came to the day the more pallid he became. His little physical vices began to add up, and one day the whole thing came to a head.

Angelegant and the Count were in a business session and I sat in the anteroom outside. I shamelessly eavesdropped whenever I could, and this time I had managed to leave the door open a crack after I had checked her into the room. Careful manipulation with my toe opened it a bit more until I could hear a murmur of their voices. An argument was progressing nicely—there were a lot of them at this time—and I could catch a word here and there. The Count was shouting and it was obvious that he wouldn't give in on some simple and necessary piece of blackmail to advance the cause. Then his tone changed and his voice dropped so I couldn't hear his words, strain as I might. There was a saccharine wheedle and whine in his voice, and Angelina's answer was clear enough. A loud and positive *no*. His bellow brought me to my feet.

"Why not? It's always *no* now and I've had enough of it!"

There was the sound of tearing cloth and something fell to the floor and broke. I was through the door in a single bound. For a brief instant I had a glimpse of a struggling tableau as he pulled at her. Angelina's clothing was torn from one shoulder and his fingers were sunk into her arms like claws. Clubbing my pistol I ran forward. Angelina was a bit faster. She pulled a bottle from the table and banged it into the side of his head with neat efficiency. The Count dropped as if he had been shot. She was pulling up her torn blouse when I came roaring to a halt.

"Put the gun away, Bent—it's all over," she said in a calm voice. I did, but only after making sure the Count was really out, hoping an extra slam might be needed. But she had done a good job. When I stood up Angelina was already halfway out of the room and I had to run to catch up with her. The only other thing she said was "Wait here," when she steamed into her room.

It took no great power of divination to see that there was trouble coming—if it hadn't already arrived. When the Count came to with a busted head he would undoubtedly have some second thoughts about Angelina and revolutions. I thought on these and related subjects while I matched coins with the guards. A few minutes later Angelina called me in.

A long robe covered her arms so the bruises he had made weren't visible. Though outwardly composed there was a telltale glint in her eyes that meant she was doing a slow burn. I spoke what was undoubtedly the uppermost thought in her mind.

"Want me to fix it so the Count joins his noble ancestors in the family crypt?"

She shook her head no. "He still has his uses. I managed to control my temper—so you had better hold yours."

"Mine's in great shape. But what makes you think you can still get work or cooperation out of him? He's going to have an awful sore head when he comes to."

Minor factors like this didn't bother her; she dismissed the thought with a wave of her hand. "I can still handle him and make him do whatever I want—within limits. The limitations are his own natural abilities, which I didn't realize were so slight when I picked him to head this revolt. I'm afraid his cowardice is slowly destroying any large hopes I might have had for him. He will still have value as a figurehead and we must use him for that. But the power and decisions must be ours."

I wasn't being slow, just wary. I chewed around her statements from all sides before I answered. "Just what is this *we* and *ours* business? Where do I fit in?"

Angelilith leaned back in her chair and tossed a lock of her lovely golden hair to one side. Her smile had about a two thousand volt charge and was aimed at me.

"I want you to come in with me on this thing," she said with a voice rich as warm honey. "A partnership. We'll keep the Count of Rdenrundt out in front until the plan succeeds. Then eliminate him and go the rest of the way ourselves. Do you agree?"

"Well," I said. Then with brilliant inspiration, "Well . . ." again. For the first time in a lifetime of verbal pyrotechnics I found the flow shut off. I paced the room and pulled my scattered wits together.

"I hate to look a gift rocket in the tubes," I told her, "nevertheless—why *me*? A simple but hard working bodyguard, who will guard your person, labor for the cause and look forward to the restoration of his stolen lands and title. How come the big jump from office boy to board chairman?"

"You know better than to ask that," she said and smiled, and the temperature of the room rose ten degrees. "I think you can handle this job as well as I can, and enjoy doing it. Working together, you and I will make this the cleanest revolt that ever took over a planet. What do you say?"

I was pacing behind her as she talked. She stood up and took me by the arm, stilling my restless walking. I could feel the warmth of her fingers burning through my thin shirt. Her face was in front of me, smiling, and her voice pitched so low that I barely heard it.

"It would be something, wouldn't it. You and I . . . together."

Wouldn't it! There are occasions when words can't say it all and your body speaks for you. This was a time like that. Without physical deliberation my arms were around her, pulling her to me, my mouth pushing down on hers.

For the briefest of instants she was the same, her arms tight on my shoulders, her lips alive. Just for a sliver of time so brief that afterwards I couldn't be sure that I hadn't imagined it. Then the warmth was suddenly drained away and everything was wrong.

She didn't fight me or attempt to push back. But her lips were lifeless under mine and her eyes open, looking at me with a sterile emptiness. She did nothing until I had dropped my arms and stepped away, then she seated herself stiffly in the chair again.

"What's wrong?" I asked not trusting myself to say more.

"A pretty face—is that all you think of?" she asked, and the words seemed pulled from her in sobs. Expressing real emotions didn't come easily with her. "Are you men all alike—all the same—?"

"Nonsense!" I shouted, angered in spite of myself. "You wanted me to kiss you—don't deny it! What changed your mind?"

"Would you want to kiss *her?*" Angelina screamed, torn by emotions I couldn't understand. She pulled at a thin chain around her neck. It snapped and she half threw it at me. There was a tiny locket on the chain, still warm from her body. It had an image-enlarger in it, and when held at the right angle the picture inside could be seen clearly. I had the chance for only a single glimpse at the girl in the photograph, then Angelina changed her mind and pulled it away, pushing me towards the door at the same time. It slammed behind me and I heard the heavy safety bolts thud home.

Ignoring the guard's raised eyebrows I stamped down the hall to my own room. My emotions had triumphed nicely over my powers of reason, and apparently Angelina's had too—for just an instant. Yet I couldn't understand her cold withdrawal or the significance of the picture. Why did she wear it?

I had only had a single glimpse of the contents but that was enough. It was the photo of a young girl, a sister perhaps? A tragic thing, one of those horrible proofs of the law of chance that an almost infinite number of combinations are possible. This girl was cursed with ugliness, that is the only way to describe it. It was no single factor of a bent back, adenoidal jaw or protruding nose. Instead it was the damning combination of traits that combined to form a single, repellent whole. I didn't like it. But what did it matter. . . .

I sat down suddenly with the clear realization that I was being incredibly stupid. Angelina had given me a simple brief glimpse into the dark motivations that had made her, shaped her life.

Of course. The girl in the picture was Angelina herself.

With this realization so many other things became clear. Many times when looking at her I had wondered why that deadly mind should be housed in such an attractive package. The answer was clearly that I wasn't looking at the original package that had shaped the mind. To be a man and to be ugly is bad enough. What must it feel like to a woman? How do you live when mirrors are your enemies and people turn away rather than look at you? How do you bear life when at the same time you are blessed—or cursed—with a keen and intelligent mind that sees and is aware of everything, makes the inescapable conclusions and misses not the slightest hint of repulsion.

Some girls might commit suicide, but not Angelina. I could guess what she had done. Hating herself, loathing and detesting her world and the people on it, she would have had no compunction about committing a crime to gain the money she wanted. Money for an operation to correct one of those imperfections. Then more money for more operations. Then someone who dared to stop her in this task, and the ease and perhaps pleasure with which she killed him. The slow upward climb through crime and murder—to beauty. And during the climb the wonderful brain that had been housed in the illformed flesh had been warped and changed.

Poor Angelina. I could be sorry for her without forgetting the ones she had killed. Poor, tragic, alone girl who in winning half the battle had lost the other half. Purchased skill had shaped the body into a lovely—truthfully an angelic—form. Yet in succeeding, the strength of the mind that had accomplished all this had been deformed until it had been made as ugly as the body had been in the beginning.

Yet if you could change a body—couldn't you change a mind? Could something be done for her?

The very pressure and magnitude of my thoughts drove me out of the small room and into the air. It was nearing midnight and the guards would be stationed below and all the doors locked. Rather than face the explanations and simple mechanical difficulties, I climbed upwards instead. There would be no one in the roofgardens and walkways this time of night; I could be alone.

Freibur has no moon, but it was a clear night and the stars cast enough light to see by. The roof guard saluted when I went by, and I could see the red spark of a cigarette in his hand. I should have said something about it, but my mind was too occupied. Passing on I turned a corner and stood leaning on the parapet, looking out unseeingly at the black bulk of the mountains.

Something kept gnawing for attention and after a few minutes I recognized what it was. The guard. He was there for a purpose, and smoking on duty wasn't considered the best behavior for a sentry. Perhaps I was being finicky, but it is a failing of mine. Take care of all the small factors and the big ones take care of themselves. In any case, simply thinking about it was bothering me, so I might as well go around and say a word to him.

He wasn't at his usual post, which was optimistic; at least he was making the rounds and keeping an eye on things. I started to walk back when I noticed the broken flowers hanging from the edge of the garden. This was most unusual because the roofgardens were the Count's special pleasure and were practically manicured daily. Then I saw the dark patch in among the flowers and had the first intimation that something was very, very wrong.

It was the guard, and he was either dead or deeply unconscious. I didn't bother to find out which. There was only one reason I could think of for someone to be here at night like this. Angelina. Her room was on the top floor, almost below this spot. Silently I ran to the decorative railing and looked over. Five meters below was the white patch of the balcony outside her window. Something black and formless was crouched there.

My gun was in my room. For one of the few times in my life I had been so disturbed that my normal precautions were forgotten. My concern over Angelina was going to cost her her life.

All of this I realized in a fraction of a second as my fingers ran along the balustrade. A shiny blob was fixed there, anchoring a strand so thin that it was invisible, yet I knew was as strong as a cable. The assassin had lowered himself with web-spinner, a tiny device that spun a thin strand like a spider. Only the strand's substance was formed of a single long-chain molecule that could support a man's weight. It would slice my hands like the sharpest blade if I tried to slide down it.

There was only one way I could reach that balcony, a tiny square above the two kilometer drop into the valley below. I made the decision even as I was leaping up onto the rail. It had a wide flat top and I sat for an instant to catch my balance. Below me the window swung open noiselessly and I dropped, my heels extended, aiming for the man below.

I turned in the air and instead of hitting him squarely I caromed off his shoulder and we both sprawled onto the balcony. It shivered under the impact, but the ancient stone held. The fall had half-stunned me, and with pain-blurred reasoning I hoped that his shoulder felt as bad as my leg. For a few moments I could do nothing but gasp for breath and try to scramble towards him. A long, thin-bladed knife had been knocked from his hand by the impact and I could see it glittering where he reached for it. His fingers clutched it just as I attacked. He grunted and made a vicious stab at me that brushed my sleeve. Before he could draw back I had his knife wrist in my hand and clamped on.

It was a silent, nightmare battle. Both of us were half-dazed from my drop, yet we knew it was life we were battling for. I couldn't stand because of my bruised leg and he was instantly on top of me, heavier and stronger. He couldn't use the arm I had landed on, but it took all the strength of both my arms to hold away the menacing blade. There was no sound other than our hoarse panting.

This assassin was going to win as weight and remorseless strength brought the knife down. Sweat almost blinded me, but I could still see well enough to notice the twisted way his other arm hung. I had broken a bone when I hit—yet he had never made a sound.

There is no such thing as fair fighting when you are struggling for your life. I squirmed my leg out from under him and managed to bend it enough to dig the knee into his broken arm. His whole body shuddered. I did it again. Harder. He twisted, trying to pull away from the pain. I heaved sideways, throwing him off balance. His elbow bent as he tried to save himself from falling and I put all my strength in both hands turning that sinewy wrist and driving the hand backwards.

It almost worked, but he was still stronger than I was and the point of the blade merely scratched his chest. Even as I was fighting to turn the hand again he shuddered and died.

A ruse would not have tricked me—but this was no ruse. I felt every muscle in his body tighten rock-hard in a spasm as he fell sideways. My grip on his wrist didn't lessen until the light came on in the room behind me. Only then did I see the ugly yellow stain halfway up the blade of the knife. A quick-acting nerve poison, silent and deadly. There, on the sleeve of my shirt, was a thin yellow mark where the blade had brushed me. I knew these poisons didn't need a puncture, they could work just as well on the naked skin.

With infinite caution, struggling against the fatigue that wanted my hands to shake, I peeled my shirt slowly off. Only when it had been hurled on top of the corpse did I let myself drop backwards, gasping for air.

My leg could work now, though it hurt hideously. It must have been bruised but not broken since it supported my weight. Turning, I stumbled to the high window and threw it open. Light streamed out on the body behind me. Angelina was sitting up in bed, her face smooth and her hands folded on the covers in front of her. Only her eyes showing any awareness of what had happened.

"Dead," I said with a dry throat, and spat to clear it. "Killed by his own poison." I stumped into the room, testing my leg.

"I was sleeping, I didn't hear him open the window," she said. "Thank you."

Actress, liar, cheat, murderess. She had played a hundred roles in countless voices. Yet when she said those final words there was a ring of unforged feeling to them. This murder attempt had come too soon after the earlier traumatic scene. Her defenses were still down, her real emotions showing.

Her hair hung to her shoulders, brushing the single ribbons of her nightgown which was made of some thin and soft fabric; intimate. This sight, on top of the events of the evening, removed any reserve I might have had. I was kneeling by the bed, holding her shoulders and staring deep into her eyes, trying to reach what lay behind them. The locket with the broken chain lay on the bedside table. I grabbed it in my fist.

"Don't you realize this girl doesn't exist except in your memory," I said, and Angelina didn't move. "It's past like everything else. You were a baby—now you're a woman. You were a little girl—now you're a woman. You may have been this girl—but you are not any more!"

With a convulsive movement I turned and hurled the thing out of the window into the darkness.

"You're none of those things of the past, Angelina!" I said with an intensity louder than a shout. "You are yourself . . . just yourself!"

I kissed her then and there was no trace of the pushing away or rejection there had been before. As I needed her, she needed me.

18

DAWN WAS JUST touching the sky when I brought the assassin's body in to the Count. I was deprived of the pleasure of waking him since the sergeant of the guard had already done this when the roof sentry had been discovered. The guard was dead too, from a tiny puncture of the same poison-tipped blade. The guardsmen and the Count were all gathered around the body on the floor of the Count's sitting room and chattering away about this mystery, the inexplicable death of the sentry. They didn't see me until I dropped my corpse down by the other one, and they all jumped back.

"Here's the killer," I told them, not without a certain amount of pride. Count Cassitor must have recognized the thug because he gave a shuddering start and popped his eyes. No doubt an ex-relative, brother-in-law or something. I imagined he hadn't believed that the Radebrechen family would really go through with their threats of revenge.

A certain uneasiness about the guard sergeant gave me my first cue that I was imagining wrong. The sergeant glanced back and forth from the corpse to the Count and I wondered what thoughts were going through his shaven and thick-skulled military head. There were wheels within wheels here and I would like to have known what was going on. I made a mental note to have a buddy-to-buddy talk with sarge at the first opportunity. The Count chewed his cheek and cracked his knuckles over the bodies, and finally ordered them dragged out.

"Stay here, Bent," he said as I started to leave with the others. I dropped into a chair while he locked the rest out. Then he made a rush for the bar and choked down about a waterglass full of the local spirits. Only when he was working on his second glass did he remember to offer me some of this potable aqua regia. I wasn't saying no, and while I sipped at it I wondered what he was so upset about.

First the Count checked the locks on all the doors and sealed the single window. His ring key unlocked the bottom drawer of his desk and he took out a small electronic device with controls and an extendible aerial on top.

"Well look at that!" I said when he pulled out the aerial. He didn't answer me, just shot a long look at me from under his eyebrows, and went back to adjusting the thing. Only when it was turned on and the green light glowed on the top did he relax a bit.

"You know what this is?" he asked, pointing at the gadget.

"Of course," I said. "But not from seeing them on Freibur. They aren't that common."

"They aren't common at all," he mumbled, staring at the green light which glowed steadily. "As far as I know this is the only one on the planet—so I wish you wouldn't mention it to anybody. *Anybody*," he repeated with emphasis.

"Not my business," I told him with disarming lack of interest. "I think a man's entitled to his privacy."

I liked privacy myself and had used snooper-detectors like this one plenty of times. They could sense electronic or radiation snoopers and gave instant warning. There were ways of fooling them, but it wasn't easy to do. As long as no one knew about the thing the Count could be sure he wasn't being eavesdropped on. But who would want to do that? He was in the middle of his own building—and even he must know that snooper devices couldn't be worked from a distance. There was distinct smell of rat in the air, and I was beginning to get an idea of what was going on. The Count didn't leave me any doubt as to who the rat was.

"You're not a stupid man, Grav Diebstall," he said, which means he thought I was a lot stupider than he was. "You've been offplanet and seen other worlds. You know how backward and suppressed we are here, or you wouldn't have joined with me to help throw off the yoke around our planet's neck. No sacrifice is too great if it will bring closer this day of liberation." For some reason he was sweating now and had resumed his unpleasant habit of cracking the knuckles. The side of his head—where Angela had landed the bottle—was covered with plasti-skin and dry of sweat. I hoped it hurt.

"This foreign woman you have been guarding—" the Count said, turning sideways but still watching me from the corners of his eyes. "She had been of some help in organizing things, but is now putting us in an embarrassing position. There has been one attempt on her life and there will probably be others. The Radebrechen are an old and loyal family—her presence is a continued insult to them." Then he pulled at his drink and delivered the punch line.

"I think that *you* can do the job she is doing. Just as well, and perhaps better. How would you like that?"

Without a doubt I was just brimming over with talent—or there was a shortage of revolutionaries on this planet. This was the second time within twelve hours that I had been offered a partnership in the new order. One thing I was sure of though—Angelovely's offer had been sincere. Cassi Duke of Rdenrundt's proposition had a distinctly bad odor to it. I played along to see what he was leading up to.

"I am honored, noble Count," I oozed. "But what will happen to the foreign woman? I don't imagine she will think much of the idea."

"What she thinks is not important," he snarled and touched his fingers lightly to the side of his head. He swallowed and got his temper back under control. "We cannot be cruel to her," he said with one of the most insincere smiles I have ever seen on a human being's face. "We'll just hold her in custody. She has some guards who I imagine will be loyal, but my men will take care of them. You will be with her and arrest her at the proper time. Just turn her over to the jailers who will keep her safe. Safe for herself, and out of sight where she can cause no more trouble for us."

"It's a good plan," I agreed with winning insincerity. "I don't enjoy the thought of putting this poor woman in jail, but if it is necessary to the cause it must be done. The ends justify the means."

"You're right. I only wish I was able to state it so clearly. You have a remarkable ability to turn a phrase, Bent. I'm going to write that down so I can remember it. The ends justify . . ."

He scratched away industriously on a note plate. What a knowledge of history he had—just the man to plan a revolution! I searched my memory for a few more old saws to supply him with, until my brain was flooded with a sudden anger. I jumped to my feet.

"If we are going to do this we should not waste any time, Count Rdenrundt," I said. "I suggest 1800 hours tonight for the action. That will give you enough time to arrange for the capture of her guards. I will be in her rooms and will arrest her as soon as I have a message from you that the first move has succeeded."

"You're correct. A man of action as always, Bent. It will be as you say." We shook hands then and it took all the will power I possessed to stop from crushing to a pulp his limp, moist, serpentine paw. I went straight to Angelina.

"Can we be overheard here?" I asked her.

"No, the room is completely shielded."

"Your former boy-friend, Count Cassi, has a snooper-detector. He may have other equipment for listening to what goes on here."

This thought didn't bother Angelic in the slightest. She sat by the mirror, brushing her hair. The scene was lovely but distracting. There were strong winds blowing through the revolution that threatened to knock everything down.

"I know about the detector," she said calmly, brushing. "I arranged for him to get it—without his knowledge of course—and made sure it was useless on the best frequencies. I keep a close watch on his affairs that way."

"Were you listening in a few minutes ago when he was making arrangements with me to kill your guards and throw you into the dungeons downstairs?"

"No, I wasn't listening," she said with that amazing self-possession and calm that marked all her actions. She smiled in the mirror at me. "I was busy just remembering last night."

Women! They insist on mixing everything up together. Perhaps they operate better that way, but it is very hard on those of us who find that keeping emotion and logic separate produces sounder thinking. I had to make her understand the seriousness of this situation.

"Well, if that little bit of news doesn't interest you," I said as calmly as I could, "perhaps this does. The rough Radebrechens didn't send that killer last night—the Count did."

Success at last. Angelina actually stopped combing her hair and her eyes widened a bit at the import of what I said. She didn't ask any stupid questions, but waited for me to finish.

"I think you have underestimated the desperation of that rat upstairs. When you dropped him with that bottle yesterday, you pushed him just as far as he could be pushed. He must have had his plans already made and you made his mind up for him. The sergeant of the guard recognized the assassin and connected him with the Count. That also explains how the killer got access to the roof and knew just where to find you. It's also the best explanation I can imagine for the suddenness of this attack. There's too much coincidence here with the thing happening right after your battle with Cassitor the Cantankerous."

Angelina had gone back to combing her hair while I talked, fluffing up the curls. She made no response. Her apparent lack of interest was beginning to try my nerves.

"Well—what are you going to do about it?" I asked, with more than a little note of peevishness in my voice.

"Don't you think it's more important to ask what *you* are going to do about it?" She delivered this line very lightly, but there was a lot behind it. I saw she was watching me in the mirror, so I turned and went over to the window, looking out over the fatal balcony at the snow-summitted mountain peaks beyond. What was I going to do about it? Of course that was the question here—much bigger than she realized.

What was I going to do about the whole thing? Everyone was offering me half-interests in a revolution I hadn't the slightest interest in. Or did I? What *was* I doing here? Had I come to arrest Angelina for the Special Corps? That assignment seemed to have been forgotten a while back. A decision had to be reached soon. My body disguise was good—but not that good. It wasn't intended to stand up to long inspection. Only the fact that Angelina was undoubtedly sure that she had killed me had prevented her from recognizing my real identity so far. I had certainly recognized her easily enough, facial changes and all.

Just at this point the bottom dropped out of everything. There is a little process called selective forgetting whereby we suppress and distort memories we find distasteful. My disguise hadn't been meant to stand inspection this long. Originally I had been sure she would have penetrated it by now. With this realization came the memory of what I had said the night before. A wickedly revealing statement that I had pushed back and forgotten until now.

You're none of these things out of the past, I had shouted. *None of these things . . . Angelina.* I had bellowed this and there had been no protest from her.

Except that she no longer used the name Angelina, she used the alias Engela here.

When I turned to face her my guilty thoughts must have been scrawled all over my face, but she only gave me that enigmatic smile and said nothing. At least she had stopped combing her hair.

"You know I'm not Grav Bent Diebstall," I said with an effort. "How long have you known?"

"For quite a while; since soon after you came here, in fact."

"Do you know who I am—?"

"I have no idea what your real name is, if that's what you mean. But I do remember how angry I was when you tricked me out of the battleships, after all my work. And I recall the intense satisfaction with which I shot you in Freiburbad. Can you tell me your name now?"

"Jim," I said through the haze I was rooted in. "James diGriz, known as Slippery Jim to the trade."

"How nice. My name *is* really Angela. I think it was done as a horrid joke by my father, which is one of the reasons I enjoyed seeing him die."

"Why haven't you killed me?" I asked, having a fairly good idea of how father had passed on.

"Why should I, darling?" she asked, and her light, empty tone was gone. "We've both made mistakes in the past and it has taken us a dreadfully long time to find out that we are just alike. I might as well ask you why you haven't arrested me—that's what you started out to do isn't it?"

"It was—but . . ."

"But, what? You must have come here with that idea in mind, but you were fighting an awful battle with yourself. That's why I hid the fact that I knew who you really were. You were growing up, getting over whatever idiotic notions ever involved you with the police in the first place. I had no idea how the whole thing would come out, though I did hope. You see I didn't want to kill you, not unless I had to. I knew you loved me, that was obvious from the beginning. It was different from the feeble animal passion of all those male brutes who have told me that they love me. They loved a malleable case of flesh. You love me for everything that I am, because we are both the same."

"We are not the same," I insisted, but there was no conviction in my voice. She only smiled. "You kill—and enjoy killing—that's our basic difference. Don't you see that?"

"Nonsense!" She dismissed the idea with an airy wave. "You killed last night—rather a good job too—and I didn't notice any reluctance on your part. In fact, wasn't there a certain amount of enthusiasm?"

I don't know why, but I felt as if a noose was tightening around my neck. Everything she said was wrong—but I couldn't see where it was wrong. Where was the way out, the solution that would solve everything?

"Let's leave Freibur," I said at last. "Get away from this monstrous and unnecessary rebellion. There will be deaths and killing and no need for them."

"We'll go—if we go someplace where we can do just as well," Angela said, and there was a hardness back in her voice. "That's not the major point though. There's something you are going to have to settle in your own mind before you will be happy. This stupid importance you attach to death. Don't you realize how completely trivial it is? Two hundred years from now you, I and every person now living in the galaxy will be dead. What does it matter if a few of them are helped along and reach their destination a bit quicker? They'd do the same to you if they had the chance."

"You're wrong," I insisted, knowing that there is more to living and dying than just this pessimistic philosophy, but unable in this moment of stress to clarify and speak my ideas. Angela was a powerful drug and my tiny remaining shard of compassionate reserve didn't stand a chance, washed under by the flood of stronger emotions. I pulled her to me, kissing her, knowing that this solved most of the problems although it made the final solution that much more difficult.

A thin and irritating buzz scratched at my ears, and Angela heard it too. Separating was difficult for both of us. I sat and watched unseeingly while she went to the vidiphone. She blanked the video circuits and snapped a query into it. I couldn't hear the answer because she had the speaker off and listened through the earpiece. Once or twice she said *yes*, and looked up suddenly at me. There was no indication of whom she was talking to, and I hadn't the slightest interest. There were problems enough around.

After hanging up she just stood quietly for a moment and I waited for her to speak. Instead she walked to her dressing table and opened the drawer. There were a lot of things that could have been concealed there, but she took out the one thing I was least suspecting.

A gun. Big barreled and deadly, pointing at me.

"Why did you do it, Jim?" she asked, tears in the corners of her eyes. "Why did you want to do it?"

She didn't even hear my baffled answer. Her thoughts were on herself—though the recoilless never wavered from a point aimed midway in my skull. With alarming suddenness she straightened up and angrily brushed at her eyes.

"You didn't do anything," she said with the old hard chill on her words. "I did it myself because I let myself believe that one man could be any different from the others. You have taught me a valuable lesson, and out of gratitude I will kill you quickly, instead of in the way I would much prefer."

"What the hell are you talking about," I roared, completely baffled.

"Don't play the innocent to the very end," she said, as she reached carefully behind her and drew a small heavy bag from under the bed. "That was the radar post. I installed the equipment myself and have the operators bribed to give me first notice. A ring of ships—as you well know—has dropped from space and surrounded this area. Your job was to keep me occupied so I wouldn't notice this. The plan came perilously close to succeeding.'' She put a coat over her arm and backed across the room.

''If I told you I was innocent—gave you my most sincere word of honor—would you believe me?'' I asked. ''I have nothing to do with this and know nothing about it.''

''Hooray for the Boy Space Scout,'' Angela said with bitter mockery. ''Why don't you admit the truth, since you will be dead in twenty seconds no matter what you say.''

''I've told you the truth.'' I wondered if I could reach her before she fired, but knew it was impossible.

''Good-by, James diGriz. It was nice knowing you—for a while. Let me leave you with a last pleasant thought. All this was in vain. There is a door and an exit behind me that no one knows about. Before your police get here I shall be safely gone. And if the thought tortures you a bit, I intend to go on killing and killing and killing and you will never be able to stop me.''

My Angela raised the gun for a surer aim as she touched a switch in the molding. A panel rolled back revealing a square of blackness in the wall.

''Spare me the histrionics, Jim,'' she said disgustedly, her eyes looking into mine over the sight of the gun. Her finger tightened. ''I wouldn't expect that kind of juvenile trick from you, staring over my shoulder and widening your eyes as if there were someone behind me. I'm not going to turn and look. You're not getting out of this one alive.''

''Famous last words,'' I said as I jumped sideways. The gun boomed but the bullet plowed into the ceiling. Inskipp stood behind her, twisting the gun into the air, pulling it out of her hand. Angela just stared at me in horror and made no move to resist. There were handcuffs locked on her tiny wrists and she still didn't struggle or cry out. I jumped forward, shouting her name.

There were two burly types in Patrol uniforms behind Inskipp, and they took her. Before I could reach the door he stepped through and closed it behind him. I stumbled to a halt before it, as unable to fight as Angela had been a minute ago.

19

"HAVE A DRINK," Inskipp said, dropping into Angela's chair and pulling out a hip flask. "Ersatz terran brandy, not this local brand of plastic solvent." He offered me a cupful.

"Drop dead, you . . ." I followed with some of the choicer selections from my interstellar vocabulary, and tried to knock the cup out of his hand. He fooled me by raising it and drinking it himself, not in the least annoyed.

"Is that any kind of language to use on your superior officer in the Special Corps?" he asked and refilled the cup. "It's a good thing we're a relaxed organization without too many rules. Still—there are limits." He held out the cup again and this time I grabbed it and drained it.

"Why did you do it?" I asked, still wracked by conflicting emotions.

"Because you didn't, that's why. The operation is over, you are a success. Before you were merely on probation, but now you are a full agent."

He grubbed in one pocket and pulled out a little gold star made of paper. After licking it carefully and solemnly he reached out and stuck it to the front of my shirt.

"I hereby appoint you a Full Agent of the Special Corps," he intoned, "by authority of the power vested in me."

Cursing, I reached to pick the damn thing off—and laughed instead. It was absurd. It was also a fine commentary on the honors that went with the job.

"I thought I was no longer a member of the crew," I told him.

"I never received your resignation," Inskipp said. "Not that it would have meant anything. You can't resign from the Corps."

"Yeah—but I got your message when you gave me a discharge. Or did you forget that I stole a ship and you set off the scuttling charge by remote to blow me up? As you see I managed to pull the fuse just before it let go."

"Nothing of the sort, my boy," he said, settling back to sip his second drink. "You were so insistent about looking for the fair

Angelina that I thought you might want to borrow a ship before we had a chance to assign you one. The one you took had the fuse rigged as it always is on these occasions. The fuse—not the charge—is set to explode five seconds *after* it is removed. I find this gives a certain independence of mind to prospective agents who regret their manner of departure.''

"You mean—the whole thing was a frame-up?" I gurgled.

"You might say that. I prefer the term 'graduating-exercise'. This is the time when we find out if our crooked novices really will devote the rest of their lives to the pursuit of law and order. When they find out, too. We don't want there to be any regrets in later years. You found out, didn't you Jim?"

"I found out something . . . I'm not quite sure what yet," I said, still not able to talk about the one thing closest to me.

"It was a fine operation. I must say you showed a lot of imagination in the way you carried it out." Then he frowned. "But that business with the bank, I can't say I approve of it. The Corps has all the funds you will need . . ."

"Same money," I snapped. "Where does the Corps get it? From planetary governments. And where do they get it from? Taxes of course. So I take it directly from the bank. The insurance company pays the bank for the loss, then declares a smaller income that year, pays less taxes to the government—and the result is exactly the same as your way!"

Inskipp was well acquainted with this brand of logic so didn't even bother to answer. I still didn't want to talk about Angela.

"How did you find me?" I asked. "There was no bug on the ship."

"Simple child of nature that you are," Inskipp said, raising his hands in feigned horror. "Do you really think that any of our ships *aren't* bugged? And the job done so well it cannot be detected if you don't know where to look. For your information the apparently solid outer door of the spacelock contains quite a complex transmitter, strong enough for us to detect at quite a distance."

"Then why didn't I hear it?"

"For the simple reason that it wasn't broadcasting. I should add that the door also contains a receiver. The device only transmits when it receives the proper signal. We gave you time to reach your destination and then followed you. We lost you for a while in Freiburbad, but picked up your trail again in the hospital, right after you played musical chairs with the corpses. We lent you a hand there, the hospital was justifiably annoyed but we managed to keep them quiet. After that it was just a matter of keeping an eye on doctors and surgical equipment since your next move was obvious. I hope you'll be pleased to know that you are carrying a very compact little transmitter in your sternum.''

I looked at my chest but of course saw nothing.

"It was too good an opportunity to miss," Inskipp went on. There was no stopping the man. "One night when you were under sedation the good doctor found the alcohol we had seen fit to include in one of your supply packages. He of course took advantage of this shipping error and a Corps surgeon made a little operation of his own.''

"Then you have been following me and watching ever since?''

"That's right. But this was your case, just as much as it would have been if you knew we were there.''

"Then why did you move in for the kill like this?" I snapped. "I didn't blow the whistle for the marines.''

This was the big question of the hour and the only one that mattered to me. Inskipp took his time about answering.

"It's like this," he drawled, and took a sip of his drink. "I like a new man to have enough rope. But not so much that he will hang himself. You were here for what might be called a goodly long time, and I wasn't receiving any reports about revolutions or arrests you had made.''

What could I say?

His voice was quieter, more sympathetic. "Would *you* have arrested her if we hadn't moved in?" That was the question.

"I don't know," was all I could say.

"Well I damn well knew what I was going to do," he said with the old venom. "So I did it. The plot is well nipped before it could bud and our multiple murderess is offplanet by now.''

"Let her go!" I shouted as I grabbed him by the front of the jacket and swung him free of the ground and shook him. "Let her go I tell you!''

"Would you turn her loose again—the way she is?" was all he answered.

Would I? I suppose I wouldn't. I dropped him while I was thinking about it and he straightened out the wrinkles in the front of his suit.

"This has been a rough assignment for you," he said as he started to put the flask away. "At times there can be a very thin line between right and wrong. If you are emotionally involved the line is almost impossible to see.''

"What will happen to her?" I asked.

He hesitated before he answered. "The truth—for a change," I told him.

"All right, the truth. No promises—but the psych boys might be able to do something with her. If they can find the cause of the basic aberration. But that can be impossible to find at times."

"Not in this case—I can tell them."

He looked surprised at that, giving me some small satisfaction.

"In that case there might be a chance. I'll give positive orders that everything is to be tried before they even consider anything like personality removal. If that is done she is just another body, of which there are plenty in the galaxy. Sentenced to death she's just another corpse—of which there is an equal multitude."

I grabbed the flask away from him before it reached his pocket, and opened it. "I know you Inskipp," I said as I poured. "You're a born recruiting sergeant. When you lick them—make them join."

"What else," he said. "She'd make a great agent."

"We'd make a great team," I told him and we raised our cups. "*Here's to crime.*"

The Stainless Steel Rat's Revenge

1

I STOOD IN LINE, as patient as the other taxpayers, my filled out forms and my cash gripped hotly in my hand. Cash, money, the old fashioned green folding stuff. A local custom that I intended to make expensive to the local customers. I was scratching under the artificial beard, which itched abominably, when the man before me stepped out of the way and I was at the window. My finger stuck in the glue and I had a job freeing it without pulling the beard off as well.

"Come, come, pass it over," the aging, hatchet-faced, bitter and shrewish female official said, hand extended impatiently.

"On the contrary," I said, letting the papers and banknotes fall away to disclose the immense .75 recoilless pistol that I held. "*You* pass it over. All of that tax money you have extracted from the sheeplike suckers who populate this backward planet."

I smiled to show that I meant it and she choked off a scream and began scrabbling in the cash drawer. It was a broad smile that showed all of my teeth, which I had stained bright red, which should have helped her decide on the proper course of action. As the money was pushed towards me I stuffed it into my long topcoat that was completely lined with deep pockets.

"What are you doing?" the man behind me gasped, eyes bulging like great white grapes.

"Taking money," I said and flipped a bundle at him. "Why don't you have some yourself." He caught it by reflex, goggled at it, and all the alarms went off at once and I heard the doors crashing shut. The cashier had managed to trigger an alarm.

"Good for you," I said, "but don't let a minor thing like that prevent you from keeping the cash coming."

She gasped and started to slip from sight, but a wave of the gun and another flash of my carmine dentures restored a semblance of life, and the flow of bills continued. People started to rush about and gun waving guards began to appear looking around enthusiastically for someone to shoot, so I triggered the radio relay in my pocket. There was a series of charming explosions all about the bank, from every wastebasket where I had planted a gas bomb, followed by the even more charming screams of the customers. I stopped stowing money long enough to slip on the gas-tight goggles and settle them into place. And to clamp my mouth shut so I was forced to breathe through the filter plugs in my nostrils.

It was fascinating to watch. Blackout gas is invisible and has no odor but it does contain a chemical that acts almost instantly, bringing about a temporary but complete paralysis of the optic nerve. Within fifteen seconds everyone in the bank was blind.

With the exception of James Bolivar diGriz, myself, man of many talents. Humming a happy tune through closed lips I stowed away the remaining money. My benefactress had finally slid from sight and was screaming incontinently somewhere behind the counter. So were a lot of other people. There was plenty of groping about and falling over things as I made my way through this little blacked out corner of bedlam. An eerie sensation indeed, the one-eyed man in the country of the blind and all that. A crowd had already gathered outside, pressing in fascinated awe against the windows and glass doors, to watch the drama unfolding inside. I waved and smiled and a shudder passed through the nearest as they pushed back in panic from the door. I shot the lock out, angling the gun so the bullets shrieked away over their heads, and kicked the door open. Before exiting myself I threw a screamer out onto the sidewalk and quickly pushed the stopples into my ears.

The screamer sounded off and everyone began to leave quickly. You *have* to leave quickly when you hear one of these things. They send out a mixed brew of devilish sounds at the decibel level of a major earthquake. Some are audible, sounds like a magnified fingernail on a blackboard, while others are supersonic and produce sensations of panic and imminent death. Harmless and highly effective. The street was otherwise empty when I walked out to the car that was just pulling up to the curb. My head was throbbing with the supersonics that got past the plugs and I was more than happy to slip through the open door and relax while Angelina gunned the machine down the street.

"Everything go all right?" she asked, keeping her eyes on the road as she whipped around a corner on the outside wheels. Sirens began to sound in the distance.

"A piece of cake. Smooth as castor oil . . ."

"Your similes leave a lot to be desired."

"Sorry. A touch of indigestion this morning. But my coat is lined with more money than we could possibly need."

"How nice!" she laughed, and she meant it. That irresistible grin, the crinkled nose. I longed to nibble it, or at least kiss her, but settled for a comradely pat on the shoulder since she needed all her concentration for driving. I popped a stick of gum in my mouth that would remove the red tooth dye and began to peel off my disguise.

As I changed so did the car. Angelina turned into a side street, slowed and then found an even quieter street to drive along. There was no one in sight. She pressed the button.

My, but technology can do some interesting things. The license plate flipped over to reveal a different number, but that was too simple a trick to even discuss. Angelina flicked on the windshield wipers as a fine spray of catalytic fluid sprang out of jets on the front of the car. Wherever it touched the blue paint turned a bright red. Except for the top of the car which became transparent so that in a few moments we were sitting in a bubble-top surveying the world around. A good deal of what appeared to be chrome plated metal dissolved and washed away altering the appearance and even the make of the car. As soon as this process was complete Angelina sedately turned a corner and started back in the direction from whence we had come. Her orange wig was locked away with my disguise and I held the wheel while she put on an immense pair of goggly sunglasses.

"Where to next?" she asked as a huddle of shrieking police cars tore by in the opposite direction.

"I was thinking of the shore. Wind, sun, sand, that sort of thing. Healthy and bracing."

"A little too bracing if you don't mind my saying so." She patted the rounded bulge of her midriff with a more than satisfied smile. "It's six months now, going on seven, so I'm not feeling that athletic. Which reminds me . . ." She flashed me a quick scowl, then turned her attention back to the road. "You promised to make an honest woman out of me so that we could call this a honeymoon."

"My love," I said, and clasped her hand in all sincerity. "At the first possible moment. I don't want to make an honest woman out of you—that would be physically impossible since you are basically as larcenous minded as I am—but I will certainly marry you and slip an expensive—"

"Stolen!"

"—ring on this delicate little finger. I do promise. But the second we try to register a marriage we'll be fed into the computer and the game will be up. Our little holiday at an end."

"And you'll be hooked for life. I think I better grab you now before I get too round to run and catch you. We'll go to your beach resort and enjoy one last day of mad freedom. And tomorrow, right after breakfast, we are getting married. Do you promise?"

"There is just one question . . ."

"Promise, Slippery Jim, I know you!"

"You have my word except . . ."

She braked the car to a skidding stop and I found myself looking down the barrel of my own .75 recoilless. It looked very big. Her knuckle was white on the trigger.

"Promise you quick-witted slippery tricky crooked lying con man or I'll blow your brains out."

"My darling, you *do* love me!"

"Of course I do. But if I can't have you all to myself I'll have you dead. Speak!"

"We get married in the morning."

"Some men are *so* hard to convince," she whispered, slipping the gun into my pocket and herself into my arms. Then she kissed me with such delicious intensity that I almost looked forward to the morrow.

2

"WHERE ARE YOU GOING, Slippery Jim?" Angelina asked, leaning out of the window of our room above. I stopped with my hand on the gate.

"Just down for a quick swim, my love," I shouted back and swung the gate open. A .75 roared and the ruins of the gate were blown out of my hand.

"Open your robe," she said, not unkindly, and blew the smoke from the gun barrel at the same time.

I shrugged with resignation and opened the beach robe. My feet were bare. But of course I was fully dressed, with my pant legs rolled up and my shoes stuffed into my jacket pockets. She nodded understandably.

"You can come back upstairs. You're going nowhere."

"Of course I'm not." Hot indignation. "I'm not that sort of chap. I was just afraid you might misunderstand. I just wanted to nip into the shops and . . ."

"Upstairs."

I went. Hell hath no fury etc. was invented to describe my Angelina. The Special Corps medics had stripped her of her homicidal tendencies, unknotted the tangled skeins of her subconscious and equipped her for a more happy existence than circumstance had previously provided. But when it came to the crunch she was still the old Angelina. I sighed and mounted the stairs with leaden feet.

And I felt even more of an unthinking fiend when I saw that she was crying. "Jim, you don't love me!" A classic gambit since the first woman in the garden, but still unanswerable.

"I do," I protested, and I meant it. "But, it's just . . . reflex. Or something like that. I love you, but marriage is, well, like going to prison. And in all my crooked years I have never been sent up."

"It is liberation, not captivity," she said and did things with her makeup that removed the ravages of the tears. I noticed for the first time that she had white lipstick on to match her white dress and a little white lacy kind of thing in her hair.

"This is just like going swimming in cold water," she said, standing and patting my cheek. "Get it over with quickly so you won't feel it. Now roll down your pants and put those shoes on."

I did, but when I straightened up to answer this last fatuous argument I saw that the door had opened and that a Marriage Master and his two witnesses were standing in the next room. She took my arm, gently, I'll say that for her, and at the same time the recorded strains of the mighty organ filled the air. She tugged at my elbow. I resisted for a moment, then lurched forward as a gray mist seemed to fall over my eyes.

When the darkness lifted the organ was bleating its dying notes, the door was closing behind the departing backs and Angelina stopped admiring her ring-decorated finger long enough to raise her lips to mine. I had barely enough strength of will left to kiss her first before I groaned.

There were a number of bottles on the sideboard and my twitching fingers stumbled through them to unerringly find a knobby flask of Syrian Panther Sweat, a potent beverage with such hideous aftereffects that its sale is forbidden on most civilized worlds. A large tumbler of this was most efficacious, I could feel it doing me harm, and I poured a second one. While I was doing this and immersed in my numbed thoughts a period of time must have passed because Angelina—*my* Angelina (suppressed groan)—now stood before me dressed in slacks and sweater with our bags packed and waiting at her side. The glass was plucked from my fingers.

"Enough private whoopee," she said, not unkindly. "We'll celebrate tonight but right now we have to move. The marriage record will be filed at any moment and when our names hit the computer it's going to light up like a knocking shop on payday. By now the police will have tied us in to most of the crimes of the past two months and will come slavering and baying after us."

"Silence," I ordered, swaying to my feet. "The image is a familiar one. Get the car and we will leave."

I offered to help with the bags but by the time I communicated this information she was halfway down the stairs with them. With this encouragement I navigated the hazard and reached the door. The car was outside humming with unleashed power, the side door open and Angelina at the wheel tapping her foot with equally unleashed impatience. As I stumbled into it the first tentacles of reality penetrated my numbed cortex. This car, like all other ground cars on Kamata, was steam powered and the steam was generated by the combustion of a specie of peat bricks fed to the furnace by an ingenious and unnecessarily complicated device. It took at least a half an hour to raise steam to get moving. Angelina must have fired up before the wedding and planned every other step as well. My solitary contribution to all this was a private drunk which had been very little aid at all. I shuddered at what this meant, yet was still driven to the only possible conclusion.

"Do you have a drive-right pill?" I asked, hoarsely.

It was in the palm of her hand even as I spoke. Small, round, pink, with a black skull and crossbones on it. A sobering invention of some mad chemist that worked like a metabolic vacuum cleaner. Short minutes after hitting the hydrochloric acid pool of my stomach the ingredients would be doing a blitzkrieg attack through my bloodstream. Not only does it remove all of the alcohol but strips away all of the side products associated with drinking as well, so that the pitiful subject is instantly cold sober and painfully aware of it.

"I can't take it without water," I mumbled, blinking at the plastic cup in her other hand. There was no turning back. With a last happy shudder I flipped the deadly thing into the back of my throat and drained the cup.

They say it doesn't take long, but that is an objective time. Subjective was hours. It is a most unusual experience and difficult to describe. Imagine if you will what it feels like to take the nozzle of a cold water hose in your mouth and then to have the water turned on. And then, an instant later, to have the water gushing in great streams from every orifice of your body, including the pores, until you are flushed completely clean.

"Wow," I said weakly, sitting up and dabbing at my forehead with my handkerchief. The houses of a small village rushed by and were replaced by farmlands. Angelina drove with calm efficiency and the boiler chunked merrily as it ate another brick of peat.

"Feeling better, I hope?" She dived into a traffic circle and left it by a different road with only a quick glimpse at the map. "The alarm is out for us, army, navy, everything. I've been listening to their command radio."

"Are we going to get away?"

"I doubt it—not unless you come up with some bright idea very quickly. They have a solid ring with aerial cover around the area and are tightening it."

I was still recovering from the heroic treatment of the drive-right pill and had not collected all my wits. There was a direct connection from my muddled thoughts to my vocal cords that had no intervening censor of intelligence.

"A great start to marriage. If this is what it is like no wonder I have been avoiding it all these years."

The car swung off the road and shuddered to a stop in the deep grass under a row of blue-leaved trees. Angelina was out, had slammed the door and was reaching for her bag before I had time to react. I tried to tell her.

"I'm a fool . . ."

"Then I'm a fool too for marrying you." She was dry eyed and cold of voice with all of her emotions strictly under control. "I tricked you and trapped you into marriage because it was what I thought you really wanted. I was wrong, so it is going to end right now before it really gets started. I'm sorry, Jim. You made an entirely new life for me and thought I could make one for you. It has been fun knowing you. Thank you and good-by."

By the time she had finished, my thoughts had congealed into something roughly resembling their normal shape and I was weak but ready. I was out of the car before she had finished talking and standing in front of her, blocking her way, holding her most gently by the arms.

"Angelina, I will tell you this but once and probably never again the rest of my life. So listen well and remember. At one time I was the best crook in the galaxy, before I was conned into the Special Corps to help catch other crooks. And I caught you. Not only were you a crook but a mastermind criminal as well and a cheerfully sadistic murderess." I felt her body shiver in my hands and held her tighter. "It has to be said, because that is what you were. You aren't any more. You had reasons to be that way and the reasons have been removed and some unhappy quirks in your otherwise pristine cortex have been straightened out. And now I love you. But I want to remember that I loved you even then during your unreconstructed days, which is saying a lot. So if I buck at the harness now, or am difficult to deal with in the mornings, just remember that and make allowances. Is it a deal?"

It apparently was. She dropped the bag—on my toe, but I dared not flinch—and wrapped her arms around me and was kissing me and knocked me over into the deep grass and I had a jolly time kissing her right back. The newlywed effect I suppose you would call it, great fun . . .

We froze, rigid, as a pair of flywheel cycles moaned and skidded to a stop by our car. Only the police used these since they move a good deal faster than the peat-powered steamers. They are tricycle affairs with a great heavy flywheel encased between the rear wheels. They plugged them in at night so their motor-generators could run the flywheel up to top speed. During the day the flywheel generated electricity to drive the motors in each wheel. Very efficient and smog-free. Very dangerous.

"This is the car, Podder!" one of the police shouted out over the constant moan of the flywheels.

"I'll call it in. They can't have gone far. We sure have them trapped now!"

Nothing infuriates me like the bland assurances of petty officials. Oh yes, really trapped now. I growled deep in my throat as the other uniformed incompetent poked his nose around the car and gaped at our cozy cuddle in the grass. He was still gaping when I lunged an arm up and around his neck with a tight squeeze on his throat and pulled him down to join us. It was fun to watch his tongue come out and his eyes pop and his head turn red but Angelina spoiled it. She whipped off his helmet and rapped him smartly—and accurately—on the temple with the heel of her shoe. He turned off and I let him drop.

"And you talk about *me*," my bride whispered. "You've got more than a touch of the old sadist in your own makeup."

"I called it in. Everybody knows. We've sure got them now . . ." the enthusiastic remaining officer said, but his voice rattled to a stop when he looked down the muzzle of his associate's riot gun. Angelina dug a sleep capsule out of her bag and snapped it under his nose.

"And now what, boss?" she asked, smiling happily at the two black-uniformed, brass-buttoned figures by the side of the road.

"I have been thinking," I said, and rubbed my jaw and frowned with deep concentration to prove it. "We have had over four months of worryless holiday, but all good things must end. We could extend our leave. But it would be hectic to say the least and people would get hurt and you—while that is a fine shape—it is not quite the shape for flight and pursuit and general nastiness. Shall we return to the service from which we fled?"

"I was hoping you would say that. Morning sickness and bank robbery just don't seem to mix. It will be fun to get back."

"Particularly since they will be so glad to see us. Considering that they turned down our request for leave and we had to steal that mail ship."

"Not to mention all the expense money we have stolen because we couldn't touch our bank accounts."

"Right. Follow me and we'll do this with style."

We stripped off their uniforms and gently laid the snoring peace officers in the rear of the car. One had pink polkadot underwear while the other's was utilitarian black—but trimmed with lace. Which might have been local custom of dress but gave me second thoughts about the police on Kamata and I was glad we were leaving. Uniformed, helmeted, and goggled we hummed merrily down the road on our flywheel cycles waving to all the tanks and trucks that roared by the other way. Before there were too many screams and shouts of discovery I braked in the center of the road and signaled an armored car to a stop. Angelina swung her cycle behind them so that they would not find the sight of a pregnant police officer too distracting.

"Got them cornered!" I shouted. "But they have a radio so keep this off the net. Follow me."

"Lead on!" the driver shouted, his mate nodding agreement while thoughts of rewards, fame, medals danced dazzlingly before their eyes. I led them to a deserted track into the woods that ended at a small lake complete with ramshackle boathouse and dock.

I braked, waved them to a stop, touched my finger to my lips and tiptoed back to their car. The driver lowered the side window and looked out expectantly.

"Breathe this," I said and flipped a gas grenade through the opening.

There was a cloud of smoke followed by gasps followed by two more silent uniformed figures snoring in the grass.

"Going to take a quick peek at their underwear?" Angelina asked.

"No. I want to maintain some illusions, even if they are false."

The cycles rolled merrily down the dock and off into the water where they steamed and shortcircuited and made a lot of bubbles. As soon as the armored car had aired out we boarded and drove away. Angelina found the driver's untouched lunch and cheerfully consumed it. I avoided most of the main roads and headed back to the city where the command post was located at the central police station. I wanted to go where the big action was.

We parked in the underground garage, deserted now, and took the elevator to the tower. The building was almost empty, except for the command center, and I found an unoccupied office nearby and left Angelina there. Innocently amusing herself with the sealed—

but easily opened—confidential files, I lowered my goggles into place ane staged a dusty, exhausted entrance to control. I was ignored. The man I wanted to see was pacing the floor sucking on a long dead pipe. I rushed up and saluted.

"Sir, are you Mr. Inskipp?"

"Yar," he muttered, his attention still on the great wall chart that theoretically showed the condition of the chase.

"Someone to see you, sir."

"What? What?" he said, still distracted. Harold Peters Inskipp, director and mastermind of the Special Corps, not quite with it this day. He followed me out easily enough and I closed the door and slipped off the heavy goggles.

"We're ready to come home now," I told him. "If you can find a quiet way of getting us off this planet without the locals getting their greedy hands on us."

His jaw clenched with anger and fractured the mouthpiece of the pipe into innumerable fragments. I led him, spitting out pieces of plastic, to the room where Angelina was waiting.

3

"ARRGH!" INSKIPP SNARLED, and shook the sheaf of papers in his hand so that they rattled like dry skeletal bones.

"Very expressive," I said, slipping a cigar from my pocket humidor and holding it to my ear. "But with a very minimal content of information. Could you be more explicit?" I pinched the cigar's small end and there was not the slightest crackle. Perfection.

"Do you know how many millions your crime wave has cost? The economy of Kamata . . ."

"Will not suffer an iota. The government will reimburse the institutions that suffered the losses and will then in turn deduct the same amount from its annual payment to the Special Corps. Which has more money than it can possibly use in any case. And look at the benefits bestowed in return. Plenty of excitement for the populace, increased sales of newspapers, exercise for the sedentary law enforcement officers—and that is an interesting story in itself—as well as field maneuvers that were a pleasure for everyone involved. Far from being annoyed they should pay us a fee for making all these exciting things possible." I lit the cigar and blew out a great cloud of fragrant smoke.

"Don't play wise with me, you aging con man. If I turned you and your bride over to the Kamata authorities you would still be in jail 600 years from now."

"Little chance of that, Inskipp, aging con man yourself. You are short of good field agents as it is. You need us more than we need you. So consider this chewing out at an end and get on with the business. I have been chastised." I tore a button off the front of my jacket and threw it across the desk to him. "Here, rip off my medals and reduce me to the ranks. I am guilty. Next case."

With a final simulated growl of anger he filed the papers in the wastebasket and took out a large red folder that buzzed threateningly when he touched it. His thumb print defused the security device and the folder dropped open.

"I have a top secret gravely important assignment here."

"What other kind do I ever get?"

"It is hideously dangerous as well."

"You are secretly envious of my good looks and have a death wish for me. Come on, Inskipp. Stop sparring and let me know what the deal is. Angelina and I can handle it better than the rest of your senile and feeble agents."

"This job of work is for you alone. Angelina is, well : . ." His face reddened and he examined the file closely.

"Whoopee!" I shouted. "Inskipp the killer, daredevil, master of men, secret power in the galaxy today. And he can't say the word *pregnant*! How about *baby*? Wait, *sex*, that is a goodie. You blush to think about it. Go ahead, say *sex* three times fast, it will do you good—"

"Shut up, deGriz," he growled. "At least you finally married her which shows you have a single drop of honesty in your other-wise rotten carcass. She stays behind. You go out on this one-man job. Probably leaving her a widow."

"She looks awful in black so you can't get rid of me that easily. Tell."

"Look at this," he said, taking a roll of film from the folder and slipping it into a slot in his desk. A screen dropped down from the ceiling and the room darkened. The film began.

The camera had been handheld, the color was off at times, and it was most unprofessional. But it was the best home movie I had ever seen because the material was so good. Authentic, no doubt about it.

Someone was waging war. It was a sunny day with white puffs of clouds against a blue sky. And black puffs of antiaircraft fire in among them. But the fire was not heavy and there was not enough of it to stop the troop carriers that came in low and fast for landing. This was at an average sized spaceport, with the buildings in the far background and some cargo ships nearby. Other craft roared in low and bomb explosions reached skyward from what must have been the defense positions. The impossibility of what was happening finally came home to me.

"Those are *spaceships*!" I gurgled. "And space *transports*. Is some numbskull government so stupid as to think that it can succeed in an interplanetary war? What happened after they lost—and how does it affect me?"

The film ended and the lights came up again. Inskipp steepled his fingers on the desk and leered over them.

"For your information, Mr. Know-it-all, this invasion suc-ceeded—and so did the other ones before it. This film was taken by a smuggler, one of our regular informants, whose ship was just fast enough to get away during the battle.''

This was a stopper. I dragged deeply on the cigar and considered what little I knew about interplanetary warfare. There was little enough to know. Because it just doesn't work. Maybe a few times in the galaxy when local conditions are right, say a solar system with two inhabited planets. If one planet is backward and the other advanced industrially the primitive one might be invaded successfully. But not if they put up any kind of a real defense. The distance-time relationships just don't make this kind of warfare practical. When every soldier and weapon and ration has to be lifted from the gravity well of a planet and carried across space the energy expenditure is considerable, the transport demands incredible and the cost unbelievable. If, in addition, the invader has to land in the face of determined opposition the invasion is impossible. And this is inside a solar system where the planets are practically touching on a galactic scale. The thought of warfare between planets of different star systems is even more impossible.

But, once again, it has been proven that nothing is basically impossible if people want to tackle it hard enough. And things like violence, warfare and bloodshed are still hideously attractive to the lurking violence potential of mankind, despite the centuries of peace and stagnation. I had a sudden and depressing thought.

''Are you telling me that a successful interplanetary invasion has been accomplished?'' I asked.

''More than one.'' That evil smirk was decorating his face as he spoke.

''And you and the League would like to see this practice stopped?''

''Right on the head, Jim my boy.''

''And I am the sucker who has been picked for the assignment?''

He reached out, took my cigar from my numb fingers and dropped it into the ashtray—then solemnly shook my hand. ''It's your job. Go out there and win.''

I slipped my hand from his treacherous embrace, wiped my fingers on my pantsleg and grabbed back my cigar.

''I'm sure that you will see that I have the best funeral the Corps can afford. Now, would you care to squeeze out a few details or would you prefer to blindfold me and shoot me out in a one-way cargo rocket?''

''Temper, my boy, temper. The situation seems to be quite clear. There has been little word about this in the news media because of a certain political confusion surrounding the invasions, plus a rigid

censorship by the planets under consideration. As we have reconstructed it—and good men have died getting this information—the
responsible world is named Cliaand, the third planet in the Epsilon
Indi system. There are two score planets orbiting this sun, but only
three are inhabitable. And inhabited. Cliaand took over both the
sister worlds some years ago, but we considered this no cause for
alarm. What is alarming is the fact that they have expanded their
scope. *Interstellar* conquest, heretofore considered an impossibility. They have invaded and conquered *five* other planets in nearby
systems and seem poised for bigger and better things. We don't
know how they are doing it, but they must be doing something right.
We have had agents on the conquered worlds but have learned little
of value. The decision has been made, a high level one I assure
you—you would stand and salute if you heard some of the names
of the people involved—that we must get a man to Cliaand to root
out the problem at the core of the woodpile and cut the Gordian
knot.''

"Other than being contained in a mixed and disgusting metaphor
I think the idea is a suicidal one. Instead of this we could . . .''

"You are going. There is no possible way to wriggle out of this
one, Slippery Jim.''

I tried. But nothing worked. I was given a copy of all the known
details, a cortex-recording of the language and the masterkey to a
fast pursuit ship to take me there. I returned gloomily to our quarters
where Angelina, tired of doing her hair and her nails, was throwing
a knife at a head-sized target on the far wall. She was very good.
Even underhand, after a quick draw from her arm sheath, she could
hit the black spot of either eye.

"Let me get a pic of Inskipp," I said. "It will make a more
interesting target and one that you can get a degree of pleasure out
of.''

"Is that evil old man sending my darling out on a job?''

"That dirty old goat is trying to get me killed. The assignment is
so top secret I can't tell a soul about it, particularly you, so here are
all the papers, read them for yourself.''

While she did this I slipped the Cliaand language recording into
the stamping machine. This recorded the material directly on my
cortex without the boring and time-consuming intermediary of any
learning process. The first session would take about a half an hour
with a dozen or more shorter reinforcing sessions after that. I would
end up speaking the language and having one hell of a headache
from all the electronic fingering of my synapses. But there was a
period of total unconsciousness while the machine operated and that

was just what I felt like at the moment. I slipped the helmet down over my ears, settled on the couch and pressed the button.

There was a flicker of no-time and Angelina was carefully lifting off the helmet and handing me a pill at the same instant. I swallowed it and kept my eyes closed while the pain ebbed away. Soft lips kissed mine.

"They are trying to kill you, but you will not let them. You will laugh and win and someday you will have Inskipp's job."

I opened one eye a crack and looked at her jubilant expression.

"Come home with my shield or on it? Go to glory or the grave? Are you worried about me?"

"All of the time. But that is a wife's job. I certainly cannot stand in the way of your career—"

"I didn't know I had one until you told me just now."

"—and will do everything I can to help."

"You can't come with me, for a very obvious and protruding reason."

"I know that. But I will be with you in spirit all the time. How are you going to land on this world?"

"Board my nimble pursuit ship, come in straight and fast behind a radar screen, zing down into the atmosphere—"

"And get blasted into your component atoms. Here, read this report by the survivor of the last ship to try this approach."

I read it. It was most depressing. I threw it back with the others.

"I heed the warning. This planet appears to be militarized to the hilt. I'll bet even the house pets wear uniforms. Bulling in like that is approaching these people on their own terms, competing in the area where they are best organized. What they are not organized against is a little bit of guile, some larceny, a smooth approach covering a devious attack. Insinuate, penetrate, operate and extirpate."

"All at once I am beginning not to like it," my love said, frowning. "You will take care of yourself, Jim? I don't think worrying would be good for me right now."

"If you wish to worry, worry about the fate of this poor planet with Slippery Jim unleashed against them. Their conquests are at an end, they are as good as finished."

I kissed her resoundingly and walked out, head high and shoulders back.

Wishing that I was one tenth as sure of myself as I had acted. This was going to be a very rough one.

4

My PLANNING HAD been detailed, the preparations complex, the operation gigantic. I had received more than one shrill cry of pain from Inskipp about the cost, all of which I dutifully ignored. It was my neck in the noose, not his, and I was hedging all the bets that I could to assure my corporeal survival. But even the most complicated plan is eventually completed, the last details sewed up, the final orders issued. And the sheep led to the slaughter.

Baaa. Here I was, naked to the world, sitting in the bar of the intersystem spacer *Kannettava*, a glass of strong drink before me and a dead cigar clutched in my fingers. Listening to the announcement that we would be landing on Cliaand within the hour. I was naked, figuratively speaking of course. It had taken an effort of will and strong discipline to force myself to leave every article of an illegal nature behind. I had never done this before in my entire life. No minibombs, gas capsules, gigli saws, fingertip drills, card holdouts, phone tappers. Nothing. Not even the lockpick that was always fixed to my toe nail. Or . . .

I grated my teeth at the thought and looked about me. The other revelers were knocking back the taxfree booze in a determined manner and none was looking at me. Slipping my wallet from my pocket I touched the seam at the top. And felt a certain stiffness. Memory, how it cuts both ways, revealing and clouding. My own subconscious was fighting against me. Only my conscious mind was at all enthusiastic about landing on Cliaand without any illegal devices. I squeezed the wallet hard in the right way and the tiny but incredibly strong lockpick dropped into my fingers. A work of art. I admired it when I raised my glass. And said good-by. On the way back to my cabin I dropped it into a waste disposal. It would go on with the ship while I landed on this singularly inhospitable world.

Every report and interview indicated that Cliaand had the most paranoiac customs men in the known universe. Contraband simply could not be smuggled in. Therefore I was not trying. I was just what I appeared to be. A salesman, representative of Fazzoletto-Mouchoir Ltd., dealers in deadly weapons. The firm existed and I was their salesman and no amount of investigation could prove otherwise. Let them try.

They did. Landing on Cliaand was not unlike going into prison. I, and the handful of other debarkees, trundled down the gangway and into a gray room of ominous aspect. We huddled together, under the eyes of watchful and heavily armed guards, while our luggage was brought and dumped nearby. Nothing happened until the gangway had been withdrawn and the *Kannettava* had departed. Then, one by one, we were called out.

I was not first and I welcomed the opportunity to examine the local types. They were supremely indifferent to us, stamping about in knee-high boots, fingering their weapons and keeping their chins up high. Their uniforms were all the same color, a color which at first glance might be mistaken for a very unmilitary hue of carmine, a purplish red. Very quickly I realized that this was almost exactly the color of blood, half arterial blue, half venous pink. It was rather disgusting and hard to avoid looking at. And, in addition, gave no small hint about the nature of the wearer.

All of the guards were on the large side and ran to protruding jaws and little piggy eyes. Their helmets looked like fibersteel, with sinister black visors and transparent faceplates that could be dropped down. Each carried a gaussrifle, a multipurpose and particularly deadly weapon. High capacity batteries stored a really impressive electrical charge in the stock. When the trigger was depressed a strong magnetic field was generated in the barrel which accelerated the missile with a muzzle velocity that equaled any explosive cartridge weapon. And the gaussrifle was superior in that it had a more rapid rate of fire, made no sound, and shot out any one of an assortment of deadly missiles, from poison needles to explosive charges. The Corps had reports about this weapon but we had never seen one. I made plans to rectify that situation as soon as possible.

"Pas Ratunkowy," someone shouted and I stirred to life as I remembered this was my cover name. I waved hesitantly and one of the guards stomped and clacked over to me. I do believe that he had metal plates on his heels to increase the militaristic effect. I looked forward to getting a pair of these boots as well: I was beginning to like Cliaand.

"You Pas Ratunkowy?"

"I am he, sir, at your service," I answered in his native tongue, being careful to keep a foreign accent.

"Get your luggage. Come with me."

He spun about and I had the temerity to call after him.
"But, sir, bags are too heavy to carry all at once."

This time he impaled me with a cold, withering look and fingered his gaussrifle suggestively. "Cart," he finally snarled and stabbed a finger at the far side of the prison yard. I humbly went after cart. This was a drably efficient motorized platform that rolled along on small wheels. I quickly loaded my bags onto it and looked for my guide. He stood by a now open door with his finger even closer to the trigger than before. The electric motor whined at top speed and I galloped after the thing towards the door.

The inspection began.

How easy that is to say. But it is one of those simple statements like "I dropped the atom bomb and it went off." This was the most detailed and thorough inspection I had ever experienced and I was exceedingly happy that I had found that lockpick first.

There were ten men waiting in the smooth-walled, antiseptically white room. Six took my baggage while the other four took me. The first thing they did was strip me mother naked and drop me onto a fluoroscope. A magnifying one. Seconds later they were conferring over a blown-up print of the fillings in my teeth. There was a mutual decision that one of them was unduly large and had a rather unusual shape. A sinister looking array of dental gadgetry emerged and they had the filling out in an instant. While the tooth was being refilled with enamel—I'll say that much for them—the original filling was being zapped by a spectroscope. They seemed neither depressed nor elated when its metallic content proved to be that of an accepted dental alloy. The search went on.

While my tender pink person was being probed one of the inquisitors produced a file of papers. Most of these were psigrams sent out after my landing application had been received. They had consulted Fazzoletto-Mouchoir Ltd., my employers, and had all the details of my job. It is a good thing that this was legitimate. I responded correctly to all the questions, inserting random sounds only twice when the physical examination probed a tender spot. This appeared to go well; at least the file was closed and put aside.

While this was going on I had been catching glimpses of the fate of my bags. They suffered more than I did. Each of them had been opened and emptied, the contents spread out on the white tables, and the bag was then methodically taken to pieces. To little pieces. The seams were cut open, the fastening removed, the handles dissected. And the resulting rubbish put in plastic bags, labeled and saved. No doubt for a later and most detailed inspection. My clothing was given only a perfunctory examination then pushed aside. I soon found out why. I would not be seeing it again until I left the planet.

"You will be issued with good Cliaand clothing," one of my inquisitors announced. "It is pleasure to wear." I doubted that very much but kept my silence.

"Is this religious symbol," another asked, holding the photograph in his fingertips at arm's length.

"It is a picture of my wife."

"Only religious symbols permitted."

"She is like an angel to me."

They puzzled over this one for awhile, then reluctantly admitted the picture. Not that I would be able to have anything as deadly as the original. It was whisked away and a photographic copy returned. Angelina seemed to be scowling in this print or perhaps that was only my imagination.

"All of your personal items, identification and so on will be returned to you when you leave," I was coldly informed.

"While on Cliaand you will wear local dress and observe local customs. Your personal items are there." Three very utilitarian and ugly pieces of luggage were indicated. "Here is your identification card." I grabbed at it, happy to be assured of my existence, still naked and beginning to get a chill.

"What is in this locked case?" an inspector called out, a ring of expectancy in his voice like that of a hound catching the scent. They all stopped work and came over as the incriminating case was held out for my inspection. Their expressions indicated that whatever answer I gave would be admission of crime to be followed by the death penalty. I permitted myself to cringe back and roll my eyes.

"Sirs, I have done nothing wrong . . ." I cried.

"What is it?"

"Military weapons—"

There were stifled cries and one of them looked around as though for a gun to execute me on the spot. I stammered on.

"But, sirs, you must understand. These are the reason I came to your hospitable planet. My firm, Fazzoletto-Mouchoir Ltd., is an old and much respected manufacturer in the field of military electronics. These are samples. Some most delicate. Only to be opened in the presence of an armament specialist."

"I am armament specialist," one of them said, stepping forward. I had noted him earlier because of his bald head and a sinister scar that drew up one eye in a perpetual wink.

"Please to meet you, sir. I am Pas Ratunkowy." He was unimpressed by my name and did not offer his. "If I can have my key ring I will open said case and display to you its contents."

A camera was swung into place to record the entire operation, before I was permitted to proceed. I unlocked the case and flipped back the lid. The armament specialist glared down at the various components in their padded niches. I explained.

"My firm is the originator and sole manufacturer of the memory line of proximity fuses. No other line is as compact as ours, none as versatile." I used tweezers to take a fuse from a holder. It was no larger than a pinhead. "This is the most minuscule, designed to be used in a weapon as small as a handgun. Firing activates the fuse which will then detonate the charge in the slug when it comes near a target of predetermined size. This other fuse is the most intelligent, designed for use in heavy weapons or missiles." They all leaned forward eagerly when I held up the wafer of the Mem-IV and pointed out its singular merits.

"All solid state construction, capable of resisting incredible pressures, thousands of G's, massive shocks. It can be preset to detonate only when approaching a specific target, or can be programmed externally and electronically at any time up to the moment of firing. It contains discrimination circuits that will prevent explosion in the vicinity of friendly equipment. It is indeed unique."

I replaced it carefully and closed the lid on the case. A happy sigh swept through the spectators. This was the kind of thing they really *liked*. The armament specialist took up the case.

"This will be returned to you when it is needed to demonstrate."

Reluctantly, the examination drew to a close. The fuses had been the highpoint of the search and nothing else could quite equal this. They had some fun squeezing the tubes and emptying the jars in my toilet kit but their hearts were not really in it. Finally tiring of this they bundled away all my goods and tossed me my new clothing.

"Four and half minutes to dress," an exiting inspector said. "Bring bags."

My garments were not what might be considered high fashion under any conditions. Underwear and such were a drab utilitarian gray and manufactured from some substance that felt like a mixture of shredded machine shop waste and sandpaper. I sighed and dressed. The outer garment was a one piece jumpsuit sort of thing that made me look like some giant form of wasp with its wide black and yellow bands. Well, if that is what the well dressed Cliaandian wore, that is what I would wear. Not that I had much choice. I picked up the two bags, their sharp handles instantly cutting into my palms, and left through the single open door.

"Car," a guard said outside, pointing to a driverless bubble-topped vehicle that stood nearby. We were now in a large room, still decorated in the same prison gray. The side door of the vehicle opened at my approach.

"I will be pleased to take car," I nodded and smiled. "But where shall I go—"

"Car knows. In."

Not the galaxy's most witty conversationalists. I threw in my bags and sat down. The door wheezed shut and the bank of lights on the robodriver lit up. We started forward and a heavy portal swung open before us. And another and another, each one thick enough to seal a bank vault. After the last one we shot up into the open air and I winced at the impact of sunlight. And looked on with great interest at the passing scene.

Cliaand, if this nameless city was any example, was a modern-ized, mechanized, and busy world. Cars and heavy lorries filled the motorways, all apparently under robot control since they were evenly spaced and moved at impressive speeds. Pedways were on both sides and crossed overhead. There were stores, signs, crowds, uniforms. Uniforms! That single word does not convey the be-medaled and multicolored glories that surrounded me. *Everyone* wore a uniform of some sort with the different colors, I am sure, denoting the different branches and services. None of them were striped yellow and black. One more handicap placed in my way, but I shrugged it off. When you are drowning who cares if a teacup of water is poured over your head. Nothing about this piece of work was going to be easy.

My car darted out of the rushing traffic, dived down into another tunnel entrance and drew to a stop before an ornately decorated doorway. The great golden letters *Zlato-Zlato* were inscribed over the entrance which, in Cliaandian, might be translated as *luxury*. This was a pleasant change. A beribboned, jeweled and elegant doorman rushed forward to open the door, then stopped and stamped away and his place was taken by a bullet-necked individual in a dark gray uniform. Little silver crossed knife-and-battle-ax insignia were on both shoulders and his buttons were silver skulls. Somehow, not very encouraging.

"I am Pacov," this depressing figure mumbled. "Your body-guard."

"A pleasure to meet you, sir, a real pleasure."

I climbed out, carrying my own bags it will be noted, and followed the grim back of my watchdog into the lobby of the hotel, which is what it proved to be. My identification was accepted with a maximum of discourtesy, a room assigned, a bellboy reluctantly prodded into showing me the way and off we went. My status as a theoretically respected offworld sales representative got me into the establishment, but that did not mean that I had to like it. My wasp colors branded me an alien, and alien they were going to keep me.

The quarters were luxurious, the bed soft, the bugs enthusiastically present. Sound and optic, they seemed to be built into every fitting and fixture. Every other knob on the knobbed furniture was a microphone and the light bulbs turned to follow me with their beady little eyes when I moved. When I went into the bath to shave an optical eye looked back at me through the lightly silvered mirror and there was another optical pickup in the end of my toothbrush—no doubt to spy out any secrets lurking in my molars. All very efficient.

They thought. It made to laugh, and I did, turning it into a snort when it emerged so my patient bodyguard would not be suspicious. He pad-padded after me wherever I went in the spacious apartment. No doubt he would sleep at the foot of my bed when I retired.

And all of this was of no avail. Love laughs at locksmiths—and so does Jim diGriz. Who knows an incredible amount, if you will excuse my seeming immodesty, about bugging. This was a case of massive overkill. So there were a lot of bugs. So what do you do with all that information? Computer circuitry would be completely useless in an observational situation like this one, which meant that a large staff of human beings would be watching, recording and analyzing. There is a limit to the number of people who can be assigned to this kind of work because a geometric progression soon takes place with watchers watching watchers until no one is doing anything else. I am sure there was a large staff keeping a keen eye on me, foreigners were rare enough to enjoy this luxury. Not only would my quarters be bugged but the areas I normally passed through, ground cars and such.

The entire city could *not* be bugged, nor was there reason to do so. All I had to do was act my normal humble cover-role self for awhile until I found the opportunity to leave the bugged areas. And cook up a plan that would permit my complete disappearance once I was out of sight. I would have only one chance at this; whatever plan I produced would have to work the first time out or I would be a very dead rat.

Pacov was always there, watching my every motion. He was

watching when I went to sleep at night and the suspicious look in those hard little eyes was the first thing I saw in the morning. Which was just the way I wanted it. Pacov would be the first to go, but until then his mere presence with me meant that my watchers were relaxed. Let them relax. I looked relaxed, too—but I wasn't. I was examining every aspect of the city that I could see, looking for that rathole.

On the third day I found it. It was one of the many possibilities I had under consideration and it quickly proved to be the best. I made plans accordingly and that night smiled into the darkness as I went to sleep. I'm sure the smile was observed with infrared cameras—but what can be read from a smile?

The fourth day opened as did all the others with breakfast served in the room.

"My, my, but I am hungry today," I told the glowering Pacov. "It must be the exhilarating atmosphere and aura of good cheer on your fine planet. I believe I will have a little more to eat."

I did. A second breakfast. Since I had no idea when my next meal might be I decided to stoke up as best I could.

Standard routine followed. We emerged from the hotel at the appointed hour and the robocar was waiting. It started at once towards its programmed destination, the war office where I had been demonstrating the effectiveness of the Fazzoletto-Mouchoir fuses. A number of targets had been destroyed, and today others would be blasted under even more exacting circumstances. It was all good fun.

We surfaced on the main road, spun down it and turned off into the side road that led to our destination. Traffic was light here—as always—and no pedestrians were in sight. Perfect. Street after street zipped by and I felt a familiar knot of tension developing. All or nothing. Slippery Jim, here we go . . .

"Ah-choo," I said, with what I hoped was appropriate realism, and reached for my handkerchief. Pacov was suspicious. Pacov was always suspicious.

"Bit of dust in nose, you know how it is," I said. "Say, look, is that not the good General Trogbar over there?" I pointed with my free hand.

Pacov was well trained. His eyes only flickered aside for an instant before they returned to me. The instant was all I needed. Knotted into the handkerchief was a roll of small coins, the only weapon I could obtain under the authority's watchful gaze. I had assembled it, coin by coin, under the bedcovers at night. As the eyes flickered my hand struck, swinging the hard roll in a short arc that ended on the side of Pacov's head. He slumped with a muffled groan.

And even as he slumped down I was leaning over into the front of the car and banging down on the emergency stop button. The motor died, the brakes locked, we squealed to a stop and the doors popped open. Not more than a dozen paces from the selected spot. A bullseye. I was out and running at the same moment.

Because when I hit my bodyguard and the stop button every alarm must have lit up on the bugging board—there were plenty of little seeing eyes in the car. The forces of the enemy were launched at the same instant I was. All I had were seconds—a minute perhaps—of freedom before the troops closed in and grabbed me.

Would it be enough time?

Running, head down as fast as I could, I turned and skidded into the narrow opening of the service street. This cut through behind a row of buildings and emerged on a different street. There were robots here loading rubbish into bins, but they ignored me as I ran by since they were simple M types programmed for nothing but this kind of work.

The robot pusher was another matter. He was human and had an electronic lash that he used to stir the robots along. It cracked out and snapped around me and the electric current crackled into my side.

5

IT WAS SHOCKING, to say the least, but I barely felt it. The voltage is kept low since it is meant to stir the robots, not to cook out their brain circuits. I grabbed the whip as soon as it hit and pulled hard.

All of this was of course according to plan. I had seen this robot pusher and his work gang in this same place every day when we passed; Cliaand does love its routine. The robot pusher, a thick-necked and thuggy looking individual, could be counted on to interfere with a running alien—and had done just as I had hoped. When I pulled on the whip I had him off balance and he staggered towards me, jaw agape, and I let him have a roundhouse right on the point of that agaping jaw. It connected.

He shook his head, growled something, and came at me with his hands ready to crunch and rend.

This was *not* according to plan. He was supposed to drop instantly so I could rush through the rest of the routine before the cavalry arrived. How could I have known that not only did he have the IQ of a block of stone but the constitution of one as well? I stepped aside, his fingers grabbed empty air, and I began to sweat. Time was passing and I had no time. I had to render this hulk unconscious in the quickest way possible.

I did. It wasn't graceful but it worked. I tripped him as he went by, then jumped on his back and rode him to the ground accelerating his fall. And held him by the head and pounded it against the pavement. It took three good knocks—I was afraid the pavement would give way before he did—before he grunted and re-laxed.

In the distance the first siren sounded. I sweated harder. Indifferent to the ways of man the robots dumped their dustbins.

The robot pusher was dressed in a uniform of a decomposed green in color, no doubt symbolic of his trade. It was closed with a single zipper which I unzipped, then began to work the clothing off his bulky and unyielding form. While the sirens grew closer. At the last moment I had to stop and tear his boots off in order to remove the trousers, a noisome operation that added nothing good to the entire affair.

The siren echoed loudly from the walls of the service street and brakes squealed nastily close by.

With what very well might be called frantic haste I pulled the uniform on over my own wasp-like garb and zipped it shut. Running feet pounded loudly towards me. I grabbed up the whip and let the nearest robot have a crack right across his ball bearings.

"Stuff this man into a bin!" I ordered and stood back as it grabbed up its former master.

The feet had just vanished from view when the first of the red uniformed soldiers burst into sight.

"An alien!" I shouted, and shook my whip towards the other end of the narrow street. "He went thataway. Fast. Before I could stop him."

The soldiers kept going fast as well. Which was a good thing since the pair of recently removed boots were lying there right in plain sight. I threw them in the bin after their owner and cracked the whip on my half dozen robots.

"We march," I ordered. "To the next location." I hoped they were programmed for a regular route—and they were. The truck-robot led the way and the others fell in behind them. I went behind, whip ready. My little procession emerged into the police gorged, soldier full street. Armored vehicles twisted around us and drivers cursed. My faithful band of robots struck straight across the street through this mess while I, with a paralyzed smile on my lips, trotted along after them. I was afraid that if I made any attempt to change the orders my mechanical team would stage a sitdown right there in the street. We passed behind the abandoned groundcar just as my old bodyguard, Pacov, was being helped from it. I turned my back on him and tried to ignore the chill prickling up and down the nape of my neck. If he recognized me . . .

The first robot entered another serviceway and I staggered after them until, after what felt like a two day walk, I entered this haven of relative safety. It was a coolish day but I was sweating heavily: I leaned against the wall to recover while my robots emptied the bins. More cars were still appearing in the street I had so recently left and a flight of jets thundered by overhead. My, but they certainly were missing me.

What next? A good question. Very soon now, when no trace of the fugitive alien could be found, someone would remember the one witness to his escape. And they would want to talk to the robot pusher again. Before that moment came I would have to be else-where—but where? My assets were very limited; a collection of garbage collecting robots, now industriously clanking away at their trade, two uniforms—one worn over the other—either of which made me a marked man, and an electronic whip. Good only for whipping robots; the feeble current it generated was just enough to close a relay to cancel a previous order or action. What to do?

There was a grating noise close behind me and I jumped aside as a rusty iron door slid upwards. A fat man in a white hat poked his head out.

"I got another barrel in here for you, Slobodan," he said, then looked suspiciously at me. "You ain't Slobodan."

"You're right. Slobodan is someone else. And he is somewhere else. In the hospital. Having a hernia removed. They're putting in a new one."

Was opportunity tapping? I talked fast and thought even faster. There was still plenty of rushing about in the street I had so recently crossed but no one was looking into the serviceway. I cracked my whip across the gearbox of the nearest robot and ordered him to me.

"Follow that man," I said, snapping my whip in the right direction. White hat popped back inside, the robot followed him and I followed the robot.

Into a kitchen. A big one, a restaurant kitchen obviously. And there was no one else in sight.

"What time do you open?" I asked. "I'm getting quite an appetite on this job."

"Not until tonight—hey! Tell this robot to stop following me and get that garbage out of here."

The cook was backing around the room with the robot trundling faithfully after him. They made a fine pair.

"Robot," I said, and cracked the whip. "Do not follow that man any more. Just reach out your implacable little robot hands and grab him by the arms so he cannot get away."

The robot's reflexes, being electronic, were faster than the cook's. The steel hands closed, the cook opened his mouth to complain—and I stuffed his hat into it. He chewed it angrily and made muffled noises deep in his throat. He kept this up all the time I was tying him into a chair with a fine assortment of towels, securing the gag in place as well. No one else had appeared and my luck was still running strong.

"Out," I ordered the robot, cracking it across the patient metal back. The others were still working away and I laid about like a happy flagellant until they were all quivering for orders.

"Return. To the place from whence you came this morning. Go now."

Like well trained troops they turned and started away. Thankfully, in the direction away from the street we had just crossed. I popped back into the kitchen and locked the door. Safe for the moment. They would trace me to the robot rubbishmen sooner or later, but would have no idea where or when I had left the convoy. Things were working out just fine.

The captive cook had managed to knock the chair over and was wriggling, chair and all, towards the exit.

"Naughty," I said, and took the largest cleaver from the rack. He stopped at once and rolled his eyes at me. I put the cleaver and the whip where they could be reached quickly and looked about. For a little while at least I could breathe easy and make some more definite plans. It had all been rush and improvise so far. There was a sudden knocking in the distance and the sharp ringing of a bell. I sighed and picked up the cleaver again. Rush and improvise was the motto of this operation.

"What is that?" I asked the cook, slipping the hat from his mouth for the moment.

"The front door. Someone there," he said hoarsely, his eyes on the cleaver I held ready over his head. I restored the gag and sidled to the swinging door on the far wall and opened it enough to peek through.

The dining room behind was dark and empty. The banging and ringing came from the entrance on the far side. No one else had appeared to answer this noisy summons so I felt safe in assuming that the cook and I were alone for the moment. Now to see what it was all about. With the cleaver at the ready I went to the front entrance, slid back the bolt and opened the door a crack.

"Whaddayawant?" I asked, aiming for the same rudimentary grammar and low accent voiced by the cook.

"Refrigerator service. You called you got trouble. What kind of trouble?"

"Big trouble!" My heart bounded with unexpected joy. "Come in and bring biggest toolbox you got."

It was a fair sized toolbox and I let him in, closed the door behind, and tapped him smartly on the back of the head with the flat of the cleaver blade. He folded nicely. His uniform was a utilitarian dark green, a great improvement on wasp, white or garbage, my only choice up to this moment. I stripped him quickly and tied him to a chair next to the cook where they commiserated in silence with each other. For the first time I was ahead of my pursuers. With luck it would be some hours before my captives were discovered and connected with my flight. I put the green uniform on, prepared a large number of sandwiches, picked up the toolbox, tipped my uniform cap to the captives in the kitchen, and slipped out the front door.

A large riding robot was standing there, another toolbox hanging from one hand, humming quietly to itself. Painted on its metallic chest was the same crest of the service company that now adorned my own chest.

"We travel in comfort," I said. "Take this." I got my fingers out of the way just in time as it reached for the toolbox.

During my rapid trips through the city I had seen a number of these riding robots from a distance, but had never been close to one before. There was a sort of saddle arrangement on their backs where the operator rode, but I hadn't the slightest idea of how to get into the seat. Did the thing kneel to be mounted or drop down a ladder or what? Cars and other robots were going by in this street and a squad of soldiers was approaching at a good clip. I found myself sweating again.

"I wish to leave. Now."

Nothing happened. Except that the soldiers were that much closer. The robot stood as stolid as a statue. There was no help here. I didn't know if it was the orthodox manner or not, I had to do something, so I put one foot on the thing's hip socket, grabbed a riding light up near its shoulder blade and swarmed up its side. Hidden motors hummed louder as it shifted balance to accommodate my added weight. I slipped into the saddle just as the squad of soldiers trotted by. They ignored me completely.

The seat was comfortable. I had a good view, with my head at least three meters above the ground, and I hadn't the slightest idea what to do next. Though leaving this vicinity would make fine openers. A compact control panel was set into the top of the robot's head and I pressed the button labeled WALK. I felt the grinding vibration of internal gears being engaged and it began to mark time in place. A good beginning. A rapid search found the button marked FORWARD. It lurched ahead and broke into an easy trot. I soon left the police and all the excitement behind.

A plan was needed. I rode my mechanical mount through the

heart of the city and considered my position. One man against a world. Very poetic and possibly disconcerting except for the fact that I had been in this position before while they had not. All of the security arrangements meant that aliens were few and far between on Cliaand and always kept under close surveillance. Perhaps they had never lost track of one before and this was sure to be a great annoyance. Heads would roll. Fine. As long as one of them wasn't mine. In a sense I had the advantage. Other than my cover identity they knew nothing about me. If I could lose myself in the depths of their depressing culture I would be impossible to find. As long as I stayed submerged. Positive action would come later. Right now I had to save my valuable hide and plan for the future.

One of the city exits was ahead and an unusually large number of uniformed individuals were involved in examining and searching everyone attempting to leave. A touch on the LEFT button started my mount down another street away from this danger. When I wanted to leave the city I would. That time had not yet arrived.

By mid afternoon I had a working knowledge of the layout of the city and was developing calluses on my bottom. The robot was going slower and evidently in need of a recharge from some handy wall socket. I needed a recharge from the sandwiches in the toolbox. We both needed a rest. And the chances were good that my prisoners had been found in the kitchen and that the new alarm was going out. Using the more vacant side streets I worked the robot back to the manufacturing district that I had noted earlier and looked for a place to hole up. I had seen some factories and warehouses with a distinctly deserted air that would fit my needs.

One did. Cobwebs on the windows and rust on the hinges of the front door. No one in sight and a lock that I could have opened in the dark with my fingernails. The door creaked open, not a soul was in sight. We slipped in and the bolt clicked behind us. Security. The place was deserted, dusty and for the most part empty. A great ancient piece of machinery brooded in one corner, as featureless and mysterious as a lost jungle idol, with sacrifices of discarded cartons about its feet. Perfect. I lunched, relaxed, searched the building, found an interior room with no windows, brought in the flashlight and a pencil from the toolbox and one of the sacrificial cartons. Time for the next step.

Pencil in hand, the blank square before me illuminated by the light, I spoke aloud.

"Now hear this. Memory is about to begin. The count will start at ten. I will become tired during the progression and by the time zero is reached I will be asleep. The memory is keyed to the word . . . xanadu!''

"Ten," I said, feeling fine. Then "Nine" and I yawned. By the time I hit five my eyelids were drooping and I have no memory at all of ever getting to zero.

6

I AWOKE TO find my fingers stiff, my arm cramped, my eyes sore. And the great square of cardboard covered with a complex wiring diagram. The subconscious is a fine place to hide things unknown to the conscious mind. I not only had the diagram but suddenly realized that I now knew just how to use it. The plan was a dazzlingly simple one and I was instantly jealous of whoever dreamed it up. It also required a bit of time, a lot of electronic wiring and equipment. All of which would have to be stolen. I sighed and stretched my cramped muscles. It had been a tiring day and my sleep during the hypnotic trance had been no sleep at all. Tomorrow would be another day, the pace of pursuit should have died down.

Tomorrow and tomorrow were nothing but work. I was a stainless steel rat gone to ground and there was much scuttling about to be done. The city continued in its business around me, and I'm sure the search for me went on unabated although it never came near my cozy retreat. I soldered and wired, stole food and other items of comfort and luxury in an almost offhand way. Cliaand seemed to have a very low level of crime because almost no precautions appeared to have been taken to prevent the sort of burglary I indulged in. Either the criminal class had all been killed off or they now ran the government. Which could very likely be the case. My solitary period would end soon and I would abandon my passive role and indulge in the espionage that I had been sent here to do.

Leaving the city was far simpler than I had imagined. By adroit loitering in the area of the checkpoint I saw that the military were in charge of the operation which appeared to proceed in a very simpleminded and military way. A certain amount of saluting and ordering, examining of papers and rubber stamping, a quick search and away. I hoped it would work that easily for me. To make the entire operation military I stole an army truck at dusk, stopping it by planting my robot in the road in front of it. The truck vibrated to a stop and the driver put his head out and cursed fluently. Most of the words had not been in my language lessons and I filed them for future use. He seemed to be alone, which was a blessing.

"And the same to you," I told him. "That is no way to talk to civilians. This is emergency."

"What emergency?" Suspiciously.

"This emergency." Enthusiastically.

The needle slammed home in the side of his neck and he slumped. I had also made a raid on a chemical supply house. I pushed him aside, put on his uniform cap, ordered the robot into the back of the truck and returned to the warehouse for my wares. They stowed neatly behind the crates of dehydrated meals, forms in triplicate, cans of boot polish and other essential military items in the truck. Dressed in the soldier's red uniform, he dozing nicely in my green, I said good-by to the robot, my only friend on this inhospitable planet. He answered nothing in return which did not hurt me. I left.

My papers and identification were accepted with military taciturnity, examined and approved, and I was free. I sped merrily out into the night and phase two of my plan. Physically this involved a lot of rushing about, stealing various vehicles to confuse my trail, and a long trek through the central desert to a certain landmark. This was a great lump of stone standing very much by itself in the sea of sand. It was shaped very much like a pot and was called *Ionac* in the Cliaand language. Which means *pot* and gives you some idea of the great scope of their imagination. The camouflage net covered the stolen groundcar, and I worked most industriously here for seven full days before I was satisfied with the results. What I had built, with my own two little hands and the help of an excavation robot, was a completely self-contained underground shelter no more than 100 meters from Pot rock. This was the last and final bit of preparation for phase three. That night I initiated this phase. My little home-wired transmitter was tuned and ready to go, the antenna pointed straight up at the zenith. Exactly at midnight I turned it on and the narrow, highly directional signal blasted up into space. I kept it going for exactly thirty seconds, then shut it off.

That was that. The die cast and the next move was up to Them. Them being a Special Corps detachment that had arranged this phase. Hopefully arranged it, I would know nothing positive until the following evening. If the plan worked, and I chewed my lip a little over the *if* as I stowed the radio back into the car, my signal should have been received by them—and only by them. Narrow band width and very directional. Impossible to detect. The Cliaandians should know nothing about it at all. But great powers would have been set into motion. Mighty computers computed and gigantic rockets fired. A selected meteorite set into motion along with a collection of accompanying space debris. Out in space beyond the Cliaand detectors. But coming this way, aimed at the solitary rock of the Pot. I had a day and a night to wait.

Knowing my attitude towards unproductive waiting I had arranged a little party for myself. There was good food, or as good as I could get in preserved rations, and better drink since I had a far wider assortment to select from. Wine with the meal and more potent distillates afterward. For closers I lit a cigar and turned on the pocket-sized screen of the miniprojector and ran a couple of the feelthy-feely-films that I had bought at an army exchange. Pretty crude stuff for the troops, though it looked pretty attractive to me in my desert nomad role. Sleep lowered its gentle blanket, day followed night and then night again in its turn. And as soon as it was dark I was out there with my field glasses quartering the sky. Nothing. It wasn't due for hours yet, but I was impatient. The entire plan was beginning to sound absurd. And I was feeling very much alone, trapped on this alien planet light years from civilization. The mood was a depressing one. I had a drink from my pocket flask.

If all were going well the great hunk of rock should be heading towards Cliaand on a collision course. When it was detected by the defenses it should be considered as just another piece of spatial debris. It would hit the atmosphere and burn. If they were tracking it, on the offchance that it might be more than it appeared, this should reassure them. The speed and temperature ruled out any living cargo. It should also be a little difficult to follow because of the accompanying debris that would also be bouncing back radar signals. The meteor would burn through the atmosphere and hit the desert with an impact enough to destroy anything living. If there were an investigation it would be dilatory, and important things would happen before the investigators arrived. I hoped. It all sounded so good in theory and seemed such an absurd piece of madness in practice.

Very close to midnight a new star flickered and burned in the clear sky above and I sighed and put away the flask. Right on time like a commuter rocket. The point grew brighter and brighter, then brighter still. Aimed right at me. I knew that computers and astronomers were good—but not that good. Was the thing going to come down right on top of me?

Not quite. As I watched it appeared to drift to one side, accelerating as it went, while a great hissing roar like a heavenly steam kettle crackled through the air. I jumped into the groundcar and kicked it to life as the burning bomb of light vanished behind the tower of the Pot to be followed instantly by a rolling explosion that lit the night air and outlined the Pot with fire. I moved.

My headlights picked out a raw pit in the ground, surrounded by debris and overhung with a cloud of smoke and dust. And at the bottom was the great glazed chunk of steaming rock. Bullseye! I backed the car behind the nearest sand dune and thumbed the transmitter. There was another explosion, infinitely smaller than the one of impact, and pieces of rock zinged above my head. When I next looked at the meteor it had been neatly cracked in half by the charges and the jelly-like liquid that had protected the contents was soaking into the sand.

At the same moment I heard the rising rumble of approaching jets and killed the headlights. They roared by overhead, triangles of darkness against the stars, and tilted into a turn. At this moment I gained new appreciation of the Cliaand powers of suspicion as well as a deep respect for their radar, computers and organization. I was going to have less time than I thought. I jumped into the hole trying to ignore the heat of the crackling rock.

The equipment was intact, sealed into flat boxes, and there was just enough light from the stars for me to drag them out and stow them into the car. The jets circled above, brought to the general area by radar triangulation and searching now for the precise point of impact. Not that they could see much, at their speed in the darkness. But slower aircraft were undoubtedly on the way. With instrumentation and lights that could quarter the area. I moved a little faster at the thought, my imagination already producing the flutter of great propellers on the horizon. Panting heavily, the last box in the groundcar, I waited until the jets were swinging away from me before starting for my hidey-hole. I went as fast as I dared, steering around the bigger obstacles and bumping over the small. When the jets swung in my direction I stopped, trying to think tiny, waiting for them to pass. On the next rush I made it to the entrance. As I dropped the first of the boxes into the hole in the ground I *did* hear engines. Strong lights were flickering in the distance—coming my way. Things were being shaved entirely too close. I hurled the boxes out one after another, not caring where or how they landed. I was ready to dive after them and stow them carefully, when great wings fluttered overhead and a sizzling light raced from behind the Pot and flashed over me, blinding me.

It moved on and I groped for the car's starting switch through a galaxy of rainbows and roaring discs of light. The groundcar started up, then leaped into motion as I kicked it into gear. As the light hit again I fell over the side and lay still.

For a considerable length of time I was motionless and bathed by the light, searing in even through my closed eyelids. It felt as though I lay there between two and three years but could only have been a fraction of a second. The ladder was in place and I climbed down it, barking my shins well on the tumbled clutter of boxes. Rooting about like a mole in the darkness I kicked and pushed them through the entranceway ahead of me. The roar of great machines was loud behind me, joined a moment later by the sound of rapid firing weapons and the boom of explosions.

"Perfect," I panted, hurling the last of the boxes. "Weapons are meant to be used, so they are using them. I was sure they would be a trigger-happy bunch and I'm most pleased to see my conclusions justified." A louder boom announced the destruction of my car. It could not have been better. I felt for the transmitter by the entrance and took it with me as I climbed up the ladder, at a much more leisurely pace.

Standing comfortably on the ladder, with my elbows resting on the ground, I had the best seat for the performance. Jets roared and propellers thrashed from the sky above. Bullets sang and bombs exploded. The groundcar burned nicely, sending up angry spurts of flame whenever the wreck was strafed. As the banging and booming began to taper off I livened it up by pressing the first button on the transmitter.

With a satisfying explosion of sound the rapidfire guns began to fire from the top of the Pot, while at occasional intervals rockets shot up out of the launcher. Every other round was tracer so the show was most impressive. The forces in the sky above zoomed away to regroup, then returned to the attack with savage vigor. The top of the Pot and the ground all about was torn with explosions. I had raided the Cliaand armory for my weapons and it was nice to see the same side shooting at itself. A bomb exploded no more than thirty meters from me and sand shook down my neck. This part of the show was over; time for the finale.

Sand was falling all around me as I dropped back to the bottom of the hole. With a certain amount of haste I pulled the ladder through the entrance, then tugged on the cables and darted inside. A good part of the sand I had dug out was piled above the entrance and held back by restraining boards. Now removed. I pushed the door shut as the sand slid down with sudden speed. Standing there in the darkness I counted slowly to ten to allow enough time for the sandslide to completely fill the hole. Then I pressed the second button.

Nothing happened.

And this was an essential part of the operation. With all the bombs going off, the ground still shook with their vibration, one more explosion would not be noticed. The second button was to have triggered a buried charge that would conceal all signs of my activities and seal my rat hole at the same time. If it did not go off I would be easily found and dug out . . .

Memory returned and I cursed my own foolishness. Of course I had made plans for this contingency. The radio signal from my little transmitter could not reach through the ground. I had known that. I groped for the flashlight I had left by the entrance, turned it on and saw the bare end of wire sticking through the wall. It was even labeled 2 so there would be no confusion if I were in a hurry.

I was in a hurry. The explosions were dying away, presumably the mechanical enemy on the Pot had been destroyed, and if my explosion did not go off soon it would look very suspicious to say the least. I wrapped the end of the wire, it extended up to ground level, around the whip aerial on the transmitter and thumbed the button again. There was silence.

Until a jarring explosion went off just overhead, shaking the bones inside my body and rattling my teeth together. My concrete cave boomed like a drum and dirt and chips rattled down. I was safe.

Snug as a roach in the rafters. I turned on the light and looked with pride on my residence for the next couple of weeks. Power supply, shielded of course, food, water, atmosphere renewal, everything a man might need. And the solid state circuitry and devices that had arrived in the meteor. I would work and assemble my equipment and emerge ready to face the world. While the desert above was searched and quartered and the chase went further away. They would never think to look right under their noses, never! I smiled and looked for a bottle to open to celebrate.

7

No LONGER A THIEF I, nor a hider under rocks. On the 13th day I had unblocked my door and dug my way back to the surface. With this symbolic act I left behind my fugitive's existence and entered Cliaandian society. With assorted identification and various uniforms I now played a wide selection of roles in this rather repellent society until I knew far more about it than I really cared. In my various identities I only brushed the periphery of the military since I wanted to save my energies for a frontal assault there in full power.

With this possibility I boarded an SST flight to Dosadanglup, the fair sized provincial city that happened to be situated adjacent to the military base of Glupost. From what I had been able to determine Glupost was also a major spaceship center and staging area for offworld expeditions. So there was more than chance to the fact that I loitered near enough to the seat reservation clerk to see who got what, and then asked for a seat next to a very attractive who.

Attractive only to me, I hasten to add. By any other standard of measurement the flight-major would win no prizes. His jaw was too big, apparently designed to project into places where it wasn't wanted, and it had a nasty little cleft built into it as though it had cracked from being poked too far. Suspicious dark eyes lurked under simian shelving brows and the cavernous nostrils were twin furlined subway tunnels. I could not care less. I saw only the black uniform of the Space Armada, the many decorations signifying active service, and the wings-and-rocket of a senior pilot. He was my man.

"Good evening, sir, good evening," I said as I slipped into the seat next to him. "A pleasure to travel with you."

He aimed the twin cannons of his nose at me and fired a broadside snort that signaled a close to the recently opened conversation. I smiled in return and buckled my belt and was slammed back into the cushions as the SST hurled itself into the night sky. At cruising altitude most of the wing area slipped back into the hull and I took out my pocket flask and detached the two small cups.

"It would be a pleasure to offer you a drink of refreshment, noble flight-major, in gratitude for your many services rendered to the glorious cause of Cliaand.''

This time he did not even bother to grunt, but instead picked at his teeth with a none too clean pinky nail until he extracted a fragment of meat from his recent dinner. Close examination convinced him that it was too large to discard so he reingested it with a certain relish. A man of simple pleasures. I offered a better one.

''Nothing too good for our boys in the service. This is narcolethe.'' I sipped at the cup and smacked my lips.

He looked directly at me for the first time and there should have been little splintering sounds as his lips moved slowly into an unaccustomed smile.

''I'll drink that,'' he said in a grating voice, and well he should since the small flask of liqueur would have cost him a month's salary. Narcolethe, the finest drink known to mankind, distilled in small quantities from a scarce botanical on a minor planet at the galaxy's rim. Soothing, charming, subtle, intoxicating, inspiring, aphrodisiac, stimulating. It was everything any other drink was, plus much more, with no side effects and no hangover. He took the proffered cup and lowered the caverns of his nose over it and sipped.

''Not bad,'' he said, and I smiled at this crude understatement as though it were sincerest flattery and offered him the false name I had assumed. He thought about it and realized that an exchange was in order.

''Flight-Major Vaska Hulja.''

''The pleasure is mine, sir, the pleasure is mine. May I top that up for you, these cups are so small.''

Very soon, as our razor nosed craft cracked the sound barrier and boomed through the sleep of the dozing citizens on the ground, I came to almost love the flight-major. He was perfect, all-around, with no bulges of doubt or pockmarks of uncertainty. Just as a spider is a perfect spider or a vampire bat a perfect vampire bat, he was a perfect freewheeling bastard. As his spirits lifted and his tongue grew thick the anecdotes became more detailed. The flight-major on strafing:

''Never make mistake of going after individuals or small groups, it is overall effect that counts. Stay to plan, hit buildings and grouped vehicles, finish the run. On a second run it's all right to hit groups of people, but only big ones, with firebombs. That spreads and splatters and gets the most.''

The flight-major on recreation:

''There was just the two of us and we had maybe a dozen bottles and case of weedstick, enough for couple of days, so we got these three girls, one as spare, you know, just in case, and took them . . .''

The flight-major on offworlders:

''Animals. You can't tell me we can even interbreed with them. Obvious that Cliaand is source of all intelligent life in the universe and only civilizing influence.''

There was more like this and I could only nod my head in rapt attention. Perfect, as I said. What had me almost pulsating with joy was the information that he had just been assigned to the Glupost station after his R & R. This was his first visit to the immense base after years of duty on the fighting front. Destiny was controlling the fall of the dice.

What I had to do next was dangerous and involved a great deal of risk—but the opportunity presented was too good to miss. In the weeks that I had been exploring the details of the Cliaand society I had come to know it in great depth. I thought. Now was the time to find out how much I really did know. For the part of society I had picked my way through was just the periphery, the non-military part and the military was the one that really counted. It dominated this world in every way and had managed to extend its dominance to other worlds as well. Despite the rules of logic, the inverse square, and history. I was going to have to apply my little bit of know-how to crack the final barrier.

I was joining the army. Enlisting in the Space Armada. With the rank of flight-major. As the ship tilted into its landing approach I put thought into deed.

''Must you report to duty at once, Vaska?'' Strong drink had put us on a first name basis. He shook his head in a shaggy *no*.

''Tomorrow I am due.''

''Wonderful. You do not wish to spend your last night of leave between the cold sheets of a solitary bed in the B.O.Q. Just think what else could be accomplished in the same time.''

I went into some imaginary detail of what could be done with silken sheets in an unsolitary bed. Good food and fine drink were mentioned as well, but these were only of contingent interest. The flask tilted once more and he nodded cheerful agreement to my plan.

As soon as we had landed and our baggage had been disgorged, a robocab took us to the Dosadan-Glup Robotnik. This was the local branch of a planet-wide chain of hotels that specialized in non-human service. Everything was mechanized and computerized. Human beings presumably visited them once in a while to check the gauges and empty the tills, but I had never seen one although I had used these hotels quite often, for many obvious reasons. I had occasionally seen other guests entering or leaving but we had avoided each other's gaze like plague carriers. The Robotniks were islands of privacy in a sea of staring eyes. They had certain drawbacks, but I had long since learned to cope with these. To the Robotnik we went.

The front door opened automatically when we approached and a sort of motorized-dolly robot slipped out of its kennel and sang to us.

"World famous since the day we opened,
The Dosadan-Glup Robotnik welcomes you.
I am here to take your luggage—
Order me and I'll help you!"

This was sung in a rich contralto voice to the accompaniment of a 200 piece brass band; a standard recording of all the Robotnik hotels. I hated it. I kicked the robot back, it was pressing close to our ankles, and pointed to the robocab.

"Luggage. There. Five pieces. Fetch."

It hummed away and plunged eager tentacles into the cab. We entered the hotel.

"Don't we have four pieces luggage?" Vaska asked, frowning those beetling eyebrows in thought.

"You're right, I must have miscounted." The luggage robot caught up and passed us, with our suitcases and the back seat torn out of the cab. "We have five now."

"Good evening . . . gentlemen," the robot at the desk murmured, with a certain hesitation before the final word as it counted us and compared profiles in its memory bank. "How may we serve you?"

"The best suite in the house," I said as I signed a fictitious name and address and began to feed 100 *boginje* bills into the pay slot on the desk. Cash in advance was the rule at the Robotnik with any balance returned upon departure. A bellboy robot, armed with a key, rolled out and showed us the way, throwing the door wide with a blare of recorded trumpets as though it were announcing the second coming.

"Very nice," I said and pressed the button labeled *tip* on its chest which automatically deducted two *boginjes* from my credit balance.

"Order us some drinks and food," I told the flight-major, pointing to the menu built into the wall. "Anything you wish as long as there are steaks and champagne."

He liked that idea and he was busily punching buttons while I arranged the luggage. I also had a bug-detector strapped to my wrist which led me unerringly to the single optic-sonic bug. It was in the same place as every other one I had found, these hotels really were standardized, and I managed to move a chair in front of it when I opened my suitcase.

The delivery door dilated and champagne and chilled glasses slid out. Vaska was still ordering away on the buttons and my credit balance, displayed in large numbers on the wall, was rolling rapidly backwards. I cracked the bottle, bouncing the cork off the wall near him to draw his inebriated attention, and filled the glasses.

"Let us drink to the Space Armada," I said, handing him his glass and letting the little green pellet fall into it at the same time.

"To Space Armada," he said, draining the glass and breaking into some dreary chauvinistic song that I knew I would have to learn, all about shining blast-tubes, gleaming guns, men of valor, burning suns. I had enough of it even before he began.

"You look tired," I told him. "Aren't you sleepy?"

"Sleepy . . ." he agreed, his head bobbing.

"I think it would be a good idea for you to lie down on the bed and get some rest before dinner."

"Lie down . . ."His glass fell to the rug and he stumbled across the room and sprawled full length on the nearest bed.

"See, you were tired. Go to sleep and I'll wake you later."

Obedient to the hypnodrug, he closed his eyes and began snoring at once. If anyone were listening at the bug they would detect nothing wrong.

Dinner arrived, enough food to feed a squad—my money meant nothing to good old Vaska—and I ate a bit of steak and salad before going to work. I snapped open the kit and spread out the materials and tools.

The first thing was of course an injection that acted as a nerve block and numbed all sensation in my face. As soon as this took effect I propped the snoring flight-major up and trained the reading light full in his face. This would not be a hard job at all. We both had about the same bony structure and build, and the resemblance did not have to be perfect. Just close enough to match the prison-camp picture on his ID card. The quality of this picture was what one learns to expect from an identification photo, looking more like a shaven ape than a human.

The chin was the biggest job in every sense and massive injections of plastic jell built mine up to Vaska's heroic size. I molded its shape before it set, cleft and all, then went to work on the eyebrows. More plastic built up the brow ridges, and implanted black artificial hair drove home the resemblance. Contact lenses matched the color of his eyes and expanding rings in my nostrils flared them to the original's cave-like size. All that remained then was to transfer his fingerprints to the skintight and invisible plastic that covered my own fingers. Nothing to it.

While I altered Vaska's best uniform to a better fit for me he rose—as instructed—and ate some of the cold dinner. Sleep overcame him soon after that and this time he retired to the bed in the other room where his snores and grumbles would not annoy me.

I mixed a stiff drink and retired early. The morrow would be a busy day in my new identity. I was going into the Space Armada.

With a little luck I might get a clue as to the nature of their remarkable military powers.

8

"I'M SORRY, SIR, but you can't get in," the guard in front of the gate said. The gate itself was made of riveted steel and was solidly set into a high stone wall capped with many strands of barbed wire.

"What do you mean I *can't* get in? I have been *ordered* to Glupost," I shouted in my best military-obnoxious manner. "Now press the button or whatever else you do to unlock that thing."

"I can't open it, sir, the base is sealed from the inside. I'm stationed with the outside guard detail."

"I want to see your superior officer."

"Here I am," a cold voice said in my ear. "What is this disturbance?"

When I turned around I looked at his lieutenant's bar and he looked at my flight-major's double cross and I won that argument. He led me to the guardhouse and there was a lot of calling back and forth on the TV phone until he handed it to me and I looked a steely-eyed colonel in the face. I had already lost this argument.

"The base is sealed, flight-major," he said.

"I have orders to report here, sir."

"You were to report here yesterday. You have overstayed your leave."

"I'm sorry, sir, must have been an error in recording. My orders read report today." I held them up and saw that the reporting date *was* the previous day. That drunkard Vaska had got me into the trouble he deserved himself. The colonel smiled with all the sweetness of a king cobra in rut.

"If the mistake were in the orders, flight-major, there would certainly be no difficulty. Since the mistake was yours, *lieutenant*, we know where the error lies. Report to the security entrance."

I hung up the phone and the guard lieutenant, grinning evilly, handed me a set of lieutenant's bars. I unclipped my double-crosses and accepted the humbler rank. I hoped promotion was as fast as demotion in the Space Armada. A guard detail marched me along the wall to a smaller airlock type of entrance and I was passed through. My credentials and orders were examined, my fingerprints taken, and in a few minutes I was through the last gate and inside the base of Glupost.

A car was summoned, a private soldier took my bags, we drove to the officers' quarters and I was shown to my room. And all the time I kept my eyes open. Not that there was anything fascinating to see. See one military base and you've seen them all. Buildings, tents, chaps in uniform doing repetitive jumping, heavy expensive equipment all painted the same color, that sort of thing. What I had to find out would not be that easy to uncover. My bags were dumped in the tiny room, salutes exchanged, the soldier left, and a voice spoke hoarsely from the other bed.

"You don't happen to have a drink on you, do you?"

I looked closely and saw that what I at first thought was a bundle of crumpled blankets now appeared to contain a scrawny individual who wore dark glasses. The effort of talking must have exhausted him and he groaned, adding another breath of alcoholic vapor to the already rich atmosphere of the room.

"It so happens that I do," I said, opening the window. "My name is Vaska. Do you prefer any particular brand?"

"Otrov."

I could think of no drink by that title so presumably it was my roommate's name. Taking the flask with the most potent beverage from my collection I poured him half a glass. He seized it with trembling fingers and drained it while shudders racked his frame. It must have done some good because he sat up in bed and held out the glass for more.

"We blast off in two days," he said, sniffing his drink. "This really isn't paint remover, is it?"

"No, it just smells that way to fool the MP's. Where to?"

"Don't make jokes so early in the morning. You know we never know what planet we're hitting. Security. Or are you with security?"

He blinked suspiciously in my direction: I would have to watch the questions until I knew more. I forced a smile and poured a drink for myself.

"A joke. I don't feel so good myself. I woke up a flight-major this morning . . ."

"And now you're a lieutenant. Easy come, easy go."

"They didn't come that easy!"

"Sorry. Figure of speech. I've always been a lieutenant so I wouldn't know how the others feel. You couldn't just tip a little more into this glass? Then I'll be able to dress and we can get over to the club and get into some serious drinking. It's going to be awful, all those weeks without drink until we get back.''

Another fact. The Cliaand fought their battles refreshed with water. I wondered if I could. I sipped and the disturbing thought that had been poking at me for some minutes surfaced.

The real Vaska Hulja was back at the hotel and would be discovered. And I could do nothing about it because I was in this sealed base.

Some of the drink went down the wrong pipe and I coughed and Otrov beat me on the back.

''I think it really is paint remover,'' he said gloomily when I had stopped gasping, and began to dress.

As we walked to the officers' club I was in no mood for communication, which Otrov probably blamed on my recent demotion. What to do? Drink seemed to be in order, it wasn't noon yet, and it would be wisest to wait until evening to crack out of the base. Face the problems as they arose. Right now I was in a perfect position to imbibe drink with my new peer group and gather information at the same time. Which, after all, was the reason that I was here in the first place. Before leaving I had slipped a tube of killalc pills into my pocket. One of these every two hours would produce a massive heartburn, but would also grab onto and neutralize most of the alcohol as soon as it hit the stomach. I would drink deep and listen. And stay sober. As we walked through the garish doorway of the club I slipped one out and swallowed it.

It was all rather depressing, particularly since I was sloshing the stuff down my throat as fast as I could drink it and buying rounds for the others and not feeling it at all. As the afternoon went on and thirsts increased other officers appeared in the club and there were soon a dozen other pilots crowded around our free-spending table. All drinking well and saying little of any interest.

''Drink, drink,'' I insisted. ''Won it gambling. Don't need it where we're going,'' and bought another round.

There was a great deal said, as one might well imagine, about the flying characteristics of various ships and I filed all relevant details. And much mumbling over old campaigns, I dived from 50,000, planted the bombs, pulled up and that sort of thing. The only thing remarkable about all this was the unsullied record of victories. I knew the Cliaand armed forces were good, but looking at this collection of drunks almost made it impossible to believe they could be *that* good. But apparently they were. There were endless boasting tales of victory after victory and nothing else, and after a period I too came to believe. These boys were good and the Space Armada of Cliaand a winner. It was all too depressing. By evening there was a literal falling away of the original drinkers, though their places at the table were filled quickly enough. When one of them slid to the floor the servants would gently carry him off. I realized that I was the last of the originals so no one would notice if I also made an exit in this apparently traditional manner. Letting my eyes close I sank deep into my chair, hoping this would do since I did not relish a trip to the debris littered floor. It took them some minutes to notice I was no longer functioning, but eventually they did. Hard hands caught me at knees and armpits and I was hauled off.

When the footsteps had rattled away I opened my eyes to a sort of dim chamber whose walls were lined with bunks. Nearby me was the gaping *O* of Otrov's mouth, snoring away in his cups. As were the others. No one noticed when I pulled on my gloves and went to the door that opened into the company street and let myself out. It was almost dark and I had to leave the camp and I had not the slightest idea of how I could do it.

The gates were impossible. I strolled along the wall to the first one. Sealed and bolted shut, solid steel, with a brace of guards to see that the locks weren't tampered with. I walked on. There were guards every hundred paces or so along the wall and I assumed that there were an equal or greater number of electronic safeguards as well. As evening approached searchlights were turned on that illuminated the outside of the wall and glinted from the barbed wire that topped it. Admittedly all this was to keep anyone from getting in—but it worked equally well in the opposite direction. I walked on, trying to fight off the black depression that still threatened to overwhelm me. I passed through a medium sized atmosphere craft area, two crossed runways and some hangars, with a collection of lumbering jet transports standing about. For a moment I considered stealing one of these—but where would I land without being captured? I had to be in this city tonight, not zipping off to parts unknown.

Beyond the aircraft was a high chain metal fence that cut off the spaceship area. Getting in there would be easy enough—but what would it accomplish? I could see the same high outer wall stretching off into the distance. There was a rumble in the sky and bright lights lanced down. I turned around and watched, sunk in gloom, as a delta wing fighter settled in heavily for a landing. It looked like one of the same type that had strafed me at Pot rock. The tires squealed when it was hit and the jets roared with reverse thrust—and I was running forward even while the idea was half-formed in my mind.

Madness? Perhaps. But in my line of business, crookery, you learn to rely on hunches and trained reflexes. And while I ran the parts all fell into place and I saw that this was It. Sweet, fast, clean and dangerous. The way I liked things. I took a false moustache out of my pocket and fixed it on my lip as I ran.

The jet turned and taxied off to a hardstand and I trotted after it. A car came out to meet it and a crew of mechanics began to service the jet. One of them unloaded a ladder and placed it next to the cockpit as the top of the canopy opened like an alligator's mouth. I ran a little faster as the pilot climbed down and made for the car. He was just climbing in when I came stumbling up and he returned my salute. A burly individual in heavy flying gear, the golden crescent of a major on his collar.

"Excuse me, sir," I gasped, "but the commandant asked me to make sure you had the papers."

"What the hell are you talking about?" he grumbled, sliding into his seat. He sounded tired. I climbed into the back.

"Then you *don't* know. Oh, God! Driver—get going as fast as possible."

The driver did, since that was his job, and I slipped the tube out of the holder in my hip pocket. When we were out of sight of the jet I raised it to my lips.

"Major . . ." I said, and he turned his head and grunted. I puffed.

He grunted again and raised his hand towards the little dart stuck in his cheek—then slumped forward. I caught him before he fell.

"Driver—stop! Something has happened to the major."

The driver, obviously not a man of much imagination, took a quick look at the slumped figure and hit the brake. As soon as we skidded to a stop, away from any buildings I was happy to see, I let him have a second narco-dart and he went off to join the major in dreamland. I laid them both on the ground and stripped off the officer's flying suit and helmet. With a little bit of struggling I managed to pull the things over my own uniform, then strapped on the helmet and pulled the tinted goggles down over my eyes. All of this took less than a minute. I left the dozing pair in each other's arms and headed the car back to the plane. So far so good. But this had been the easiest part. I stood on the brakes so that the car screeched, bucked and skidded to a stop on the hardstand.

"Emergency!" I shouted, leaping from the car and running to the ladder. "Unhook this thing so I can take off."

The mechanics merely gaped at me, making no move towards the umbilical wires and hoses that connected the plane to the servicing pit. I wheeled the nearest one about and used the toe of my boot to move him in the right direction. He got the message clearly and the others now understood as well. They went to work. All except a grizzled noncom with a sleeve covered with hashmarks and stripes and a face covered with suspicion. He rolled over and looked me up and down.

"This is Major Lopta's personal plane, sir. Haven't you made a mistake?"

"Not as big a mistake as you are making interfering with me. How long has it been since you were a private?"

He looked at me in thought for a moment, then turned away without another word. I headed for the plane. As I climbed the ladder I saw that the noncom was busy at the radio in the car. This was a mistake on my part; I should have done something about that radio. As I was getting into the cockpit he dropped the radio and bellowed.

"Stop that man! He has no orders for this flight."

The man steadying the ladder reached for my leg and I put my foot on his chest and pushed. I sent the ladder after him and dropped into the seat.

This situation had rapidly developed in a direction that was not to my liking. I had planned on having enough time to familiarize myself with the controls before I fired up the engines; although I had plenty of jet hours I had never been in a Cliaandian one before. Not only didn't I know where the starter was but I did some pretty desperate fumbling before I even found the switch for the instrument lights. As I flicked it on the ladder smacked back against the side of the plane. I hated old efficient noncoms, the backbone of the military. Now I had to take out time to open the flying suit and grope inside it for my pockets.

A few happy-gas and sleep grenades cleared away the mechanics for the moment. Some lay cheerfully unconscious while the others laughed themselves sick. The noncom had cowardly stayed out of range and was back on the radio again. I studied the instruments. There! The little black knob with PALJENJE on it. When I slapped it the jets whined and rumbled to life. A rocket slug crashed through the open canopy above my head and I ducked cursing. As I kicked in the throttle I saw the noncom kneeling to take careful aim. The plane began to move—slowly.

His gun flared again and I felt the vibration as the slug buried itself in the seat. Which was probably armored. My first bit of luck.

I flipped the tail so it pointed at the gunman, which put the armor between me and him and gave him a good blast of jet exhaust in the face. The plane bucked and shuddered and moved forward again—and I saw the torn fuel hose flapping in the windstream and pumping out its vital juices. Those idiots hadn't disconnected it! I didn't know where the fuel gauge was on the cluttered instrument board, nor did I want to look at it. Logic told me that gravity would bleed the fuel out a lot slower than the pumps had forced it into the tanks—but logic had nothing to do with this. I had a vision of the jets dying out here in the middle of the field while the forces of the enemy closed in around me. I could feel my blood pressure going up like an express elevator.

My busy little noncom friend was obviously still working on the radio, because when I turned onto the runway I saw that some trucks were moving into position to block it and something that looked suspiciously like an armored car was roaring up in the background. I cut the throttle back almost all the way and ducked my head down to read the instrument panel again.

What I was looking for wasn't there! Then I noticed another bank of switches on one side and painfully spelled out their dim messages in the bad light. ISBACIVANJE. There it was!

I looked up and saw that I was about to crash into the first truck. Men were bailing out and running in all directions. My feet paddled about as I groped for the wheel brakes and I threw the rudder hard over. I finally found the brakes, stood on the right one and did a shuddering turn. About a half meter of wing tip tore off on the front of the truck. There was the orange blast of a gun as someone fired at me, but I have no idea where the slug went. Then the jet was around and I was belting back in the opposite direction. This time at full throttle.

The runway lights were streaming by, faster and faster, and I had to keep one hand on the wheel while I groped for the belts and harnesses with the other. One of the buckles was missing and the end of the runway was coming up before I found out that I was sitting on it. I clicked it into place and grabbed the wheel with both hands as I ran out of runway.

The jet did not have flying speed. The nose was mushy and would not lift when I pulled back on it.

Then I was bumping across the graded dirt heading straight for that stone wall I had been looking at all evening.

Faster and faster to a certain collision.

9

THE TIMING HAD to be just right. Too early or too late would be just as disastrous. When the wall loomed up above the jet and I could see the joints between the blocks I figured it was about right and I hit the eject button.

Bam! The sequence was almost too fast to follow—but it worked. A transparent shutter snapped down over my face, the still tilted up canopy blew away with a crack of explosives, and the seat slammed up so hard against me that it felt like my spine had shortened to half its length. Almost in slow motion I sailed up and out of the jet and, for a hideously long second, saw the raw stone of the wall directly in front of me. Then I was over with only the dark sky ahead.

At the highest point in my arc there was another sharp crack at my back and I looked up to see the white column of the parachute swirling up above me. I was falling and the roofs of some buildings looked very close below.

The chute opened with a rustling snap, the seat pushed up against me and, a moment after this jarring deceleration, the wall of a building was rushing past and the seat hit the ground and rolled over. The chute settled slowly down and draped me in its enveloping folds.

I am chagrined to report that I did nothing at all at that moment. Events had moved even faster than I had planned and this final bit had been simply stunning. I gaped and gasped and shook my head and finally had enough sense to bang the quick release and throw off the harness straps. After that I kept my head down and crawled and finally got out from under the chute.

A man and a woman had stopped on the opposite side of the street and were goggling in my direction. No one else was in sight. The only sign of activity seemed to be coming from the other side of the great black wall that loomed behind me. Flames lit the sky and smoke roiled and I could hear the loud popping of burning ammunition. Lovely.

"Testing new equipment," I called out to the spectators and turned and trotted out of sight around the corner. In a dark doorway I stripped off the flying suit and dropped the helmet on top of it. Unidentified and free I strolled away towards the Robotnik. *Brilliantly conceived, Jim,* I told myself and gave myself a little pat on the shoulder.

At the same moment I realized that now that I was out of the base I would have to find a way to get back in before dawn, but I pushed this depressing revelation out of sight. First things first. I had to dispose of the real Vaska Hulja in order to take over his identity.

He was stirring when I came in, thrashing about in the bed and rocking his head back and forth. The hypnotic trance was wearing thin and he was fighting against it. Not that the robot cleaner was helping. It had dusted and cleaned the room and was now trying to make the bed with Vaska in it. I booted the thing in its COME BACK LATER button and ordered dinner for two. To take Vaska's subconscious mind off his troubles I gave him the strong suggestion that he had gone two days without eating and that this was the best meal he had ever had in his lifetime. He smacked and chortled and gurgled with delight while he ate; I just picked at my food. In the end I pushed it away and ordered Strong Drink in the hopes that the alcohol would stimulate or depress my thoughts into some coherent plan.

What was I to do with my companion here, happily shoveling food into his gaping gob? His existence was a constant threat to my existence; there was room enough for only one Vaska Hulja in the scheme of things. Kill him? That would be easy enough. Dismember him in the bathtub and feed the parts and gallons of blood into an easily constructed arc furnace until I was left with a handful of dust. It was tempting, he had certainly killed enough people in his short and vicious lifetime to call this justice. But not tempting enough. Cold-blooded killing is just not my thing. I've killed in self-defense, I'll not deny that, but I still maintain an exaggerated respect for life in all forms. Now that we know that the only thing on the other side of the sky is more sky, the idea of an afterlife has finally been slid into the history books alongside the rest of the quaint and forgotten religions. With heaven and hell gone we are faced with the necessity of making a heaven or hell right here. What with societies and metatechnology and allied disciplines we have come a long way, and life on the civilized worlds is better than it ever was during the black days of superstition. But with the improving of here and now comes the stark realization that here and now is all we have. Each of us has only this one brief experience with the bright light of consciousness in that endless dark night of eternity and must make the most of it. Doing this means we must respect the existence of everyone else and the most criminal act imaginable is the terminating of one of these conscious existences. The Cliaandians did not think this way, which was why I intensely enjoyed dropping gravel in their gearboxes, but I still did. Which meant that I couldn't take the easy way out of reducing gravy-stained Vaska to his component molecules. If I did this I would be no better than they and I would be getting into the old game of the ends justifying the means and starting on that downward track. I sighed, sipped, and the diagrams I had been visualizing for an arc furnace faded and vanished.

Well what then? I could chain him in a cave with an automatic food dispenser if I had a cave and so forth. Out. Given time and hard work I could alter his appearance and plant false memories that would last at least six months and get him into a prison or a work gang or a mental home or such. Except I did not have the time for anything this complex. I had until morning—or less—unless I wanted to abandon all the work I had already done in creating the false Vaska and having him accepted. They were probably getting involved in roll calls right now so I really should be thinking about ways of getting back into Glupost rather than worrying about my swinish companion. I noticed his stomach beginning to bulge so I turned off his appetite. He sat back and sighed and belched, with good reason. There was a rustling on the far wall as a panel slid back and the robot cleaner trundled in.

"May I give you a good cleaning?" it whispered in a sexy contralto voice. I told it what it could do, but it wasn't equipped to take this kind of instruction and only clicked and whirred until I ordered it to go to work. I watched it gloomily as it bustled about and made the bed—and the first spark of an idea began to glimmer in the darkness.

Vaska had stayed in the Robotnik for an entire day without any trouble. How long would it be possible to hold him here? Theoretically forever if enough money were deposited to the room's account. But he could not be kept subjugated by hypnosis for more than a day or two if I were not there to reinforce the suggestion. Or could he . . . ? I would have to find the control center of the hotel before I could make any final decisions. But this could be the right idea.

I left Vaska watching an historical space opera on TV, with the suggestion that this was the finest entertainment he had ever witnessed, which might possibly be the truth. Loaded with instruments and tools I went on the prowl. There would be a serviceway for the robots behind the rooms, but it was undoubtedly small, dark and dusty. That was a last resort. As mechanized as this hotel was, human beings had built it and could repair it if they had to. A quick prowl of the lower hallways near the entrance uncovered a concealed door with a disguised keyhole. It was flush with the wall and outlined with paneling, designed to be unobtrusive to maintain the fiction that the Robotnik was a hundred percent robot run. I spent more time with my instrumentation, making sure there were no bugs on the door, than I did opening it. The lock was a joke. There was no one in sight when I slipped through the door and closed it behind me.

I felt like a roach inside a radio. Electronic components hung, projected and bulged out on all sides; cables and wires looped and sagged in a profusion of electric spaghetti. Rolls of tape clicked and whirred on the computers, relays opened and closed, and gear trains chattered. It was a very busy place. I worked my way through it examining the labels and stepping over the little hutches where off duty robots rested, until I found what might be called a control center. There was even a chair here before a console, that was designed for the human form, and I dropped into it. And set to work. I had been mulling my new plan over while tripping through this mechanical jungle and now knew what had to be done.

First, the electronic bugs in Vaska's room. I did not want him observed or listened to. The bugging circuits were easy enough to find and there was even a monitor screen that could be connected to any of them. I tested this out and apparently there was a bug in every room in the hotel and some interesting things were going on, but I have never been much of a voyeur, preferring participation to observation, and a married man now as well. And time was passing quickly. All of the bugging circuits came together into a cable that vanished through the wall, to the local police station or other government bureau. Which gave me the idea. I had no time to fix a tape and soundtrack that would pump phoney information into the bugging circuit, I had to improvise. This was done easily enough by feeding the signal from the bugging circuit of another room into the wire from the room Vaska was occupying. From the way this setup was arranged it was obvious that the bugs were used to watch only one room at a time, for reasons best known to the people who built it. There was about one chance in ten thousand that it would ever be noticed that the same signal was coming from two rooms. And these odds were good enough for me. Over half of the rooms were empty in any case, which improved the odds even more.

Vaska could neither be seen nor heard now. The room and

associated pleasures had to be paid for, but before I left I would deposit enough money (all stolen) to last a year if needs be.

A way to keep him in the room for that length of time was now needed and I—with my usual fertile imagination and basically nasty nature—had already devised that scheme. A small tape recorder was wired into the speaker circuit for the room, a timer attached, and the whole device concealed in the maze of other circuits and components. I programmed the tape, set the timer and started it up. Then rushed back to the room to watch my creation begin its job.

Vaska still had his eyes glued to the TV screen, panting with passion as mighty spaceships locked in frenzied destruction. Blaster cannon sizzled and ravening energies raved, and through this cut my recorded voice.

"Now here this, Vaska, now hear this. You have had a long day and you are sleepy. You are yawning. You are going to turn off the lights and retire now, to sleep the sound sleep of the blessed for tomorrow is another day."

And that was the big lie. For tomorrow would not be another day, not for dear Vaska. It was going to be the same one all over again. He would be lulled into a deep sleep and an even deeper trance by my soothing voice. And while there it would be explained to him that he would forget this day so he could wake up on the morning of his last day of leave before reporting for active duty. He would wake up with a slight hangover from the celebrations of the night before and would make an easy day of it. Just lie around the hotel room, read a bit, eat some food, watch TV, and retire early. He would enjoy himself. He would enjoy himself the same way every day until the program was broken.

It was a wonderful plan and as foolproof as possible. I fed over half of my liquid funds into the paying hopper and the balance of the wall indicator shot up to an enormous number.

Slowly and happily, I reached out and hung the DO NOT DISTURB sign on the outside of the door.

And then I got depressed and turned the lights back on and looked around for the bottle that had provided me with so much inspiration so far. Vaska was well taken care of.

But how did I get back into the thrice-guarded and now doubly wakeful military base?

That high stone wall loomed as large in my brain as it did in reality. I had made a fuss going over it and alerted everyone. It would be nice if I could return without anyone knowing, sneaking under it perhaps. Out of the question, digging and earth moving and things like that could not be accomplished in a few hours. Steal a plane, fly over, parachute in? And be shot down before I hit the ground. There could be no worse time than the present to try to enter or leave the base. The guards would be suspicious and reinforced and the place crawling with troops. Which of course gave me the clue as to what I had to do. Turn their strength against them, use their own numbers to defeat them, judo on a giant basis. But how?

The answer came quickly enough once the problem had been correctly stated. I put together the equipment I would need, it was quite bulky, then stowed it all into a large suitcase and fitted the suitcase with a destruct apparatus. A disguise would be needed, nothing complex, just something to hide my real-assumed identity. Ahh, the levels of deception we must enter into. A long coat buttoned high concealed my uniform, my cap went into my pocket to be replaced by a floppy black hat, and my old faithful gray beard muzzled my face in anonymity. I was ready. I took a deep breath and a small drink and slipped out, locking the door behind me and pocketing the key. As I went out I slipped this into a waste chute and the flare of instant destruction brightened my way. Going a good distance from the hotel I signaled and a robocab stopped and I heaved in my suitcase.

"Main entrance, Glupost base," I ordered and away we went.

Madness? Perhaps. But it was the only way.

Not that I didn't have a trapped butterfly or two beating for release from my stomach. This was only to be expected as we rolled up the approach street under the high lights, towards the suspicious and heavily armed guards who stood about fondling their weapons. Dawn was already lightening the sky.

"The base is closed!" a lieutenant shouted, pulling open the door of the cab. "What are you doing here?"

"Base," I quavered in a very bad imitation of an old man's falsetto. "Isn't this the Carrot Juice Center for Natural Health? This cab has done me wrong . . ."

The officious lieutenant snorted through his nostrils and turned away—and I rolled a pair of gas grenades out through his bowed legs. And heaved five more after them. As the first ones went off I pulled the gas mask down out of my hat and slapped it over my face, beard and all.

My but things got busy. The grenades were a fine mixture of blackout gas, smoke and happygas. Blind, laughing, cursing, coughing men stumbled about on all sides and a few guns went off. I worked my way through their confused ranks, sowing more confu-

sion as I went, and up to the main gates and put down my suitcase
and opened it. The shaped charges had adhesive bases and stuck to
the steel of the gate when I slapped them into place.

A rocket slug burst against the gate and pieces of shrapnel tore at
my flapping coat. I hit the ground. Tearing out two smoke grenades
and dropping them behind me. Just as the smoke roiled up I had a
quick glimpse of a squad coming up on the double, still outside the
gassed area, firing as they came. Two more blackout gas bombs in
that direction helped a lot. Now, as much in the dark as everyone
else, I pushed in the caps by touch and linked them with fuse wire to
the radio igniter.

Time was passing too quickly. They were alert inside the gate
now and would be waiting for me. But I had come too far to back
out. I closed the suitcase, again by touch, grabbed it up and inched
my way along the wall and pressed the transmitter switch in my
pocket.

Explosions banged out in the darkness and were followed by the
clang of steel.

Hopefully an opening had been blasted in the gate.

I stumbled back towards it with all the sounds of bedlam in the
darkness around me.

10

THE HOLE WAS there all right, with glimpses of lights on the other side as the smoke cloud roiled through it. There were troops there too because a hail of small arms fire clanged against the door with some chance slugs coming through the new-blasted opening. Screams sounded behind me as someone was hit. The fools were shooting each other, helping to spread the confusion I had sown. Keeping out of the line of fire from inside the gate I hurled grenade after grenade through and, when the smoke was at its thickest there, went through myself as fast and low as I could.

It really sounded great. Sirens were moaning, men shouting, weapons barking: the voices of utter confusion. I threw more grenades in all directions, throwing them as far as I could to widen the area of cover, until only a half dozen were left. These I saved for possible emergencies, which were sure to emerge, jamming them into my coat pockets. The self-destruct on the suitcase had a five second delay which I tripped, then hurled the suitcase away in the opposite direction. I crept along the wall, my only point of reference in the blackout, towards the guardhouse I had noticed when I had first examined the gate. There had been a clutch of vehicles parked there—at the time—and I muttered prayers that at least one of them still remained. The cloud thinned and I hurled two more grenades ahead of me. In the darkness I heard a motor start up.

Forgetting caution, I ran. Someone slammed into me and fell heavily but I kept my feet and stumbled on. Then I tripped over a curb and did fall, but did a quick roll and came up running minus my hat. The engine was louder and then I saw the squarish van just beyond the edge of the smoke cloud. It was turning to start down the road and I threw two of my remaining four grenades as far ahead of it as I could. The driver hit the brakes as the mushrooming clouds sprang out, then I was at the door tearing it open. He was in cook's white, cap and all, and I reached out and dragged him to me, landing a swift right cross on his gaping jaw as he went by. Then I was in the driver's seat and pushing the thing into gear and jumping the deadweight of the vehicle forward as fast as I could, letting the door swing shut with the sudden acceleration. Once out of the smoke I saw that daylight had arrived.

Well done, I congratulated myself, then slowed down to avoid being conspicuous. More soldiers were coming down the street towards me, running at the double, so I slipped down as far as I could and began to tug at the gray beard. It was just about time to resume my Vaska identity.

A ringing pain possessed the side of my head and I fell over, shouting aloud at the sudden agony, pulling on the steering tiller as I went. The van rushed at the squad of soldiers who scattered in all directions. Something shiny flashed in the corner of my eye and I moved aside so the second blow caught me on the shoulder and was scarcely felt through all the clothing. A white clad arm holding a heavy pot projected in from the rear of the truck. I jammed the steering tiller hard over and the arm vanished from sight as its owner fell. In the rush I had forgotten there might be others in the van.

Just before the truck a frightened officer was spread-eagled against the wall. I pushed the tiller again and narrowly avoided him and we had a good look at each other as the van rushed by. He was sure to be impressed by my gas mask and beard and would instantly report it on his radio. Time was running out. Arm and pot reappeared and I chopped the wrist with the edge of my hand and gained possession of the pot. As soon as I had whipped the van around another corner, foot hard down on the throttle now, I threw the pot back to its owner with a blackout grenade inside, silencing at least this source of trouble for the moment. I straightened the weaving course of the van, gently touched the growing knot on my head, and noticed a brace of armored vehicles that appeared in the road ahead and turned in my direction. Buildings rushed by and I braked and turned into the next crossroad. The van was becoming more of a liability than an asset and I had to get rid of it.

But what then? I did not want to be found away from my quarters, this would bring instant suspicion, and the officers' buildings were in the opposite direction. But the officers' club was not too far away in the recreation area. Could I get there? Was it possible that the unconscious drunks of the previous evening's festivities still lay on the bunks where I had left them? This was too good a chance to miss, because if I could get back into my bunk I would certainly not be suspect.

This was close enough. There were vehicles coming towards me—and undoubtedly more behind me—but none close for the moment. I twisted the van into a narrow street, braked to a stop and hit the ground running. Shedding my disguise as I went, coat, beard, gas mask marking the trail behind me. I stuffed the remaining grenade into my pocket, pulled on my cap, squared my shoulders in a military manner, and strolled around the corner. A squad of soldiers were pouring out of barracks and forming ranks, but they ignored me, just another uniform among uniforms. The officers' club was not too far away. Two more corners and there it was. The front door sealed, but I knew the bunkroom entrance would be open.

Just as I was about to turn the corner I heard the men talking and I held back.

"Is that all?"

"Just a few more, sir, a couple that are hard to wake up. And one who won't get out of his bunk."

"I'll talk to him."

I took a quick look, then drew back.

I was too late. An officer was just entering the bunkroom door and plenty of soldiers were milling about, guiding hungover officers to a waiting truck. One of the officers was sitting on the ground, holding his head and ignoring the soldiers who were trying to entice him into the waiting transportation. Another was flipping his cookies against the wall of the building.

Think quickly, diGriz, time is running out. I bounced the last smoke grenade in my palm, then flipped the actuator with my thumb. If I could join the drunk team I would be safe; it would be worth the risk. I stepped around the corner, arm back, and no one was looking in my direction; with a quick heave I threw the grenade over the truck as far as it would go.

It exploded nicely, thud, boom, clouds of smoke and startled cries from the soldiery. And everyone looking in the same direction. Eight fast paces took me up behind them, to the seated officer who mumbled unhappily to himself, ignoring all else. I bent over, agreeing sympathetically with his half-heard complaints, helping him to his feet.

Then the soldiers were helping me, holding me as well since I seemed none too steady on my feet, guiding us both to the waiting truck. I tripped and almost fell and they caught and righted me. Now the stage was set—because there was one more thing I had to do. The cook in the truck would report that he had hit the spy on the head. So the word would be out to look for a head wound—like the one I had. I couldn't get rid of the knob on the side of my skull, but I could camouflage it. It would be painful, but it was necessary.

The soldiers helped me to the first step and I started up. As soon as they let go I missed the next step—and plummeted over backwards between them cracking my head on the ground.

I hit harder than I had planned and the blow on my already sore noggin felt like molten lead had been poured on it and I must have passed out for a moment. When I recovered I was sitting up with blood running down the side of my face—I hadn't planned that but it certainly made a nice touch—and a soldier was running up with a first aid kit. I was bandaged and calmed and this time helped all the way into the truck: I felt awful which was fine. With dragging feet I groped my way to the far end, as far from the entrance as I could get, where a voice called out hollowly to me.

"Vaska . . ." It changed to a hollow coughing.

My roommate Otrov was there, looking rumpled and miserable.

"You don't have a drink?" he asked, his usual morning salutation.

I gave him sympathy, if not beverage, during our brief ride.

There were aggrieved cries when the wheeled drunk tank was unloaded and the officers saw that they had not been returned to their quarters, but had been brought instead to one of the administration buildings. I complained along with the others, although I had been expecting something like this. Someone had escaped from the Glupost base, someone else had entered. Every head would have to be counted until the missing and/or extra party could be found. We were guided, stumbling, into a waiting area, to be called out one by one to confer with a battery of tired clerks. While we waited there was a brisk amount of business back and forth to the latrine and I joined the queue. Mainly to leave a little soap on my fingers when I washed my hands, so I could rub some of it into my eyes. It burned like acid, but I let it stay for a moment before I rinsed it out. My eyes glared back at me from the mirror like twin coals of fire. Perfect.

On cue, I found the clerk, showed my identification and had my name checked off a roster. I hoped, like all the others, that we would be allowed to leave soon. Many of them had gone to sleep on the benches and I joined their number. It had been a strenuous night. What better disguise for the spy than sleeping in the heart of the enemy?

It was the sudden silence that shook me awake. I had been lulled off by the grumbles and complaints of my fellow officers, the coming and going of soldiers, the busy whir of office machines. These noises had all stopped, and had been replaced by silence. Through the silence, first distant, than louder and louder, came the sound of a single set of footsteps approaching slowly and steadily. They came towards me—and passed by, and I kept my eyes closed and forced myself to breathe regularly. Only when they were well past did I open my eyes a crack.

I wondered at the silence. All I saw was the back of the man, a nondescript back slightly bent, a wrinkled uniform of unimpressive pale gray and a cap of the same fabric. I could not recall seeing this particular uniform before. I wondered what the fuss was about. Yawning, I sat up and scratched my head below the bandage, watching as the man reached the end of the room and turned to face us all. He was no more prepossessing from the front than from the back. Sandy hair getting a little thin on top, an incipient roll of fat and double chin, clean shaven with an unmemorable face. Yet when he spoke, in the tones of a stern schoolmaster, all of the veteran officers present remained dead silent.

"You officers, the few among you who were sober enough that is, may have heard an explosion and seen a cloud of smoke while you were on the way here. This explosion was caused by an individual who entered this base and is still undetected in our midst. We know nothing about him, but suspect that he is an offworld spy . . ."

This drew a gasp and a murmur as might be expected and the gray man waited a moment until he continued.

"We are making an intensive search for this individual. Since you gentlemen were in the immediate vicinity I am going to talk to you one at a time to find out what you might know. I also may discover . . . which one of you is the missing spy."

This last shaft exacted only a shocked silence. Now that he had everyone in the right mental condition for cross-examining the gray man began calling officers forward one at a time. I was doubly grateful for the foresight that had dropped me off the truck onto the side of my head.

It was no accident that I was the third man called forward. On what grounds? General resemblance in build to the offworld spy Pas Ratunkowy? My delayed arrival at Glupost? The bandage? Some basis of suspicion must have existed. I dragged forward with slow speed just as the others had done. I saluted and he pointed to the chair next to the desk.

"Why don't you hold this while we talk," he said in a reasonable voice, passing over the silver egg of a polygraph transmitter.

The real Vaska would not have recognized it, so I didn't. I just looked at it with slight interest—as though I did not know it was transmitting vital information to the lie detector before him—and clutched it in my hand. My thoughts were not as calm.

I'm caught! He has me! He knows who I am and is just toying with me!

He looked deep into my bloodshot eyes and I detected a slight curl of distaste to his mouth.

"You have had quite a night of it, Lieutenant Hulja," he said quietly, his eyes on the sheaf of papers—and on the lie detector readout as well.

"Yes sir, you know . . . having a few last drinks with the boys." That was what I said aloud. What I thought was *They will shoot me, dead, right through the heart!* and I could visualize that vital organ spouting my life's blood into the dirt.

"I see you recently had your rank reduced—and where are your fuses, Pas Ratunkowy?"

Am I tired . . . wish I was in the sack I thought.

"Fuses, sir?" I blinked my red orbs and reached to scratch my head and touched the bandage and thought better of it. His eyes glared into mine, gray eyes almost the color of his uniform, and for a moment I caught the strength and anger behind his quiet manners.

"And your head wound—where did you get that? Our offworld spy was struck on the side of the head."

"I fell, sir, someone must have pushed me. Out of the truck. The soldiers bandaged it, ask them . . ."

"I already have. Drunk and falling down and a disgrace to the officer corps. Get away and clean yourself up, you disgust me. Next man."

I climbed unsteadily to my feet, not looking into the steady glare of those cold eyes, and stared off as though I had forgotten the device in my hand, then turned back and dropped it on his desk, but he was bent over the papers and ignoring me. I could see a faint scar under the thin hair of his balding crown. I left.

Fooling a polygraph takes skill, practice and training. All of which I had. It can only be done in certain circumstances and this one had been ideal. A sudden interview without normalizing tests being run on the subject. Therefore I began the interview in a near panic—before any questions had been asked. All of this must have peaked nicely on his graph. I was afraid. Of him, of something, anything. But when he had asked the loaded question meant to uncover a spy—the question I knew was coming—I had relaxed and the readout had shown this. The question was a meaningless one to anyone but the offworlder. Once he saw this the interview was over, he had plenty more to do.

Otrov was sitting up, cold sober, eyes as big as plates when I came back and dropped onto the bench next to him.

"What did he want?" He spoke in a hollow whisper.

"I don't know. He asked me something or other that I didn't know about and then it was over."

"I hope he doesn't want to talk to me."

"Who is he?"

"Don't you *know!*" With shocked incredulity. I tread warily, covering my complete lack of information.

"Well you know I just came here . . ."

"But *everyone* knows Kraj."

"Is that *him* . . . ?" I gasped it out and tried to look as frightened as he did and it seemed to work, because he nodded and looked over his shoulder and quickly back again. I rose and went to the latrine again to terminate the conversation at this spot. Everyone knew about Kraj.

Who was Kraj?

11

EMBARKING FOR THE invasion came as a relief to everyone; better a nice quiet war than the suspicions and fears that swept the Glupost base during the following days. There were sudden inspections, midnight searches, constant alarms and the sound of marching boots at all hours. I would have been proud of my efforts at sowing the seeds of disorder if I had not been a victim of that disorder at the same time. The invasion plans must have gone ahead too far to alter because, in the midst of all the excitement, we still adhered to schedule. On B Day minus two all the bars closed so that the sobering up process of the troops could begin. A few reluctant ones, myself and Otrov included, had concealed bottles which carried us a bit further, but even this ended when our lockers and bags were put into storage and we were issued pre-packed invasion kits. I had a small can of powdered alcohol disguised as tooth powder that I was saving for an emergency and the emergency instantly presented itself as the thought of the coming weeks without drink, so Otrov and I finished the tooth powder on B Day minus one and that was that. After one last midnight spot check and search we were assembled and marched to the departure area. The fleet, row after row of dark projectiles, stood waiting beyond the gates. We were called out, one at a time, and sent to our assigned places.

In the beginning I had thought that this was a rather stupid way to run an invasion. No plans, no diagrams, no peptalk, no training, no maneuvers—no nothing. It finally dawned on me that this was the ideal way to mount an invasion that you wished to keep secret. The pilots had plenty of piloting experience, and would get more on the outward voyage. The troops were ready to fight; the sources of supply supplied. And somewhere at the top there were locked boxes of plans, course tapes and such. None of which would be opened until we were safe in warpdrive and outside communication would be impossible. All of which made life easier for me since there were few opportunities to trip me up in my knowledge of things Cliaandian.

It was with a great deal of pleasure that I found myself assigned as pilot of a troop transport. This was a role I could fill with honor. My earlier assignment of a roommate had not been accidental either, because Otrov climbed into the navroom a few minutes later and announced that he was going to be my copilot.

"Wonderful," I told him. "How many hours do you have on one of these Pavijan class transports?"

He admitted to an unhappily low figure and I patted him on the shoulder.

"You are in luck. Unlike most First Pilots your old Uncle Vaska is without ego. For an old drinking buddy no sacrifice is too great. I am going to let you fire the takeoff and if you do the kind of job I think you will do, then I might let you shoot the landing as well. Now hand me the check list."

His gratitude was overwhelming, so much so that he admitted that he had been saving his fountain pen for a real emergency since it was filled with 200 proof alcohol and we both had a squirt. It was with a feeling of contentment—and scarred throats—that we watched the troops marching up and filing into the loading ports far below. A few minutes later a grizzled fullbearded colonel in combat uniform stamped into the navroom.

"No passengers allowed here," I said.

"Shut your mouth, lieutenant. I have your course tapes."

"Well let me have them?"

"What? You must be either mad or joking—and both are shooting offenses in combat."

"I must be on edge, colonel, not much sleep, you know . . ."

"Yes." He relented slightly. "Allowances must be made, I suppose. It hasn't been easy for anyone. But that's behind us now. Victory for Cliaand!"

"Victory for Cliaand!" we entolled ritually. There had been a lot of this the last couple of days. The Colonel looked at his watch.

"Almost time. Get the command circuit," he ordered.

I pointed to Otrov, who pressed the right button instantly. A message appeared on the comscreen. STAND BY. We stood. Then it began blinking quickly and changed to the harsh letters, SET COURSE. The colonel took the tape container from his pouch and we had to sign as witnesses on a form stating that the tape was sealed when we received it. Otrov inserted the tape into the computer and the colonel grunted in satisfaction, his work done, and turned to leave. He fired a parting shot over his shoulder on the way out.

"And none of those 10 G landings that you moronic pilots seem to enjoy. I'll courtmartial you both if that happens."

"Your mother knits sweaters out of garbage," I shouted after him, waiting, of course, until the door was closed. But even this feeble effort stirred enthusiasm in Otrov who was beginning to respect me more and more.

Hurry up and wait is common to all military forces and that is what we did next. The check lists were complete and we saw ship after ship take off until most were gone. The transports were last. The green BLASTOFF signal came as a relief. We were on our way. To a nameless planet circling an unknown star as far as any of us were concerned. The tape told the computer where we were going but did not condescend, nor had it been programmed, to inform us.

This security blanket lasted right up to the invasion itself. We were seven boring days en route with nothing to drink and the ship piloted by the computer and the frozen rations barely edible. On a long term basis, without the ameliorating effects of alcohol, Otrov proved to be less than a sparkling companion. No matter where the conversation began it invariably ended up in repetitive anecdotes from his school days. I slept well, I'll say that, and usually while he was talking but he never seemed to mind. I also checked him out on the instruments with drills and dry runs, which may have done him some active good and certainly acquainted me with the controls and operation of the ship.

Since the ship was completely automated, Otrov and I were the only crew members aboard. The single doorway to the troop area was sealed and my friend the surly colonel had the only key. He visited us once or twice which was no pleasure at all. On the seventh day he was standing behind us glowering at the back of my neck when we broke out of warpdrive and back into normal space.

"Take this, inspect here, sign that," he snapped and we did all those things before he broke the seal on the flat case. This was labeled INVASION in large red letters which rather suggested that things would be hotting up soon. My instructions were simple enough and I switched on the circuits as ordered so the ship could home in on the squadron leader. A yellowish sun shone brightly off to one side and the blue sphere of a planet was on the other. The colonel glared at this planet as though he wanted to reach out and grab it and take a bite out of it, so future developments seemed obvious enough without asking questions.

The invasion began. Most of the fleet was ahead of us, lost in the night of space and visible only occasionally as a network of sparks when they changed course. Our squadron of transports stayed together, automatically following the course set by the lead ship, and the planet grew in the screens ahead. It looked peaceful enough from this distance, though I knew the advance units of the fleet must be attacking by this time.

I was not looking forward to this invasion—who but a madman can enjoy the prospect of approaching war?—but I was hoping to find out the answer to the question that had brought me here. I believed that interplanetary invasions were *still* impossible, despite the fact that I was now involved in one myself. I felt somewhat like the man who, upon seeing one of the most exotic animals in the zoo, said 'there ain't no such animal.' Interplanetary invasions just don't work.

The interplanetary invading force rushed on, a mighty armada giving the lie to my theories. As the nameless planet grew larger and larger, filling the forward screens, I could see the first signs of the war that I knew was already in progress; tiny sparkles of light in the night hemisphere. Otrov saw them too and waved his fist and cheered.

"Give it to them boys," he shouted.

"Shut up and watch your instruments," I snarled. Suddenly hating him. And instantly relenting. He was a product of his environment. As the twig is bent so grows the bough and so forth. His twig had been bent nicely by the military boarding school into which he had been stuffed as a small child. Which, for some unknown reason, he still thought well of although every story he told me about it had some depressing or sadistic point to make. He had been raised never to question, to believe God had created Cliaand a bit better than all the other planets, and that they were therefore ordained to take care of the inferior races. It is amazing the things people will believe if you catch them early enough.

Then we were turned loose as the individual transports scattered to home in on their separate targets. I fiddled with the radio and silently cursed the Cliaandian passion for security and secrecy. Here I was landing a shipload of troops—and I didn't even know where! On the planet below, surely, they could not very well disguise that fact, but on what continent? At what city? All I knew was that pathfinder ships had gone in first and planted radio beacons. I had the frequency and the signal I was to listen for, and when I detected it I was to home in and land. And I knew that the target was a spaceport. With the final instructions I had received some large and clear photographs—the Cliaandian spies had obviously been hard at work—of a spaceport; aerial and ground views. A big red *X* was marked near the terminal buildings and I had to set the ship down as close to this site as I could. Fine.

"That's the signal!" The dah-dah-dit-dah was loud and clear.

"Strap in—here we go," I said, and fed instructions to the computer. It worked up landing orbit almost instantly and the main jets fired. "Give the colonel the first warning, then feed him proximity and altitude reports while I bring her in."

We were dropping towards the terminator, flying into the dawn. The computer had a fix on the transmitter and was bringing us down in a slow careful arc. When we broke through the cloud cover and the ground was visible far below I saw the first sign of any resistance. The black clouds of explosions springing up around us.

"They're shooting at us!" Otrov gasped, shocked.

"Well it's a shooting war, isn't it?" I wondered what kind of a veteran he was to be put off by a little gunfire, and at the same time I hit the computer override and turned off the main jets. We dropped into free fall and the next explosions appeared above and behind us as the gun computer was thrown off by our deceleration change.

I caught sight of the spaceport below and hit the lateral jets to move us in that direction. But we were still falling. Our radar altimeter readings were being fed into the computer which kept flashing red warnings about the growing proximity of the ground. I gave it a quick program to hold landing deceleration as long as possible, to drop us at 10 G's to zero altitude. This meant we would be falling at maximum speed and slowing down for minimum time, which would decrease the time we would be exposed to ground fire. And I wanted the colonel to have the 10 G's he had once warned me about.

The jets fired at what looked like treetop height, slamming us down into our couches. I smiled, which is hard to do with ten gravities pulling at you, thinking about the expression on the colonel's face at that moment. Watching the screen I added some lateral drift until we were just over the hardstand which was our target area. After this it was up to the computer which did just fine and killed the engines just as our landing struts crunched down. As soon as all the engines cut off I hit the disembark button and the ship shivered as the ramps blew out and down.

"That takes care of our part," I said, unbuckling and stretching.

Otrov joined me at the viewport as we watched the troops rush down the ramps and run for cover. They did not seem to be taking any casualties at all which was surprising. There were some bomb craters visible nearby and heaps of rubble, while fighter-bombers still roared low giving cover. But it didn't seem possible that all resistance had been knocked out this quickly. Unless this world did not have much of a standing army. That might be one answer to explain the Cliaandian invasion success; only pick planets that are ripe for plucking. I made a mental note to look into this. Well behind his troops came the colonel in his command car. I hoped that his guts were still compressed from the landing.

"Now we have to find some drink," Otrov said, smacking his lips with anticipation.

"I'll go," I said, taking my sidearm from the rack and buckling it on. "You stay with the radio and watch the ship."

"That's what all the first pilots always say," he complained, so I knew I had called this one right.

"Privilege of rank. Someday you will be exercising it too. I shouldn't be long."

"Spaceport bar, that's where it usually is," he called after me.

"Don't teach your grandpa to chew cheese," I sneered, having already figured that one out.

All of the interior doors had unlocked automatically when we landed. I climbed the ladders down to the recently vacated combat deck and kicked my way through the discarded ration containers to the nearest ramp. The fresh sweet air of morning blew in, carrying with it the smell of dust and explosives. We had brought the benefits of Cliaandian culture to another planet.

I could hear firing in the distance and a jet thundered by and was gone, but after this it was very quiet. The invasion had fanned out from the spaceport leaving a pocket of silence in its wake. Nor was anyone in sight when I walked, unexamined, through the customs area and, with reflex skill, found the bar. The first thing I did was to drain a flask of beer, then poured a small Antarean *ladevandet* to hold it down. There were ranked bottles behind the bar, new friends and old ones, and I made a good selection. I needed something to carry them in and opened one of the sliding doors beneath, looking for a box or a bag, and found myself staring into the frightened eyes of a young man.

"*Ne mortigu min!*" he cried. I speak Esperanto like a native and answered in the same tongue.

"We are here to liberate you so mean you no harm." Word of this conversation might get to the authorities and I wanted to make the right impression. "What is your name?"

"Pire."

"And the name of this world?" This seemed sort of a dim

question for an arrogant invader to ask, but he was too frightened to question it.

"Burada."

"That's fine, I'm glad you decided to be truthful. And what can you tell me about Burada?"

Badly phrased, admittedly, and he was too stunned to answer. He gaped for a moment, then climbed out of the cabinet and turned to root about in it. He came up with a booklet that he passed over in silence. It had a 3D cover of an ocean with graceful trees on the bordering shore, that sprang to life as soon as the heat of my hand touched it; the waves crashed silently on the golden sands and the trees moved to the touch of unfelt breezes. Letters formed of clouds moved across the sky and I read BEAUTIFUL BURADA . . . HOLIDAY WORLD OF THE WESTERN WARP . . .

"Looting and consorting with the enemy," a familiar, and detested, voice said from the doorway. I turned slowly to see my friend the colonel from our ship standing there fingering his gauss-rifle with what can only be termed a filthy grin on his face.

"And 10 G landing too," he added, undoubtedly the real cause of his unhappiness. "Which is not a shooting offense although the other two are."

12

PIRE SHRIEKED IN a muffled manner and drew back, not understanding the colonel's words but recognizing his manner and his
weapon. I smiled, as coldly as I could, as I saw that my hands were
out of sight below the bar. Turning to the youth I pointed to the far
end of the room and ordered him there. He scuttled nicely and while
this bit of mis-direction was going on I slipped the tourist book into
my pocket and eased my gausspistol out of its holster. When I
turned back to the colonel I saw that he had half raised his rifle.

"You are wrong," I said, "and insulting as well to a fellow
officer who recently was a flight-major. I am aiding our invading
forces by securing this drinking establishment to prevent any of
your troops from becoming drunk on duty and therefore injuring our
all-out efforts. And while in this place I took a prisoner who was
hiding here. That is what happened and it is my word against yours,
colonel."

He raised his gun barrel towards me and said, "It is only my word
that I caught you looting and was forced to shoot you when you
resisted arrest."

"I am a hard one to shoot," I said, letting the muzzle of my pistol
slide up over the edge of the bar until it was centered between his
eyes. "I am an expert shot and one of these explosive slugs will take
the top of your head off."

Apparently he had not expected this kind of instant response from
a flying officer and he hesitated for a moment. Pire squealed faintly
and there was a thud. I assumed he had fainted but was too busy to
look. This murderous tableau held for a moment and there was no
way of knowing how it might have ended if a soldier had not rushed
into view with a field radio. The colonel took the phone and went
back to the war while I stuffed two bottles into the back of my jacket
and went out the other exit, stepping over Pire who was unconscious
on the floor and undoubtedly better off that way. I was gone before
the colonel realized it and I took the drink back to the ship and sent it
up the service lift to Otrov." And don't drink more than one," I

ordered and his voice responded with a happy cry over the intercom.

I was on my own now and I meant to make the most of the opportunity. With the battle still being waged my movements would not be watched and I could make my observations. Of course I might also be killed, but that is one of the occupational hazards of the service. Once the invasion had succeeded movement would be sharply restricted and I would probably be on my way back to Cliaand. The guide booklet was still in my pocket, the heat of my hip keeping the action going on the cover. I opened it and flipped through the pages which were heavy on pictures and short on copy. This was the hard sell all right with low music coming from the illustration of the floating orchestra on beautiful Sabun Bay and the scent of flowers from the Kanape fields. I expected some snow to fall out of the picture of skiing in the Kar mountains, but the technology of advertising did not extend this far. There was a map showing the airport and the city, diagrammatic and worthless for the most part, though it did tell me I was standing in Sucuk Spaceport close by Sucuk City. I threw away the book and went to see the sights.

Depressing. It would be a long time before the tourists came back to these sunny shores. I walked through the empty streets, pocked by explosions and charred by fire, and wondered what the purpose of this could possibly be. War, always a foolish business, seemed even more infantile at this moment. Horrible might be a better word; I saw my first corpses. There was the sound of dragging feet and a horde of prisoners appeared in the street ahead, guarded on all sides by alert Cliaandian troops. Many of the prisoners were wounded and few bandaged. The sergeant in charge saluted when they went by and gave a wave of victory. I smiled in return but it took an effort. What I had to do now was to find some responsible citizen of Sucuk City who was not yet a prisoner or dead and get the answers to some questions.

The citizen found me first. I left the main road and turned down a narrow winding street ominously labeled Matbaacilik-sasurtmek—any street with a name like that could not be all good. My suspicions had some justification in fact. I discovered this when I turned a sharp corner and found myself facing a young woman who was pointing a large bore hunting rifle at me. I was waving my little fingers in the air even before she spoke.

"Surrender or die!"

"I've surrendered—can't you see! Long live Burada, rah-rah . . ."

"None of your sickening jokes, you foul war-mongering male, or I'll shoot you on the spot."

"I'm on your side, believe me. Peace on Burada, good will to men—and women too of course."

She snorted at this and waved me towards a dark doorway with the gun. Even in anger she was a handsome woman, wide-faced with flaring nostrils and black hair hanging straight to her shoulders. She wore a dark green uniform, high boots, leather straps and all, with some kind of insignia on the sleeve. She was feminine despite this; no uniform could be made to disguise the magnificent swell of that bosom. I entered the doorway as she demanded and she reached to take my pistol as I passed. I could have done some quick business then with her arm and the gun barrel and ended up with both weapons, but I restrained myself. As long as she felt she was in charge she might talk more easily. We entered a dark inner room with a single window, an office of some kind, where another girl in uniform was stretched out on the desk. Her eyes were closed and the leg of her uniform had been cut away to disclose an ugly wound now bound with clumsy bandages. Blood had seeped through them and pooled upon the desk top.

"You have medicine?" my captress asked.

"I do," I said, opening the medpack at my waist. "But I don't think it will do much good. She appears to have lost a lot of blood and needs medical attention."

"Where will she get it? Not from you swine invaders."

"Perhaps." I was busy with pressure points, tearing off the old bandages, sprinkling on antiseptic powder and applying better bandages. "Her pulse is slow and very weak. I don't think she will make it."

"If she doesn't—you killed her." Tears were in my opponent's eyes, though this did not stop her from keeping the blunderbuss pointed at my midriff.

"I'm trying to save her, remember? And you can call me Vaska."

"Taze," she said automatically. "Sergeant in the Guard before *they* took over."

"They?" I felt slightly confused. "You mean them, *us*, the army of Cliaand?"

"No, of course not. But why am I talking to you when I should be killing you . . ."

"You shouldn't. Kill me I mean. Would you believe me if I told you I was a friend?"

"No."

"That I was a spy from elsewhere now working against the Cliaands although I am in their Space Armada?"

"I would say that you are a worm pleading for your worthless life and willing to say anything."

"Well it's true, anyway," I grumbled, realizing she wasn't going to take my revelations on faith.

"Taze . . ." the girl on the table said weakly and we both turned that way. Then "Taze" again and died.

I thought I was dead as well. Taze swung the rifle up and I could see her knuckles whiten as she squeezed. I did a lot of things quickly, starting with a dive to get under the gun and a roll right into her. The gun fired—the blast almost taking my head off in the confined space—but I wasn't hit. Before she could fire again I had the barrel in my hand and did a quick chop at the muscles in her arm and a few other things one does not normally do to women except in an emergency like this. Then I had the rifle, as well as my pistol back, and she was lying against the wall with something to really cry about this time. It would be a number of minutes before she could use her fingers again; I had stopped just short of breaking the bone.

"Look I'm sorry," I said, putting my pistol away and fumbling with the archaic mechanism of the rifle. "I just didn't feel like getting killed at the moment and this was the only way that I could stop you." I worked the bolt and ejected all the cartridges, then squinted inside to make sure I hadn't missed any. "What I told you was true. I am on your side and want to help you. But you will have to help me first."

She was puzzled, but I had her attention. She wiped her eyes on her sleeve when I handed back her rifle, then widened them when I passed over the ammunition.

"I would appreciate it if you would keep that weapon unloaded for the moment. I'll trade you information if you don't want to give it freely. There is an organization you probably never heard of who is very interested in what the Cliaand are doing. And what they are doing is interstellar invasion—Burada is the sixth on the list and it looks as though it will be as successful as the others."

"But why do they do this?"

I had her interest now and I rushed on.

"The why isn't important, at least not for the present, since evil ambitions are not unusual among the varied political forms of mankind. What I want to know is the *how*. How did they get away with this invasion in the face of the defences of the planet?"

"Blame the Konsolosluk," she said with vehemence, shaking the rifle. "I'm not saying that the Women's Party didn't make mistakes, but nothing like theirs."

"Could you fill in some background detail, because I'm afraid that you've lost me."

"I'll give you detail. Men!" She spat and her eyes glowed with anger and she was beginning to look attractive again. "The Women's Party brought centuries of enlightened rule to this planet. We had prosperity, there was a good tourist trade, no one suffered. So maybe men voted a few years later than women or couldn't get the best jobs. So what? Women suffered through this sort of thing—and worse—on other planets, and they didn't revolt. Those Konsolosluk, sneaking around everywhere, whispering lies. Men's rights and down with oppression and that kind of thing. Getting people worked up, winning a few seats in parliament, disturbing the country. Then their one day revolution, seizing everything, getting control. And all their promises. All they wanted to do was strut around and act superior. Some superior! Worthless all of them. Know nothing of Government or fighting. When your pigs landed more of these *men* ran away than fought, weak fools. And surrendering rather than fighting. I would never have surrendered."

"Perhaps they had to."

"Never. Weaklings, that's all."

All of which gave me pause to think, and with thought came suspicion and after this the dawning light of discovery. Pieces began to fall into shape in my mind and I tried not to get too excited. It was a formless idea yet—but if it worked—if it worked!

Then I would know how the Cliaandians managed their invasion trick. Simple, like all good ideas, and foolproof as well.

"I'll need your help," I told Taze. "I'll stay in the Space Armada, at least for the moment, since I can learn more there. But I won't leave this planet. This is where the Cliaandians are the weakest and this is where they are going to be beaten. Have you ever heard of the Special Corps?"

"No."

"Well you have now. It is, well, it is the group that is going to help you. I work for them and they should be keeping an eye on me. They saw the fleet leave Cliaand and are certain to have followed it here. That was one of the developments we had planned for. Right now a message drone should be circling this planet. It will relay any messages to the Corps and we will have all the help we need. Can you get access to a medium powered radio transmitter?"

"Yes—but why should I? Why should I believe you? You could be lying."

"I could be—but you can't take the chance." I scratched feverishly on a message form. "I'm leaving you now, I have to get back to my ship before they begin to wonder where I have gone. Here is the message you are to transmit on this frequency. You can do it without getting caught, it's easy enough. And you lose nothing by doing it. And you may save your planet."

She was still doubtful, looking at the paper.

"It's so hard to believe. That you are really a spy—and want to help us."

"You can believe he is a spy, take my word for it," a voice said from the doorway behind me and I felt a cold hand clamp down on my heart. I turned, slowly.

Kraj, the man in gray was standing there. Two other gray uniformed men stood behind him leveling their weapons at me. Kraj pointed his finger like a third gun.

"We have been watching you, spy, and waiting for this information. Now we can proceed with the destruction of your Special Corps."

13

"PEOPLE SEEM TO be popping up in doorways a lot today, ha ha," I said with a joviality I certainly did not feel. Kraj smiled a very wintry smile.

"If you mean the colonel, yes, I had him watching you. Now try to act the fool, Pas Ratunkowy, or whatever your name really is."

"Hulja, Vaska, Lieutenant in the Space Armada."

"Flight-Major Hulja has been found in the Dosadan-Glup Robotnik Hotel, which discovery put us on your trail. Yours was a most ingenious plan and might have succeeded had not an optical pickup burned out. The repairman sent to order the matter discovered the Flight-Major and his delusion about the date and this was brought to my attention. I'll take that."

Kraj lifted the message form from Taze's unresisting fingers. He seemed very much in control of the situation. I clutched my chest in the area of my heart, rolled up my eyes and staggered backwards.

"Too much . . ." I muttered. "Heart going . . . don't shoot . . . this is the end."

Kraj and his two men looked on coldly while I was going through all this for their benefit, until the dramatic moment when I clutched at my throat and shrieked with pain, my body arched and every muscle taut, then fell over backwards through the window.

It was nicely done with plenty of crashing glass, and I flipped in midair and landed on my shoulder and did a roll and came up to my feet, ready to run.

Looking right up the barrel of a gaussrifle held by another silent and unsmiling man in gray. He scored zero as a conversationalist and for the moment I could think of nothing bright to say myself. Kraj's voice came clearly through the broken window behind me.

"Take the girl to the prison camp, we have no further need for her. The rest of us will return with the spy. Be on guard constantly, you have seen what he can do."

Not very much, I thought to myself in a sudden gloomy depression. Not very much at all. I had penetrated all right, and found out what I wanted to know, but I had not been able to get my information out. Which made it useless. Worse than useless. Kraj might be able to turn my message to his own ends which I was sure were pretty nasty ones. This dark state of mind persisted while the rest of the doom-faced gray men surrounded me and trotted me off to a waiting truck. There was no chance at all to escape: they were very efficient with those guns.

It was a brief trip, though a remarkably uncomfortable one. The vehicle was a captured Burada truck that must have been used for the transport of garbage or something worse. I was the only one who seemed bothered by the permeating smell. The gray men neither commented on it nor took their eyes from me once during the trip. At least the vehicle was silent and smooth; it burned gas in a fuel cell to generate electricity—supplied to a separate drive motor in each wheel. I considered desperate plans of ripping up one of the cables where it passed by my feet, of leaping out of the rear of the truck and so forth. None of this was much good and we reached our destination with our relative positions unchanged. At gunpoint I was herded into a commandeered building, into an empty room where, still at gunpoint, I was ordered to strip. With a portable fluoroscope and cold probes, most humiliating, they removed all devices and gadgetry from my person, then gave me new clothes.

These clothes were something else again. A single-piece overall made of soft and flexible plastic they provided protection and warmth for the wearer. Yet they were the ideal prison dress because they were completely transparent. This continual shielded-nakedness was certainly not morale building and I began to have even more respect for the gray men. And everything done in silence despite my attempts at conversation. The final sartorial touch was a metal collar that locked around my neck. A cable ran from the collar to a box one of the gray men held. All of this had a very ominous look to it. My suspicions were justified when the others left with all of the weapons and he faced me, box in hand.

"I can do this," he said in a voice as gray as his garb and pressed a button on the box.

The thing I experienced next was quite unexpected and singularly painful. In a single instant I was blinded by exploding lights of a color and fury I had never seen before. Sound greater than sound filled my ears and every square inch of my skin burned with fire as though I had been dropped into an acid bath. These interesting things went on for a longer time than I really appreciated and then suddenly vanished as quickly as they had begun. Sight and hearing returned and I found myself lying on the floor with a sore spot on the back of my head where I had cracked it when I fell. It felt rather good just to lie there. That little box must generate neural currents on selected frequencies. No need to torture the body when you can feed specific pain impulses into the nervous system.

"Stand," my captor said, and I did rather quickly.

"If you wish to convey the message that you can do that whenever you want, and right now you want me to behave—the message has been received. But speak and I shall obey. I'll be a good boy."

For the time being. Until I found a way to get out of this stainless steel rat trap. I trotted along docilely to another room where Kraj waited for me behind a large metal desk. The room was dusty and blank areas on the wall showed where pictures and pieces of furniture had been removed. The only new item, other than the desk, was a shining hook recently affixed in the ceiling. I was not at all surprised when the hook fitted into a ring on the box and I was leashed, standing before my captor.

Kraj looked me up and down, examining me closely, a very easy thing to do considering the transparent condition of my clothing. I have never suffered from a nudity taboo so this did not bother me. It was the cold and unemotional look in his eyes that was more offputting. At the present moment I was, to use the classical term, completely at his mercy. I had no idea of what nastiness he had in mind for me and I determined to at least attempt to ameliorate it a bit.

"What would you like to know?" I asked.

"A number of things, but that will come later."

"What's wrong with now? Considering the state of modern hypnotic techniques, drug therapy and old-fashioned torture—like your nerve machine here—it is impossible to keep facts from a determined interrogator. Therefore ask and I shall answer." What little I knew about the Special Corps he was welcome to. All of the locations of the bases were kept secret from us, undoubtedly with an interrogation like this in mind. I was surprised when he shook his head in a slow no.

"You will give me the information later. First you must be convinced of the seriousness of my aims. I intend to question you, then to enlist your services in our cause. Voluntarily. In order to convince you of this I must begin by saying you will not be killed. Strong men face death bravely. It is an easy escape from their problems. You have no such escape."

I was becoming less and less intrigued all the time by what he had to say. I had expected a rough questioning session, but he had bigger things in mind. So I dropped the bantering tone and gave it to him straight.

"Forget it. Face the fact that I do not like you or your organization or what you stand for, and I do not intend to change my mind. Even if I promise to aid you you can never be sure that I mean it—so let us not get involved in this sort of farcical position to begin with."

"Quite the contrary," he said, and touched a button on his desk. The box above hummed and reeled in the thick wire pulling me upward until I had to stand on tiptoe in order to breathe, the collar biting into my neck. "Before I am through with you you will be begging me for the opportunity to cooperate and will cry when I do not permit it, until you reach the happiest moment in your life when you are at last granted your single wish. Let me demonstrate one of our simpler but most convincing techniques."

My feet vibrated with pain but I had to stay on my toes or I would have been strangled by the collar. Kraj rose and walked behind me where I could not see him—then seized both my wrists and pushed them down against the edge of the metal desk. The desk obliged him by snapping two cuffs about my wrists, clamping them there. Not about my wrists, this isn't exactly true, but about my lower arm, leaving my wrists and hands free. Not that I could do anything more than drum my fingertips on the tabletop. Kraj reappeared and bent to take something from a drawer in the desk.

It was an ax. A long handled, steel edged ax of a primitive and efficient sort that could be used to chop down trees. He took it in both hands and raised it high over his head.

"What are you doing? Stop!" I shouted in sudden fear, writhing in the metal embrace, unable to do anything except stare while he held the ax high for a moment. Then brought it down with a vicious, forceful chop.

I suppose I screamed when it hit, I must have, the pain was large and consuming.

As was the sight of my right hand severed from the wrist, lying unmoving on the desk top, the spout of blood from my wrist pumping out and drenching it. The ax went up again and this time I am sure I shouted aloud, screamed, all the time it went up and flashed down and my left hand was severed like the right and my life's blood spouted out all over the desk and ran down to the floor.

And through the pain and the terror that possessed me I was aware of Kraj's face. Smiling. Smiling for the first time.

Then I was unconscious. Blacking out, dying, I couldn't tell. The world rushed away from me down a dark tunnel and I was left with the sensation of pain alone and then even that was gone.

When I opened my eyes I was lying on the floor and a period of unmeasured time had gone by. My thoughts were thick with sleep or something else and I had to work to dredge up the memory of what had happened. Only when the startling vision of my severed hands came to me clearly did I open my eyes and sit up, rubbing one hand with the other. They felt perfectly normal. What had happened?

"Stand up," Kraj's voice said, and I realized that I was sitting on the floor before his desk and that the collar was still in place about my neck with its wiring running up to the device on the ceiling. I stood, slowly, and looked at his clean desk. There was no blood.

"I would have sworn . . ." I said and my voice died away as I saw the two great grooves in the metal top of the desk as though it had been hit twice with some heavy blade. Then I lifted my hands before my face and looked at my wrists.

Each wrist was circled by a red weal of healing flesh with the sharp red points of removed stitches along the edges. Yet my hands felt as they always did. What had happened?

"Are you beginning to understand what I mean?" Kraj asked, once more seated behind the desk, his voice as gray as his clothing.

"What did you do? You couldn't have amputated my hands and sewed them back. I could tell, it would take time, you couldn't . . ." I realized that I was starting to babble and I shut up.

"You don't believe it happened? Should I do it again?"

"No!" I said, almost shouting the word, drawing back from him. He nodded approvingly at this.

"So the training begins. You have lost a little bit of reality. You do not know what happened—but you do know that you do not wish it to happen again. This is the way it will go. Eventually you will lose all touch with the reality you have known all your life, and then will lose contact with the person you have been all your life. When you reach that state we will accept you as one of us. Then you will go into great detail about your Special Corps, not only racking your memory for crumbs of fact you may have missed, but in actively originating plans for their destruction."

"It won't work," I said with a great deal more sincerity than I really felt. "I am not alone. The Corps is onto you now and actively working against you, so that it is now just a matter of time before they pull the plug and all your little invasion schemes go down the drain."

"Quite the opposite," Kraj said clasping his hands together on the desk before him like a teacher about to lecture a class. "We have been aware of their attention for a long time and have forestalled them at every turn. We have captured, tortured and killed a number of the Corps people to get information. We know that everything is geared to follow the lead of a field agent, such as yourself, and we have been waiting for one to come along. You have come, and we have you. It is that simple. You are the weapon with which we will destroy the Special Corps."

He had me half believing him. The plan he proposed sounded like a reasonable one and I put that thought away as fast as it arrived. I was going to have to stop agreeing with him, attack rather than defend.

"That is very ambitious of you and I hope you don't bite off more than you can chew. Aren't you forgetting the hundreds of planets that support the league and what they can do to you when they find out the kind of trouble you are causing?"

"There are hundreds of planets only in theory, in reality they are just one after the other. We pluck them in that manner, they fall before us, we cannot be stopped, and the process is an accelerating one. As our empire expands we move faster and faster."

"And there is a limit to that speed," I broke in, trying to work a sneer into my words. "I know how your invasion technique works. You don't invade a planet until they have already *lost*. Isn't that right?"

"Perfectly correct." He nodded agreement and I rushed on.

"You find a planet that is ripe for the picking with some dissident element in the population; there are people who would complain about paradise so you have no problem in finding a group on any world. Here on Burada it was the men, the Konsolosluk party. They were hot for male rule. You backed them with whatever they needed. Your underground operators supplied them with money, weapons, propaganda, all the essentials of a takeover—and it worked. And you asked nothing in return for all this aid, other than only a token resistance when the invasion began. Your agents saw to it that the armed forces surrendered after only the briefest show of force. This invasion was won before it began! No wonder your military people aren't used to taking losses."

"Very observant of you. This is exactly what we do, your analysis is a masterly description of the way in which we operate."

"There, I have you," I said happily.

"On the contrary—we have you. You are the only one who

knows about our techniques and you will never report them to your superiors.''

''Oh, I don't know,'' I said with a bravado I did not feel.

''Perhaps you do not know, but we do. We have intercepted the report you made and it will never be sent. They will wait in vain for any word from you and time will pass and soon it will be too late for them to do anything because we will move into phase two of our operation. With the many allies we have gained by occupying planets with governments now friendly to us, we will have a considerable number of troops available to us. Mercenaries I believe they are called. They will be invasion troops and great numbers of them will be killed, but we will always win because our supply will be relatively inexhaustible. It presents an interesting picture, does it not?''

''It will never work,'' I shouted, with the sinking feeling at the same time that it would. ''The Corps will stop you.'' How, with their only agent run to earth and trapped? I was having a hard job convincing myself and getting nowhere at all in convincing him.

Kraj rose and started around the desk.

''Now it is time for your indoctrination to begin.''

I cannot express the fear that overwhelmed and possessed me when I heard those words.

14

I WAS TAKEN to a cell. A bare, windowless room whose only furnishing was an empty bucket. A ceiling hook had recently been installed here and my attendant gray man obligingly hooked me up to it.

"There is little chance of my starving to death," I told him. "Because I'll die of thirst first."

He gave no spoken answer but he did return with a soft plastic water bottle and a standard Cliaand field ration. Not the world's most inspiring food, but it would keep me alive.

As I chewed and sipped I clamped hard on that last thought. Keep me alive. They would do anything except kill me. They wanted me, actually needed me. They knew that the Special Corps was breathing hot on their trail and they would have to exert an all-out effort to stop them. Kraj had talked big and half convinced me; I looked at my wrists and shuddered. He *had* convinced me. But why had he tried so hard?

Because I was obviously more than a pawn in this game. I was the factor that could swing the outcome either way. Right now Cliaand was doing well in the invasion business—but they could be stopped. With what I knew the Special Corps could start work as counter-insurgents and prevent expansion to other planets. Cliaand might even be stopped here. If I were to change sides my specialized knowledge might not defeat the Corps, but it could surely slow it down long enough for the second phase of the invasion operation to go into effect.

Which means the gray men had made a mistake. They should have killed me as soon as they discovered who I was. If I could be tortured and convinced to change my mind I might be a weapon in their hands. Two maybes. That ignored the fact that as long as I was alive I was the most deadly and potent weapon against them.

They had made a mistake. I grabbed to that conclusion and worried it just as I worried the jaw-breaking ration. I did not consider that I was their prisoner in every way. Every way? Ha! Physically, yes. Mentally—a resounding no. They had almost had

me there for a while with the nerve torture and the positive assurance
that I would fall into their hands. At the thought of amputation my
stomach gave a heave and I suddenly lost my appetite. I had put the
sight of my severed hands out of my mind. For good reasons.

Now I would have to remember and think about it. But not in the
way they wanted. It was a trick, it *had* to be a trick, and that was the
supposition I must hold on to. While I chewed and glugged down
the rest of my unappetizing meal I gave myself the hard sell. Listen
diGriz, you know enough about reality to be able to tell when it has
been tampered with. You are always tampering with it yourself for
your own benefit and others' discommoding. So now someone has
turned the same trick on you. *The severed wrists pumping blood!*
Down, boy. Drain away some of the emotion. We'll get to the
memories after a while. But let us first look at the realities.

Reality. Marvelous as medicine is it cannot repair amputation in a
couple of hours or a couple of days.

Now where did that figure come from? At some unconscious
level I felt that only a brief time had passed between the amputation
and the recovery. We all have a clock ticking away down deep in the
brain, it controls the circadian rhythms of sleeping and waking and
it works all of the time. Right now it was trying to tell me that only a
brief time had passed since I had been brought here by the gray men.
But did I have any real evidence to back it up? I felt my face and my
hair. I needed a shave, but not badly, and my hair felt about the right
length. But I could have had a haircut and a shave, no evidence
there.

My fingernails? I kept them trimmed short, and one trimmed
fingernail looks like any other one. Wait, think. Memory. Something. Small. Yes—during the landing, plenty of tension, plenty of
distractions. I had broken the little fingernail on my left hand. No,
don't look yet, sit on the thing and remember. Broken nail . . . distraction . . . bit it off. A rather unappetizing bit of self-consumption
that most of us indulge in at one time or another. The offending
particle of nail torn free, right down to the quick, a minor ouch and a
tiny drop of blood. Completely forgotten in the rush of subsequent
events.

With careful motions I released my left hand from its prisoning
buttock and held it before me. Little finger, short nail—and a tiny
clot of blood.

Got you, Kraj, you old faker!

From the look of the thing I had been a prisoner for a day or two at
the most, surely no longer than that. The red marks on my wrists

were just that—red marks on my wrists. There were a hundred different ways this could have been done. And the amputation? Kraj had tampered with my reality, hypnosis perhaps, it didn't really matter.

Kraj and his crew were not as bright as they looked. They had undoubtedly used this mind-cracking torture many times before and had really impressed themselves with the success of the technique. Perhaps this was the way they converted recruits to their nasty ends on the planets they were to invade. Very possible. But Kraj's cutthroats were used to working on solid citizens, one dimensional peasants who mistook the painted flats and props of their existence as the only reality. Their world was the only real world, their town the really best town. Pull them out of the familiar environment and put pressure on their minds and their brains ran out of their ears like jelly. Jelly men, prey for the gray men.

Not noble, upright, flexible, dishonest, chameleon-like Slippery Jim diGriz. Man of a thousand faces, familiar of a hundred cultures, linguistically competent in scores of tongues. And they wanted to louse up *my* reality? It made me laugh. I laughed.

I not only laughed but I scampered and danced. I ran in circles shouting Yippee! and Victory! and other cries of happiness. Because of my collar and cable I was forced to run in circles but I found that I could vary this by swinging in circles. The cable was too thin to climb, deliberately designed so I am sure, but I could coil a loop of it and hang from this. I made the loop as high above my head as I could reach, grabbed it, kicked off and swung freely. At the bottom of the swing I kicked hard and went higher. Great fun. Until my hand slipped and the loop unlooped.

Everything almost ended at that moment as all of my weight came on the metal collar about my neck. That's the way they kill people, you know, by hanging. Not by suffocating them. By giving that sudden jerk to the noose that breaks the spinal cord.

This thought was uppermost in my mind as I clutched and scrabbled at the cable and managed to grip it before the snap came. And it came on the front of my neck, not the side, or I might very well have heard that sharp *crack* that signals the end. It hurt and everything went around in circles for a minute and when I said *Wow!* it was in a whispered voice because I had not done my vocal cords any good either.

Eventually I sat up and drank some water and felt a little better—and wondered why no one had come to investigate all the recent nonsense. I was sure they had the room bugged to watch me, but perhaps they were not impressed by my acrobatics. Or maybe they were so busy with the invasion that they did not have time to keep that careful an eye on me. If this latter supposition were correct, then perhaps I might be able to capitalize on it.

The food wrappings and the water bottle wadded together to make excellent padding for my hands. Around this I wrapped a double loop of the cable, close against my neck. Then, clutching the cable tightly, I jumped as high as I could and let my weight crash down on the cable.

And on my arms. By the tenth time I had done this I was beginning to feel as though my arms would be torn off at the sockets before any vital part of my emprisoning mechanism gave way. The theory was certainly sound enough. A metal box, a cable, a handle, a hook, a number of components the failure of any one of which might grant me freedom. Though my components were failing much faster. I panted a bit, wiped my forehead with my forearm, and jumped up for try number thirteen.

Lucky thirteen! Something snapped with a sharp metallic crack and the box came down and bounced off my head.

I was out, how long I don't know, probably only a few moments, and came to shaking my head and trying to stand. *Move* was the pressing thought, get out of here before they came for me. But first I had to deactivate the torture box since it could be worked by remote radio control. I turned it over and saw that the metal loop by which it was suspended had fractured. There was a control section here with about 50 small red buttons arranged in a grid. I shivered at the thought of pressing any of them. Above the grid were two large buttons, one red, one black. The red was depressed. This seemed obvious enough. Logically I should push the black one and turn the box off, but memories of the pain kept intruding. Finally I stabbed down on the black button.

Nothing happened. That I could feel. With this security I lightly touched one of the small red buttons, then another and another. Nothing. The box was now so much dead metal. I hoped. I coiled up the extra cable until the box dangled handily. Then tried the door. Which proved to be unlocked. Inefficient warders or great faith in their torture machines. Putting my eye close to the edge of the door I opened it a crack.

And closed it even more swiftly. Coming down the corridor towards me were two of the gray men carrying a sinister looking object between them. I had not seen enough of it to capture any details, though what I had seen had given me a definitely crawling sensation. The next step in the diGriz pacification program? This seemed highly probable when the door handle started to turn.

There was a surprise in store for this pair and I wanted to keep it from them as long as I could. As the door opened I stepped behind it and waited while they struggled with the bulky torture machine. Only when I heard one of them gasp in alarm did I put my shoulder to the door and ram it into them with all my weight and strength. As soon as they crunched and howled I jumped around the door, the metal control box swinging at the end of its cable.

One of them was bent over, more interested in the weight of the machine on his foot than in anything else and I let my weapon bounce off the top of his skull. While it rebounded the second man tried for his gun and actually had it halfway out of its holster before my knee caught him low in the stomach and he folded on top of his associate. I plucked the gun from his limp fingers as he went down and now I was armed.

During most of my stay in the building I had been conscious and I thought I knew my way out. Back through the main entrance which was sure to be guarded. It was one flight down and in the opposite direction from Kraj's chambers. The gausspistol had a full charge of power and a filled magazine as well. There was no time to check what kind of ammunition it was loaded with, but it was surely something lethal which was fine by me. I was in a lethal mood. I wrapped the cable up close to the box so it wouldn't swing and get in my way, took a deep breath—and dived out the door.

The hallway was empty, a good beginning. I trotted to the stairs without seeing anyone, then went down them two at a time. The next floor would be the ground floor since they had only taken me up one story. This memory was opposed by the reality that there was a large stairwell beside me that did not end at the next floor. When this fact finally registered on my tardy synapses I skidded to a stop and looked carefully over the edge of the railing.

There were at least eight more stories below this one.

They *had* been running through my cerebral cortex with their little leaden boots. This certainly proved my theoretical stance that a good deal of what had happened to me was illusion or false memory. What had been real? Was this 'escape' real at the present moment? This was a chilling thought; everything that was happening could be a generated series of unreal events to prove to me that I could not escape. I could keep going down these stairs forever or wake up at any moment back in my room still attached to my pendent box. Well, if this were true, there was absolutely nothing I could do about it. I had to treat this illusion like reality until it proved otherwise. Unless this was an endless dream building these stairs had to end somewhere, and I was going to find out.

Four floors down, just when I was beginning to get dizzy from the constant circling, I met another man coming up. A gray man with a rifle and a very surprised look. Since I had been expecting this encounter and he hadn't I got in the first shot.

Quite a shot. The gausspistol was loaded with explosive slugs. They blasted a gaping hole in the staircase and hurled the gray man against the wall where he slumped, crumpled and unconscious. The echoes were still booming and the dust unsettled when I leaped the gaping hole and hurled myself down the stairs at a suicidal pace. It would be more certain suicide to wait around.

The stairs ended, I was at the bottom, and I slammed into the wall I was going so fast. There was much shouting from above me and the hammer of running feet. My gun at the ready I pushed open the door and walked into blackness.

It was a bit of a shock and I almost fired off a couple of rounds on general principle but, as my eyes adjusted, I saw a dim light in the distance. There were rough walls and dust and other indications that I had bypassed the ground floor and ended up in a cellar. Which was all right too since there was undoubtedly a warm reception waiting for me a flight above. If I could get out of the basement I was still one jump ahead of the competition. Gun ready, metal box swinging, shins bruised by unseen obstacles, I stumbled towards the far off light. I was not enthused when I reached it after running the invisible obstacle course. It was a window.

But a small window, high on the wall, coated with insect corpses and dirt. And heavily barred.

Behind me in the darkness there were shouts, running feet, crashing noises and healthy curses. What to do?

Obvious. Get out. I stepped back, raised the gun, shielded my face, and blew the window out. And part of the wall around it and some of the street outside until my gun clicked empty. I dropped it, slung my box over my shoulder and used my free hand to help me scrabble up the slope of rubble and out into the street.

To start running again. Someone saw me and shouted but I did not shout back. I ran harder even though I was getting winded and more than a little fatigued by the effort. It is one thing to escape, it is another thing altogether to stay free once out. Barefooted, dressed in totally transparent clothes with a collar and some meters of wire about my neck, not to mention the control box, I must have presented a rather unusual and unmistakable sight. I needed to hide, hole up, change, get rid of the collar, a lot of things. And I was getting very tired.

I went around a corner as fast as I could and slammed into someone coming in the opposite direction. We both went down and I rolled on my back like a bug, near exhaustion, gasping for air. Then I saw the face of the man I had run into and had a last little burst of hope.

"Otrov," I gasped. "Old friend, old roommate, old copilot. I am in trouble and need your help. The locals, you see . . ."

I saw Otrov, a mild man at the worst of times, turn into a very angry animal. Twisted face, bulging eyes, the works. He dived on me and pinned me to the cold ground.

"Locals nothing," he shouted. "Kraj has been asking after you, Kraj wants you. What have you done?"

15

I STRUGGLED A BIT, but it did me no good. My heart wasn't in it and I was close to exhaustion. Though I did manage to catch my ex-friend Otrov a good one on the side of the head with my torture box. His eyes crossed but he didn't let go and by that time a small squad of gray men were upon us, peeling him off and prodding me to my feet with their rifle barrels. I prodded slowly. Sunk in dark despair and limp with fatigue I was certainly in no hurry.

There were six of them and Otrov, who had a look on his face of wishing to be elsewhere.

"Kraj talked to me, you see. About Vaska here, said he wanted him . . ." His voice ran down and expired when the stony faced men completely ignored him. I didn't.

"What did you expect—gratitude? You rat. Starting your own bomb-your-buddy week, aren't you?" I tried to sneer but it turned to a gurgle when one of my captors jerked on my cable. One of my five captors. I blinked and looked again because I could swear there had been six there a moment ago.

While I was still counting a pair of hands reached up and closed around the neck of number five. His eyeballs bulged and his mouth gaped and I worked to keep my expression calm and not to bulge my own eyes in the same manner. The hands scrunched, the eyes closed, and number five vanished from sight. I struggled a bit so the survivors would keep their attention on me, even lashing out a foot and getting Otrov in the ankle to keep him occupied as well.

"You didn't have to do that," he complained. I smiled as number four went the way of the others.

There was something to be admired in the efficient and quiet disposal of the enemy. It reminded me of a hunter I once worked with on a planet whose name I forget. He was a professional and very good at his job. He would go out at dawn when a flock of birds was going over and shoot the last bird in the flight. Then the next one and the next one. He could get four or five sometimes without the other birds even knowing what was happening. The same principle was being applied here in an equally professional way.

The system broke down with number four who thrashed a bit and drew the attention of one of the others, human beings being slightly smarter than birds after all. I waited until they had turned towards the disturbance then let the nearest gray man have it in the side of the neck with the edge of my hand. Fatigue weakened the blow so that he didn't drop at once and I had to let him have a few more to quiet him. And while I worked I was aware of thuds and cut-off screams from the others.

When I straightened up I saw that Otrov and all but one of the gray men were dozing happily in a heap, while my rescuers put down the final one. He was a big bruiser and fought well, but he was outclassed and soon unconscious. Which was interesting because both of his attackers were women—dressed in skimpy and colorful Burada shifts and the high-heeled local shoes. The nearest one turned and I recognized Sergeant Taze and some of the pieces began to fall into place.

The other woman was smaller and quite neatly formed, with a figure I remembered and a face I could not forget. My wife.

"There, there," Angelina said, patting me on one cheek and giving me a quick kiss on the other. "I hope you can run a bit, darling, because more of these thugs are on the way." A projectile of some kind whined by to punctuate the statement.

"Run . . ." I said hoarsely and staggered off, still not quite sure what had happened but at least still bright enough to not ask any questions. Taze put her arm around me, getting me going in the right direction and pulling me along, while my Angelina relieved me of the weight of box and cable. We rushed away like that and I'm sure we made a charming sight, me in my transparent coveralls and the girls in their neat little frocks, except no one was on the street to appreciate the scene.

"Keep going!" Taze shouted as she dragged me around a corner. There were explosions close behind us. I ignored everything except putting one foot in front of the other as fast as I could and wondered just how long I would last.

Taze seemed to know what she was doing. Before we had gone very far in this new direction she turned, half carried me up a few steps and into a building. She threw the bolts on the heavy door and we staggered on, a little slower now, through deserted offices of some kind, to the rear where the windows faced on a courtyard. There was a good sized drop here and Taze went first, lithe as a big cat, then helped me down with Angelina lowering from above. I was as putty in their hands, and a very nice sensation it was too.

Taze ran ahead to open a large door. Inside was a Cliaand command car with a general's flag still flying from the antenna.

"That's more like it," I said, walking over on rubbery legs.

"In the back you two," Taze ordered, pulling on a military jacket and pushing her hair up under a Cliaand helmet. I did not ask what had happened to the original owner. Angelina was right behind me when I crawled into the back and collapsed on the floor, snuggling her warm round curves up against me. I felt very comfortable as the car bounced forward. I enjoyed a good hug and a kiss before I could get in any questions.

"Your figure has improved," I managed to gasp when I came up for air.

"You'll be so happy to know that you are now the proud father of twins. Both boys. With big mouths and hearty appetites like their father. I've named them James and Bolivar after you."

"Anything you say, my sweet. I suppose you would not mind telling me how you came to be here at this most opportune moment?"

"I came to take care of you, and as you can see I was right."

"Yes, of course," I said, and nodded dimly at this fine bit of female logic. "Mechanically, I mean. The last I saw you were headed for the hospital with a bulge in your midriff and the light of motherhood in your eyes."

"Well that all worked out fine as I've told you, weren't you listening? Then I heard that these filthy Cliaand people were off to invade another planet and that you were probably taking part in the invasion."

"Inskipp told you all this?"

"Of course not!" She sniffed delicately at the thought. "I broke into his files and found the records. He was very angry but did not try to stop me when I came here with the follow-up team. I imagine he knew better than to interfere. In fact he promised to keep an eye on the nurse and the children for me. We went into orbit, received the message and I came down, that's about all there is to it. Let me try this lockpick on that horrid collar thing you're wearing. I don't know why you ever let them treat you like this."

"There are one or two gaps in your story," I insisted. "Like what message?"

"My message," Taze said, who had been shamelessly eavesdropping while she drove. "You forget that I am a sergeant in the Guard and I had seen the message you prepared, the one they took away. So of course I had memorized it as well as the radio frequencies. Those swine took me to a prison camp for *civilians* so I left it that same night." Taze was quite sure of herself and, looking back at the record, I realized she had cause to be.

"I came down in a scout ship as soon as the call was heard." Angelina diddled with the lockpick while she talked. "I had to shoot my way in which certainly was not hard to do. For galaxy conquerors these people are very indifferent pilots. Then I met Taze." Angelina touched her lips to my ear and hissed coldly. "How well do you know this girl?" She twisted the collar at the same time.

"Just met her that once." I gasped, and the pressure let off. "Not my type at all."

"You like them buxom like that, don't lie to me Jim diGriz."

I blinked rapidly and tried to restore the conversation to its original direction.

"But then, how did you find me? What did you do?"

"Simple enough." There was a click and the collar snapped open. I rubbed my sore neck with relief. "There is only one building where these men in gray uniforms operate. We watched it, trying to find a way in. Our only trouble was the soldiers, trying to pick us up all the time. But we extracted information from them. And this car."

I had a vision of these two murderous cuties slowly decimating the Cliaandian invasion with their own secret weapons, and knew enough not to ask about the fate of the driver and his friends.

"Now tell us what happened to you," Angelina said, and snuggled down to hear a good story. "I'm dying to find out what this thing is they had on your neck and why in heaven you are wearing that awful transparent suit."

I told them all right, and was rewarded with a number of girlish gasps, and at least one screech when I got to the wrist part. Taze even stopped the car so she could look at the scars too. After that they listened in cold-eyed stillness and I almost felt sorry for any of the gray men they might meet in the future. By the time I had finished my fascinating and slightly repulsive story we had arrived at wherever we were going. A wide door opened at our approach and closed behind us. Other girls were there, well armed and attractive for the most part, and I wondered how the Konsolosluk party had ever managed to muster up a resistance to a government like this. Thank the Cliaandians for that. When it comes to governments and armies I'm pretty much of an anarchist and think least is best in both departments. But if you have to have them it sure helps if they are pretty. I shook my head, realizing that my thoughts still hadn't a firm grip on reality, and let myself be led to a room where there was a very enticing army cot. I dropped onto it.

"Clothes," I said, "and drink, and not necessarily in that order." I tucked a corner of the blanket coyly over me. Not out of shame, rather that these alert amazons should not be subject to temptation. And besides, my wife was there. She knew very well what I meant by drink and pushed aside the glass of water one of the ladies was trying to force on me and passed over a small flask of potent brew. It burned sweetly down my throat and sent tendrils of fire into my brain.

"I'm afraid my thoughts . . . my sense of reality is still a little confused," I admitted, and from the look on Angelina's face I knew that she was already aware of it. "They did something to me, don't know what, but it'll wear off soon I'm sure."

"I'll kill them, every one, terribly," Angelina said through tight-clenched teeth and there was a murmur of agreement from all the listeners. I closed my eyes for a moment to rest them and when I opened them again the room was empty except for Angelina; a light had been lit and the window was dark. It was like a spliced break in a film with a chunk left out. I respected Kraj's mental diddling techniques and roundly loathed him for it.

"Hungry," I told Angelina and she came over and sat by me and held my hand.

"You've been asleep—and talking. Some awfully strange things."

"I feel better for it. When we get back to base I'll have the medics vacuum out all the dark corners. But there are more important things for the present. We have to organize the resistance here before the Cliaand get a tight grip on everything. And . . ."

"No."

"What do you mean *no?*"

I had the feeling that I had missed some important part of the conversation. Was this more results of the brain fiddling—or just female conversation?

"I mean no, we won't do that. While you were sleeping I sent a long report to Inskipp, everything you told me about the Cliaand plans and how they work their invasions and how they are out to get the Corps, everything."

"Did you at least sign my name?" I asked, petulantly.

She patted my hand. "Of course, darling. It was *your* work and I wouldn't *think* of trying to get credit for it."

I was filled with instant regret for speaking like that, and apol-

ogized, then she apologized because my ill temper probably had to
do with the brain business, and we had a drink and that was settled
and I tried to get back to the business at hand.

"So you sent the report. And then—?"

"Then it went to a relay ship on the other side of this sun and was
sent out as a psigram to Inskipp. His answer came in and he said
'message received, congratulations, return at once.' So you see you
will have to go back."

I snorted through my nose, then sipped my drink.

"Do you think I'll go back?"

"You're not well, you need medical attention, you've done what
you came to do—"

"That's not what I asked. Do *you* think I'll go back now?"

Angelina tried to look fierce, which she cannot do unless she
really means it—then shrugged her shoulders in a very resigned
way.

"Of course not. If you did you would not be the man I married.
So now we wipe out these fiends and save Burada and stop the
invasions."

"Not quite all at once, but that is sort of what I had in mind. A
resistance movement will have to be organized, with our advice and
material help Taze should be able to handle that, but there is one
thing that takes priority over even that. We must capture Kraj or one
of his gray men."

"What a wonderful idea! If they think they know about torture
they will soon learn a thing or two. I remember . . ."

"Angelina! That is not what I had in mind. For a moment there a
lot of the old reconstructed you was shining through."

"Nonsense. I admit I could use one or two techniques I learned in
those days, but my motives are the purest. Lioness defending her
mate and that sort of thing. Perfectly justified."

"Yes, that might be so, but it is not quite what I was talking
about. I want one of those gray men in a laboratory and I want
exhaustive tests run on him. When you were beating up on that
bunch earlier today did you notice anything strange about them?"

"Nothing particular, I was otherwise occupied you might say.
Just the fact that they weren't wearing enough clothing or something, because their skins felt so chill."

"Exactly so. And they never laugh or show emotion, they don't
gossip or talk unless there is something important to say, and have a
number of other little traits that draw the attention."

"Just what are you trying to say, darling, that they are zombies or robots or something? I thought that sort of thing appeared only on space operas for the kiddies.''

"Laugh now, while there is still time. Not robots or such, these types are alive enough. I just don't think that they are human, that's all. There are aliens among us.''

"Perhaps you better have some more sleep. I'll turn down the light.''

"Don't humor me, damn it! I have been thinking about this ever since I first met Kraj, so it is no figment of a recently tortured mind. There is all sort of evidence. The Cliaand soldiers are deathly afraid of Kraj and his thugs and won't even talk about them. The gray men are cut off from normal Cliaandian life and different in every way from them. Almost as though they were not the same people. I can visualize these gray men doing a survey of the human planets and finding Cliaand just ripe for their picking. A stratified, militarized way of life with everyone in uniform. All they had to do was take over at the top and they would be in control. And this they seem to have done. They appear in none of the tables of organization or charts so dear to the military mind—yet they seem to be running things most of the time.''

"Well . . .''

"There. You're not convinced but you are beginning to doubt. Then you'll help me get a specimen gray man?''

"Help?'' She clapped her hands with sheer girlish enthusiasm. "I'm simply looking forward to it. Of course he might get a little damaged while I'm bringing him in, but as long as he still works that is really all that matters, isn't it?''

Before I could answer Taze ran in and threw an armload of clothing onto the bed.

"Get dressed, quickly,'' she ordered. "The boots are the biggest we could find and I hope they fit.''

"Is there any reason for all this rush?'' I asked.

"There certainly is. There are troops and heavy weapons on all sides. This building is completely surrounded by the enemy.''

16

THE BOOT WAS tight and delicately pointed, but I squeezed my foot in as fast as I could. "Were we followed here?" I asked Taze.

"No—of course not. I am no beginner at this business. Nor is the stolen car here any longer."

I cudgeled my sluggish brain into thought while I struggled with the second boot. The telephone rang and I froze—as did the two women—staring at it like a poison snake. It rang just once more then the tiny inset screen lit up and Kraj stared out of it, as emotionless as ever.

"You know that you are surrounded," he said. "Resistance is useless, diGriz. Surrender quietly and none of your friends will be hurt . . ."

My boot hit the screen and Kraj's image flared and died; I ripped the entire instrument out by the roots and hurled it against the wall. A fine cold sweat dotted my skin. I knew that most phones can be turned on from central with the right equipment, but this was a bad time to see the theory proven.

"Don't panic!" I shouted, mostly to myself I imagine, because Angelina and Taze were perfectly calm. I hopped about the room getting on the other boot and tried to jar some clear thought into my tangled brain. The last hop ended me up sitting on the cot, panting, counting off on my fingers.

"Let us forget that call for a moment and figure out what is happening. One, we were not followed when we came here. Two, our transportation is gone so that could not be traced. Three, Kraj knew that I was here, which means they may have planted a directional radio transponder in me. In which case the services of a surgeon and a good x-ray machine will be needed as soon as we get out of here."

"You are forgetting a simpler explanation," Angelina said.

"Don't keep it a secret. If you can think better than I can—which is no compliment right now—let's have it."

"The torture box. You said it was radio controlled."

"Of course! A directional apparatus is probably an integral part of the mechanism. Is the thing still here, Taze?"

"Yes, below. We thought there might be a use for it."

"There is now. When we leave the box stays here. Maybe this will keep their attention on the building—and once away they won't find me this easily again. Now brief me, Taze, what kind of a building is this—and how do we get out of it?"

"It is a factory, owned by one of our members. And there is no possible way out, we are doomed to fight and die, but when we do we will sell our lives well and take many of those swine-pig-dogs with us . . ."

"That's fine, yes indeed. But we'll sell our lives dearly only if we have to. DiGriz can find escape routes where others only despair. Is your factory owner here? Good, send her up as quickly as possible."

Taze left on a run and I turned to my wife.

"I assume you brought the usual equipment with you? The sort of thing we had on our honeymoon."

"Bombs, grenades, explosives, gas charges, of course."

"Good girl. With you for a wife I have a growing sense of security."

Taze ran back in followed by another uniformed amazon. A little older perhaps, with a very attractive touch of gray to her hair, yet full-bosomed and round-limbed in a maturely fascinating way . . . I caught the cold look frosting in Angelina's eyes and quickly put my thoughts on more pressing matters.

"I am James diGriz, interstellar agent and spy."

"Fayda Firtina of the Guard," she barked and snapped a salute.

"Yes, very good Fayda, glad to meet you. At ease. I understand that you own this building."

"That is correct. Firtina Amalgamated (construction) Robutlers, Limited. The finest product on the market."

"What is?"

"Robutlers."

"You wouldn't think me dense if I asked what a robutler is?"

"A luxury product that is a necessity for the proper home. A robot that is programmed, trained, articulated and specially designed for but a single function. A butler, a servant, a willing aid around the house that makes the house a home, relieving the lady of the establishment of the chores and cares and stresses of modern living . . ."

There was more like this, obviously quotes from a sales brochure, but I did not hear it. A plan was forming in my mind, taking shape—until the sound of firing broke through my train of thought.

"They have made a probing attack," Taze said, a com-radio to her ear. "But were repulsed with losses."

"Keep holding them. They shouldn't try the heavy stuff for awhile since they still hope to get me alive." I waved over the factory owner who seemed ready to go on with her sales talk. "Fayda, will you give me a quick sketch of the ground plan of the building and the immediate area around it."

She drew quickly and accurately, military training no doubt, indicating doors and windows and the surrounding streets.

"What do your robutlers look like?" I asked.

"Roughly humanoid in form and size, the optimum shape for a home environment. In addition—"

"That's fine. How many do you have ready to go, field tested or whatever you call it, with their little power packs charged?"

She frowned in thought. "I'll have to check with shipping, but at a rough guess I would say between 150 and 200."

"That will be just perfect for our needs. Would you be terribly put out—your insurance might cover it—if they were destroyed in the cause of Burada freedom?"

"Every Firtina robutler would willingly die, happily, if it had any emotions for the cause. Though of course they are incapable of bearing arms or of violent acts of any kind."

"They don't have to. We can take care of that. Our robutler brigade will be the diversion that gets us out of here. Now come close girls and I'll tell you the plan."

The old diGriz brain was really turning over at last. The firing in the background only stimulated me to grander efforts, while I was buoyed up on a wave of cheerful enthusiasm. Within minutes the preparations were being made, and within a half an hour the troops were ready to attack.

"You know your orders?" I asked the dimly lit shipping bay full of robots.

"That we do sir, yes sir, thank you sir," they all answered in the best of cultured accents.

"Then prepare to depart. What you do now is a far far better thing than you would have ever done in an electronic lifetime of domestic service. When I say leave, each to its appointed task."

"Very kind sir, thank you sir."

There were over a hundred here in the shipping bay of the factory, our main diversionary attack. They stood in neat rows, humming and eager to go. The front ranks were dressed in all the excess garments we had been able to assemble; some with uniform hats, others with jackets, still fewer wearing slacks. Most of the clothing had been donated piecemeal by the female shocktroops, which fact was not doing me much good in my new marital status. There was entirely too much tanned flesh around for a man to completely ignore. It was almost a pleasure to be with the robots for a change. Their forms were sleek but hard, their dress inconsistent and reveal- ing of nothing of interest. And each of them clutched a length of pipe or plastic or some other object resembling a weapon. In the confusion that was soon to come my hope was that they would be mistaken for human attackers. I looked at my watch and raised the com-radio to my mouth.

"Stand by all units. Fifteen seconds to zero. Bombers stand ready. Keep away from the windows until the last second. Ready, keep low . . . trigger your bombs . . . *THROW!*"

There was a series of dull explosions from the street outside, that would be echoed on all sides of the building, as the girls heaved the bombs from the upper stories. Smoke bombs for the most part, though there were some irritants and sleep gas mixed in with them. I gave the bombs five seconds to maximum density then hit the garage door switches. The doors rumbled up to reveal little other than twisting coils of smoke that instantly began to pour into the garage.

"Go, my loyal troops, go!" I ordered and every left foot shot forward as one, and the ranks of my robot brigade surged forward.

"Thanking *you* sir!" mellifluously sounded in perfect tones from those metallic throats, and I retreated as they ran by.

There was firing now, from the windows above, echoed instantly by the troops outside. According to plan. I looked at my watch as I ran. Fifteen seconds from zero, time for the second wave.

"All other robutler units—*now!*" I ordered into the com-radio.

At that moment, from the other doors and exits of the factory, into the shroud of smoke and gas, the remaining robots should be going into action. I had not taken the time to try and rig an eavesdropping circuit on the enemy's command net, but I could just imagine what was happening now. What I hoped was happening now.

The building was surrounded, all their troops alert, our stronghold visible in all details in the warm afternoon sunlight. Then the sudden change, smoke, chemical irritants, shrouding the building on all sides. A breakout obviously—and there it was! Dim figures in the smoke, firing, get them, shoot to kill. Zoing, zoing!

Take that you rotten Burada guerrilla fink! What fighters these Burada are—men of steel!—shoot them and they don't fall. Panic in the smoke. The word that there are other breakouts. Which was the real one, which a cover? How to mass the troops? Where should the reserves be sent?

I figured that it would take about one minute for the first confusion to have reached its peak. After this the smoke would begin to thin and the dead bodies would be discovered to be robots and the word would get out. We wanted to get out before this word did. Once the bombs had been thrown Taze and her troops would be hurrying to get into position—and one minute was not very much time to reach the back of the factory from the upper floors. Yet most of them were there before me with Taze checking them off as they ran up.

"That's the lot," she said, making a final tick on her list.

"With five seconds to go." I looked at my watch and raised my hand.

"*Now!* Angelina stand ready with the grenades."

The small fire exit was unlocked and dragged open and Angelina hurled her smoke grenades out to intensify the gloom before us. There was no more talking, and in the sudden silence the shooting and shouting could clearly be heard. I was sure that I could detect an occasional *Thank you, sir* among the voices. Fayda led the way and we followed in line, hands on the shoulders of the preceding marchers. I was in the middle of the line and Angelina just before me, so I held to her. This placement was accidental, I am sure, since she wouldn't have cared if I clutched one of the half-naked Burada cuties.

It was a little disconcerting moving helplessly like this through the darkness, particularly when the occasional missile whined by. By accident, I hoped. This street was narrow and blocked at both ends by Cliaand troops. If they knew what was happening they could sweep the street with a deadly crossfire. But hopefully they were involved with the robutlers for the moment. All we had to do was quietly cross the 20 meters or so of open road, to the apartment dwelling on the other side. If we reached this unnoticed we had a good chance of going through it to the mixed business and residential plaza on the other side. From here we would break up and scatter through the warren of streets and walkways and tunnels, hopefully merging into the civilian population and disappearing before our absence was noticed. Hopefully.

I was counting my steps so knew I had almost reached the

building—which meant half of our number were safe—when the voice called out nearby.

"Is that you, Zobno? What did the sergeant say about robots? It sounded like robots?"

The line stopped, instantly, in breath-holding silence. We were so close. The voice was male and it spoke Cliaandian.

"Robots? What robots?" I asked as I pulled the hand from my shoulder and placed it on Angelina's shoulder before me. "*Move*," I whispered in her ear. Then left the line and stamped heavily towards him in my new boots.

"I'm sure he said robots," the voice complained. Behind me I was aware of the faint stir as the line started forward again. I stamped and coughed and moved closer to the unseen speaker. My hands before me ready for a quick clench and crush as soon as he spoke again.

All of which would have worked fine, and have given me a little sadistic pleasure, if the evening breeze had not sent eddies around the corners of the building. The wind moved coolly on my face and a rift opened in the smoke. I was looking at a Cliaand trooper, helmed and armed with his gaussrifle at the ready, a shocked expression stamped on his face. With good reason. Instead of gazing upon a fellow trooper he saw an unknown individual with snapping fingers, red eyes and unshaven jaw, dressed in totally transparent dungarees and ladies' boots, with bundles and packs slung on his shoulders. Gape was about all he could do.

This paralysis lasted just long enough for me to reach him. I grabbed him by the throat so he couldn't shout a warning, and by the gun so he couldn't shoot me. We danced around like this for a bit and the smoke closed over us again. My opponent wasn't shouting or shooting—but neither was he submitting. He was burly and well muscled and holding his own. Luckily he wasn't too bright and kept both his hands on the gun and tried to get it away from me. Just about the time he realized he could hold it with one hand and slug me with the other I got a foot behind his heel and went down on top of him. Before he hit the ground he managed to get two quick punches into my midriff which did me no good. Then we landed and I knocked all the air out of him. This freed my throat hand and, before he could suck in enough breath to shout with, I rendered him unconscious.

I sat on him, waiting for my head to stop spinning and for the knot of pain in my gut to ease, when another voice sounded close by.

"What's that noise? Who is it?"

I breathed in a deep shuddering breath, let a bit of it out and worked for control of my voice.

"It's me." Always a good answer. "I tripped and fell down. I hurt a finger . . ."

"Then you'll get a medal for it. Now shut up."

I shut up, took the gaussrifle from my limp companion and stood up—and realized that I was completely lost in the smoky darkness.

Not a pleasant sensation at all. The smoke was thinning and I was alone with no sense of direction. If I walked in the wrong direction it would be suicide.

Panic! Or rather a moment of panic. I always allow myself at least a brief panic in any tight situation. This flushes out the bloodstream, starts the heart pumping faster, releases a jolt of adrenalin and provides other nice things for an emergency. But only a little panic, time was pressing. And after the basic bestial emotion drained away, lips dropped back over fangs and hair on neck down again and all that, I put the old logic center to work.

ITEM: I was not alone. The silent line of escapees may have marched into the building and safety, but my Angelina would not desert me. I knew, as clearly as if I could see her, that she was outside that door to survival and waiting for me.

ITEM: She had her sense of direction, I didn't. Therefore she would have to come to me.

"This finger is killing me, Sarge," I whined, then whistled in supposed agony. One short whistle and one long one. The letter *a* for Angelina in the code that I knew she knew well. That I needed help I knew she would figure out for herself.

"Stop that whistling and noise," the other voice growled back, ending in a note of suspicion. "Say, who are you?"

I groped through my memory for the name I had heard a few moments earlier.

"It's me, Sarge. Zobno. This finger . . ."

"That's not Zobno!" a second voice called out. "I'm Zobno . . ."

"No, *I* am," I shouted. "Who's that said that?"

"Both of you come here—*now!*" the sergeant ordered. "I'm going to start shooting in five seconds."

The real Zobno stumbled through the smoke and I didn't dare say a thing or move. And I could already feel the slugs tearing through me—when something plucked at my sleeve and I jumped.

"Angelina?" I whispered, and received a silent answer when she threw her arms about me. I reached for her but she wasn't waiting;

taking my hand she pulled me after her. There were voices behind us in the smoke then the sudden whine of a gaussrifle and shouts of command.

I stumbled over an invisible step and waiting hands pulled me through the doorway.

17

"SEARCH PARTY . . . SEARCH PARTY . . ."

The words came dimly through the throaty growls of the attacking teddy bears. I could have fought them off, even though the candy canes I was using for swords kept breaking on me. But even without a candy cane give a teddy a quick kick in the gut and over he goes, no staying power. The teddies I could have handled alone if they hadn't got those damn wooden soldiers on their side. They would make a good bonfire and that is just what I had in mind, fumbling for matches, when one of them got me in the arm with the bayonet on his toy rifle. It stung and I blinked and opened my eyes to look up at the whiskery face of Doctor Mutfak who was staring back at me.

"An alarm, that was, very badly timed indeed I must say. I have given you an injection to cancel the hypnotic drug." He held up the hypodermic and I rubbed my arm where it had stung me. "Very badly timed."

"I didn't arrange it that way," I mumbled, still only half awake and wishing I could have finished off the teddy bears.

"The treatment is going well and it will be time consuming to start over again. I have regressed you to your childhood and— my!—you have had an interesting, not to say repellent childhood! You must give me permission to write up this case. The symbol of the teddy bear, normally one of warmth and comfort, has been transmogrified by your obnoxious subconscious into . . ."

"Later, doctor, if you please," Angelina said, coming to my rescue. A picture of golden charm, she had been sunning herself on the balcony and the wisps of fabric she wore for this operation had about the same surface area as a butterfly's wing.

I sat up and shook my head, still foggy with the traces of the drug. The room was colorful and luxurious, with one entire wall opening onto the balcony, with the blue sky and bluer ocean beyond, perched high on top of the Ringa Baligi Hotel. This hotel, supposed to be the best one on Burada and I could well believe it, was in the center of a lagoon and approachable only by water or air. This gave us advance warning of any unwanted visitors—and the warning had just been given. The drill was carefully worked out. I had worn swim trunks during the brain-bending session, just in case of an emergency like this one, so I took Angelina's hand and we trotted to the private elevator. As we got into it the sound of engines on the landing platform above was loud and clear. We held the grips as the high-speed elevator dropped out from under us.

"Do you feel up to this?" Angelina asked.

"Just a little foggy, but that will go away. Do you think this brain-drainer is any good?"

"He's supposed to be the best on the planet. He'll straighten out the kinks Kraj put in if anyone can."

"He could work a bit faster. Three days now and we're still in my childhood."

"You must have been a *terrible* little boy. Some of the things I've heard . . ."

Before I could think of a snappy comeback the elevator whoosed to a stop and we emerged at water level. Steps led down into the ocean from an enclosed diving room. The attendant was waiting with our scuba gear ready and we buckled it on and dove in. Straight to the bottom and out among the coral reefs. Even if they came looking they would never find us here. I snapped on the sonar communicator and called in.

"Not much of a search," the operator told me. "I'll let you know when they reach the lower level."

Angelina and I dove deep. Rainbow-hued fish burst out and around us, green plants bowed to our passing. The water was clear and warm and was rapidly restoring my thoughts and good spirits. We swam to a grotto, completely surrounded by coral, that we had found on an earlier visit during an alert, and settled down on the golden sand. I put my arm around Angelina and she snuggled up to me, both for the fun of it and to get our masks touching so we could talk.

"Anything new come in on Kraj and his boys while the doc was slogging through my gray matter?"

"They've been located, but that's all. Now that the first stage of invasion is over the Cliaand forces seem to be settling down for the occupation. They've taken over this immense office building, the Octagon it's called probably because it has eight sides, and have cleared everyone out. They seem to have moved most of their administrative operations there—and one of Kraj's gray men was seen coming out of the building. This must be where they are holed up.''

"I wonder why they left the last building?"

"Afraid of you and your relentless revenge, no doubt."

I snorted. Hard to do in a face mask. "You're only saying that, but by Belial there is more than an element of truth in it. The Cliaand operation in general has to be knocked out, but those gray men need special attention. But first we have to grab one of them. I'll have to get inside the building."

"You'll do nothing of the sort." She pinched the skin over my ribs and I tried to slap her hand away but you can't do this under water. I settled for a pinch myself, and she was surely far more pinchable than I, and we played around like this for awhile until I remembered why she had distracted me and returned ruthlessly to the interrupted conversation.

"Why can't I try to get into the building? I'll be disguised, I speak Cliaandian, I know the ropes . . ."

"And they know yours. They'll have cameras on every entrance feeding data to the computers. Which will know your height, your build, your weight, manner of walk, retinal pattern, the works. You can't disguise everything and you know it. They'll have you in the bag the instant you walk into the place."

"You're just saying that because it is true," I muttered. "So I suppose you have a better plan?"

"I do. I speak Cliaandian and they have no records on me at all. And I'm an experienced field operator, the only one on this planet besides you."

"No!"

"Why the instant no?" She scowled at me and the next pinch hurt. "You're my husband, not my owner—remember? I'm as good at this business as you are, maybe better, and there is a job that needs doing. Let's have none of your male superiority and possessiveness."

She was right of course, but I couldn't let her know it.

"I was only worried about your safety."

She melted at this, even the smartest woman is a sucker for the loving attention, and rubbed against me. I felt like the heel I was.

"You do love me, Jim, in your own horrible way. But I'll be all right, you'll see. There are some women among the Cliaandian supporting echelons—I don't see how they can wear those ugly uniforms—and the girls and I will grab onto one. With her uniform and identification I'll get into the building, find Kraj—"

"You won't do anything foolish?"

"Of course not. This is too important to bungle by trying it alone.
I told you I wanted to give him my *personal* attention at my leisure.
This will be a scouting trip only. I'll locate the gray men, map the
layout and take a look at the detection devices—and leave at once."

"Great." I was getting enthusiastic now and trying to put my
fears for her safety aside. "That is all we will need to mount a quick
kidnapping. Hit them fast and hard, walk right in and grab Kraj and
right out again. Foolproof."

The sonar communicator buzzed and I flicked it on.

"The search party has gone. You may return."

We swam back slowly, hand in hand, enjoying the moment.
Doctor Mutfak was waiting when we climbed out of the water.

"Good, we pick up where we left off." There was no warmth at
all in his smile. "The teddy bears, we must probe the symbolism
here so we can move on to more recent things."

He tapped his foot impatiently while Angelina and I clutched in a
nice wet embrace and kissed with abandon. Wearing the masks had
been quite frustrating. Then back to the room. I let the doctor put me
under at once since I didn't want Angelina to catch my jumpiness
before she left. The mission would be difficult enough without my
giving her things to worry about. She waved and went to dress and I
waved back and Mutfak stuck a needle in my arm. No romance in
his soul.

We must have moved along nicely because when I awoke next the
teddy bears had long since vanished and the last dream I remembered had something to do with exploding spaceships and solar
flares. Dr. Mutfak was packing up his instruments and the last
glimmer of daylight was fading in the night sky outside.

"Very good," he said. "Coming along nicely."

"Have you uncovered any traces of Kraj's tampering yet?"

"Traces!" His nostrils flared and he puffed out his cheek. "They
are like heavy boot marks all through your cortex! Butchers, those
people, simply butchers! Lucky in a way because their traces are so
easy to find. Memory blocks all over, areas of amnesia with connec-
tions to patterns of false memory. These memories are the only
thing of any clinical value and I must find out what techniques they
use. They were placed there very quickly, you told me that, yet they
are incredibly complete, all senses involved, and detailed as well."

"I'll vouch for that."

"I think you will have found them impossible to tell from real
memories, that is the strength of their technique. I have removed

some major ones that seemed to be disturbing you and in later sessions I will take care of the others. Now—look at your wrists and tell me about the red lines you see there.''

''They look just like red lines,'' I said. Then I remembered waking up in the cell and, for some reason believing that my hands had been cut off. I don't know why. They were just red lines.

''A false memory?'' I asked.

''Yes, and an outstandingly repulsive one. I'll tell you about it at the next session. But right now you need rest.''

''A fine idea, after I get something to eat . . .''

The door flew open and Taze ran in and, as she passed, I had a quick glimpse of the horrified expression on her face. Sudden fear hit me in the stomach and I sat, watching her, saying nothing while she turned on the TV. The Cliaandians had a propaganda station operating now, though no one bothered to watch it.

The screen lit up and I found myself looking at Kraj. He almost smiled as he spoke.

''It's a tape, it keeps repeating,'' Taze said.

''. . . that we want him to know. Someone out there must know the man known as James diGriz. Contact him. Tell him to listen to this broadcast. This message is for you, diGriz. We want you back here. I have Angelina here. She is unharmed—as *yet*—and will remain that way until dawn. I suggest you contact me and see me.

''Welcome home, Jim.''

18

I HAD A number of moments of numb shock after this, during which period I wished to be alone. Taze was understanding enough to leave when I pointed at the exit, but the doctor tried to start a conversation which I terminated by clutching his neck and the seat of his trousers and heaving through the door which she obligingly held open. Then I kicked in the TV set, an act of wanton destruction that helped a bit, before I poured a stiff cogitating drink. With this in hand I dropped into the chair, looked out unseeingly at the star spread sky, and worked out a plan. This was not going to be simple—and dawn was not that far away.

The thought that kept nibbling at the edge of my awareness was finally faced. I was going to have to surrender and get a collar back on—there was no way of avoiding that. My memories of what that was like were not very nice, in fact my brain sort of twitched a bit inside the bone case at the thought. There had been entirely too much traffic through my gray matter of late and I was not looking forward to any more. Yet it was unavoidable. The collar and torture box had to be part of any plan, and they had to be neutralized. Not a very easy thing to accomplish. I mumbled over all the possibilities, and when the attack plan was blocked out I sent for Taze and told her what I was going to do.

"You can't," she said, and I swear those large lovely eyes were filled with tears, "turn yourself over to those fiends. To save a woman. If only the *men* on this planet were like you. Impossible to believe . . ."

I resisted the impulse to enjoy a little warm female solace and turned to snapping open some of the weapon containers. At the sight of the grenades Miss Taze retreated and Sergeant Taze looked on with interest.

"This will be a two part operation," I told her. "I'll take care of the first part myself, which will be the penetration of the building and freeing Angelina. I hope to grab a gray man as well, but if that slows me down we'll save that part of the job for another time. The second part of the operation will be getting out of the Octagon, and for that I am going to need your help. I'll need plans of the building, I want to talk to someone who knows his way around it well, someone on the custodial staff if possible, so I can find an area of vulnerability. Can you do this now?''

''At once,'' she called back over her shoulder as she left. A reliable girl our Taze. I dug into the equipment containers.

Dawn was only two hours away before we were ready to move. I had completed my part of the operation, but setting up the escape afterwards wasn't that simple. The Octagon was very much like a fortress in the eyes of the small forces we could muster quickly. And we were hampered by our lack of any aircraft or heavy equipment. There seemed no way out by air or on the ground. It was one of the maintenance staff, finally located and dragged in shivering, who found the exit and pointed it out with a trembling finger on the blueprints.

''Cable tunnel, sir and mam, goes under the street and under the walls and comes up in sub-basement 17. Big tunnel for wires and telephone and that kind of thing.''

''It's sure to be bugged,'' I said. ''But if we plan this right it won't matter. Take notes, ladies, because I don't want to repeat myself. This is how the operation is going to work.''

By the time everything had been taken care of it was less than twenty minutes to dawn and I was in a cold sweat. The first units were moving into position when I put the viewphone call in to Kraj. We were connected at once and I talked before he could say anything.

''I want to see Angelina instantly, and talk to her. I have to be absolutely sure she has not been harmed.''

He didn't argue, he had been expecting this. She came into focus and I saw that hated collar with its cable leading up out of the picture.

''Are you all right?''

''As fine as I could possibly be while in the same room with this creature,'' she said calmly.

''They've done nothing to you?''

''Nothing as yet, other than to clap this collar around my neck and hook the thing up to the ceiling so I wouldn't run away. But you can just imagine the threats this repulsive man has made. I don't think I could live for a moment with a mind like his . . .''

She stiffened then and her eyes rolled up out of sight although her lids didn't close. Kraj had given her a shot of the nerve torture. I knew at that moment that he would never live if I could get my hands on him. His face reappeared on the screen and it took an effort I did not think myself capable of to stare at him calmly and say nothing.

"You'll come to me now, diGriz, and surrender. You only have a few minutes left. You know what will happen to your wife if you don't. If you surrender she will be released at once."

"What proof do I have that you will keep your word?"

"None whatsoever. But you don't have a choice, do you?"

"I'll be there," I said as calmly as I could manage and turned the phone off—but not before I heard Angelina's shouted *no* in the background.

"Are those clothes dry yet?" I asked, tearing off my shirt and kicking out of my boots at the same time.

"Just about," Taze said. She and another girl were holding hot air blowers to a Cliaand uniform that I thought was just right for this occasion. It had been soaked in a chemical bath and was now being force dried.

"Almost is good enough, we can't wait any longer."

There were some damp patches, but nothing that mattered. We left, and the powerboat was waiting at the hotel dock below, motor rumbling. So far so good. And the car was there on shore with Dr. Mutfak in the back, black bag on his knees, muttering to himself.

"I don't like it," he said. "It is really a violation of my medical code of ethics."

"War is a violation of any code of ethics or morality, a monstrosity against which any weapons must be used. Do what you have been asked."

"I'll do it, that goes without saying, but a man is allowed to comment upon the ethics involved."

"Comment. But fill the needle at the same time."

We parked in a side street, in the darkness, with the Octagon just around the corner.

"Catalyst," I said, "and don't spill any. Under my arms where the dampness won't be noticed."

I raised both arms and felt the warmth of the liquid from the insulated container, then quickly lowered my arms to trap the wet fabric between my upper arms and my sides. Then I climbed out of the car and put my hand back in through the window. The needle bit into my flesh and that was that. As I started around the corner I heard the car pull away.

The Octagon loomed up like a mountain before me, the sky beginning to lighten behind it. We had cut this very close. There was an entrance ahead, the one I had been directed to, and two of the gray men were waiting. Both wore gausspistols which were still in the holsters. They were very sure of themselves. I walked up to them silently and one of them clamped a come-along cuff on my wrist and led me in through the doors and past the silent guards. I stumbled going up the stairs and after that looked down carefully to see where I put my feet. The injection was beginning to take effect. There was nothing I wanted to say and my captors, they in their usual fashion, had nothing to say to me. They prodded me in the direction they wanted me to go and pushed me through the doorway of the room they wanted me to enter. Once inside they covered me with their guns while the wrist-cuff was unlocked.

"Clothes off," one of them ordered.

It was an effort not to smile. There was the fluoroscope off to one side and the other test equipment. These characters were running true to type, following the same routine they had used when I had first been captured. Didn't they realize that routine was a trap and a losing game? No they did not. I fumbled off my clothes and let them work their will upon me.

They found nothing of course, since there was nothing there to find. Or rather there was one thing that I was sure they would not find. And they didn't. They slowly plodded through their routine examinations and I began to wish they would finish and be done. My head was getting a little foggy from the drug and I felt as though I were wrapped in cotton wool. The injection must be reaching the peak of its effectiveness and would be tapering off soon. What I had to do must be done when the drug was at the height of its power—or close to it—or all the preparations would be useless.

"Put these on," a wooden faced captor said and threw me the familiar transparent dungarees. I bent to pick them up and to cover the smile that I could no longer resist. Done it! They did not seem impatient when I fumbled with the closings on the clothes. I had to watch my fingers carefully to be sure they did their job. When the collar locked around my neck I almost heaved a sigh of relief. We were getting close, and the timing was just about perfect. As one of the guards took the torture box and led me out I lowered my head so I could see where I put my feet so I would not stumble. If this generated an illusion of defeat all the better. We went down a wide corridor and past a staircase, and I made a mental note of its location, even counting the paces after it to get some estimate of its distance from our destination.

Which was Kraj's lair. He was waiting behind his desk, as

patiently and as emotionlessly as a spider in its web. Angelina sat before him, her torture box hooked to the ceiling.

"Are you all right?" I asked as I came through the door.

"Of course. Nothing has happened. You shouldn't have come."

As soon as I had this reassurance I turned my attention to Kraj, aware at the same time of the guard closing the door behind us.

"You'll release her now, won't you?" I asked.

"Naturally not. There would be no advantage in that." His expression never changed while he spoke.

"I didn't think you would. Is there any reason why you shouldn't tell me how you caught her?"

"Your memory contained an exact description of your wife. When we discovered that two women had aided your escape we naturally assumed that one might have been this Angelina. The computer identified her as soon as she entered the building."

"We were foolish to take the risk," I said, apparently turning to face her, but looking at the guard instead. He was about to hook my torture box to another hook in the ceiling—and if he did we were trapped.

All I could do was make a dive for him.

"Stop him!" Kraj shouted and the guard looked at me and pressed a quick pattern on the red keys on the box.

I can't pretend that it felt nice. Enough pain leaked through to tear at my stomach with nausea and to knot my muscles. I stumbled and fell at the man's feet, not quite reaching him. The drug I had taken blocked most of the pain, but not all of it. There still had to be nerve pathways open for motor control. My eyes filled with tears and I could not wipe them so my vision blurred and swam. There was a shoe before me and that was no good, and a uniform leg, bad as well.

And then the guard's hand as he bent over to take hold of me. I lashed out with my extended middle finger and scratched the skin on the back of his hand.

He shivered just a bit and kept on bending, almost in slow motion, until he crumpled on the floor next to me, dropping the control box. It was just close enough to reach out and tap the *off* button.

The pain was over, instantly. And Kraj was behind my back. I scrambled and rolled, fighting my knotted muscles, climbing to my feet.

In the few moments since I had attacked the guard the situation had changed drastically. Angelina lay across Kraj's desk, holding to her collar, writhing in pain. Kraj was on his knees behind the desk reaching for his gun. I dived for him just as he raised it. I was not going to make it, I was too late, he was going to fire and that was that.

But at precisely that moment the distant explosion went off and the floor heaved, dust and bits of plastic shook down from the ceiling and the lights flickered. Kraj had not been expecting this—and I had—and his attention wavered for that vital instant as I slithered across the desk towards him and my fingernail nicked his skin.

He fired, but the slug plowed into the far wall because he was falling, unconscious even as he pulled the trigger.

Angelina must have attacked him as soon as I had dived for the guard. By hanging from the cable she had brought her feet up high enough to get in the one good kick that had sent Kraj over. He had retaliated by going to the radio control before his gun—and this little bit of excess sadism had given me the chance to reach him. But Angelina was paying for this now.

I could not look at her twisting body as I climbed up on the desk beside her. There were a number of controls before Kraj's chair but I was not going to take the time to try to figure them out. Instead I unhooked the box and turned it off. Angelina opened her eyes and lay still, just staring at me as I went through the drawers in the desk.

"Darling, you are a genius," she said weakly. I found a key and bent to unlock her collar. "How did you do it?"

"I out-thought them, that's all. They couldn't find any weapons in my clothing because the clothing itself was the weapon. The fabric was soaked in tanturaline which transformed it into a powerful explosive. I put the liquid catalyst on the cloth under my arms where my body heat would keep it from reacting. As long as I was in the uniform nothing happened, but as soon as they made me strip it off—as I was sure they would—the catalyst began to cool and when it reached the critical temperature . . ."

"Boom the whole thing exploded. My genius." She reached up and pulled me to her as the collar clicked open, and bestowed a warm and passionate kiss that I returned for a bit until I remembered where we were and disentangled gently. She sat up shakily and tried the key in my collar.

"And I suppose you have some wonderfully ingenious explanation of how you killed these fiends?"

"Not dead yet, just unconscious. I filed one fingernail to a point sharp enough to scratch skin, then painted it with callanite.''

"Of course! Invisible to the eye and it would take a spectometric test to find the tiny trace. But more than enough to render the scratchee instantly unconscious. What next?''

"A phone call to get the rest of the operation going in case that explosion wasn't heard outside the building. But they have listening devices . . .''

– Before I could finish the sentence the lights went out. Since the room had no windows we were in complete darkness and I was lost, falling, out of contact with reality.

"Angelina!'' I called out, aware of the hoarseness of my voice. "I am juiced to the eyeballs with narco drugs that cut off almost all pain sensation, which is why I could polish off the guard even though he was jazzing me with his shock box. But this also means I can't feel anything at all—I'm completely numb. All I can do is hear in the darkness. You'll have to help.''

"What should I do?''

"Find Kraj and drag him over to me. I'm going to see if we can't get him out with us.''

She pulled him out from behind the desk, none too gently from the sounds I heard, and helped me get him up on my shoulders.

"Now lead us out of here. You'll have to guide me because I have no way at all of moving around in this darkness. Across to the other side of the hall, then left for about 45 meters until you come to the stairs. Then down, all the way.''

Angelina took my hand and we were off. I slammed into a couple of things but that wasn't her fault since I still had no sense of touch. It was easier and faster in the hall where she could follow the wall with one hand. There were voices shouting in the distance as well as one or two satisfying screams. My exploding wardrobe was providing plenty of distraction, coupled with the electrical failure. Then, just as I was congratulating myself on how well things were going, the lights flickered and came back on dimly.

We stopped, frozen, blinking in the sudden illumination and feeling as though we were in the middle of a spotlit stage. There must have been at least a dozen people in sight.

But they were all ignoring us, involved in their own troubles, barely aware of each other. A uniformed fat official actually ran by us, eyes wide with fear after the explosion and the darkness, not even seeing us.

"The stairway, quick,'' I said and lumbered forward as fast as I could with Kraj bounding on my shoulders.

Of course it was too good to last. The emergency lights flickered and dimmed redly and seemed about to expire at any minute. A soldier coming towards us had enough time to look and to think about what he was seeing. It finally dawned on him that something was wrong and he raised his gaussrifle and shouted to us to stop.

Angelina had Kraj's pistol and she fired just once. The soldier folded and we were at the stairs—when the lights went out again and stayed out.

The stairs were difficult to maneuver, though some sensation was coming back and I could feel a certain amount. But I dropped Kraj once, we both laughed a little at this and rolled him down an extra step or two for good measure, and a moment later I fell against Angelina and almost toppled us both headlong. After this we went more carefully and one flight down someone spoke.

"We've been waiting to take you out. Just stand still."

It was a girl's voice, and not speaking Cliaandian, or Angelina would have blown the whole stairwell up. We waited and I felt someone's hands touching my head, putting on a pair of heavy glasses. Then I could see again, with everything in harsh contrast. They were infrared goggles and the girl who was waiting for us had a hand projector. We went down almost at a run after that, while she called on her com-radio. Taze was waiting at the foot of the stairs.

"We sent people up all the staircases to try and contact you. They are coming back now. This way."

They took Kraj from me. I couldn't feel any pain or fatigue, but I was sure from the way my muscles were vibrating that I would ache all over when the drug wore off. We went at a fast trot to the open mouth of the service tunnel.

"In," Taze ordered. "There are cars waiting at the other end."

19

WHENEVER I MOVED I GROANED. A little more hollowly and theatrically than was really called for by my condition, but it made Angelina feel wanted and took her mind off her troubles. She clucked about like a mother hen, plumping the pillows under my head, pouring me soothing drinks, peeling sweet fruits and cutting them into tiny pieces for me to nibble on. I hoped that these wifely ministrations would keep her from remembering the torture box of the day before, and if she were thinking about this she never mentioned it. The air that moved in through the open windows was warm and the sky its usual brilliant blue.

"Were there any casualties?" I said. "I meant to ask when I woke up but my head is still swimming in slow circles."

"None to speak of. Some burns and scrapes and a few superficial wounds among the rear guard. Apparently everything went off just as you had planned. As soon as the explosion was heard they shorted all the phone and power lines that led to the Octagon and made a fearful mess of the wiring. Then the girls came through the tunnel and knocked out the emergency generator. You know the rest since you were obliging enough not to keel over until we reached the cars."

"I would have been happy to do it earlier but I did not relish the thought of being dragged through the pipes by Taze's amazons. They still don't seem to think much of men. Maybe they'll make me an honorary girl."

"Let's see that is all they make you. Dr. Mutfak phoned a little while ago to say that he had Kraj almost to the point where we could talk to him."

"Then let's go. This is a conversation I have been looking forward to for a long time."

When I got out of the bed my muscles creaked and snapped and I felt a thousand years old. I was wearing swimming attire, as was Angelina; informality was the order of the day at the luxurious Ringa Baligi. This also enabled us to do our dive for life if any troops came nosing around. Which made me think.

"What happens if any interfering Cliaandians come this way? I assume plans have been made to hide Kraj."

"Hide is the correct word. Since he is unconscious he can be stowed in the back of one of the refrigerators. A good idea, particularly if they forget and leave him there."

"Vengeance later, information now. I wonder what fascinating facts the good doctor has uncovered about our alien?"

"He's not an alien," Dr. Mutfak insisted. While I slept he had been working in the small but complete laboratory that was part of the mini-hospital in the hotel. "I will stake my reputation on it."

"The only reputation that you have that I know of is as a brainsqueezer," I said. "Can you be sure . . ."

"I will not be insulted by foreigners!" The doctor shouted, drawing himself up in anger so the top of his head almost reached my shoulder. "Insults from females I am used to, but from off-worlders I will not bear. Even on the nameless planet where you were spawned it must be known that the basis of all medical training is a sound grounding in biology and physiology. It so happens that cytology is a bit of a hobby of mine—I could show you cells that would have you crying aloud with wonder—so I know what I am about. This man's cells are human, so he is human. A viable homo sapiens."

"But the differences, so alien, his low body temperature, the lack of emotions, all that."

"All well within the realm of human variation. Mankind is quite adaptable, and generations of survival in various environments produce suitable adaptations. There are many more exotic instances cited in the literature than are represented by this individual."

"Then he couldn't be a robot either?" Angelina asked with wide-eyed innocence, skittering away when I reached to grab her. My theories didn't seem to be holding up too well.

"When can we talk to him?" I asked.

"Soon, soon."

"Is it permitted to ask what you have done to him that will make him amenable to questioning?"

"A good question." Mutfak fingered his silvery beard and concentrated on interpreting the mysteries of medicine for the layman.

"Since this is the man who appears to be responsible for the major and harmful tampering with your brain I did not feel what might be called the usual moral responsibility of doctor to patient, particularly when the patient has helped arrange the ruthless invasion of my planet as well."

"Good for you, Doc."

"Therefore I have been quite single-minded and have circumvented his normal thought processes for our benefit and not for his. I did not do this easily, and feel it is just as much a moral crime as what was done to you, but I will take the responsibilities of the act. The fact that he was unconscious when brought here was a help. I have planted false memories and caused regression in areas of attitude and emotions, put in memory blocks and in general have done some terrible things for which I will carry shame until the day I die."

Dr. Mutfak looked as though he might cry at any moment and I patted him on the shoulder.

"You're a front line soldier, Doctor, going into battle. Doing what you have to do to win. We all respect you for it."

"Well I don't, but I shall worry about that later." He shook himself and was the man of science again. "In a few minutes I shall bring the patient up from the deep trance. He will appear to be awake but his conscious mind will have little or no awareness of what is happening. His emotional attitudes will be those of a child of about age two who wants to help. Remember that. Do not force questions or act hostile. He wants to aid you in every way he can, but many times won't have access to the information easily. Be kind and rephrase the question. Don't push too hard. Are you ready?"

"I guess so." Though I found it hard to think of Kraj as a cooperative kiddy.

Angelina and I trooped along behind the doctor, into the dimly lit hospital room. A male nurse who had been sitting by the bed stood up when we came in. Mutfak arranged the lighting so most of it fell on Kraj while we sat in half darkness, then gave the man an injection.

"This should work quite fast," he said.

Kraj's eyes were closed, his face slack and unmoving. White bandages wrapped his skull and a handful of wires slipped out from under them to the machines beside the bed.

"Wake up, Kraj, wake up," the doctor said.

Kraj's face stirred, his cheek twitched and his eyes slowly opened. His expression was one of calm serenity and there was the trace of a shy smile on his lips.

"What is your name?"

"Kraj." He spoke softly in a hoarse voice that reminded me of a young boy's. There were no traces of resistance.

"Where do you come from?"

He frowned, blinking at me, and stammered some meaningless sounds. Angelina leaned forward and patted his hand and spoke in a friendly tone.

"You must be calm, don't rush. You have come here from Cliaand, haven't you?"

"That's right." He nodded and smiled.

"Now think back, you have a good memory. Were you born on Cliaand?"

"I—I don't think so. I have been there a long time, but I wasn't born there. I was born at home."

"Home is another world, a different planet?"

"That's right."

"Could you tell me what it is like at home."

"Cold."

When he said it his voice was as chill as the word, more like the Kraj we knew, and his face worked constantly, expressions echoing his words.

"Always cold. Nothing green, nothing grows, the cold doesn't stop. You have to like cold and I never did though I can live with it. There are warm worlds and many of us go to them. But there are not many of us. We don't see each other very much, I don't think we like each other and why should we? There is nothing to like about snow and ice and cold. We fish, that is all, nothing lives on the snow. All the life is in the sea. I put my arm in once but I could not live in the water. They do and we eat them. There are warmer worlds."

"Like Cliaand?" I asked, quietly as Angelina had done. He smiled.

"Like Cliaand. Warm all the time, hot too, too hot, but I don't mind that. Strange to see living things on the land other than people. There is a lot of green."

"What is the name of home, of the cold world?" I whispered.

"The name . . . the name . . . ."

The transformation was immediate. Kraj began to writhe on the bed, his face twisting and working, his eyes wide and staring. Dr. Mutfak was shouting at him to forget the question, to lie still, while he tried to get a hypodermic needle into his thrashing arm. But it was too late. The reaction I had triggered went on and, just for an instant, I swear there was the light of intelligence and hatred in his eyes as the conscious Kraj became aware of what was happening.

But only for that moment. An instant later his back arched in a silent spasm and he collapsed, still and unmoving.

"Dead," Dr. Mutfak pronounced, looking at his telltale instruments."

"That was useful," Angelina said, walking to the window and throwing open the curtains. "Time for a swim if you feel up to it, darling. Then we'll have to think of a way to get another gray man for Dr. Mutfak. Now that we know the area to avoid we can make him last longer while he is questioned."

The doctor recoiled. "I couldn't, not again. We killed him, I killed him. There was an implanted order, an irresistible order, to die rather than reveal where this planet is. It can be done, the death wish, I have seen it now. Never again."

"We have been raised differently, doctor," Angelina said, calmly and without passion. "I would shoot a creature like Kraj in battle and I feel no differently about his dying in this manner. You know what he is and what he has done."

I said nothing because I agreed with them both. Angelina who saw the galaxy as a jungle, as survival a matter of eating or being eaten. And the doctor, a humanitarian who had been raised in a matriarchy, stable and unchanging, peaceful and at peace. They were both right. An interesting animal is man.

"Take a rest, Doc," I said. "Take one of your own pills. You have been up for a day and a night and that can't be doing you any good. We'll see you when you wake up, but have a good rest first."

I took Angelina's arm and guided her out, away from the sad little man who was staring, unseeing, at the floor.

"You don't feel sorry for that Kraj creature?" Angelina asked, giving me her number two frown which means something like I'm not looking for trouble, but if you are you are certainly going to get it.

"Me? Not much chance, love. Kraj is the man who unreeled the barbed wire in my brain awhile back and tried to do the same to you. I'm only sorry we couldn't get more from him before he left us."

"The next one will tell more. At least we know now that your idea was right. They may not be aliens, but they certainly aren't natives of Cliaand. If we can root them out of there we might be able to stop the entire invasion thing."

"Easier visualized than accomplished. Let's have that swim and brood about it over a drink when we come out."

The water loosened up my muscles and made me profoundly aware of a great hunger and thirst. I called in on my sonar communicator so that a small steak and a bottle of beer were waiting at the water's edge when we emerged. These barely brushed the fringes of my appetite yet gave me the strength to make it back to our room for a more elaborate meal.

And elaborate it was, seven courses beginning with a fiery Burada soup, going on to fish and meat and other delicacies too numerous to mention. Angelina ate a bit then sipped at her wine while I finished most of the food in sight. Finally replete I ordered the soiled dishes away and settled back with a sigh.

"I have been thinking," I said.

"You could have fooled me. I thought you were eating like a pig with both trotters in the trough."

"Just save the bucolic humor. A hard night's work deserves a good day's food. Cliaand, that's our problem. Or rather the gray men who have her war economy so firmly under control. I'll bet if we could get rid of them the original Cliaandians would not have this same burning interest in interstellar conquest."

"Simple enough. A program of planned assassination. There can't be too many of them, Kraj said as much. Polish them off. I'll be glad to take on the assignment."

"Oh no you won't. No wife of mine hires out as a contract gun. It is not that simple—physically or morally. The gray men can guard themselves well. And that the ends justify the means is a bankrupt statement. You saw what happened to Dr. Mutfak when he worked for a good end but used means that ran counter to his moral beliefs. You and I are of tougher fabric, my love, but we would still be affected if we went in for mass slaughter . . ."

She went white and I was sorry I had said it. I took her hand.

"I didn't mean it that way. I wasn't talking about the past."

"I know, but it still stirred up some unwholesome memories. Let's forget assassination. What else can be done?"

"A number of things, I am sure, if we can only ask just the right questions. There must be a way to break apart the constantly expanding Cliaand empire."

Angelina touched the wine glass to her lips and a highly attractive concentration line appeared between her eyes.

"What about starting counter-revolutions or rebellions on all the conquered worlds?" she said. "If we kept the Cliaandians busy fighting on the presently conquered planets they couldn't very well go seeking for new territory."

"You're nibbling close to the idea there, but it's not quite right yet. We can't expect much from the resistance movements on these different worlds if the example of Burada is at all relevant. You heard what Taze said, the fighting is dying down because of the massive reaction by the Cliaand forces. If one of them is killed in a raid they slaughter twenty Buradans in return. These people, after generations of peace, are not mentally equipped to fight a ruthless guerrilla war. I even doubt if the Cliaandians would react so viciously if they weren't forced on by the gray men who organized and order everything. The soldiers just follow orders, and following orders has always been a Cliaand strength. We'll never stop these people by trying to incite minor revolts behind their backs. But you are right about causing them trouble on the various worlds. The entire Cliaandian economy and culture is set up on a continuing wartime basis. It is like some demented life form that must keep expanding or die. Cliaand itself can't possibly build or supply its fleets but must depend on the conquered worlds. These worlds are in the absolute control of the Cliaand so they take orders and turn out the goods and the invasions roll on and nothing can stop the advance.''

"I wish the Cliaand invasion was that demented life form you talk about, some sort of ugly green growing thing. We could tear it up by the roots, break off the limbs—'' She broke a hard roll in half to demonstrate what she meant, then nibbled at it. When she started to speak again I held up my hand.

"Stop," I ordered. "Say nothing. I think. I see something. It is almost there."

Then I paced the room, putting two and two together and getting four and adding four and getting eight and performing equally skilled problems of mathematics and logic. It was clear, all clear, and the pieces fell into place and I fell into my chair and grabbed up my drink.

"I am a genius," I said.

"I know. That's why I married you. Physically you are very unattractive.''

"You will soon be apologizing for that remark, woman. For the moment we will drink to my Plan and to victory.''

We clinked and sipped.

"What plan?" she asked.

"I cannot tell you yet. Aside from the fact that you scoffed, it is not detailed in all its ramifications and must be worked out. But the first step is clear and will begin at once or sooner. Do you think the gray men have made a public announcement of Kraj's kidnapping?''

"I doubt it. We've heard nothing on the command circuits we

monitor. And I'm sure this is not the kind of news they would want the Cliaandian man-in-the-spaceship to know about.''

"Just my thinking. Add to this the exaggerated aloofness and self-centered attitude that they have, even towards each other. I am going to gamble on the fact that there has been no widespread announcement about Kraj.''

"How?''

"Get the makeup and facelifting kit. I am going to get into the military base disguised as Kraj. I have some important things to do there.''

She started to protest, but I raised my finger and she was silent. Just as I had been when she went to the Octagon. There was nothing she could say and she knew it.

Without a word she went for the disguise materials.

20

I NEEDED CLIAANDIAN transportation and I got it in the simplest way possible. From the enemy. Since I wasn't outrageously happy about the makeup job we had done I decided to operate after dark when the dim lights would help the illusion. Then, wearing Kraj's uniform and carrying my own case, I went with Hamal to the Octagon, scene of the earlier festivities. Hamal was a member of the auxiliary police, male that is, since the women made up most of the force. I would have preferred one of the girls, they seemed much more sure of themselves, but there were only male Cliaand troops on the planet at this time. The handful of Cliaand women stayed out of sight. Hamal looked a little nervous and I didn't like the way he rolled his eyes from time to time, but he would have to do.

"You understand your part?" I asked him, pushing him into the shadowed entrance to the deep doorway.

"I do, sir, sure I do."

Were his teeth chattering? It was hard to tell. I took out the vial Dr. Mutfak had given me for use in case of emergency.

"Take two of these, chew and swallow. They're happy pills that should raise your morale without sending you dancing through the streets."

"I don't . . ."

"You do now. Take."

He took and I scuttled away towards the Octagon, keeping to the shadows, and looking carefully around the corner before I made my play. There was a certain amount of traffic in and out of the building even at this hour of the night, but nothing that would help me. Finally a small ground car pulled up and dropped two officers off, then started away. In my direction. All systems go. I stepped into the street in front of it and waved my hand; it squealed to a stop with the front bumper almost touching me. The driver looked frightened and I kept him that way.

"Do you always drive like that?"

"No, sir, but . . ."

"Save your excuses, they don't interest me." I climbed into the

257

car next to him while he was still gaping. "Drive on, I'll tell you
where I want to go."

"Sir, this car, I mean . . ."

A single, cold, Krajian look wilted him like a spring flower in a
blizzard and he shot the car forward. As soon as we were out of sight
of the building I ordered him to stop and broke a sleep capsule under
his nose. I'm sure he could use the rest. Then I drove him to the
place where Hamal was waiting. He had pried open the door to the
stationery store in which he was hiding, and we carried the Cliaand
trooper inside. He would sleep until morning after that capsule and I
arranged reams of paper comfortably under his head and feet while
Hamal changed into his uniform.

"Do you know how to drive this car?" I asked him when we
emerged.

"I should. It's one of ours. They stole it and painted their dirty
flag on it."

"Spoils of war regained. Now drive me to the spaceport. And
don't stop completely at the gate, just slow down and keep rolling.
It's all bluff so keep your chin up and try not to look as scared as you
are. Be a man."

"I am," he moaned. "But this is a woman's job. I don't know
how I ever got myself talked into it."

"Shut up and drive on. And take a couple more of these pills."

The spaceport was ahead and I was more worried about my driver
than I was about anyone there. I had seen the way they stayed out of
Kraj's way. Perhaps that would help to explain my driver's obvious
fear. I sighed. Roll on the car. Everyone was supposed to know
Kraj—and now I was putting that theory to the test. The guards
snapped to attention when we appeared and the sergeant started to
say something, but I talked first.

"Stay away from that phone. I want to talk to some people and I
don't want you telling them I'm coming. You know what will
happen to you if you do." I had to shout the last words since, in his
near panic, Hamal had not slowed enough and we zipped right by
the guards. But they must have heard because they made no attempt
that I could see to get near their phone. Step one.

"I can't do it!" Hamal sobbed and spun the wheel on the car until
we were headed back towards the gate. "I'm going home. I was
never cut out for the police, it was all my mother's idea, she wanted
me to be like a daughter to her and made a tomgirl out of me. When
all I ever wanted to be was a simple househusband like my
father . . ."

The gate was coming up at a great rate and I cursed fluently and jumbled out a sleep capsule to crack in front of his face, then tugged at the wheel. I had to hold him up with the other hand and we made another turn and zipped off into the night again. I hesitated to think what the guards at the gate thought about all this. Struggling with the controls I managed to guide the car to the rear of one of the big hangars before Hamal's foot slipped off the accelerator and the engine died.

There were crates of some kind in the rear of the car as well as a bundle of army blankets. I heaved everything out except the blankets which I used to cover Hamal, now curled up sweetly on the floor. Perhaps I should have shot him or just dumped him out. But it really wasn't his fault that he was born low man in a matriarchy. As long as no one came near the car we were safe, and I did not feel that anyone would show that much interest in Kraj's car. I drove to the nearest spacer, a great cargo transport, and parked well away from the lights around the entrance. Now for step two.

"You know who I am?" I said to the master at arms stationed at the foot of the gangway. My voice cold and empty.

"Yes, sir, I do." He stood at attention staring directly ahead of him.

"All right, then have the Chief Engineer meet me on A deck."

"He's not aboard, sir."

"I've made a note of that dereliction of duty and you will tell him of it when he returns. His assistant then."

I went by him without a further look and he sprang to the telephone. By the time I had reached A deck an engineer in greasy coveralls was waiting for me, nervously wiping his hands on a cloth.

"I'm sorry, we were taking down one of the generators . . ." his voice ran out and expired as I glared at him.

"I know you have trouble, and that is why I am here. Take me to the engine room."

He hurried away and I followed heavily after him. This was going to be easier than I thought. Three white-faced ratings looked up from the guts of the generator when we came in.

"Get them out of here," I said and did not have to repeat myself.

I looked at the open generator and nodded sagely as if I had any idea what the repairs were about. Then I began a slow tour of the engine room, tapping dials and squinting into observation ports while the engineer trotted after me. When I reached the warpdrive generator I looked at the nameplate covered with incomprehensible numbers, then turned to the engineer.

"Why is this model being used?"

I have never seen an engineer yet who didn't have something to say about every piece of equipment under his care and this one was no different.

"We know it is the older model, sir, but the replacement didn't arrive in time to install and balance before the flight."

"Bring me the tech manual."

As soon as his back was turned I squeezed the handle of my case and the bomb dropped into my hand. I set the delay for forty minutes, armed it, and activated the sticky molecules on the base. Then I bent down and pushed it up under the thick housing of the warpdrive generator where it could not be seen. I was examining another piece of equipment by the time the engineer returned with the manual. A quick flip through the pages and a grunt or two over the identification numbers satisfied him, and I handed it back. I felt ashamed because the job was so easy.

"See that the work is done quickly," I said as I left, specifying nothing, but receiving in return his fervent assurances that it would be so.

I repeated this maneuver at the next spacer, parking my car in the shadows near it. Just about the time I realized that there was something familiar about the ship, Otrov came down the gangway and turned to face me.

This sudden confrontation startled me as much as it did him. But his eyes bulged and he stopped dead while I, being deep in the Kraj role, only stared coldly at him. Would he recognise me? I had bunked with him and drunk with him during my Vaska Hulja days, and I had piloted this ship. The Kraj disguise was good—but could it be expected to stand up to this close an examination by someone who knew me so well?

"Well?" I whispered finally, when he showed no intention of moving or speaking or doing anything other than stare.

"I'm sorry, sir, you surprised me. I didn't expect to see you here, if you know what I mean." He began to sweat and I stayed silent. "Your voice," he said finally. "Is there anything wrong?"

Of course there was. I knew I couldn't make my voice sound like the real Kraj's to someone who had talked with him recently as Otrov had. I also knew that one whisper sounds very much like any other whisper. But I wasn't telling him that.

"A wound," I husked. "After all there is a war on—and some of us are fighting it."

"Yes, of course, I understand."

He jittered back and forth from one foot to the other and I had enough of this and pushed on by. But he called after me and I turned with cold impatience to face him again.

"I'm sorry to bother you. I was just wondering if you have heard anything about the whereabouts of Vaska . . ."

"That is not his name. He is a spy. You aren't trying to become familiar with a spy are you?" Otrov flushed red, but went on.

"No, of course not, spy, that's what he is. But we were friends once, he wasn't a bad sort then. I was just inquiring."

"I'll do the inquiring, you do the piloting."

I turned after these appropriately Krajian words and stamped into the ship. Otrov had surprised me standing up to Kraj like that. Somewhere inside his alcoholic hide there was a human being struggling for release.

This bomb was as easy to plant as the first one had been and I set it to go off at roughly the same time. Working fast now I drove quickly from ship to ship and managed to plant seven more bombs before the first one went boom. I was in engine room number nine when the alarm sounded.

"What is that?" I asked, hearing the distant moan of sirens.

"I have no idea," the elderly engineer said, and pointed back to the engines. "These liner tubes, second rate and shoddy and I can't get replacements . . ."

"I'm no supply officer," I snarled, suddenly very much in a hurry. "Go find out what the trouble is."

As soon as he left I slipped the bomb into place, set it for three minutes and followed him out.

"What is it?" I asked, meeting him at the top of the gangway.

"An explosion in one of the ships, in the engine room."

"Where? I must look into this!"

I shouted the words and exited as fast as I could. Almost all of the bombs should have gone off by now and the reports would be pouring in. At first it would all be confusion, and it was during this period that I had to make my exit from the base. Because soon after that would come the realization that all of the explosions had occurred in the same place in a number of ships, followed by the unbelievable news that Kraj had recently been in all of these engine rooms. Kraj would not be suspected, not at first, but the authorities would certainly like to have a little chat with him. I wanted to get out before this final stage was reached. Walking as fast as I could without attracting attention, I headed for my car.

And saw the two military policemen standing there, holding the sagging Hamal between them.

"Is this your car, sir?" one of them asked.

"Of course. What are you doing here?"

"It's this man, we saw him sitting in the back talking to himself. We thought he was drunk until we heard him speak. Some foreign language, sir, sounds like the one they talk on this planet. Do you know who he is?"

I didn't hesitate. This was war and troops die for a lot of reasons.

"Never saw him before in my life."

My voice penetrated Hamal's drugged brain because he looked up, blinking. Weak as his nerve was, he must have the physical constitution of an ox to be even moving after the amount of gas he had breathed. Then he groped for me shouting aloud.

"You must help me, they are going to kill me, get me out of here, it was a mistake bringing me in the first place . . ."

"What's he saying?" one of the military policemen asked.

"I have no idea—though I think he might be the spy who has been causing the engine room sabotage." Time was going by too quickly; how soon before they thought of Kraj? "Put him in the back of the car and come with me. I know how to make him talk sense."

While they were doing this I started the engine and pulled away, even before they sat down. This tumbled them about a bit and if they noticed the blankets on the floor they did not mention them. Throttle wide open I headed for the exit.

Towards the officer who stood blocking the way, holding up his hand for me to stop. I kept going but had to brake hard at the last instant because he did not move.

"You cannot leave. The base is closed." He was coldeyed, hardfaced and mean. So was I.

"I am leaving. Save your orders for others."

"My orders were to close the gate to *everyone* without exception."

"I have a prisoner who may be a saboteur and I have two men to guard him. I am taking him to the Octagon for questioning. Your professional zeal is commendable, Captain, but you must know that I am the one who issues orders, not obeys them."

"You cannot leave."

Either he was bullheaded to an insane degree—or he had specific orders about me. I had not time to find out. Through the window I could see one of the men answering the phone and I had a sharp suspicion what that call might be. I drew my pistol and pointed it at the captain.

"Move or I will kill you," I said, in as bored a monotone as I could manage.

He half reached for his gun—then stopped. For a moment more he hesitated and I could see the worried fear in his eyes. Then he stepped aside reluctantly and I gunned the car forward. I had a brief glimpse of a soldier running out of the guardhouse, pointing at the car, shouting something that was drowned in the roar of the engine. After that I did not look back, though the military policemen obviously did. In the rear view mirror I saw them whispering together and they might have been reaching for their guns. I took no chances. As soon as we turned the first corner I threw a gas grenade into the back seat, then stopped just long enough to unload my brace of sleeping beauties.

Hamal was also now very soundly asleep and I strongly wished that I were as well. I yawned broadly and, following the side roads, headed for the dock.

21

"EXPLAIN, DIGRIZ, explain and make it good."

Inskipp was in his usual charming humor, growling and snarling and pacing the length of the spacer's lounge.

"First tell me how the children are, my sons, never seen by their father, how do they do?"

"Yes, how are they?" Angelina asked, sitting back comfortably in one of the lounge chairs. Inskipp sputtered a bit but had to answer.

"Doing fine. Putting on weight. Eat a lot just like their father. You'll see them soon. Now enough of that. I come I don't know how many light years to supervise this operation because it seems to have ground to a full stop. And what do I find? My two agents have had enough and have deserted the planet of their assignment and meet me here in orbit—even though said planet is clamped beneath the iron heel of the Cliaand. Explain."

"We have won."

"No jokes, diGriz. I can have you shot."

"You won't hurt me, you have too much invested in my hide. And I meant what I said. We have won. Burada, clamped under the iron heel, doesn't know it yet. The Cliaandian clampers don't know it yet. Just we privileged few."

"I'm not one of that happy number. Talk faster."

"A demonstration is in order. Angelina my sweet, do you have our little toy?"

She opened a box next to her chair and handed over the Thing. It was smooth and black and no bigger than my hand. There were small openings on its bottom and at each end, while one end had a cluster of tiny lenses as well. I held it out to Inskipp who looked at it suspiciously.

"Do you know what this is?" I said.

"No. And I can't say that I really care to."

"This is the tombstone on the grave of all the Cliaandian expansionist ambitions. What type of space vessel is this we are aboard?"

"A light destroyer, Gnasher class. And what relevancy does that have?"

"Patience, and all will be revealed."

I next took the small control box from Angelina and inserted the end of the spiked rod projecting from it into the matched opening in the Thing. Then I tapped out the serial number for Gnasher class destroyers on the keyboard. With the control box still attached I carried the Thing to the lounge exit where we could see the bulky disc of the main airlock. Angelina followed, leading the protesting Inskipp.

"We must imagine," I said, "that this ship is on the ground and that the lock is open. All airlocks open sooner or later and when they do the Thing is waiting. And so is the operator, watching from up to three kilometers away. The lock opens and he activates the Thing. It soars straight at the open lock through it, and—"

I pressed the *go* button and it went. Tiny jets screamed and it darted off like an impassioned hummingbird, down the hallway towards the stern.

"After it!" I shouted and led the way at a dead run.

We caught up with it two decks down where it had been stopped by a closed door—but not stopped for long. The thermal lance in the Thing's nose burned a quick hole through the metal and it was off again. When we reached the engine room it had almost eaten its way through this thicker door and there was just time to throw the door open as it went through. It zoomed once around the room as though getting its bearings, so small and fast it was almost impossible to follow, then it dived.

Right at the warpdrive generator where it exploded in a puff of black smoke.

"A harmless smoke charge," I said. "To be replaced in field operation by high explosive, more than enough to destroy the warpdrive generator, yet small enough not to cause any other damage. A humane weapon indeed."

"You're mad."

"Only at the Cliaand and the gray men for pursuing this futile war. If we can go back for that drink now I'll tell you how it is going to be stopped."

Comfortably seated, throat cooled, I explained.

"I personally polished off the warpdrive generators in nine of the Cliaand ships, just to see if it could be done and if there would be any unusual problems in ship design or construction. There were none. Cliaandian ships are just like other ships, only more so since they like a good deal of uniformity which makes our job that much easier. The Thing has been designed to do that job. The Thing operator can sit at his ease outside of a spaceport, watching the Cliaand ships through high powered glasses. When the observed ship opens its port the Thing strikes. The operator must merely aim it, feed in the type of ship, and start it on its way. The Thing has a molecular level memory bank and computer circuitry. It zeroes in on the ship at high speed, finds the port and enters and then, using its programmed knowledge of the vessel's interior, it makes its way to the engine room, stopping for nothing. Where it blows up the warpdrive generator. End of the Cliaand invasion.''

''End of one warpdrive generator,'' Inskipp said, a sneer in his voice. ''They order up another one and that is that.''

''That is not that. Generators are complex and not easy to build. There are very few factories that turn them out because most people are satisfied to buy them from someone else. I am sure the Cliaand have at least one factory, but that can be found and knocked out from space.''

''So they get one from the warehouse.''

''There is a limit to the number they can have, and quite soon the warehouse will be empty. Because we are going to have agents on every planet now ruled by the Cliaand and they are going to blow up every warpdrive generator on every ship on those planets. We won't have to go anywhere near the home planet. The warpdrive will be knocked out of cargo ships, war ships, any and all within the Cliaand area of control. Nor will they be able to get any from the outside since this is one embargo that it will be easy for the Corps and the cooperating planets to enforce. End of an empire.''

''How?''

''Think, Inskipp, age couldn't have withered your brain as much as your leathery hide. Angelina gave me the clue. The Cliaandians must keep expanding or perish. They don't have enough food or raw materials on their single planet to carry on this kind of continual expansion. So they conquer a planet, put it to work on their behalf, then restored and resupplied go on to bigger and better things. Only not any more. They still have the planets and the materials—but what good are they if they can't be transported to where they are needed? The expansion will have to stop, and as the ships grow scarce they will have to pull back. Further and further back until they are on their home planet again and that will be the end of that. Any single planet can support itself with raw materials and food, at least enough to survive. But an empire cannot survive with its trade arteries cut. I give them a year, no more, before Cliaand is just another backwater planet with a lot of guys in uniforms and out of jobs. When it is all over normal trade can be started again. A year at the outside. What do you think."

"I think you did it again, my boy, as I knew you would."

He beamed at me and I winked at Angelina and we drank to that.

22

WE WERE STANDING at the inner lock, ready to disembark from the spaceship, when one of the pursers hurried over and handed me a psigram. Angelina blasted it with a withering look.

"Tear it up," she said. "If that is from foul Inskipp canceling the one little vacation we have ever had . . ."

"Relax," I said, glancing through it quickly. "Our holiday is still safe. This is from Taze . . ."

"If that topheavy hussy is still chasing you she is in for trouble."

"Have no fear, my love. The communication is of a political nature. The results of the first election to be held since the Cliaandian withdrawal are in. The men's Konsolosluk party has been swept from office and the girls are back at the helm. Taze has been appointed Minister of War, so I don't think future invasion will be as easy as the last. The psigram further states that we have both been awarded the Order of the Blue Mountains, First Class, and there will be much ceremony and medal pinning when next we get to Burada."

"Just see you don't try going there on your own, Slippery Jim."

I sighed as the massive outer lock of the spaceship ground open and the militant oompah of band music was carried in by the outside air. The sky was clear and empty of anything other than the puffy white clouds and a copter towing a banner that read WELCOME WELCOME.

"Very nice," I said.

"Urgh urgh," Bolivar said, or something like that, or was it James who had spoken? They were hard to tell apart and Angelina took a very antipathetic view towards my suggestion that we paint a B on one little forehead and J on the other. Just for awhile. She bent over their tiny forms in the robopram, tucking in blankets and doing other unessential maternal things. Only I knew that she had a gun in her girdle and a knife in the nappies. My Angelina is just as motherly as any female tiger: she takes care of her cubs but also keeps her claws sharp just in case. Pity the poor kidnapper who tried to swipe the diGriz babies!

"That's an improvement over the usual rattling escalator," I said, pointing to the platform outside.

A shipyard repair stage had been polished and decorated with flags and turned into a passenger elevator. It not only held all the people disembarking but there was plenty of room left over for the military band. Who were now thumping and trumpeting and generally having a good time. We strolled out onto the platform and the robopram rolled after us. James—or was it Bolivar?—tried to hurl himself out of it but a padded tentacle pushed him back to the pillows.

"It doesn't look so bad," Angelina said, looking out across the spaceport to the city while the stage slowly descended. "I can't understand what you were complaining about."

"Let's say the reception was a bit different last time I was here. Isn't that a pleasant sight?"

I pointed to the row upon row of abandoned spaceships, the streaks of rust on their sides visible even from here.

"Very nice," she said, not looking, tucking in an infant that the robopram had already done an excellent job on. Like all new fathers I was more than a little jealous of the attention lavished on the kiddies, and I looked forward to the next joint assignment when I might get a little closer to center stage in her affections. I was being broken to the marriage harness, and, despite my basic loathings and thrashings, was beginning to enjoy it.

"Isn't that dangerous?" Angelina asked as we reached the ground and the double row of soldiers of the honor guard snapped to attention with a resounding crash and clatter. There must have been at least a thousand of them and each one was armed with a gauss-rifle.

"Weapons have been incapacitated, that was part of the agreement."

"But can we trust them?"

"Absolutely. One thing they know how to do is take orders."

We strolled on towards the reception buildings, between the rows of gaudy glittering soldiers, erect as statues with their rifles at present arms.

"I'll show you," I said and led her over to the nearest soldier while the pram turned to follow us. He was tall, erect, big-jawed, steel-eyed, everything a soldier should be.

"Right shoulder-HARMS!" I barked in my best parade ground manner. He obeyed instantly with a great deal of snappy exactitude. Gray haired too, he must have been at the game for a long time.

"Inspection . . . wait for it . . . HARMS!"

He snapped the weapon down across his chest and with a double clack-clack opened the inspection port and extended the rifle. I seized it and looked inside the receiver. Spotless. I held it up to the sky and looked down the barrel and saw only unrelieved blackness.

"There's something blocking the barrel."

"Yes, sir, Orders, sir."

"What is it?"

"Lead, sir. Melted it and poured it in myself."

"An excellent weapon. Carry on trooper." I hurled it back at him and he caught and rattled it efficiently. There was something about him.

"Don't I know you, trooper?"

"Perhaps, sir, I've done duty on many planets. I was a colonel once."

There was a distant glint in his eyes when he said this, but it quickly faded. Of course. I hadn't recognised him without his beard. He was the officer that Kraj had watching me, who tried to shoot me when we first landed on Burada.

"I knew that man, high ranking officer," I told Angelina as we strolled on.

"Very little chance for that kind of work now. He should be happy he has a job that keeps him out in the fresh air. It's amazing that they all seem to be taking it so well."

"They have little choice. When their empire collapsed they flocked back here to Cliaand—and found out that all their mineral and power resources had been exhausted during the invasion years and they had never noticed it. So it was either farm or go hungry. I understand that the agriculture is going just fine right now. And the gray men are gone, Inskipp sent agents in and found they had all packed up and left. To cause trouble elsewhere I suppose. We are going to have to track them to their home planet one of these days."

"Nasty people. That's where a globe-buster bomb would do some good."

"Not in front of the children," I said, patting her hand. "You don't want them to get wrong thoughts about their mother."

"They'll get some right ones. And I'm still suspicious of these ex-warrior types."

"Don't be. We had political agents in here after the breakdown. Issuing orders, and orders are one thing they know how to take. All things considered they have been quite good about it."

Angelina sniffed, still not convinced. "I wonder what bright boy thought up the tourist routine—and suggested we come on the first tour ship?''

''I did. Guilty on both counts. And don't look daggers at me. They need something that will keep them busy and bring in foreign exchange and that sort of thing, and tourism is about all a planet without resources can manage. They have swimming and skiing and all the usual things, plus a deadly sort of fascination for the people they once invaded. It will work out, you just wait and see.''

Hordes of uniformed porters jostled for our baggage, then led the way with the bags to the surface transportation. Things had changed mightily since my first visit to this planet. They seemed to be enjoying themselves, too. I don't think they were ever cut out to be a warrior race and interstellar conquerors. For old times' sake I had registered us at the Zlato-Zlato where I had first stayed, still the most luxurious hotel in town. The doorman's manners were far better this time and the desk clerk even bowed as we came up.

''Welcome to Cliaand, General and Mrs. James diGriz and sons. May your stay here be an enjoyable one.''

Traveling with a title always helps, even more so on this world. I looked around the lobby and then at the clerk.

''Otrov! Is that you?'' I said. He bowed again.

''I am Otrov, indeed sir, but I am afraid you have the better of me.''

''Sorry. Couldn't expect you to recognize me with my own face, or a reasonable facsimile. The last time you talked to me you thought I was a creature named Kraj, and before that you knew me as Vaska Hulja.''

''Vaska—can it be you! It is, I do believe, the voice of course.'' Then his own voice sank. ''I hope you will accept my apology at this late date. I never did feel right about helping that Kraj to capture you. Even though I was unconscious for a day and a half, I was still rather happy you had escaped. I know you were a spy and all that, but . . .''

''Say no more. The matter is closed and I prefer to think of you as the roommate of our drinking days.''

''Most kind. Would you grant me the courtesy of shaking your hand?''

We shook and I looked at him curiously.

''You've changed, for the better I think. Put on a little weight, polished up the old manners.''

''Thank you, Vaska. Most kind. Stopped drinking so I have to watch my diet now. And I don't have to worry about flying those filthy spaceships any more. My family were always innkeepers, traditional trade and all that. Until the draft got me. A pleasure to return to something I know, and right at the top too as you can see. Shortage of good hotel men now. If you will sign here.''

He handed me the pen and continued in the same neutral voice, only not as loudly.

''I hope you will pardon my saying this is a bit of emergency, so please don't jump or turn around. But there has been a man staying here ever since we opened, one of Kraj's men I do believe, and he has the staff terrified. I didn't know what he wanted until this moment. I believe he is after you and I hope you are armed. He is coming from the right, behind you, wearing a plum jacket and yellow striped hat.''

It was a holiday—and I was unarmed. For the first time in a long time I swore silently that it would be the last. Then I remembered Angelina and saw her bending over the robopram again.

''I don't wish to bother you dearest,'' I said, smiling, an itchy feeling crawling up my back and into my skull. ''But the man in the plum jacket coming up behind me is an assassin. Do you think you could do anything about it—and keep him alive if possible?''

''How sweet of you to ask!'' she said, laughing, patting the pile of diapers in the pram.

I stepped back to the desk, watching her. Charming, relaxed, smiling, touching her hair.

Taking her time too. I opened my mouth to mention this fact—just as her arm snapped down. There was a muffled shriek behind me and I turned and ducked.

It was all over. Plum coat had lost his striped hat—and his pistol as well which was lying on the rug. He was reaching for the knife that projected from his upper arm, making little scrabbling motions. Then Angelina was at his side, chopping his neck and lowering his unconscious figure to the floor.

''Holiday world, indeed,'' she sniffed, but I knew she was enjoying herself.

''You'll get a medal for this, my sweet. The Corps will take care of this lad and I imagine they will extract information about his home planet, which will be a relief.'' I turned back to Otrov.

''Thanks for saving my life.''

''Not at all, sir. I always believe that it is the little extra services that count. Now—may I show you your room?''

''You may, and a drink as well. You'll join us in a glass won't you?''

"Well, just this once, seeing as how it is a special occasion. And I must say that you are a lucky man to have a wife who shares your same enthusiasm and talents."

"It was a match made in crime and some day I may tell you all about it."

I looked on fondly while my Angelina neatly wiped her knife off on the unconscious man's shirt, then stowed it back among the diapers. I was sure that when the children got older they would appreciate her talents.

She was the sort of mother every boy should have.

The Stainless Steel Rat
Saves the World

1

"YOU ARE A CROOK, James Bolivar diGriz," Inskipp said, making animal noises deep in his throat while shaking the sheaf of papers viciously in my direction. I leaned back against the sideboard in his office, a picture of shocked sincerity.

"I am innocent," I sobbed. "A victim of a campaign of cold, calculating lies." I had his humidor behind my back and by touch alone—I really am good at this sort of thing—I felt for the lock.

"Embezzlement, swindling and worse—the reports are still coming in. You have been cheating your own organization, our Special Corps, your own buddies—"

"Never!" I cried, lockpick busy in my fingers.

"They don't call you Slippery Jim for nothing!"

"A mistake, a childish nickname. As a baby my mother found me slippery when she soaped me in the bath." The humidor sprang open, and my nose twitched at the aroma of fragrant leaf.

"Do you know how much you have stolen?" His face was bright red now, and his eyes were beginning to bulge in a highly unattractive manner.

"Me? Steal? I would rather die first!" I declaimed movingly as I slipped out a handful of the incredibly expensive cigars destined for visiting VIP's. I could put them to a far more important use by smoking them myself. I am forced to admit that my attention was more on the purloined tobacco than on Inskipp's tedious complaints so I did not at first notice the change in his voice. Then I suddenly realized that I could barely hear his words—not that I really wanted to in any case. It wasn't that he was whispering; it was more as though there were a volume control in his throat that had suddenly been turned down.

"Speak up, Inskipp," I told him firmly. "Or are you suddenly beset with guilt over these false accusations?"

I stepped away from the sideboard, half turning as I moved in order to mask the fact that I was slipping about 100 credits' worth of exotic tobacco into my pocket. He rattled on weakly, ignoring me, shaking the papers soundlessly now.

"Aren't you feeling well?"

I asked this with a certain amount of real concern because he was beginning to sound rather distant. He did not turn his head to look at me when I moved but instead kept staring at the place where I had been, nattering away in an inaudible voice. And he was looking pale. I blinked and looked again.

Not pale, transparent.

The back of his chair was very definitely becoming visible through his head.

"Stop it!" I shouted, but he did not appear to hear. "What games are you playing? Is this some sort of three-D projection to fool me? Why bother? Slippery Jim's not the kind who can be fooled, ha-ha!"

Walking quickly across the room, I put out my hand and poked my index finger into his forehead. It went in—there was slight resistance—and he did not seem to mind in the least. But when I withdrew it, there was a slight popping sound and he vanished completely while the sheaf of papers, now unsupported, fell to the desktop.

"*Whargh!*" I grunted, or something equally incomprehensible. I bent to look for hidden devices under the chair when, with a very nasty crunching sound, the office door was broken down.

Now this was something I could understand. I whirled about, still in the crouch, and was ready for the first man when he came through the door. The hard edge of my hand got him in the throat, right under the gas mask, and he gurgled and dropped. But there were plenty more behind him, all with masks and white coats, wearing little black packs on their backs, either barefisted or carrying improvised clubs. It was all very unusual. Weight of numbers forced me back, but I caught one of them under the chin with my toe while a hard jab to the solar plexus polished off another. Then I had my shoulders to the wall, and they began to swarm over me. I smashed one of them across the back of the neck, and he fell. And vanished halfway to the floor.

This was very interesting. The number of people in the room began to change rapidly now as some of the men I hit snuffed out of sight. This was a good thing that helped even the odds except for the fact that others kept appearing out of thin air at about the same rate. I struggled to get to the door, could not make it, then the club got me in the side of the head and scrambled my brains nicely.

After that it was like trying to fight slow motion under water. I hit a few more of them, but my heart wasn't really in it. They had my arms and legs and began to drag me from the room. I writhed about a certain amount and cursed them fluently in a half dozen languages, but all of this had just about the results you would expect. They rushed me from the room and down the corridor and into the waiting elevator. One of them held up a canister, and I tried to turn my head away, but the blast of gas caught me full in the face.

It did nothing for me that I could feel, though I did get angrier. Kicking and snapping my teeth and shouting insults. The masked men mumbled back in what might have been irritated mumbles, which only goaded me to greater fury. By the time we reached our destination I was ready to kill, which I normally do not find easy to do, and certainly would have if I hadn't been strapped into a gadgety electric chair and had electrodes fastened to my wrists and ankles.

"Tell them that Jim diGriz died like a man, you dogs!" I shouted, not without a certain amount of slavering and foaming. A metal helmet was lowered over my head, and just before it covered my face I managed to call out, "Up the Special Corps! And up your—"

Darkness descended, and I was aware that death or electrocution or brain destruction or worse was imminent.

Nothing happened, and the helmet was raised again, and one of the attackers gave me another shot in the face from a canister, and I felt the overwhelming anger draining away as fast as it had arrived. I blinked a bit at this and saw that they were freeing my arms and legs. I also saw that most of them had their masks off now and were recognizable as the Corps technicians and scientists who usually puttered about this lab.

"Someone wouldn't like to tell me just what the hell is going on, would they?"

"Let me fix this first," one of them said, a gray-haired man with buckteeth like old yellowed gravestones caught between his lips. He hung one of the black boxes from my shoulder and pulled a length of wire from it that had a metal button on the end. He touched the button to the back of my neck where it stuck.

"You're Professor Coypu, aren't you?"

"I am." The teeth moved up and down like piano keys.

"Would you think me rude if I asked for an explanation?"

"Not at all. Only natural under the circumstances. Terribly sorry we had to rough you up. Only way. Get you off-balance, keep you angry. The angry mind exists only for itself and can survive by itself. If we had tried to reason, to tell you the problem, we would have defeated our own purpose. So we attacked. Gave you the anger gas as well as breathed it ourselves. Only thing to do. Oh blast, there goes Magistero. It's getting stronger even in here.''

One of the white-coated men shimmered and grew transparent, then vanished.

"Inskipp went that way," I said.

"He would. First to go, you know."

"Why?" I asked, smiling warmly, thinking that this was the most idiotic conversation I had ever had.

"They are after the Corps. Pick off the top people first."

"Who?"

"Don't know."

I heard my teeth grating together but managed to keep my temper. "Would you kindly explain in greater detail or find someone who can make more sense of this affair than you have been doing."

"Sorry. My fault entirely." He dabbed at a beading of sweat on his forehead, and a whisk of red tongue dampened the dry ends of his teeth. "It all came about so fast, you know. Emergency measures, everything. Time war, I imagine one might call it. Someone, somewhere, somewhen, is tampering with time. Naturally they had to pick the Special Corps as their first target, no matter what other ambitions they might have. Since the Corps is the most effective, most widespread supranational and supraplanetal law enforcement organization in the history of the galaxy, we automatically become the main obstacle in their path. Sooner or later in any ambitious time-changing plan they run against the Corps. They have therefore elected to do it soonest. If they can eliminate Inskipp and the other top people, the probability of the Corps' existence will be lowered and we'll all snuff out, as poor Magistero did just then."

I blinked rapidly. "Do you think we could have a drink that might act as a bit of lubricant to my thoughts?"

"Splendid idea, join you myself."

The dispenser produced a sickly sort of green liquid that he favored, but I dialed for a large Syrian Panther Sweat, most of which I drained with the first swallow. This frightening beverage—whose hideous aftereffects forbade its sale on most civilized worlds—did me nothing but good at this moment. I finished the glass, and a sudden memory popped up out of the tangled jumble of my subconscious.

"Stop me if I'm wrong, but didn't I hear you lecture once about the impossibility of time travel?"

"Of course. My specialty. Smoke screen that talk, I think you might call it. We've had time travel for years here. Afraid to use it, though. Alter time tracks and all that sort of trouble. Just the kind of thing that is happening now. But we have had a continuing project of research and time investigation. Which is why we knew what was happening when it began to happen. The alarms were going off, and we had no time to warn anyone—not that warnings would do any good. We were aware of our duty. Plus the fact that we were the only ones who could do anything at all. We jury-rigged a time-fixator around this laboratory, then made the smaller portable models such as the one you are wearing now."

"What does it do?" I asked, touching with great respect the metal disk on the nape of my neck.

"Has a recording of your memory that it keeps feeding back to your brain every three milliseconds. Telling you you are you, you see, rebuilding any personality changes that time line alterations in the past may have shifted. Purely a defensive mechanism, but it is all we have." Out of the corner of my eye I saw another man wink out of sight, and the professor's voice grew grim. "We must attack if we are to save the Corps."

"Attack? How?"

"Send someone back in time to uncover the forces waging this time war and destroy them before they destroy us. We have a machine."

"I volunteer. Sounds like my kind of job."

"There is no way to return. It is a one-way mission."

"I withdraw the last statement. I like it here." Sudden memory— restored no doubt three milliseconds earlier—grabbed me and a prod of fear pumped a number of interesting chemical substances into my blood.

"Angelina, *my* Angelina! I must speak to her. . . ."

"She is not the only one!"

"The only one for me, Prof. Now stand aside or I'll go through you."

He stepped back, frowning and mumbling and tapping his teeth with his fingernails, and I jabbed the code into the phone. The screen beeped twice, and the few seconds crawled by like lead snails before she answered the call.

"You're there!" I gasped.

"Where did you expect me to be?" A frown crossed her perfect features, and she sniffed as though to get the aroma of booze from the screen. "You've been drinking, and so early too."

"Just a drop, but that's not why I called. How are you? You look good, great, not transparent at all."

"A drop? Sounds more like a whole bottle." Her voice chilled, and there was more than a trace left of the old, unreformed Angelina, the most ruthless and deadly crook in the galaxy before the Corps medics straightened out the knots in her brain. "I suggest you hang up. Get a drive-right pill, then call me back as soon as you are sober." She reached out for the disconnect button.

"*Don't!* I am cold sober and wish I weren't. This is an emergency, red. A top priority. Get over here now as absolutely fast as you can and bring the twins."

"Of course." She was on her feet instantly, ready to go. "Where are you?"

"The location of this lab, quick!" I said, turning to Professor Coypu.

"Level one-hundred and twelve. Room thirty."

"Did you get that," I said, turning back to the screen.

Which was blank.

"*Angelina. . . .*"

I jabbed the disconnect, tapped her code on the keys. The screen lit up. With the message "This is an unconnected number." Then I ran for the door. Someone clutched at my shoulder, but I brushed him aside, grabbed the door and flung it open.

There was nothing outside. A formless, colorless nothing that did strange things to my brain when I looked at it. Then the door was pulled from my hand and slammed shut, and Coypu stood with his back to it, breathing heavily, his features twisted by the same unnamable sensations I had felt.

"Gone," he said hoarsely. "The corridor, the entire station, all the buildings, everything. Gone. Just this laboratory left, locked here by the time-fixator. The Special Corps no longer exists; no one in the galaxy has even a memory of us. When the time-fixator goes we go as well."

"Angelina, where is she, where are they all?"

"They were never born, never existed."

"But I can remember her, all of them."

"That is what we count upon. As long as there is one person alive with memories of us, of the Corps, we stand a microscopic chance of eventual survival. Someone must stop the time attack. If not for the Corps, for the sake of civilization. History is now being rewritten. But not forever if we can counterattack."

A one-way trip backward to a lifetime on an alien world, in an alien time. Whoever went would be the loneliest man alive, living thousands of years before his people, his friends, would even be born.

"Get ready," I said. "I'll go."

2

"FIRST WE MUST find out where you are going. And when."

Professor Coypu staggered across the laboratory, and I followed, in almost as bad shape. He was mumbling over the accordion sheets of the computer print-out that were chuntering and pouring out of the machine and piling up on the floor.

"Must be accurate, very accurate," he said. "We have been running a time probe backward. Following the traces of these disturbances. We have found the particular planet. Now we must zero in on the time. If you arrive too late, they may have already finished their job. Too early and you might die of old age before the fiends are even born."

"Sounds charming. What is the planet?"

"Strange name. Or rather names. It is called Dirt or Earth or something like that. Supposed to be the legendary home of all mankind."

"Another one? I never heard of it."

"No reason you should. Blown up in an atomic war ages ago. Here it is. You have to be pushed backward thirty-two thousand five hundred and ninety-eight years. We can't guarantee anything better than a plus or minus three months at that distance."

"I don't think I'll notice. What year will that be?"

"Well before our present calendar began. It is, I believe, A.D. 1975 by the primitive records of the aborigines of the time."

"Not so aboriginal if they're fiddling with time travel."

"Probably not them at all. Chances are the people you are looking for are just operating in that period."

"How do I find them?"

"With this." One of the assistants handed me a small black box with dials and buttons on it, as well as a transparent bulge that contained a free-floating needle. The needle quivered like a hunting dog and continued to point in the same direction no matter how I turned the box.

"A detector of temporal energy generators," Coypu said. "A less sensitive and portable version of our larger machines. Right now it is pointing at our time-helix. When you return to this planet Dirt, you will use it to seek out the people you want. This other dial is for field strength and will give you an approximation of the distance to the energy source.''

I looked at the box and felt the first bubbling and seething of an idea. "If I can carry this, I can take other equipment with me, right?''

"Correct. Small items that can be secured close to your body. The time field generates a surface charge that is not unlike static electricity.''

"Then I'll take whatever weapons or armament you have here in the lab.''

"There is not very much, just the smaller items.''

"Then I'll make my own. Are there any weapons technicians working here?''

He looked around and thought. "Old Jarl there was in the weapons sections. But there is no time to fabricate anything.''

"That's not what I had in mind. Get him.''

Old Jarl had taken his rejuvenation treatments recently so he looked like a world-soiled nineteen-year-old with an ancient and suspicious look in his eye as he came closer.

"I want that box," I said, pointing to the memory unit on his back. He whinnied like a prodded pony and skittered away clutching at the thing.

"Mine, I tell you mine! You can't have it. Not fair to even ask. Without it I'll just fade away." Tears of senile self-pity rose to his youthful eyes.

"Control yourself, Jarl! I don't want to fade you out; I just want a duplicate of the box. Get cracking on it.''

He shambled away, mumbling to himself, and the technicians closed in.

"I don't understand," Coypu said.

"Simple. If I am gunning after a large organization, I may need some heavy weapon. If I do, I'll plug old Jarl into my brain and use his memories to build them.''

"But—he will be *you*, take over your body, it has never been done.''

"It's being done now. Desperate times demand desperate measures. Which brings us to another important point. You said this would be a one-way trip through time and that I couldn't return.''

"Yes. The time-helix hurls you into the past. There will be no helix there to return you.''

"But if one could be built there, I could return?"

"Theoretically. But it has never been tried. Much of the equipment and materials would not be available among the primitive natives."

"But if the materials were available, a time-helix *could* be built. Now who do you know that could build it?"

"Only myself. The helix is of my own construction and design."

"Great. I'll want your memory box, too. Be sure you boys paint your names on the outside so I don't hook up with the wrong specialist."

The technicians grabbed for the professor.

"The time-fixator is losing power!" one of the engineers shouted in a voice filled with rising hysteria. "When the field goes down, we die. We will never have existed. It can't be. . . ." He screamed this, then fell over as one of his mates gave him a faceful of knockout gas.

"Hurry!" Coypu shouted. "Take diGriz to the time-helix, prepare him!"

They grabbed me and rushed me into the next room, shouting instructions at one another. They almost dropped me when two of the technicians vanished at the same moment. Most of the voices had hysterical overtones—as well they might with the world coming to an end. Some of the more distant walls were already becoming misty and vague. Only training and experience kept me from panicking too. I finally had to push them away from the emergency space suit they were trying to jam me into in order to close the fastenings myself. Professor Coypu was the only other cool one in the whole crowd.

"Seat the helmet, but leave the faceplate open until the last minute. That's fine. Here are the memories, I suggest the leg pocket would be the safest place. The grav-chute on your back. I assume you know how to operate it. These weapon canisters across your chest. The temporal detector here. . . ."

There was more like this until I could hardly stand. I didn't complain. If I didn't take it, I wouldn't have it. Hang on more.

"A language unit!" I shouted. "How can I speak to the natives if I don't know their language?"

"We don't have one here," Coypu said, tucking a rack of gas containers under my arm. "But here is a memorygram—"

"They give me headaches."

"—that you can use to learn the local tongue. In this pocket."

"What do I do, you haven't explained that yet? How do I arrive?"

"Very high. In the stratosphere, that is. Less chance of colliding with anything material. We'll get you there. After that—you're on your own."

"The front lab is gone!" someone shouted, and popped out of existence at almost the same instant.

"To the time-helix!" Coypu called out hoarsely, and they dragged me through the door.

Slower and slower as the scientists and technicians vanished from sight like pricked balloons. Until there were only four of them left and, heavily burdened, I staggered along at a decrepit waddle.

"The time-helix," Coypu said, breathlessly. "It is a bar, a column of pure force that has been warped into a helix and put under tension."

It was green and glittered and almost filled the room, a coiled form of sparkling light as thick as my arm. It reminded me of something.

"It's like a big spring that you have wound up."

"Yes, perhaps. We prefer to call it a time-helix. It has been wound up . . . put under tension, the force carefully calculated. You will be placed at the outer end and the restraining latch released. As you are flung into the past, the helix will hurl itself into the future where the energies will gradually dissipate. You must go."

There were just three of us left.

"Remember me," the short dark technician called out. "Remember Charli Nate! As long as you remember me, I'll never. . . ."

Coypu and I were alone, the walls going, the air darkening.

"The end! Touch it!" he called out. Was his voice weaker?

I stumbled, half fell toward the glowing end of the helix, my fingers outstretched. There was no sensation, but when I touched it, I was instantly surrounded by the same green glow, could barely see through it. The professor was at a console, working the controls, reaching for a rather large switch.

Pulling it down. . . .

3

EVERYTHING STOPPED.

Professor Coypu stood frozen at the controls with his hand locked on the closed switch. I had been looking in his direction, or I would not have seen this because my eyes were fixed rigidly ahead. My body as well—and my brain gave a flutter of panic and tried to bounce around in its bony pan as I realized that I had stopped breathing. For all I knew, my heart wasn't beating either. Something had gone wrong, I was sure of that, since the time-helix was still tightly coiled. More soundless panic as Coypu grew transparent and the walls behind him took on a definitely hazy quality. It was all going, fading before my eyes. Would I be next? There was no way to know.

A primitive part of my mind, the apeman's heir, jibbered and wailed and rushed about in little circles. Yet at the same time I felt a cold detachment and interest; it isn't everyone who is privileged to watch the dissolving of his world while hanging from a helical force field that may possibly whip him back into the remote past. It was a privilege I would be happy to pass on to any volunteers. None presented themselves, so I hung there, popeyed and stiff as a statue while the laboratory faded away around me and I was floating in interstellar space. Apparently even the asteroid on which the Special Corps base had been built no longer had any reality in this new universe.

Something moved. I was tugged in a way that is impossible to describe and moved in a direction I never knew existed before. The time-helix was beginning to uncoil. Or perhaps it had been uncoiling all the while and the alteration in time had concealed my awareness of it. Certainly some of the stars appeared to be moving, faster and faster until they made little blurred lines. It was not a reassuring sight, and I tried to close my eyes, but the paralysis still clutched me. A star whipped by, close enough so that I could see its disk, and burned an afterimage across my retina. Everything speeded up as my time speed accelerated, and eventually space became a gray blur as even stellar events became too fast for me to see. This blur had a hypnotic effect, or my brain was affected by the time motion, because my thoughts became thoroughly muddled as I sank into a quasi-state somewhere between sleep and unconsciousness that lasted a very long time. Or a short time, I'm not really sure. It could have been an instant, or it could have been eternity. Perhaps there was some corner of my brain that remained aware of the terrible slow passage of all those years, but if so, I do not care to think about it. Survival has always been rather important to me, and as a stainless steel rat in among the concrete passages of society I look only to myself for aid. There are far more ways to fail than to succeed, to go mad than to stay sane, and I needed all my mental energies to find the right course. So I existed and stayed relatively sane during the insane temporal voyage and waited for something to happen. After an immeasurable period of time something did.

I arrived. The ending was even more dramatic than the beginning of the journey as everything happened all at once.

I could move again. I could see again—the light blinded me at first—and I was aware of all the bodily sensations that had been suspended so long.

More than that, I was falling. My long-paralyzed stomach gave a twist at this, and the adrenalin and like substances that my brain had been longing to pour into my blood for the past 32,598 years—give or take three months—pumped in and my heart began to thud in a healthily excited manner. As I fell, I turned, and the sun was out of my eyes, and I looked out at a black sky and down at fluffy white clouds far below. Was this it? Dirt, the mysterious homeland of mankind? There was no telling, but it was still a distinct pleasure to be somewhere and somewhen without things dissolving around me. All my equipment seemed to still be with me, and when I touched the control on my wrist, I could feel the tug of the gravchute taking hold. Great. I turned it off and dropped free again until I felt the first traces of thin atmosphere pulling at the suit. By the time I came to the clouds I was falling gently as a leaf, plunging feetfirst into their wet embrace. I slowed the rate of fall even more as I dropped blind, rubbing at the condensation on the faceplate of the space suit. Then I was out of the clouds, and I turned the control to *hover* and took a slow look around at this new world, perhaps the home of the human race, surely my home forever.

Above me the clouds hung like a soft wet ceiling. There were trees and countryside about 3,000 meters below with the details blurred by my wet faceplate. I had to try the atmosphere here sooner or later, and hoping my remote ancestors were not methane breathers, I cracked the faceplate and took a quick sniff.

Not bad. Cold and a little thin at this height, but sweet and fresh. And it didn't kill me. I opened the faceplate wide, breathed deeply, and looked down at the world below. Pleasant enough from this altitude. Rolling green hills covered with trees of some kind, blue lakes, roads cutting sharply through the valleys, some sort of city on the horizon boiling out clouds of pollution. I'd stay as far away from that as possible for the time being. I had to establish myself first, see about. . . .

The sound had been pushing at my awareness, a thin humming like an insect. But there shouldn't be insects at this altitude. I would have thought of this sooner if my attention hadn't been on the landscape below. Just about the time I realized this the humming grew to a roar and I twisted to look over my shoulder. Gaping. At the globular flying craft supported by an archaic rotating airfoil of some kind, behind the transparent sides of which there sat a man gaping back at me. I slammed the wrist controller to *lift* and shot back up into the protecting cloud.

Not a very good beginning. The pilot had had a very good look at me, although there was always the chance that he might disbelieve what he saw. He didn't. The communicators in this age must be most sophisticated, the military's preparedness or paranoia equally so, because within a few minutes I heard the rumble of powerful jets below. They circled a bit, roaring and bellowing, and one even shot up through the clouds. I had a quick glimpse of an arrowlike silver form; then it was gone, the clouds roiling and seething in its wake. It was time to leave. The lateral control on a grav-chute isn't too precise, but I wobbled off through the clouds to put as much room between myself and those machines as I could. When I had not heard them for some time, I risked a drop down just below the cloud level. Nothing. In any direction. I snapped my faceplate shut and cut all the power.

The drop in free fall could not have taken very long, though it seemed a lot longer. I had unhealthy visions of detectors clattering, computers digesting the information and pointing mechanical fingers, mighty machines of war whistling and roaring toward me. I rotated as I fell, squinting my eyes for the first sight of shining metal.

Nothing at all happened. Some large white birds flapped slowly along, veering off with sharp squawks as I plunged by. There was the blue mirror of a lake below, and I gave a nudge of power that moved me toward it. If the pursuit did show up, I could drop under the surface and out of detection range. When I was below the level of the surrounding hills with the water rushing up uncomfortably close below, I slammed on the power. I shuddered and groaned and felt the straps cutting deep into my flesh. The grav-chute on my back grew uncomfortably warm, though I began to sweat for a different reason. It was still a long fall, to water hard as steel from this height.

When I finally did stop moving, my feet were in the water. Not a bad landing at all. There was still no sign of pursuit as I lifted a bit above the surface and drifted toward the gray cliff that fell directly into the lake on the far side. The air smelled good when I opened the faceplate again, and everything was silent. No voices, no sounds of machines. Nor signs of human habitation. When I came closer to the shore, I heard the wind in the leaves, but that was all. Great. I needed a place to hole up until I got my bearings, and this would do just fine. The gray cliff turned out to be a wall of solid rock, inaccessible and high. I drifted along its face until I found a ledge wide enough to sit on, so I sat. It felt good.

"Been a long time since I sat down," I said aloud, pleased to hear my voice. *Yeah*, my evil subconscious snapped back, *about thirty-three thousand years*. I was depressed again and wished that I had a drink. But that was the one essential supply I had neglected to bring, a mistake I would have to rectify quickly. With the power cut the space suit began to warm up in the sun, and I stripped it off, placing all the items of equipment against the rock far from the edge.

What next? I felt something crunch in my side pocket and pulled out a handful of hideously expensive and broken cigars. A tragedy. By some miracle one of them was intact, so I snapped the end to ignite it and breathed deep. Wonderful! I smoked for a bit, my legs dangling over the drop below, and let my morale build up to its normal highly efficient level. A fish broke through the surface of the lake and splashed back; some small birds twittered in the trees, and I thought about the next step. I needed shelter, but the more I moved around to find it, the more chance I had of being discovered. Why couldn't I stay right here?

Among the assorted junk I had been draped with at the last minute was a laboratory tool called a masser, I had started to complain at the time, but it was hung on my waist before I could say anything. I considered it now. The handgrip that contained the power source blossomed out into a bulbous body, which thinned again into a sharp, spikelike prod. A field was generated at the end that had the interesting ability of being able to concentrate most forms of matter by increasing the binding energy in the molecules. This would crunch them together into a smaller space, though they of course still had the same mass. Some things, depending upon the material and the power used, could be compressed up to one-half their original size.

At the other end the ledge narrowed until it vanished, and I walked along it as far as I safely could. Reaching out, I pressed the spike to the surface of the gray stone and thumped the button. There was a sharp crack as a compressed slab of stone the size of my hand fell from the face of the cliff and slid down to the ledge. It felt heavy, more like lead than rock. Flipping it out into the lake, I turned up the power and went to work.

Once I got the knack of the thing the job went fast. I found I could generate an almost spherical field that would detach a solid ball of compressed stone as big as my head. After I had struggled to roll a couple of these heavyweights over the edge—and almost rolled myself with them—I worked the rock away at an angle, then cut out above this slope. The spheres would crunch free, bang down onto the slope, and roll off the edge in a short arc, to splash noisily into the water below. Every once in a while I would stop and listen and look. I was still alone. The sun was close to the horizon before I had a neat little cave in the rock face that would just hold all my goods and myself. An animal's den that I longed to crawl into. Which I did, after a quick floating trip down to the lake for some water. The concentrates were tasteless but filling, so my stomach knew that I had dined, though not well. As the first stars began to come out, I planned the next step in my conquest of Dirt, or Earth, whichever the name was.

My time voyage must have been more fatiguing than I had thought because the next thing I realized was that the sky was black and a great orange full moon was sitting on the mountains. My bottom was chilled from contact with the cold rock, and I was stiff from sleeping in a cramped sitting position.

"Come, mighty changer of history," I said, and groaned as my muscles creaked and my joints cracked. "Get out and get to work."

That was just what I had to do. Action would bring reaction. As long as I holed up in this den, any planning I might do would be valueless since I had no facts to operate with. As yet I didn't even know if this was the right world, or the right time—or anything else. I had to get out and get cracking. Though there was one thing I could do—that I should have done first thing upon arrival. Mumbling curses at my own stupidity, I dug through the assorted junk I had brought with me and came up with the black box of the time energy detector. I used a small light to illuminate it, and my heart thudded down on top of my stomach when I saw that the needle was floating limply. Time was not being warped anywhere on this world.

"Ha-ha, you moron," I called out loudly, cheered by the sound of the voice I liked the most. "This thing would work a lot better if you turned on the power." An oversight. Taking a deep breath, I threw the switch.

Still nothing. The needle hung as limp as my deflated hopes. There was still a good chance that the time triflers were around and just happened to have their machine turned off at the present moment. I hoped.

To work. I secreted a few handy devices about my person and disengaged the grav-chute from the space suit. It still had about a half charge in its power pack, which should get me up and down the cliff a number of times. I slipped my arms through the straps, stepped off the ledge, and touched the controls so that my free fall changed to an arc that pointed in the direction of the nearest road I had seen on the way down. Floating low over the trees, I checked landmarks and direction constantly. The outsize and gleamingly bedialed watch I always wear on my left wrist does a lot more things than tell the time. A touch of the right button illuminated the needle of the radio compass that was zeroed in on my home base. I drifted silently on.

Moonlight reflected from the smooth surface that cut a swath through the forest, and I floated down through the trees to the ground. Enough light filtered through the boughs so that I didn't need my flash as I made my way to the road, going the last few meters with extreme caution. It was empty in both directions, and the night was silent. I bent and examined the surface. It was made of a single slab of some hard white substance, not metal or plastic, that appeared to have tiny grains of sand in it. Most uninteresting. Staying close to the edge, I turned in the direction of the city I had glimpsed and started walking. It was slow, but it saved the power in the grav-chute.

What happened next I can attribute only to carelessness, tempered with fatigue, and seasoned by my ignorance of this world. My mind wandered, to Angelina and the children and my friends in the Corps, all of whom existed only in my thoughts. They now had no more reality than my memory of characters I had read about in a novel. This was a very depressing idea, and I brooded over it rather than rejected it, so I was taken completely unaware by the sudden roar of engines. At this moment I was rounding a turn in the road that had apparently been cut through a small hill, since there were steep banks on each side. I should have considered being caught in this cut and have planned some means to avoid it. Now, while I considered the advisability of climbing the slope, of lifting up by grav-chute or of some other means of escape, bright lights shone around the turn ahead and the roar grew louder. In the end I only dropped to one side of the road, in the ditch that ran there, and lay down and tried to think small, burying my face in my arm. My clothing was a neutral dark gray and might blend into the ground.

Then the stuttering roar was upon me, next to me, and bright lights washed over me and were gone. As soon as they were by, I sat up and looked after the four strange vehicles that had passed. Details were not clear, since I saw them only as silhouettes against their own headlights, but they seemed very narrow, like monocycles, and each had a little red light at the back. Their sound quieted and was mixed with a kind of honking like some animal and a shrill screeching. They were slowing. They must have seen me.

Cracking, barking sounds echoed in the cut as the lights turned full circle and headed back in my direction.

4

WHEN IN DOUBT, let the other guy make the first mistake, one of my older mottoes. I could attempt to escape, climbing or floating, but whoever these people were, they might have weapons, and I would make a peachy target. Even if I did escape, I would only draw attention to this area. Better to see who and what they were first. Turning my back so their lights wouldn't blind me, I waited patiently as the machines rumbled up and stopped in an arc around me, motors coughing and lights pointed at me. I closed my eyes to slits to shield them from the glare and listened to the strange sounds the riders made gabbling to one another, not one word of which I found comprehensible. The chances were good that my clothing was on the exotic side as far as they were concerned. They must have reached some agreement because the engine on one of the invisible conveyances clattered into silence and the driver stepped forward into the light.

We exchanged looks of mutual interest. He was a little shorter than I but looked taller because of the bucket-shaped metal helmet he was wearing. It was studded with rivets and bore a tall spike on the top, very unattractive, as was the rest of his dress. All black plastic with shining knobs and clasps, brought to the acme of vulgarity by a stylized skull and crossbones on the chest that was picked out with fake gems of some kind.

"*Kryzl prtzblk?*" he said in a very insulting manner, allowing his jaw to protrude at the same time. I smiled to show that I was a friendly, good-natured fellow and responded in the warmest fashion.

"You'll look uglier dead than alive, bowb, and that's what you will be if you keep talking to me that way."

He looked puzzled at that and there was more incomprehensible chitchat back and forth. The first driver was joined by one of the others, equally strangely garbed, who pointed excitedly to my arm. All of them looked at my wrist chronometer, and there were shrill cries of interest that changed to anger when I put my hand behind my back.

''*Prubl!*'' the first thug said, stepping forward with his hand out. There was a sharp snick, and a gleaming blade appeared in his other fist.

Now this was language I understood, and I almost smiled at the sight. No honest men these, unless the law of the land decreed drawing weapons on strangers and attempting to rob them. Now that I knew the rules I could play by them.

''Prubl, prubl?'' I cried, shrinking away and raising my hands in a gesture of despair.

''*Prubl drubl!*'' the evilly grinning lout shouted, jumping toward me.

''How's that for prubl?'' I asked as I kicked up and caught him on the wrist with my toe. The knife sailed away into the darkness, and he squeaked with pain, the squeak turning into a vanishing gurgle as my pointed fingers stabbed him in the throat.

By this time all the eyes must be on me, so I triggered a miniflare into my hand from my sleeve holdout and dropped it on the ground before me, closing my eyes just before it exploded. The glare burned hot on my lids, and I saw little floating blobs of light when I opened them again. Which was a lot better than my attackers, who were all temporarily blinded if their groans and complaints meant anything. None of them stopped me as I walked behind them and gave them, each in turn, a sharp boot toe where it would do the most good. They all yiped with pain and ran in little circles until two collided by chance and began to beat each other unmercifully. While they were amusing themselves in this manner, I examined their conveyances. Strange things with only two wheels and no sign of a gyro to stabilize them in motion. Each had a single seat on which the operator sat, straddling the thing to make it go. They looked very dangerous, and I had no desire at all to learn to operate one.

What was I to do with these creatures? I had never enjoyed killing people, so they couldn't be silenced that way. If they were the criminals they appeared to be, there was a good chance they would not report the event to the authorities. Criminals! Of course, just the kind of informants I needed. One would be enough, the first one preferably since I would have no compunction about being stern with him. He was moaning his way back to consciousness, but a whiff of sleepgas put him well under. Around his waist was a wide, metal-studded belt that looked fairly strong. I fastened this to one of my belt clips and held him in friendly embrace under the arms. Then thumbed the grav-chute control.

Silently and smoothly we lifted, floating up and away from the noisy little group, arrowing back toward my lakeside retreat. Their companion's vanishing act would be singularly mysterious, and even if they reported it to the authorities, it would accomplish nothing. I was going to hole up with my dozing companion for a few days and learn the speech of this land. My accent was sure to be of the lowest, but that could be corrected later. My retreat gaped its welcoming mouth at me, and I zipped in, dropping my limp burden ungracefully on the stone.

By the time he came groaning back to awareness I was completely prepared and had all the equipment laid out. I puffed pleasurably on a cigar from my pocket humidor and said nothing while he went through a painful series of adjustments. There was plenty of lip smacking before he opened his eyes and sat up—only to moan and clutch at his head. My sleepgas does have some painful aftereffects. But memory of his knife aimed at me did much to steel me to his suffering. Then came the wild look around, the eye boggling at me and my equipment, the crafty look at the black opening of the entrance and the apparently accidental way he got his legs beneath him. To spring out of the opening. To land smash on his face as the cable that secured his ankle to the rock brought him down.

"Now the games are over and we get to work," I told him, not unkindly as I sat him back against the wall and tightened the device about his wrist. I had rigged it while he slept, and it was simple but effective. It contained a blood pressure and skin resistance gauge with readouts on the control box that I held before me. A basic form of lie detector. It also contained a negative reinforcement circuit. I normally wouldn't use this technique on a human being—it was usually reserved for training laboratory animals—but this present human being was an exception. We were playing by his rules, and this shortcut would save a lot of time. When he began shouting, what I am sure were obnoxious insults, and started to tear at the box, I pressed the reinforcement button. He shrieked and thrashed about enthusiastically as the electric current hit him. It wasn't really that bad; I had tried it on myself and set the level at slightly painful, the sort of pain one could easily endure but would prefer not to.

"Now we begin," I said, "but let me prepare myself first."

He looked on in wide-eyed silence while I adjusted the metal pads of the memorygram on my temples and activated the circuit.

"The key word is"—I looked at my companion—"ugly. Now we begin."

There was a pile of simple objects at my side, and I picked up the first one and held it out before me so he could see it. When he looked at it, I said "rock" loudly, then was silent. He was silent as well, and after a moment I triggered the reinforcement circuit and he jumped at the sudden burst of pain and looked around wildly.

"Rock," I repeated in a quiet, patient voice.

It took him awhile to get the idea, but he learned. There was a shock for cursing or saying anything irrelevant and a double shock when he tried to lie about a word; my polygraph kept me informed about that. He had enough of this quite quickly and found it easier to supply the word I wanted. We quickly ran through my supply of objects and shifted to drawings and acted-out motions. I accepted the phrase "I don't know," as long as it wasn't used too often, and my store of words grew. Under the pressure of the microcurrents of the memorygram the new vocabulary was jammed into my cortex, but not without some painful side effects. When my head began to throb, I took a painpill and went on with the word games. It didn't take long to file away enough words to switch to the second part of the learning process, grammar and structure. "What is your name?" I thought to myself and added the code word "ugly."

"What . . . name?" I said aloud. A very unattractive language indeed.

"Slasher."

"Me . . . name . . . Jim."

"Lemme go, I ain't done nuttin' to you."

"Learn first . . . leave later. Now tell, what year?"

"What year what?"

"What year now, dum-dum?"

I repeated the question in different ways until realization of what I was asking finally penetrated the solid bone of his skull. I was beginning to sweat.

"Oh, the *year*. It's 1975. June the nineteenth, 1975."

Right on target! Across all those centuries and millennia the time-helix had snapped me with precise accuracy. I made a mental note of thanks to Professor Coypu and the other vanished scientists, and since they lived on only in my memory, this was probably the only way to send the message. Much cheered by this information, I got on with the language lesson.

The memorygram clutched onto everything he said, organized it, and jammed it deep into my bruised synapses. I stifled a groan and took another painpill. By sunrise I felt I had enough of a command of the language to add to it by myself and switched off the machine.

My companion fell over asleep and clunked his head on the rock without waking. I let him sleep and disentangled us both from the electronic equipment. After the nightlong session I was tired myself, but a stimtab took care of that. Hunger growled plaintively in my gut, and I broke out some rations. Slasher awoke soon after and shared my breakfast, eating one of the bars only after he saw me break off the end and consume it myself. I belched with satisfaction, and he echoed eructatingly. He eyed me and my equipment for some time before he made a positive statement.

"I know who you are."

"So tell me."

"You're from Mars, dat's what."

"What's Mars?"

"The planet, you know."

"Yeah, you might be right. It don't matter. You gonna do what I said, help me get some loot?"

"I told you, I'm on parole. If I'm grabbed, they'll throw the key away."

"Don't let it bug you. Stick with me and they won't lay a finger on you. You'll be rolling in bucks. Do you have any of these bucks? I want to see what they look like."

"No!" he said, and his hand went to a bulge in a flap of material affixed to his lower garments. By this time I could detect his simple lies without my equipment.

Sleepgas quieted him, and I worked a sort of hide envelope from his clothing that contained flimsy scraps of green paper, undoubtedly the bucks he had referred to not having. To look at them was to laugh! The cheapest copying machine could turn out duplicates of these by the barrelful—unless there were hidden means of authentification. To check I went over them with the most delicate equipment and found no trace of chemical, physical, or radioactive identification. Amazing. The paper did appear to contain short threads of some kind of substance, but a duplicator would print replicas of these on the surface which would do fine. If only I had a duplicator. Or did I have a duplicator? Toward the end there they were hanging every kind of equipment on me that they could. I rooted through the pile, and sure enough, there was a tiny desk model duplicator. It was loaded with a block of extremely dense material that was expanded in some cellular fashion inside the machine to produce a sheet of smooth white plastic on which the copies were made. After a number of adjustments I managed to reduce the quality of the plastic until it was as rough and crumpled as the bucks. Now when I touched the copy button, the machine produced a buck that appeared a duplicate of the original. The largest denomination Slasher had was a ten-buck note, and I made a number of copies of this. Of course, they all had the same serial number, but my experience has been that people never look very closely at the money they accept.

It was time to move into the next phase of my penetration of the society of this primitive planet, Earth. (I had discovered that Dirt was not correct and had another meaning altogether.) I arranged about my person the equipment I might need and left the remainder in the cave with the space suit. It would be here whenever I needed it. Slasher mumbled and snored when I floated him back across the lake and low over the trees toward the road. There was more traffic on it now during the day, I could hear the vehicles rumbling by, so I once more dropped down into the forest. Before waking Slasher, I buried the grav-chute with a radio transponder that would lead me back to it if needs be.

"What, what?" Slasher said, sitting up as soon as the antidote took effect. He looked around uncomprehendingly at the forest.

"On your hooves," I told him. "We gotta move out of here."

He shambled after me, still half-asleep, though he woke up rather quickly when I ruffled the wad of money under his nose.

"How do these bucks look to you?"

"Great—but I thought you didn't have any bread?"

"I got enough food, but not enough money. So I made these. Are they OK?"

"A-OK, I never seen better." He flipped through them with the appraising eye of the professional. "The only way you can tell is that the numbers are all the same. This is high-class green."

He parted with them only reluctantly. A man of little imagination and no compunction; just what I needed. The sight of the bucks seemed to have driven all fear of me from him and he actively joined in planning to obtain even more money as we trudged along the road.

"That outfit you're wearing, it's OK from a distance, like now, no one in the cars notices nuttin'. But we gotta get you some threads. There's kind of a general store foot of this hill. You wait away from the road while I go in and buy what you need. In fact, maybe we get some wheels before that; my feet are killing me. There's some kind of little factory there with a parking lot. We'll see what they're selling."

The factory proved to be a squat, squarish building with a number of chimneys that were puffing out smoke and pollution. An assortment of multicolored vehicles were arranged to one side, and following Slasher's example, I bent low as we moved quickly to the nearest one in the outside row. When he was sure we were unobserved, my companion released a catch on a swollen purple thing, with what appeared to be a row of metal teeth at one end, and lifted a large lid. I looked in and gasped at the excessively complex and primitive propulsion engine it contained. I was indeed in the past. In response to my questions, Slasher described it as he shorted some wires that seemed to control the ignition.

"An intoinal-combustion engine we call it. Almost new, should be three hundred horses there. Climb in and we'll make tracks out of here before anybody sees us."

I made a mental note to inquire later about the theory behind this intoinal combustion. From earlier conversation I had understood that horses were a rather large quadruped, so perhaps it was an animal miniaturizing process to get a large number of them into the machine. But primitive as the device looked, it certainly moved quickly enough. Slasher manipulated the controls and twisted the large wheel, and we shot out onto the road and were away—apparently without being detected. I was more than satisfied to let Slasher drive while I observed this world that I had arrived on.

"Where is all the money kept? You know, like the place where they lock it up."

"You must mean the banks. Places with thick walls, big vaults, armed guards. They got at least one in every town."

"And the bigger the town, the bigger the bank?"

"You're catchin' on."

"Then drive on to the nearest big town and find the biggest bank. I need plenty of bread. So we'll clean it out tonight."

Slasher gaped in awe. "You can't mean it! They got all kinds of alarms and stuff."

"I laugh at their Stone Age gadgets. Just find the town, find the bank, then find some food and drink. Tonight I'll make you rich."

5

IN ALL TRUTH I have never robbed a bank more easily or cracked a simpler crib. The establishment I selected was in the center of a city with the improbable-sounding name of Hartford. It was severely constructed of gray stone, and all the openings were covered with thick metal bars—but these defenses were negated by the fact that there were other buildings joined to the bank on both sides. A rat rarely enters by the front door. It was early evening when we set out, and Slasher was jittery and nervous despite the large quantity of low-quality alcoholic beverage he had consumed.

"We oughta wait until later," he complained. "There are still plenty of people in the street."

"Just how I want it. They won't pay no attention to a couple more. Now park this heap around the corner where we planned and bring the bags."

I carried my tools in a small case while Slasher followed me with the two large pieces of luggage we had purchased. The building ahead, on the left of the bank, was dark, and the outer door was surely locked. No trouble. I had looked at the lock earlier in the day and had determined that it presented no problem at all. The device in my left hand neutralized the alarm while I inserted the lockpick with my right. It opened so easily that Slasher did not even have to stop but went right on by me with the bags. Not a soul in the street paid us the slightest attention. A corridor led to some more locked doors, which I passed through with the same ease, until we reached an office in the rear.

"This room should share a wall with the bank. Now I'm gonna find out," I said.

I whistled under my breath as I went to work. This was by no means my first bank robbery, and I had no intention of making it my last. Of all the varied forms of crime, bank robbery is the most satisfactory to both the individual and to society. The individual of course gets a lot of money, that goes without saying, and he benefits society by putting large amounts of cash back into circulation. The economy is stimulated, small businessmen prosper, people read about the crime with great interest, and the police have a chance to exercise their various skills. Good for all. Though I have heard foolish people complain that it hurts the bank. This is arrant nonsense. All banks are insured, so they lose nothing, while the sums involved are minuscule in the overall operation of the insuring firm, where the most that might happen is that a microscopically smaller dividend will be paid at the end of the year. Little enough price to pay for all the good caused. It was as a benefactor of mankind, not a thief, that I passed the echo sounder over the wall. A large opening on the other side; the bank without a doubt.

There were a number of cables and pipes in the wall, power and water I presumed, along with some that were obviously alarms. I marked their positions on the wall until the pattern was clear. There was one area that was free of all obstructions that I outlined.

"We go in here," I said.

"How we gonna break the wall down?" Slasher swung between elation and fear, wanting the money, afraid he would be caught. He was obviously a petty criminal, and this was the biggest job he had ever been on.

"Not break, dum-dum," I said, not unkindly, holding up the masser. "We just convince it to open before us."

Of course he had no idea what I was talking about, but sight of the gleaming instrument seemed to reassure him. I had reversed the device so instead of increasing the binding energy of molecules, it reduced their attraction close to zero. With slow precision I ran the point of the device completely over the chosen area of wall, then turned it off and stowed it away.

"Nuttin' happened," Slasher complained.

"Sometin' will now." I pushed the wall with my hand, and the entire area I had prepared fell away with a soft whoosh, sliding down like so much fine dust. Which it had become. We looked through into the brightly lit interior of the bank.

We were invisible from the street when we crawled through and crept along behind the high counter where the tellers normally sat. The builders had thoughtfully put their vault in the lower depths of the building and out of sight of the street, so once down the steps, we could straighten up and go about our task in comfort. In rapid sequence I went through a pair of locked doors and a grille made of thick steel bars. Their locks and alarms were too simple to discuss. The vault door itself looked more formidable, yet proved the simplest of them all.

"Look at dat," I called out enthusiastically. "There is a time lock here that opens automatically sometime tomorrow."

"I knew it," Slasher wailed. "Let's get out before the alarms go off. . . ."

As he ran for the stairs, I tripped him and put one foot on his chest while I explained.

"That is what they call good, dum-dum. All we have to do to open the thing is to advance the clock so it thinks it is the morning."

"Impossible! It's sealed behind a couple of inches of steel!"

Of course, he had no way of knowing that an ordinary serviceman's manipulator is designed to work through casings of any kind. When I felt the field engage the cogs, I rotated it, and the dials whirled, and his eyes bulged—and the mechanism gave a satisfied click, and the door swung open.

"Bring da bags," I ordered, entering the vault.

Whistling and humming gaily, we packed the two bags solid with the tightly wrapped bundles of crisp notes. Slasher closed and sealed his first, then mumbled impatiently at my slowness.

"What's da rush?" I asked him, closing the case and assembling my tools. "You gotta take the time to do things the right way."

As I put the last of my instruments away, I noticed a needle jump, then hold steady. Interesting. I adjusted the field strength, then stood with it in my hand and looked around. Slasher was on the other side of the vault, fumbling with some long metal boxes.

"And what are you doing?" I asked in my warmest voice.

"Takin' a shufty to see if maybe there are some jewels in these safe-deposit boxes."

"Oh, that is what you are doing. You shoulda asked me."

"I can do it myself." Surly and cocksure.

"Yes, but I can do it without setting off the silent alarm to the police station." Cold and angry. "As you have just done."

The blood drained from his face nicely; his hands shook so he dropped the box; then he jumped about to bend and pick up the satchel of money.

"Dum-dum yo-yo," I snarled and booted hard in the inviting target presented. "Now get that bag and get out of here and start the car. I'm right behind you."

Slasher stumbled and scrambled up the stairs, and I followed more calmly after, taking a moment to close all the gates and grilles behind me in order to make things as difficult as possible for the police. They would know the bank had been entered but would not know it had been robbed until they rousted out some bank official and opened the vault. By which time we would be long vanished.

But as I came up the stairs, I heard the squeal of tires and saw, through the front windows, a police car pulling up outside.

They had certainly been fast, incredibly so for an ancient and primitive society like this one. Though perhaps that was why; certainly crime and crime detection must consume a large part of everyone's energies. However, I wasted no time philosophizing over their arrival but pushed the bags ahead of me as I crawled behind the tellers' counter. As I was going through the hole to the other building, I heard keys rattling in the outer door locks. Just right. As they came in, I would go out—and this proved to be the case. When I looked out at the street, I saw that all the occupants of the police car had entered the bank while a small, but curious, crowd had gathered. With their backs toward me. I exited slowly and strode toward the corner.

The Neolithic fuzz were certainly fast on their feet. It must come from running down and catching their own game or something. Because I had not reached the corner before they popped out of the door behind me, tooting painfully on shrill whistles. They had entered the bank, seen the hole in the wall, then retraced my path. I took one quick look at them, all shining teeth, blue uniforms, brass buttons and guns, and started running myself.

Around the corner and into the car.

Except that the street was empty and the car was gone.

Slasher must have decided that he had earned enough for one evening and had driven away and left me for the law.

6

I AM NOT suggesting that I may be made of sterner stuff than most men. Though I do feel that most men when presented with a situation like this—32,000 years in the past, a load of stolen money, the law in hot pursuit—might give way to more than a little suggestion of panic. Only conditioning, and the fact that I had been in this position far too often during my life, kept me running smoothly while I considered what to do next. In a few moments some heavy-footed minions of the law would come barreling around the corner while, I am sure, a radio alarm would be drawing in reinforcements to cut me off. Think fast, Jim.

I did. Before I had taken five more paces, my entire plan for escape was outlined, detailed, set into type, printed, and bound into a little booklet with page one open in my mind's eye before me.

First—get off the street. As I jumped into the next doorway, I dropped the money and let a minigrenade fall into my fingers from my holdout. This fitted into the round opening of the keyhole very nicely, and with an impressive thud, it blew out the lock and part of the frame. My pursuers were not in sight yet, so I hesitated until they appeared before pushing open the ruined door. Hoarse shouts and more whistle blowing signaled that I had been observed. The door opened into a long corridor, and I was at the far end of it, hands raised in surrender, when the gun-toting law hesitatingly peeked in through the opening.

"Don't shoot, coppers," I shouted. "I surrender, a poor young man led to crime by evil companions."

"Don't move or we'll hole you," they growled happily, entering warily with strong lights flashing into my eyes. I simply stood there, fingers groping for empty air, until the lights slid away and there was the double thud of falling bodies. There should have been since there was more sleepgas than air in that hallway.

Being careful to breathe through the filter plugs in my nostrils, I stripped the uniform from the snoring figure that was closest to my size, cursing the crude arrangement of fastenings, and put it on over my own clothes. Then I took the hand weapon he had been carrying and restored it to its holster, picked up my bags again and left, walking back up the street toward the bank. Frightened civilians peered out of doorways like animals from their burrows, and at the corner I was met by another police car. As I had guessed, a number of them were converging on this spot.

"I have the loot," I called in to the solid figure behind the wheel. "I'm takin it back to da bank. We have them cornered, da rats, a whole gang. Through that door. Go get them!"

This last advice was unneeded because the vehicle had already left. The first police conveyance still stood where I had last seen it, and under the cowlike eyes of the spectators, I threw the bags into the front seat and climbed in.

"Gowan, beat it. Da show's over," I shouted as I groped among the unfamiliar instruments. There were an awful lot of them, enough to fly a spaceship with, much less this squalid groundcar. Nothing happened. The crowd milled back, then milled forward. I was sweating slightly. Only then did I notice that the tiny keyhole was empty and remembered—belatedly—something Slasher had said about using keys to start these vehicles with. Sirens grew louder on all sides as I groped and fumbled through the odd selection of pockets and wallets on the uniform I wore.

Keys! An entire ring of them. Chortling, I pushed one after another into the keyhole until I realized that they were all too big to fit. Outside, the fascinated crowd pressed close, greatly admiring my performance.

"Back, back," I cried, and struggled the weapon from its holster to add menace to my words.

Evidently it had been primed and was ready to be actuated, and I inadvertently touched the wrong control. There was a terrible explosion and cloud of smoke, and it jumped from my hand. Some kind of projectile hurtled through the metal roof of the car and my thumb felt quite sore.

At least the spectators left. Hurriedly. As they ran in all directions, I saw that one of the police cars was coming up behind me, and I felt that things were just not going as well as they should. There must be other keys. I groped again, throwing the miscellaneous items I discovered onto the seat beside me until there were no more. The other car stopped behind mine and the doors opened.

Was that a glint of metal in that small hide case? It was. A pair of keys. One of them slid gently into the correct orifice as the two minions of law and order walked up on both sides of the car.

"What's going on here?" the nearest called out as the key turned and there was the groaning of an engine and a metallic clashing.

"Trouble!" I said as I fumbled with the metal levers.

"Get outta there, you!" he said, pulling out his weapon.

"Matter of life and death!" I shouted in a cracked voice as I stamped on one of the pedals as I had seen Slasher do. The car roared with power; the wheels squealed; it leaped to life, hurtling.

In the wrong direction, backward.

There was an intense crashing and clanging of glass and metal, and the police vanished. I groped for the controls again. One of the fuzz appeared ahead, raising his weapon, but jumped for his life as I found the right combination and the car roared at him. The road was clear, and I was on my way.

With the police in hot pursuit. Before I reached the corner, the other car started up and tore forward. Colored lights began rotating on top of it, and its siren wailed after. I drove with one hand and fumbled with my own controls—spraying liquid on the windscreen, then seeing it wiped away by moving arms, hearing loud music, warming my feet with a hot blast of air—until I also had a screaming siren and perhaps, a flashing light. We tore down the wide road in this manner, and I felt that this was not the way to escape. The police knew their city and their vehicles and could radio ahead to cut me off. As soon as I realized this, I pulled at the wheel and turned into the next street. Since I was going a bit faster than I should, the tires screeched and the car bounced up onto the sidewalk and caromed off a building before shuddering back into the roadway. My pursuers dropped behind with this maneuver, not willing to make the turn in this same dramatic manner, but were still after me when I barreled around the next corner. With these two right-angle turns I had succeeded in reversing my course and was now headed back toward the scene of the crime.

Which may sound like madness but was really the safest thing to do. In a few moments, siren wailing and lights going, I was safe in the middle of a pack of screaming, flashing blue and white vehicles. It was lovely. They were turning and backing and getting in one another's way, and I did what I could to increase the confusion. It was quite interesting with much cursing and the shaking of fists from windows, and I would have stayed longer if reason had not prevailed. When the excitement reached its merriest, I worked my way out and slid my vehicle around the corner. I was not followed. At a more reasonable pace, siren silenced and lights lowered, I trundled along the street looking for a haven. I could never escape in the police car, and I had no intention of doing so; what I needed was a rathole to crawl into.

A luxurious one; I do not believe in doing things halfway. Not very much farther on I saw my goal, ablaze with lights and signs, glittering with ornament, a hotel of the plush and luxury class almost a stone's throw from the site of the crime. The last place where I would be looked for. I hoped. Certain chances have to be taken always. At the next turning I parked the car, stripped off the uniform, put a bundle of bills in my pocket, then trundled back toward the hotel with my two bags. When the car was found, they would probably think I had changed vehicles, an obvious ploy, and the area of search would widen.

"Hey, you," I called out to the uniformed functionary who stood proudly before the entrance. "Carry these bags."

My tone was insulting, my manners rude, and he should have ignored me had I not spoken in another language and pressed a large denomination banknote into his hand. A quick glimpse of this produced smiles and a false obsequiousness as he grabbed for my bags, shuffling after me as I entered the lobby.

Glowing wood paneling, soft rugs, discreet lighting, lovely women in low-cut dresses accompanied by elderly men with low-hung bellies; this was the right place. There were a number of raised eyebrows at my rough clothing as I strode across to the reception desk. The individual behind looked coldly down a long patrician nose, and I could see the ice already starting to form. I thawed it with a wad of money on the counter before him.

"You have the pleasure of meetin' a rich but eccentric millionaire," I told him. "This is for you." The bills vanished even as I offered them. "I have just come back from the boonies, and I want the best room you got."

"Something *might* be arranged, but only the Emperor Suite is available and that costs. . . ."

"Don't bodder me with money. Take this loot and let me know when you want more."

"Yes, well, perhaps something can be arranged. If you would be so kind as to sign your name here. . . ."

"What's *your* name?"

"Me? Why, it's Roscoe Amberdexter."

"Ain't that a coincidence—that's my name, too, but you can call me sir. Must be a very common name around here. So you sign for me since we both got the same name." I beckoned, and he leaned forward, and I spoke in a hoarse whisper. "I don't want no one to know I am here. Everyone's after my loot. Send up the manager if he wants more information." What he would get would be money, which I was sure would do just as well.

Buoyed on a wave of greenbacks, the rest was clear sailing. I was ushered to my quarters, and I bestowed largess on my two bag carriers for being so smart they didn't drop them. They opened and shut things and showed me all the controls, and I had one of them call room service for much food and drink, and they left in the best of humors, pockets bulging. I put the bag of money in the closet and opened the smaller case.

And froze.

The indicator needle on the time energy detector had moved and was pointing steadily toward the window and the world outside.

7

MY HANDS WANTED to shake, but I would not let them as I took out the detector and placed it gently on the floor. The field strength was 117.56, and I made a rapid note of this. Then I dropped and sighted along the needle at the exact spot under the window where it pointed. Running over quickly, I marked a big X on this spot, then rushed back to check it. As I took the second sight, the needle began to drift, and the meter dropped to zero.

But I had them! Whoever they were, they were operating out of this era. They had used their time apparatus once, and they were sure to use it again. When they did, I would be waiting for them. For the first time since I had been whipped back to this crude barbarian world I was warmed by a small spark of hope. Up until now I had been operating by reflex, just staying alive and learning to make my way in this strange place, and all of the time keeping my thoughts away from the future that would not exist unless I could bring it into being. And that was just what I was going to do.

After a hearty dinner and a snowfall of fluttering banknotes I went to sleep. Not for long though, a two-hour zonk pill put me under in the deepest possible sleep, with almost constant dreaming, and I awoke feeling much more human. There were a number of interesting bottles in the bar in the next room, some of them rather palatable; and I sat down with a filled glass in front of a glass-eyed instrument called a TV. As I had guessed, my accent in the local language left a lot to be desired, and I wanted to listen to someone who spoke a better form of it.

This was not easy to find. To begin with, it was hard to tell which were the educational channels and which were there for entertainment. I found what appeared to be a morality play in historical form where all the men wore wide-brimmed hats and rode on horses. But the total vocabulary used could not have been more than 100 words, and most of the characters were killed by shooting before I could discover what it was all about. Guns seemed to play an important role in most of the dramas I watched, though this was varied with sadism and assorted kinds of mayhem. All this violence and hurtling from one place to another in various conveyances did not leave the people much time for intersexual activity; a brief kiss was the only manifestation of affection or libido that I saw. Most of the dramas were also difficult to follow since they kept being interrupted by brief playlets and illustrated lectures about the purchase of various consumer goods. By dawn I had had enough of this and my speech had improved only microscopically, so I kicked in the glass picture tube as fitting comment and went to wash myself in a pink room filled with museum pieces out of the history of plumbing.

As soon as the shops opened in the morning, I had a number of hotel employees at work with a great deal of money and my purchases soon poured in. New clothes to fit my high station, with expensive luggage to carry it in. Plus a number of maps, a carefully made gadget called a magnetic compass, and a book on the principles of navigation. It was simplicity itself to determine the exact direction that the detector had pointed and to transfer this to a local map and to get a fairly accurate measurement of the distance in the measurement units called miles to the source of the time energy field. A long black line on the map gave me my direction, a slash across it to show distance—and I had my target. The two lines crossed at what appeared to be a major center of population, in fact, the largest one on this map.

It was called, quaintly, New York City. There was no indication where Old York City was, and it did not matter. I knew where I had to go.

Leaving the hotel was more like a royal abdication than a simple parting, and there were many glad cries for me to hurry back. As well there might be. A hired car whirled me out to the airport, and ready hands rushed my luggage to the proper exit. Where a rude shock was awaiting me since I had completely forgotten about the bank robbery. Others had not.

"Open up da bags," a grim-looking defender of law and order said.

"Of course," I said, very cheerily. I noticed that all of the passengers were being subjected to this same search. "Might I ask what you are looking for?"

"Money. Bank robbery," he muttered, poking through my possessions.

"I'm afraid I never carry large sums," I said, holding the bag with my massed banknotes tight to my chest.

"These are OK. Let's see that one."

"Not in public if you please, officer. I am a high-placed government official, and these papers are top secret." I quoted this word for word from the TV.

"In the room," he said, pointing. I was almost sorry I had kicked the thing in since it had been so educational.

In the room he looked shocked when I opened a sleepgas grenade rather than the bag, and he slumped nicely. There was a large metal locker against the wall filled with the numerous forms and papers so dear to the bureaucratic mind, and by rearranging them, I managed to make room for my snoring companion. The longer he remained undiscovered, the better. Unless there were unforeseen delays I would be in New York City before he regained consciousness—a process that would have to be a natural one since there would be no known antidote for my gas.

When I left the room, another of the uniformed officials was glowering at me, so I turned and called back through the still open door. "Thank you for your kind aid, no trouble at all, I assure you, no trouble at all." I closed the door and smiled at him as I passed. He raised a reluctant fingertip to the visor of his cap and turned away to grab at the luggage of an elderly passenger. I went on with my bag, not too surprised to notice the finest of pricklings of sweat upon my brow.

The flight was brief, uninteresting, noisy, and rather too bumpy, in a great fixed-wing craft that appeared to be powered by jets burning a liquid fuel. Though the smell of this fuel was everywhere, and familiar, I could not bring myself to believe that they were burning irreplaceable hydrocarbons. I had a moment of expectation when we disembarked, but there did not seem to be any alarm. Reaching the center of the city from the outlying airport was a painful ordeal of hurtling vehicles, shouts, noise of all kinds, and it was with a feeling of great relief that I finally fell through the door of a cool hotel room. But once reason was restored by the quiet, plus a couple of belts of the distilled organ destroyer I was becoming attached to, I was more than ready for the next step.

Which would be what? Reconnoiter or attack? Sweet reason dictated a careful stalk of the time energy source to determine what I was up against; who and what. I had half settled on this course and was berating myself mildly for even considering attack before the force of logic clanked through to its last link. I turned and pointed at myself in the mirror.

"You are a dum-dum." I shook a disgusted finger at myself. "What the cabdriver called the other cabdriver. A joick and woise."

There was only one advantage that I had—and that was surprise. Any bit of reconnoitering might tip my hand, and the time warriors would know that they were under investigation, perhaps attack. Since they had launched the time war, they were surely prepared for possible retaliation. But how can guards stay alert for weeks and months, possibly years? Once they knew I was around, at this time and place, all sorts of extra precautions would be taken. To prevent this, I had to hit and hit hard—even though I had no idea whom I was hitting.

"Does it make a difference?" I asked, snapping open a grenade case. "It might be nice to satisfy my curiosity and find out who has attacked the Corps—and why? But is it relevant or important? The answer is no." I glared across a small atomic fusion bomb at my red-eyed mirrored image and shook my head. "No, and no again. They must be destroyed, period. Now. Quickly."

There was no other course open to me, so calmly and surely I fitted about my body the most potent weapons of destruction ever devised by millennia of weapons research, always a favorite of mankind. Normally I am no believer in the kill-or-be-killed school of thought; affairs are usually not that black and white. They were now, and I felt not the slightest guilt over my decision. This was undeclared war against all mankind of the future—or why else had the Special Corps been the first target of attack? Someone, some group, wanted control of *everything*, probably the most selfish and insane plan ever conceived, and it did not really matter who or what they were. Death for them, before they killed everything of value.

When I left the hotel, I was a walking bomb, an army of destruction. The black box of the time energy detector was in the attaché case I carried, the indicators visible through holes I had cut in the lid. Somewhere out there was the enemy, and when he moved, I would be waiting.

It was a short wait. There was an unseen burst of time energy unleashed, close by if the action of the needle was any indication, and I was on the trail. Direction and distance, I worked out the vector as I plunged ahead, almost ignorant of the people and vehicles around me, but slowing and becoming more careful after a close miss by a lumbering truck.

Now a wide thoroughfare with green in the center of it, tall buildings of a uniformly depressing design, great slabs of metal and glass looming up in the polluted air. One very much like the other. Which one did I want?

The needle swung again, quivering with the intensity of its

reaction, turning as I walked, the meter rising to a distance reading right at the top of its scale.

There. In that building, the copper and black one.

In I went, prepared for anything.

Anything that is except what happened next.

They were locking the doors behind me, lining up and blocking them even as they did so. *Everyone*. The visitors to the building, the elevator starters—even the man behind the cigar counter. Running, pressing forward, coming toward me with the cold light of hatred in their eyes.

I had been discovered; they must have detected *my* detector; they knew who I was. They were attacking first.

8

IT WAS A nightmare, come alive. At some time in our lives we are all touched by incipient paranoia and feel that everyone is against us. Now I was faced with the reality. For a single instant this basic fear possessed me; then I shrugged it off and tried to win.

But that slight hesitation had been enough. What I should have done was shoot, kill, fire, destroy, just as I had planned. But I had not planned to face all these people in this manner; therefore, I could not win. Of course, I did some damage, gas and bombs, a bit of violence, but it wasn't enough. More and more hands tore at my clothing, and there was no end to them. Nor were they gentle about it, coming at me with the same raw hatred I felt for them, opposite sides of the coin, both seeing destruction in the other. I was pursued and run down, and unconsciousness was almost a blessing when it dropped.

Not that I was allowed this peace for long. Pain and a sharp smell burning in my nostrils drew me back to face unpleasant reality. A man, a large, tall man, standing and facing me, his features blurred by my unfocused eyes. It seemed that many hands held me, squeezing tight and shaking me. Something moist was pulled across my face clearing away whatever had obscured my vision, and I could see. See him as he saw me.

Twice as tall as a normal man, so much bigger than me that I had to lean back to look up at him towering there. His skin a suffused red, his eyes angled and dark, many of his teeth pointed when he opened his mouth.

"When are you from?" he asked, his voice a harsh drum, speaking the language we used in the Corps. I must have reacted to that because he smiled, with victory but not with warmth.

"The Special Corps, it had to be. The one flare of energy before darkness. How many of you came? Where are the others?"

"They . . . will find you," I managed to say. A very minor success for my side weighed against the victories of the other. As yet they did not know that I was alone, and I would stay alive until they discovered it. Which would not be long. I had been stripped efficiently, all my devices removed. My defenses gone. They would backtrack me to the hotel and find out soon enough that there was no more to fear.

"Who are you?" I asked, words my only weapon. He did not answer but instead raised both fists in a victorious gesture. The words came automatically to my lips. "You're mad."

"Of course," he shouted exultantly and the hands holding me pulled and swayed at the same time. "That is our condition, and though they killed us once for it, they will not kill us again. This time we will be victorious because we will destroy our enemies even before they are born, doom to nonlife oblivion the ones who did it."

I remembered something Coypu had said about this Earth being destroyed in the far past. Had it been done to stop these people? Was it being undone now? His screamed words cut off the thought.

"Take him. Torture him most profoundly for my pleasure and to weaken his will. Then suck all the knowledge from his brain. Everything must be discovered, everything."

As the hands tore me from the room, I knew what I had to do. Wait. Get away from this man, away from the crowds, to the specialized skills of the torturers, to some needed privacy. The opportunity came as technicians in a white laboratory beat at the people who held me and dragged me from them. They were as brutal to one another as they had been to me, a hierarchy of hatred. They must be mad as he had said. What perversion of human history had brought these people upon the scene? There was no way to imagine.

Again I waited. Calm in the knowledge that I had only a single opportunity and I should not throw it away. The door was closed. I was pressed back against a table, and my ankles were secured to it. There were five men in the room with me. Two had their backs turned, attention on their instruments; the others were pushing me down. I moved my jaw forward and bit down as hard as I could upon the last tooth.

This was my final weapon, the ultimate weapon, one that I had never used before. I normally did not even carry it, considering the normal life-and-death dustups not worth this price of winning. The present situation was different. When I bit, the artificial tooth cracked and the drops of bitter liquid it contained ran down my throat.

As the pain hit, it was obliterated, engulfed even as it began by the nerve-deadening drug that enabled me to withstand the on-slaught of the other ingredients. They were a devil's brew that the

Corps' medics had worked out at my suggestion, that had only been tested before in smaller quantities on test animals. Here were all the stimulants ever discovered, including the new class of synergators, the complex chemicals that enabled the human body to perform the incredible feats of hysterical strength that had been long known but impossible to duplicate.

Time speeded up, and the men hovering above me moved slowly. Seeing this, I waited those fractions of a second more for the drugs to take complete effect before reaching out my hands. Though each of the heavyset men had his full weight on one of my arms, it did not matter. There was no feeling of weight or even effort as I lifted them each clear of the floor at the same time and drove their skulls together before hurling them bodily at the third man at the foot of the table. All of them impacted, rolled, fell, their faces twisted in strange contortions of pain and fear. I sat up even as they dropped and seized the solid metal bands that bound my ankles and tore them free. It appeared to be the easiest and most obvious thing to do. This seemed to cause some damage to my fingers, but I was aware of it only as a passing comment and of no real importance. There were two more men in the room who were still turning toward me as though the destruction of the other three had only taken a few moments. Which it surely had. Seeing them still unprepared, one with a weapon half-raised, I threw myself at them, sparing a fist or a clutching hand for each, striking them down and hurling them toward the others into the writhing bundle of twisting bodies. They were five to my one, and I could afford to show them not even the slightest mercy even had I cared to. I struck, with my feet now since my hands were not so good, until there was no more motion in the heap, and only then could I permit the cold thoughts of logic to penetrate the hot berserker rage.

Next? Escape. My own clothes were rags, and I tore them from me in strips. My torturers were dressed in white garments, and I took the time to open all the unfamiliar fastenings and dress myself in the least soiled of their clothing. There was a ragged wound in my forehead, which I covered with a neat dressing—there would be other bandages here after the battle in the entrance—then put wrappings about my hands. I was not interrupted, it could not have taken long, and when I was done, I left the room and went hurriedly back down the hallway, retracing the course over which I had been so recently dragged. There was a buzz like a disturbed hive in the building, and everyone I passed seemed too preoccupied to notice me, even the people milling about in the anteroom where my weapons had been spread out on a large table to be examined. If it had been a time for smiling, I would have smiled.

Gently, without disturbing anyone, I reached over and actuated a rack of gas bombs, holding my breath as I groped for the nose filters. It is a fast gas, and even those who had seen what I had done had no time for warnings before they fell. The air was hazy with the concentration of the gas when I picked up a gausspistol and threw open the great door to the next room.

"*You!*" he called out, his massive red body standing even as the gas felled the others around him. He swayed and reached for me, fighting the gas that should have dropped him instantly, until I slammed the pistol into the side of his head until he stopped. Yet his eyes, murderous with hatred, were on me all the time as I bound him in the chair. Only when the door was sealed behind me did I take the time to look him in the face again and see that he was still conscious.

"What kind of man are you?" The words were on my lips, unasked. "Who are you?"

"I am He who will rule forever, the mind that never dies. Release me."

There was such a power in his words that I felt myself drawn closer, swaying despite myself, the roundness of his eyes growing before me. I was hazy, the effects of my own drugs wearing off perhaps, and I shook my head and blinked rapidly. But another part of me was still alert, still unimpressed by great power, great evil.

"A long rule, but not a comfortable one." I smiled. "Unless you do something about that bad case of sunburn."

It could not have been better spoken. This monster was utterly humorless and must have been used to nothing except slavish obedience. Just once he howled, a speechless animal sound, and then there was speech enough, a torrent of babbled insanity that washed around me as I made preparations to end the time war.

Mad? Of course he was, but with some kind of organized madness that perpetuated and grew and infected those around him. The body was artificial. I could see the scars and grafts now, and he spoke to me about it. A fabricated body, a transplanted, stolen body, a metal-framed monstrosity that told me all too much about the manner of mind that would choose to live in a case like this.

There were others like him, he was the best, he was alone—it was hard to make sense of everything, but I remembered what I could for future reference. And all the time I was taking off the ventilating grille and dusting my powders into the air system and making preparations to throw a large monkey wrench into this satanic mill.

He and his followers had been destroyed once in the fullness of time. He had told me that. In some unknown manner they had planned a second chance at the mastery of the universe—but they were not to have it. I, Slippery Jim diGriz, single-minded freebooter of no fixed address had been called upon for many big tasks before, and I had always delivered. Now I was asked to save the world, and if I must, I must.

"They could not have picked a better man," I said proudly as I looked in at the great workings of a time laboratory neatly peppered with sprawled bodies. The great green coiled spring of a time-helix glowed at me, and I smiled back.

"Bombs in the works and you for a ride," I called out happily as I made just those preparations. "Wipe out the machinery and leave the nuts here for the local authorities, though perhaps Big Red deserves a special treatment."

He certainly did, and I wondered what I was waiting for. I was waiting to do it in the heat of passion, I imagine, no cold killer I even of the coldest of killers. Though I would have to be this time. I steeled myself to this realization, thumbed the selector on the gausspistol to explosive charges, and turned to the other room.

Opportunity presented itself far more quickly than I had imagined. A great red form was on top of me, striking out, hitting me. I rolled with the blow, across the room to the wall, twisting and bringing up the gun.

He was moving fast, tripping a switch and hurling himself at the end of the time-helix.

Bullets move fast, too, and mine hissed out of the gausspistol and into his body, exploding there.

And then he was gone. Pulled into time, forward or backward I did not know because the machinery was glowing and melting even as I ran. Would he be dead when he arrived at his destination? He had to be. Those were explosive charges.

Some of the drugs were beginning to wear off, and rattling fingers of pain and fatigue were already beginning to scratch at the edge of my awareness. It was time to go. Get my equipment first, then get out. To the hotel and then to a hospital. A little rest cure while they patched me up would give me the time to consider what to do next. The technology of this era might be advanced enough for the construction of a time-helix, and I still had the professor's memory locked in that black box. I would probably need a lot more money, but there were always ways of getting that.

I exited with an unhealthy stagger.

9

I CARRIED AN attaché case filled with the usual things: grenades, gas bombs, explosives, nose filters, a gun or two—just the normal tools of the trade. My back was straight, my shoulders square, and I entered the paymaster's office in a most martial manner. If only to do the uniform justice, a spanking-new gold-striped and beribboned uniform of a commander in the United States Navy.

"Good morning," I snapped briskly, closing the door behind me and locking it at the same time, swiftly and silently, with the tool concealed in my hand.

"Yes, sir."

The grizzled chief petty officer behind the desk spoke politely enough, but it was obvious that his attention was really upon his work, the papers that piled neatly upon his desk, and strange officers just had to wait their turn. Just as sergeants do in all armies, the chiefs run the navies. Sailors hurried about on naval financial matters, and through a doorway opposite I had a view of the gape-mouthed gray form of a government issue safe. Lovely. I put my case on the chief's desk and snapped it open.

"I read about it in the newapaper," I said. "How the military always rounds its figures upwards to the next million or billion dollars when asking for appropriations. I admire that."

"Aye, aye, sir," the chief muttered, his fingers punishing the comptometer keys, uninterested either in my reading ability or in any comments from the press.

"I thought you would be interested. But that gave me the idea. Share the wealth. With such liberality there should be plenty to spare for me. That is why I am going to shoot you, Chief."

Well, that got his attention. I waited until the eye widening and jaw gaping reached their maximum, then pulled the trigger on the long-barreled pistol. It went *shoof* and thudded in my hand, and the chief grunted and slipped from sight behind the desk. All of this had taken but a moment, and the others in the office were just becoming aware that something was wrong when I turned and picked them off one by one. Stepping over the litter of bodies, I poked my head into the inner office and called out.

"Hoo-hoo, Captain, I see you."

He turned from the safe, growling some nautical oath, and caught the needle in the side of his neck. He folded as quickly as the others. My drug is potent, swift-acting, and soporific. Already snores were rising from the room behind me. The payroll was there, stacks of crisp bills arranged neatly in a nest of trays. I snapped open my folding suitcase and was reaching for the first bundle of green goodness when the glass crashed out of the window and the gun hammered bullets in my direction.

Only I wasn't there. If they had fired through the glass, I would have been thoroughly punctured by the lead slugs the people of this time favored, but they had not. Breaking the glass before firing gave me that fraction of a second to take action, action that my well-tuned and always-suspicious reflexes were constantly waiting for. I was over and back in a tumbling roll, minibombs from my sleeve holdout dropping into my fingers even before I hit the floor. Both flash and smoke. They thudded and flared, and the air was instantly opaque. I sent more after the first, and the firing stopped. I wriggled along the floor like a snake and, with the bulk of the safe between myself and the window, began stuffing the bag full of money, working by touch. Just because I was discovered, trapped, and in mortal danger was no reason to leave the loot. If I was going to all this trouble, I ought to at least be paid for it.

Dragging both bags behind me, I crawled toward the outer office and was about to go through the doorway when the loudhailer blared outside.

"We know you're in there. Come out and surrender or we'll gun you down. The building is surrounded—you don't have a chance."

The smoke thinned out near the door, and standing in the darkness, I could see through the windows that the voice had been speaking the truth. There were trucks out there, presumably loaded with hard-eyed well-armed SP's. As well as jeeps with large-caliber machine guns mounted in their rears. Quite a reception committee.

"You'll never take me alive, you rats!" I shouted, sowing smoke and flare bombs in all directions, as well as a larger explosive grenade that took out part of the rear wall. Under cover of all this excitement I crawled over to the sleeping chief and peeled off his jacket by touch. A lad of long service, he had more stripes than a tiger and hash marks up to his elbows. I threw my jacket aside and donned his, then traded hats as well. The people outside seemed to have set an elaborate trap, which meant they knew more about me than I cared to have them know. But this knowledge could be turned against them by a swift change in rank. I flipped about a few more bombs, put my gun into my pocket, picked up both bags, and unlocked and flung the front door open.

"Don't shoot!" I called out in a hoarse voice as I stumbled out into the fresh air and stood in the open doorway, a perfect target. "Don't shoot—he's got a gun in my back. I'm a hostage!" I tried to look terrified, which required little effort when I saw the small army facing me.

After this I staggered forward a half step and looked over my shoulder, letting everyone get a good view of me. Attempting to ignore the feeling that I had a bull's-eye painted on my chest with the big black spot right over my heart.

No one fired.

I stretched the moment a bit further—then dived off the steps and rolled to one side.

"Shoot! Get him! I'm clear!"

It was most spectacular. All the guns let go at once and blew the door from the frame and the glass from the windows, and the front of the building became as perforated as a colander.

"Aim high!" I called out, crawling for the protection of the nearest jeep. "All our guys are on the floor."

They shot high and vigorously and began to separate the top of the building from the bottom. I crept past the jeep and an officer came over to me and collapsed as I broke a sleepgas capsule under his nose.

"The lieutenant's hit," I cried as I shoved him and the bags into the back of the jeep. "Get him out of here."

The driver was very obliging and did as ordered, barely giving me time to get in myself. Before we had gone five meters, the gunner was sleeping next to the lieutenant, and as soon as the driver shifted into high gear, he dozed as well. It was tricky getting him out of the seat and getting myself into it while bouncing along at a good clip, but I managed it. Then I stood on the gas pedal.

It did not take them long to catch on. In fact, the first of the jeeps was after me even as I was stuffing the driver in back with the others. This barrier of bodies was a blessing because no more guns were going off. But they certainly were in hot pursuit. I did a sharp turn around a building and sent a platoon of boots jumping for cover, then took a fast look at the pursuers. My! Twenty, thirty vehicles of all kinds tore along after me. Cars, jeeps, trucks, even a motorcycle or two, passing one another, horns and sirens going, having a wonderful time. Jim diGriz, benefactor of mankind. Wherever I go, happiness follows. I turned into a large hangar and rushed between rows of parked helicopters. Mechanics dived aside in a cloud of flying tools as I skittered between the machines in a tight turn and back toward the open front of the hangar. As I emerged on one side, my followers were rushing in at the other. Very exciting.

Helicopters—why not? This was Bream Field, the self-proclaimed helicopter capital of the world. If they could fix the things, they could fly them. By now the entire naval station would be locked tight and surrounded. I had to find another way out. Off to one side the green glass form of the tower loomed up, and I headed in that direction. The flight line was before me, and a fat-bellied helicopter stood there, motor rumbling and blades swishing in slow circles. I squealed the jeep to a stop below the gaping door. When I stood up to throw my bags through it, a heavy boot kicked out at my head.

They had been alerted by radio, of course—as probably had everyone else in a hundred-mile radius. It was annoying. I had to duck under the blow, grab the boot, and wrestle with its owner while my horde of faithful followers roared up behind me. The boot owner knew entirely too much about this kind of fighting, so I cheated and shortened the match by shooting him in the leg with one of my needles. Then I threw the money in, hurled some sleepgas grenades after it, and finally myself.

Not wanting to disturb the pilot, who was snoring at the controls, I slipped into the copilot's seat and bugged my eyes at the dials and knobs. There were certainly enough of them for such a primitive device. By trial and error I managed to find the ones that I wanted, but by this time I was surrounded by a solid ring of vehicles, and a crowd of white-hatted club- and gun-bearing SP's were fighting to be first into the copter. The sleepgas dropped them, even the ones wearing gas masks, and I waited until I had a full load, then pulled the throttle full on.

There have been better takeoffs, but as an instructor once told me, anything that gets you airborne is satisfactory. The machine shuddered and shimmied and wallowed about. I saw men diving for safety below and felt the crunch of the wheels against the top of a truck. Then we were up and sagging away in a slow turn. Toward the ocean and the south. It was not chance alone that had led me to this particular military establishment when my funds ran low.

Bream Field is situated in the lower corner of California with the Pacific Ocean on one side and Mexico on the other. Which is as far south and as far west as you can go and stay in the United States. I no longer wished to stay in the United States. Not with what looked like all the Navy and Marine helicopters in the country rumbling up after me. I'm sure the fighter planes were on the way. But Mexico is a sovereign nation, a different country, and the pursuit could not follow me there. I hoped. At least it would pose some problems. And before the problems had been solved, I would be long gone.

As the white beaches and blue water flew by beneath me, I worked on a simple escape plan. And familiarized myself with the controls. After a bit of trial and error and a few sickening lurches, I found the automatic pilot. A nice device that could be set to hover or to follow a course. Just what I needed. The mere sight of it provided my plan, complete and clear. Below me the border rushed up, then the bullring and the pink, lavender, and yellow houses of the Mexican beach resort. They swept by quickly enough, and the grim coastline of Baja California instantly began. Black teeth of rocks in the foam, sand and sharp gorges cutting down to the sea gray mesquite, dusty cactus. An occasional house or campsite. Dead ahead a rocky peninsula jutted out into the ocean, and I pulled the machine up over it and down on the other side. The rest of the copters were only seconds behind me.

Seconds were all I needed. I set the controls to hover and climbed down among the sleeping defenders of the law. The ocean was about ten meters below, the great spinning rotors sending up clouds of spray from it. I threw both my bags out into the water and had turned to inject the pilot in the neck even before they had hit. He was stirring and blinking—the sleepgas antidote is almost instantaneous—as I set the robot pilot for forward flight and dived for the open door.

It was a close-run thing. The copter was moving forward at full blast as I tumbled into the air. It wasn't much of a dive, but I did manage to get my feet down so they hit first. I went under, swallowed some water, coughed, swam up, and banged my head on one of the floating bags. The water was far colder than I had thought it would be, and I was shivering and a cramp was beginning in my left leg. The bag gave me some support so that, kicking and floundering, I splashed over and grabbed the other one. Just as I did this, there was a mighty roar from overhead as the rumbling crowd of helicopters hurtled past like avenging angels. I'm sure that none of them were looking down at the water; all eyes were fixed upon the single copter rushing away ahead of them to the south. Even as I looked, this machine began to bob and turned off in a slow arc. A delta-wing jet appeared suddenly, diving past it and up and around. I had a little time but not very much. And there was absolutely no place to hide on the exposed rock of the peninsula or the bare sand of the shore.

Improvise, I told myself as I paddled and puffed toward the shore. They don't call you Slippery Jim for nothing. Slip out of this one. The cramp took over, and all I felt like doing was slipping under the water. Then there was firm sand under my feet, and I staggered, gasping, up onto the beach.

I had to hide without being hidden. Camouflage, one of mother nature's original tricks. The angry copters were still buzzing about on the horizon as I began to dig furiously at the sand with my bare hands.

"Stop!" I ordered myself and sat up, swaying. "Use your brains, not your muscles, lesson number one."

Of course. I slipped an explosive grenade into my hand, triggered it and dropped it into the shallow hole, then dived aside. It whoomphed satisfactorily and sent up a spray of sand. And left a tidy crater that was just the right size for the two bags. I hurled them into it and began to undress frantically, throwing my clothes after the bags. The copters must have been chatting with each other; they were turning and starting back down the beach.

Just by chance, vanity had goaded me this morning into putting on purple underwear which could easily pass for swimming attire from a distance. I stripped down to these shorts and kicked sand into the hole covering everything.

By the time the first copter swished by overhead I was lying facedown and sunning myself, just another swimmer on a beach. They went by overhead in a line, making a sweep. I sat up and looked at them as anyone would with all this going on. Then they were past, bobbing up over the rocky spine and gone, their motors rumbling out of hearing.

But not for long, that was certain. What should I do? Nothing. Just stay pat and think innocent. I had elected my role, and now I had to play it out.

They didn't take much time. Whoever was in charge ordered a sweep in line abreast covering the ocean, beach, and hills. Now they were slower, searching every inch of the way, undoubtedly with high-powered glasses. Time for another swim. I shivered when the spray curled around my ankles and I knew I was turning blue as the water crept ever upward. A wave broke over my head, and I was swimming with a stately dog paddle.

The copters were back, and one hovered over me, sending up clouds of spray. I shook my fist up at it and shouted realistic curses into the sound of its engine. Someone was leaning out of the open doorway, calling to me, but I was not listening. After a certain amount of fist shaking I submerged and swam underwater, trying to make my one uncramped leg do the work of two. The copter was swinging away after the others as I painfully made my way ashore again and sprawled on the sand so the wind and sun could dry me.

Now how did I get out of here?

10

AS SOON AS the copters were out of sight, I dug like a mole and unearthed my clothing and the bags, rushing them up the beach above the highwater mark. Another bomb and another interment, only this time I put on my trousers and shoes—and made sure some of my equipment went into the pockets. A few quick cuts transformed the long-sleeved uniform shirt into a short-sleeved sport shirt. As this clothing began to dry, it lost all resemblance to any part of a military dress, which was all for the best. Before leaving, I scuffed and dragged the sand to obliterate my digging and took careful triangulations of some large inland peaks so I could find the spot again. Then I headed for the coast road that passed a few hundred meters away.

My luck held. I had no sooner climbed over into the northbound lane when a beetlelike open machine with high wheels came rushing toward me. I raised my thumb in the universal gesture and was answered by a squealing of brakes. I saw now that there were powered surfboards sticking out of the back and there were two tanned young men in the front, their garments even more disarrayed than mine. A fashion, I knew, so perhaps they took me for one of their own.

"Man, you look wet," one commented as I climbed into the back.

"Man, I was high and took a watery trip."

"Gotta try that some time," the driver answered, and the machine hurled itself down the road.

Less than a minute later two hulking black sedans with flashing lights and howling sirens tore down the road in the opposite direction. The large letters "POLICIA" were painted on their side, and it took very little linguistic knowledge to translate that. My new friends, refusing the offer of refreshment, let me off in downtown Tijuana, then raced away. I sat at an outside table with a large tequila, lime, and salt and realized that I had just escaped from a carefully planned trap.

And a trap it was. That was obvious now that I had the time to stop and think about it. All those jeeps and trucks had not appeared out of thin air, and it is doubtful if that amount of firepower could have been organized so quickly even if an alarm had gone off. I went back over my motions, step by step, and was absolutely sure that I had actuated no alarms.

So how had they known what was going to happen?

They knew because some time-hopper had read the newspapers after the event, then had jumped back in time to give the warning. I had been half expecting this to happen—but that did not mean I had to enjoy it. I licked the salt from the base of my thumb, downed the bulk of the tequila, and bit hard into the lime. The combination tasted marvelous as it burned a course of acid destruction down my throat.

He was alive. I had wiped out his organization in this happy year of A.D. 1975, but He had gone on to bigger and worse nastiness in another era. The time war was on again. He and his madmen wanted to control all history and all time, an insane idea that might very well succeed, since they had already wiped out the Special Corps in the future, the one law-abiding organization that might have beaten them. Or rather they had wiped out all of the Corps except me, while I had bounced into the past to wipe out the wiper-outers and in doing so restore the Corps to the probable paths of future history. Big assignment, which I had accomplished 99.9 percent of. It was the vital .1 percent that was still causing trouble, the monster He who had escaped me at the end of a time-helix even though he had been nicely peppered with exploding slugs from my gun. Probably had armored guts. Next time I would use something stronger. An atomic bomb on his breakfast tray or suchlike.

To work. I *had* hoped that a time-helix could be built to whip me back to the future, or rather ahead to the future; grammar leaves a certain amount to be desired when it comes to time travel. Back/ahead to the arms of my Angelina and the acclaim of my peers. But not right now since they didn't even exist. Time war is a tricky thing and can be very confusing at times. All of the time might be more accurate. I was very glad that I did not need to know the theory but could just be whipped back and forth by others, like a temporal paddle ball, to do my violent best at whatever assignment was required.

There was little difficulty in obtaining a car and digging up the money early the next morning, although certain plainclothes observers had to be induced to sleep soundly instead of doing their jobs. Smuggling the money back into the United States was even easier, and before noon I was in the offices of Whizzer Electronics, Inc., in San Diego. A large and complete laboratory, a small front office with a not too bright receptionist, and that was it. I had set the place up as best I could, and it was up to Professor Coypu now to take over.

"Do you understand, Prof?" I said, talking to the small black box with his name on it. "All set up and ready to go." I shook the box. "Someday you must tell me how your memories can exist in this recorder if you don't exist or won't exist in this galaxy because He and his nuts have destroyed the Corps. Better someday you don't tell me. I'm not sure I really want to know." I held the box up and gave it a scan around the room.

"The finest equipment stolen money can afford. Every up-to-date research tool I could lay my hands on. Stocks of spare parts of all kinds. A supply of raw material. Catalogs from all the electronic, physical, and chemical manufacturers. A large bank balance to draw upon to buy what you need. A pile of signed checks waiting to be filled out. Language lessons neatly taped. Instructions, a history of what has happened, the works. Over to you, Prof, and take it easy with this body. It's the only one we have."

Before I could change my mind, I lay back on the couch, stuck the contact from the memory box to the back of my neck, and turned on the switch.

"*What's happening?*" Coypu said, slithering into my mind.

"A lot. You're in my brain, Coypu, so don't do anything dangerous."

"*Most interesting. Yes, your body indeed. Let me move that arm now, stop interfering. In fact, why don't you go away for a bit while I see what is happening?*"

"I'm not so sure that I want to."

"*Well, you must. Here, I'll push.*"

"No!" I shouted, not that it did any good. A formless blackness pressed down on me, and I spiraled out of sight into a greater darkness below, pushed away by Coypu's electronically magnified memories. . . .

time
   goes
      by
        so
          slowly

• • •

The black box was in my hand; the name "Coypu" written in rough white letters across its front; my fingers were on a switch that was turned to *off*.

Memory returned, and I staggered mentally and looked around for a chair so I could sit down. Until I discovered that I was already sitting down, so I sat harder.

I had been away, and someone else had been running my body. Now that I was back in charge I could detect faint traces of memories of work, a lot of work, a great period of time, days, perhaps weeks. There were burns and calluses on my fingers and a new scar on the back of my right hand. A tape recorder rustled to life—it must have had a timer to turn it on—and Professor Coypu spoke to me.

"To begin with—do not do this again. Do not allow this recorded memory of my brain into control of your body. Because I can remember everything. I remember that I no longer exist. This brain-in-a-box is all there may ever be of me. If I turn off the switch on it, I cease to be. The switch may never be turned on again. Probably won't. This is suicide, and I am not the suicidal type. Impossibly hard to touch the switch. I think I can do it now. I know what is at stake. Something a lot bigger than the pseudolife of this taped brain. So I will do my best to turn the switch. I doubt if I could do it a second time. As I said, don't do this again. Be warned."

"I'm warned. I'm warned," I muttered, turning off the tape while I found myself a drink. Coypu was a good man. The bar was stocked as I had left it, and a treble malt whiskey on the rocks cleared some of the muzziness from my head. I settled down and turned the tape on again.

"To business. Once I began investigating, it became obvious why these temporal criminals chose this particular epoch. A society just bursting into the age of technology, yet the people still with their minds in the Dark Ages. Nationalism, sheer folly; pollution, criminal; intraglobal warfare, madness—"

"Enough lecturing, Coypu, on with the show."

"—but there is no need to lecture on this subject. Suffice to say that all the materials for a time-helix are available here. And the societal setup is such that a major operation of time tinkering can successfully be concealed. I have constructed a time-helix, and it is coiled and set. I have also built a time tracer and with it have ascertained the temporal position of this creature called He. For reasons best known to him He is now operating out of the fairly recent past of this planet, some one hundred and seventy years ago. I am only guessing now, but I think his entire present operation is a trap. Undoubtedly for you. In some manner I cannot discover he has erected a time block before the year 1805. So you cannot return to an early enough period to catch him as he is building his present establishment. Be wary, he must be working with a large force. I have marked the controls so you can pick any of the five years after 1805 during which they are operating. In a city named London. The choice is yours. Good luck.''

I flicked off the recorder and went after more drink, depressed. Some choice. Pick my own year to get blasted. Nip back into the prescientific past and shoot it out with the minions of He. Even if I won—so what? I would be stranded there for life, stuck in time. A dismal prospect. Yet I had to go. In reality I only had the illusion of choice. He was tracking me down in the year 1975, and the next time he might very well succeed in polishing me off. Far better to carry the fight to him. Rah-rah. I took more drink and reached for the first book on the long shelf.

Coypu had not wasted his time. In addition to wiring up all the hardware, he had collected a neat little library about the years in question, the opening decade of the nineteenth century. London was my destination and as soon as that was realized, the name of one man became of utmost importance.

Napoleoni Buonaparte. Napoleon the First, Emperor of France and most of Europe and almost the world. His megalomaniacal ambitions rang a bell, for they differed hardly at all from He's own ambition. There was no coincidence here; there had to be a connection. I did not know yet what it was, but I was dismally sure that I would find out quickly enough. In the meantime, I read through all the books on the period until I felt I knew what I had to know. The only bright spot in the whole affair was the fact that England spoke a variety of the same speech as America, so I would not have to put up with any more brain-puncturing language lessons with the memorygram.

Of course, there was the matter of local dress, but there were more than enough illustrations from the period to show me what was needed. In fact a theatrical outfitter in Hollywood supplied me with a complete wardrobe, from knee pants and buttoned jackets to great cloaks and beaver hats. The styles of the time were quite attractive, and I took to them instantly, concealing a number of my devices in their voluminous folds.

Since I would return to the same time in time whatever time I left the present time, I took my time with the arrangements. But eventu-

ally, I ran out of excuses. The time had come. My weapons and
tools were adjusted and ready; my health was perfect; my reflexes
were keen; my morale was low. But what must be done must be
done. I appeared in the front office, and the receptionist gaped up at
me chewingumily from over her confession magazine.

"Miss Kipper, draw up a salary check for four weeks for yourself
in lieu of notice."

"You don't like my work?"

"Your work has been all that I desired. But owing to mismanage-
ment, this firm is now bankrupt. I am going abroad to dodge my
creditors."

"Gee, that's too bad."

"Thank you for your solicitude. Now if I can sign that
check. . . ."

We shook hands, and I ushered her out. The rent was paid for a
month ahead, and the landlord was welcome to the equipment left
behind. But I had fixed a destruct on the time-helix apparatus that
would operate after I had gone. There was enough tinkering with
time as it was, and I felt no desire to bring any more players into the
game.

It was a labor to jam myself into the space suit with all my clothes
on, and in the end, I had to take off both boots and jacket and strap
these outside with the rest of my equipment. Heavily laden, I
waddled over to the control board and braced myself for a final
decision. I knew where I would arrive and, following Coypu's
instructions, had set the proper coordinates into the machine days
earlier. London was out of the question; if they had any detection
apparatus at all, they would spot my arrival. I wanted to arrive far
enough away geographically so they would not spot me, but close
enough so I would not have to suffer a long journey by the primitive
transportation of the time. Everything I had read about it caused me
to shudder. So I compromised on the Thames Valley near Oxford.
The bulk of the Chilterns would be between me and London and
their solid rock would absorb radar, zed rays, or any other detection
radiation. Once I had arrived, I could make my way to London by
water, a matter of some one hundred kilometers, rather than by the
ghastly roads of the period.

That was where I was arriving—when was another matter. I
stared intensely at the neatly numbered dials as though they could
tell me something. They were mute. A time barrier set up at 1805, I
could not arrive earlier. The year 1805 itself seemed too much of a
trap; they would surely be ready, waiting and alert at that time. So I

had to arrive later. But not too much later, or they would have accomplished whatever evilness they had in mind. Two years then, not too long for them to work, but enough time so that they might—hopefully—be a little off guard. I took a deep breath and set the dials for 1807. And pressed the actuator. In two minutes the time would cut in full power. With leaden feet I shuffled toward the glowing green coil of the time-helix and touched the barlike end.

As before, there was no sensation, just the glow surrounding me so that the room beyond was hard to see. The two minutes seemed closer to two hours, although my watch told me there were more than fifteen seconds to go to springoff. This time I closed my eyes, remembering the uneasy sensations of my last time-hop, so I was tense, nervous, and blind when the helix released and hurled me back through time.

Zoink! It was not enjoyable. As the helix unwound, I was whipped into the past while its energy was expended into the future. An interesting concept that did not interest me in the slightest. For some reason this trip churned up my guts more than the last one had, and I was very occupied with convincing myself that whoopsing inside a space suit is a not nice thing. When I had this licked, I realized that the falling sensation was caused by the fact that I *was* falling, so I snapped open my eyes to see that I was in the midst of a pelting rainstorm. And dimly seen, close below, were sodden fields and sharp-looking trees rushing up at me.

After some panicky fumbling with the wrist control for the grav-chute, I managed to turn it on full, and the harness creaked and groaned at the sudden deceleration. I creaked and groaned, too, as the straps felt as though they were slicing through my flesh to the bone beneath—which they would quickly abrade away. I honestly expected my arms to drop off and my legs to fly by when I crashed down through the small branches of a waiting tree, caromed off a larger branch, and crashed into the ground below. Of course the grav-chute was still working on full lift, and as soon as the grassy slope had broken my fall, I was up and away again, hitting the branch a second lick for luck on the way by and springing up out of the treetop in a great welter of twigs and leaves. Once more I fumbled for the control and tried to do a better job of it. I drifted down, around the tree this time, and dropped like a sodden feather onto the grass and lay there for a bit.

"A wonderful landing, Jim," I groaned, feeling all over for broken bones. "You ought to be in the circus."

I was battered but sound, which fact I realized after a painpill had cleared my head and numbed my nerve endings. Belatedly, I looked around through the lessening rain but could see no one—or any sight of human habitation. Some cows in the adjoining field grazed on, undisturbed by my dramatic appearance. I had arrived.

"To work," I ordered myself, and began to unburden myself under the shelter of the large tree. The first thing off was the collapsible container I had constructed with great ingenuity. It opened out and assembled into a brassbound leather chest typical of the period. Everything else, including the space suit and grav-chute, fitted into it. By the time I had loaded and locked it the rain had stopped and a frail sun was working hard to get through the clouds. Midafternoon at least, I judged by its height. Time enough to reach shelter by nightfall. But which way? A rutted path through the cow field must lead someplace, so I took that downhill, climbing the drystone fence to reach it. The cows rolled round eyes in my direction but otherwise ignored me. They were large animals, familiar to me only through photographs, and I tried to remember what I had heard about their pugnacity. These beasts apparently did not remember either and did not bother me as I went down the path, chest on shoulder, setting out to face the world.

The path led to a stile which faced onto a country lane. Good enough. I climbed over and was considering which direction to take when a rustic conveyance made its presence known by a great squeaking and a wave of airborne effluvium carried by the breeze. It clattered into sight soon after, a two-wheeled wooden artifact drawn by a singularly bony horse and containing a full load of what I have since determined to be manure, a natural fertilizer much valued for its aid to crops and its ability to produce one of the vital ingredients of gunpowder. The operator of this contrivance was a drab-looking peasant in shapeless clothes who rode on a platform in front. I stepped into the road and raised my hand. He tugged on a series of straps that guided the pulling beast and everything groaned to a stop. He stared down at me, chomping empty gums in memory of long-vanished teeth, then reached up and knuckled his forehead. I had read about this rite, which represented the relationship of the lower class to the upper classes, and knew that my choice of costume had been correct.

"I am going to Oxford, my good man," I said.

"Ey?" he answered, cupping one grimy hand behind his ear.

"Oxford!" I shouted.

"Aye, Oxford," he nodded in happy agreement. "It be that way." He pointed back over his shoulder.

"I'm going there. Will you take me?"

"I be going that way." He pointed down the lane.

I took a golden sovereign out of my wallet, purchased from an old coin dealer, more money in one lump than he had probably seen in his entire lifetime, and held it up. His eyes opened wide and his gums snapped nicely.

"I be going to Oxford."

The less said about this ride, the better. While the unsprung dungmobile tortured the sitting part of my anatomy, my nose was assaulted by its cargo. But we were at least going in the correct direction. My chauffeur cackled and mumbled incomprehensibly to himself, wild with glee at his golden windfall, urging the ancient nag to its tottering top speed. The sun broke through as we came out of the trees, and ahead were the gray towers of the university, pale against the darker slate gray of the clouds, a very attractive sight indeed. While I was admiring it, the cart stopped.

"Oxford," the driver said, pointing a grubby finger. "Magdalen Bridge."

I climbed down and rubbed my sore hams, looking at the gentle arch of the bridge across the small river. There was a thud next to me as my chest hit the ground. I started to protest, but my transportation had already wheeled about and was starting back down the road. Since I was no more desirous of entering the city in the cart than he was of taking me, I didn't protest. But he might at least have said something. Like good-bye. It didn't really matter. I shouldered the chest and strode forward, pretending I did not see the blue-uniformed soldier standing by the shack at the end of the bridge. Holding a great long gunpowder weapon of some sort that terminated in what appeared to be a sharp blade. But he saw me well enough and lowered the device so it blocked my way and pushed his dark-bearded face close to mine.

"*Casket vooleyfoo?*" he said, or something like that. Impossible to understand, a city dialect perhaps since I had no trouble understanding the rustic who had brought me here.

"Would you mind repeating that?" I asked in the friendliest of manners.

"*Koshown onglay*," he growled and whipped the wooden lower end of his weapon up to catch me in the midriff.

This was not very nice of him, and I showed my distaste by stepping to one side so the blow missed and returned the favor by planting my knee in his midriff instead. He bent in the middle, so I chopped him in the back of the neck when that target presented itself. Since he was unconscious, I seized his weapon so it would not be actuated when it dropped.

All this had happened in the shortest of times, and I was aware of the wide-eyed stares of the passing citizenry. As well as the ferocious glare of another soldier in the door of the ramshackle building, who was raising his own weapon toward me. This was certainly not the way to make a quiet entrance into the city, but now that I had started I had to finish.

With the thought the deed. I dived forward, which enabled me to put down my chest while I avoided the weapon at the same time. There was an explosion, and a tongue of flame shot by my head. Then the butt of my own weapon came up and caught my latest opponent under the chin, and he went back and down with me right behind him. If there were others inside, it would be best to tackle them in the enclosed space.

There certainly were other soldiers, a goodly number of them, and after taking care of the nearest ones with a little dirty infighting, I triggered a sleepgas grenade to silence the rest. I had to do this— but I didn't like it. Keeping a wary eye on the door, I quickly mussed the clothing and kicked the ribs of the men who had succumbed to the gas in order to suggest that they had been felled by violence of some kind.

Now how did I get out of this? Quickly was the best idea since the citizenry would have spread the alarm by now. Yet when I reached the doorway, I saw that the passersby had drawn close and were trying to see what had happened. When I stepped out, they smiled and shouted happily, and one of them called out loudly.

"A cheer for his lordship! Look what he done to the Frenchies!"

Glad cries rang out as I stood there, dazed. Something was very wrong. Then I realized that one fact had been nagging at me ever since I had my first look at the colleges. The flag, flying proudly from atop the nearest tower. Where were the crossed crosses of England?

This was the tricolor of France.

11

WHILE I WAS trying to figure this one out, a man in plain brown leather clothes pushed through the cheering crowd and shouted them into silence.

"Get home, the lot of you, before the frogs come and kill you all. And don't say a word about this or you'll be hanging from the town gate."

Looks of quick fear replaced the elation, and they began to move at once, all except two men who pushed past to pick up the weapons strewn about inside. The sleepgas had dispersed, so I let them pass. The first man touched two fingers to his cap as he came up to me.

"That was well done, sir, but you'll have to move out quick because someone will have heard that shot."

"Where shall I go? I've never been to Oxford before in my life."

He looked me up and down quickly, in the same way I was sizing him up, and came to a decision.

"You'll come with us."

It was a close-run thing because I heard the tread of heavy marching boots on the bridge even as we nipped down a side lane burdened with the guns. But these men were locals and knew all the turnings and bypaths, and we were never in any danger that I could see. We ran and walked in silence for the better part of an hour before we reached a large barn that was apparently our destination. I followed the others in and put my chest on the floor. When I straightened up, the two men who had been carrying the guns took me by the arms while the man in leather held what appeared to be an exceedingly sharp knife to my throat.

"Who are you?" he asked.

"My name is Brown, John Brown. From America. And what is your name?"

"Brewster." Then, without changing the level tone of his voice: "Can you give me reason why we should not kill you for the spy you are?"

I smiled calmly to show him how foolish the thought was. Inside, I was not calm at all. Spy, why not? What could I say? Think fast,

Jim, because a knife kills just as thoroughly as an A-bomb. What did I know? French soldiers were occupying Oxford. Which meant that they must have invaded England successfully and occupied all or part of it. There was resistance to this invasion, the people holding me proved that, so I took my clue from this fact and tried to improvise.

"I am here on a secret mission." Always good. The knife still pressed against my throat. "America, as you know, sides with your cause. . . ."

"America helps the Frenchies; your Benjamin Franklin has said so."

"Yes, of course, Mr. Franklin has a great responsibility. France is too strong to fight now, so we side with her. On the surface. But there are men like me who come to bring you aid."

"Prove it?"

"How can I? Papers can be forged, they would be death to carry in any case, and you wouldn't believe them. But I have something that speaks the truth, and I was on my way to London to deliver it, to certain people there."

"Who?" Had the knife moved away the slightest amount?

"I will not tell you. But there are men like you all over England, who wish to throw off the tyrant's yoke. We have contacted some of the groups, and I am delivering the evidence I spoke of."

"What is it?"

"Gold."

That stopped them all right, and I felt the grip on my arms lessen ever the slightest. I pressed the advantage.

"You have never seen me before and will probably never see me again. But I can give you the help you need to buy weapons, bribe soldiers, help those imprisoned. Why do you think I assaulted those soldiers in public today?" I asked with sudden inspiration.

"Tell us," Brewster said.

"To meet you." I looked slowly around at their surprised faces. "There are loyal Englishmen in every part of this land who hate the invaders, who will fight to hurl them from these green shores. But how can they be contacted and helped? I have just shown you one way—and have provided you with these arms. I will now give you gold to carry on the struggle. As I trust you, you must trust me. If you wish, you will have enough gold to slip away from here and live your lives out happily in some kinder part of the world. But I don't think you will. You risked your lives for those weapons. You will do what you know is right. I will give you the gold and then go away. We will never meet again. We must go on trust. I trust you. . . ." I let my voice dwindle away, allowing them to finish the sentence for themselves.

"Sounds good to me, Brewster," one of the men said.

"Me too," said the other. "Let's take the gold."

"*I'll* take the gold if there's any to be taken," Brewster said, lowering the knife but still uncertain. "It could all be a lie."

"It could be," I said quickly, before he started punching holes in my flimsy story. "But it isn't—nor does it matter. You'll see that I'm well away tonight, and we will never meet again."

"The gold," my guard said.

"Let's see it," Brewster said reluctantly. I had bluffed it through. After this he couldn't go back.

I opened the chest with utmost care while a gun was kept pressed to my kidney. I had the gold; that was the only part of my story that was true. It was divided into a number of small leather bags and intended to finance this operation. That is just what it was doing now. I took one out and solemnly handed it over to Brewster.

He shook some of the glittering granules into his hand, and they all stared at it. I pushed.

"How do I get to London?" I asked. "By river?"

"Sentries on every lock of the Thames," Brewster said, still looking at the golden gravel upon his palm. "You wouldn't get as far as Abingdon. Horse, the only way. Back roads."

"I don't know the back roads. I'll need two horses and someone to guide me. I can pay, as you know."

"Luke here will take you," he said, finally looking up. "Used to be a drayman. But only to the walls; you'll have to get by the Frenchies yourself."

"That will be fine." So London was occupied. And what about the rest of England?

Brewster went out to take care of the horses, and Guy produced some coarse bread and cheese, as well as some ale, which was more welcome. We talked, or rather they talked and I listened, occasionally putting in a word but afraid of asking any questions that might prove my almost total ignorance. But a picture finally developed. England was completely occupied and pacified, had been for some years; the exact number was not made clear, although fighting was still going on in Scotland. There were dark memories of the invasion, great cannon that did terrible damage, the Channel fleet destroyed in a single battle. I could detect the cloven hoof of He behind a lot of it. History had been rewritten.

Yet this particular past was not the past of the future I had just come from. My head started to ache just thinking about it. Did this world exist in a loop of time, separate from the mainstream of history? Or was it an alternate world? Professor Coypu would know, but I did not think he would enjoy being plucked out of his memory tape again just to answer my questions. I would have to work it out without him. Think, Jim, put the old brainbox into gear. You take pride in what you call your intelligence, so apply it to something besides crookery for a change. There must be some form of logic here. Statement A, in the future this past did not exist. B, it sure existed now. But C might indicate that my presence here would destroy this past, even the memory of this past. I had no idea how this might be accomplished, but it was such a warm and cheering thought that I grabbed onto it. Jim diGriz history changer, world shaker. It made a pleasant image, and I treasured it as I dozed off on the hay—and woke up not too long afterward scratching at the invading insect life that was after my hot body.

The horses did not arrive until after dark, and we agreed that it would be best to leave at dawn. I managed to get some bug spray out of my chest to kill off my attackers, so I enjoyed a relatively peaceful night before the ride in the morning.

The ride! We were three days en route, and before we reached London, even my saddle sores had saddle sores. My primitive companion actually seemed to enjoy the trip, treating it as an outing of sorts, chatting about the country we passed through and getting falling down drunk each evening at the inns where we stopped. We had crossed the Thames above Henley and made a long loop to the south, staying away from all sizable centers of population. When we reached the Thames again at Southwark, there was London Bridge before us and the roofs and spires of London beyond. A little hard to see because of the high wall that stretched along the opposite riverbank. The wall had a crisp, clean look to it, far different from the smoke-stained gray of the rest of the city—and a sudden thought struck me.

"That wall, it's new, isn't it?" I said.

"Aye, finished two years back. Many died there, women and children, everyone driven like slaves by Bony to put it up. Right around the city it goes. No reason for it, just that he's mad."

There was a reason for it, and ego-flattering as it was, I still didn't like it. That wall was built for me, to keep me out. "We must find a quiet inn," I said.

''The George, right down here.'' He smacked his mouth loudly. ''Good ale, too, the best.''

''You enjoy it. I want something right on the river, within sight of that bridge there.''

''Knows just the place, the Boar and Bustard on Pickle Herring Street, right at the foot of Vine Lane. Fine ale there.''

The foulest brew was fine by Luke as long as it contained alcohol. But the Boar and Bustard suited my needs perfectly. A disreputable establishment with a cracked signboard above the door depicting an improbable-looking swine and an even more impossible-looking bird squaring off at each other. There was a rickety dock to the rear where thirsty boatmen could tie up—and a room I could have that looked out on the river. As soon as I had arranged for the stabling of my horse and argued over the price of the room, I bolted the door and unpacked the electronic telescope. This produced a clear, large, detailed, depressing picture of the city across the river.

It was surrounded by that wall, ten meters high of solid brick and stone—undoubtedly bristling with detection apparatus of all kinds. If I tried to go under or over it, I would be spotted. Forget the wall. The only entrance I could see from this vantage point was at the other end of London Bridge, and I studied this carefully. Traffic moved slowly across the bridge because everything and everyone was carefully searched before they were allowed to enter. French soldiers probed and investigated everything. And one by one the people were led through a doorway into a building inside the wall. As far as I could tell, they all emerged—but would I? What happened inside that building? I had to find out, and the ale room below was just the place.

Everyone loves a free spender, and I was all of that. The one-eyed landlord muttered and snaffled to himself and managed to find a drinkable bottle of claret in his cellar which I kept for myself. The locals were more than happy to consume blackjack after blackjack of ale. These containers were made of leather covered with tar which added a certain novelty to the flavor, but the customers did not seem to mind. My best informant was a bristle-bearded drover named Quinch. He was one of the men who moved the cattle from the pens to the knackers' yard where he also assisted the butchers in their bloody tasks. His sensibilities, as one might suspect, were not of the highest, but his capacity for drink was, and when he drank, he talked, and I hung on every word. He entered and left London every day, and bit by bit, through the spate of profanity and abuse, I put together what I hoped was an accurate picture of the entrance procedures.

There was a search; that much I could see from my window. At times a close search, at other times superficial. But there was one part of the routine that never varied.

Every person entering the city had to put his hand into a hole in the wall of the guardhouse. That was all, just put it in. Not touch anything at all, just in up to the elbow and out.

Over this I brooded, sipping my wine and ignoring the roars of masculine cheer around me. What could they detect from this? Fingerprints perhaps, but I always wore false fingerprint covers as a matter of routine and had changed these three times since the last operation. Temperature? Skin alkalinity? Pulse or blood pressure? Could these residents of, what to me was, the dim past differ in some bodily composition? It was not unreasonable to expect some changes over a period of more than 30,000 years. I had to find out the present norms.

This was done easily enough. I constructed a detector that could record all these factors and hung it inside my clothing. The pickup was disguised as a ring that I wore on my right hand. The next evening I shook hands with everyone I could, finished my wine, and retired to my chamber. The recordings were precise, accurate to ± 0.006 percent and very revealing. Of the fact that my personal readings fell well inside all the normal variations.

"You are not thinking, Jim," I accused myself in the warped mirror. "There *has* to be a reason for that hole in the wall. And the reason is a detection instrument of some kind. Now what does it detect?" I turned away from the accusing stare. "Come, come, don't evade the question. If you cannot answer it that way, turn it on its head. What is it possible to detect?"

This was more like it. I pulled out a piece of paper and began to list all the things that can be observed and measured, going right down the frequencies. Light, heat, radio waves, etc., then off into vibration and noise, radar reflections, anything and everything, not attempting to apply the things detected to the human body. Not yet. I did this after I had made the list as complete as possible. When I had covered the paper, I shook hands with myself triumphantly and reread it for human applications.

Nothing. I was depressed again. I threw it away—then grabbed it back. Something, what was it, something relating to something I had heard about Earth. What? Where. *There!* Destroyed by atomic bombs Coypu had said.

Radioactivity. The atomic age was still in the future, the only radioactivity in this world was natural background radiation. This did not take long to check.

Me, creature of the future, denison of a galaxy full of harnessed radiation. My body was twice as radioactive as the background count in the room, twice as radioactive as the hot bodies of my friends in the bar when I slipped down to check them out.

Now that I knew what to guard against I could find a way to circumvent it. The old brain turned over, and soon I had a plan, and well before dawn I was ready to attack. All the devices secreted about my person were of plastic, undetectable by a metal detector if they had one working. The items that were made of metal were all in a plastic tube less than a meter long and no thicker than my finger, which I coiled up in one pocket. In the darkest hour before the dawn I slipped out and stalked the damp streets looking for my prey.

And found him soon enough, a French sentry guarding one of the entrances to the nearby docks. A quick scuffle, a bit of gas, a limp figure, a dark passageway. Within two minutes I emerged at the opposite end wearing his uniform with his gun on my shoulder carried in the correct French manner. With my tube of devices down its barrel. Let them find *that* metal with a detector. My timing was precise, and when, at the first light, the straggling members of the night guard returned to London, I was marching in the last row. I would enter, undetected, in the ranks of the enemy. A foolproof scheme. They wouldn't examine their own soldiers.

More fool I. As we marched through the gate at the far end of the bridge I saw an interesting thing that I could not see with my telescope from my window.

As each soldier marched around the corner of the guardhouse he stopped for a moment, under the cold eyes of a sergeant, and thrust his hand into a dark opening in the wall.

12

"MAYERD!" I SAID as I tripped over the uneven footing on the bridge. I did not know what it meant, but it was the most common word the French soldiers used and seemed to fit the occasion. With this I stumbled into the soldier next to me, and my musket caught him a painful blow on the side of the head. He yelped with pain and pushed me away. I staggered backward, hit my legs against the low railing—and fell over into the river.

Very neatly done. The current was swift, and I went beneath the surface and clamped the musket between my knees so I wouldn't lose it. After that I surfaced just once, splashing at the water and screaming wordlessly. The soldiers on the bridge milled about, shouting and pointing, and when I was sure I had made the desired impression, I let my wet clothes and the weight of the gun pull me under again. The oxygen mask was in an inside pocket, and it took only seconds to work it out and pull the strap over my head. Then I cleared the water from it by exhaling strongly and breathed in pure oxygen. After that it was just a matter of a slow, easy swim across the river. The tide was on the ebb so the current would carry me well downstream from the bridge before I landed. So I had escaped detection, lived to regather my forces and fight again, and was totally depressed by my complete failure to get past the wall. I swam in the murky twilight and tried to think of another plan, but it was not exactly the best place for cogitation. Nor was the water that warm. Thoughts of a roaring fire in my room and a mug of hot rum drove me on for what seemed an exceedingly long time. Eventually I saw a dark form in the water ahead which resolved into the hull of a small ship tied up at a dock; I could see the pilings beyond. I stopped under the keel and worked my tube of instruments out of the musket and also took everything out of my coat. The gun stuffed into the jacket sleeve made a good weight, and both vanished toward the river bottom. After some deep breathing I took off the oxygen mask and stowed that away as well, then surfaced as quietly as I could next to the ship.

To look up at the coattails and patched trousers of a French soldier sitting on the rail above me. He was industriously involved polishing the blue-black barrel of a singularly deadly-looking cannon that projected next to him. It was far more efficient looking than any of the nineteenth-century weapons I had seen, which was undoubtedly caused by the fact that it did not belong to this period at all. Out of more than casual interest I had made a study of weapons available in the era I had recently left, so I recognized this as a 75-millimeter recoilless cannon. An ideal weapon to mount on a light wooden ship, since it could be fired without jarring the vessel to pieces. It could also accurately blow any other wooden ship out of the water long before the other's muzzle-loading cannon were within range. Not to mention destroying armies in the field. A few hundred of these weapons brought back through time could alter history. And they had. The soldier above turned and spat into the river, and I sank beneath the surface again and vanished among the pilings.

There were boat steps farther downriver out of sight of the French ship, and I surfaced there; no one was in sight. Dripping, cold, depressed, I climbed out of the water and hurried toward the dark mouth of the lane between the buildings. There was someone standing there, and I scuttled by—but then decided to stop.

Because he put the muzzle of a great ugly pistol into my side.

"Walk ahead of me," he said. "I will take you to a comfortable place where you can get dry clothing."

Only he did not say clothing, it sounded more like cloth-eeng. My captor very positively had a French accent.

All I could do was follow instructions, prodded on by the primitive hand cannon. Primitive or not, it could still blow a nice hole in me. At the far end of the lane a coach had been pulled up, blocking the lane completely, the door gaping open in unappreciated welcome.

"Get in," my captor said, "I am right behind you. I saw that unfortunate soldier fall from the bridge and drown and I thought to myself, what if he had been on the surface? What if he were a good swimmer and could cross the river, where would he land when moved along by the current? A neat mathematical problem which I solved, and *voilà!* there you were coming out of the water."

The door slammed, the coach started forward, and we were alone. I fell forward, dropped, turned, lunged, grabbed out for the pistol—and seized it by the butt because my captor now had it by the barrel and was holding it out to me.

"By all means you hold the gun, Mr. Brown, if it pleases you; it is no longer needed." He smiled as I gaped and scowled and leveled the pistol at him. "It seemed the simplest way to convince you to join me in the carriage. I have been watching you for some days now and am convinced that you do not like the French invaders."

"But—you are French?"

"But of course! A follower of the late king, a refugee now from the land of my birth. I learned to hate this pipsqueak Corsican while people here were still laughing at him. But no one laughs any longer, and we are united in one cause. But, please, let me introduce myself. The Count d'Hesion, but you may call me Charles since titles are now a thing of the past."

"Pleased to meet you, Charley." We shook on it. "Just call me John."

The coach clattered and groaned to a stop then, before this interesting conversation could be carried any further. We were in the courtyard of a large house and, still carrying the pistol, I followed the count inside. I was still suspicious, but there seemed little to be suspicious of. The servants were all ancient and tottered about muttering French to one another. Knees creaking, one aged retainer poured a bath for me and helped me to strip, completely ignoring the fact that I still held the pistol while he soaped my back. Warm clothes were provided, and good boots, and when I was alone, I transferred my armory and devices to my new clothing. The count was waiting in the library when I came down, sipping from a crystal glass filled with interesting drink, a brimming container of the same close by him. I handed him the pistol, and he handed me a glass of the beverage in return. It glided down my throat like warm music and sent a cloud of delicate vapor into my nostrils the like of which I had never inhaled before.

"Forty years old, from my own estate, which as you can tell instantly is in the Cognac."

I sipped again and looked at him. Nobody's fool. Tall and thin with graying hair, a wide forehead, lean, almost ascetic features.

"Why did you bring me here?" I asked.

"So we could join forces. I am a student of natural philosophy, and I see much that is unnatural. The armies of Napoleon have weapons that were made nowhere in Europe. Some say they come from far Cathay, but I think not. These weapons are served by men who speak very bad French, strange and evil men. There is talk of even stranger and more evil men at the Corsican's elbow. Unusual things are happening in this world. I have been watching for other unusual things and am on the lookout for strangers. Strangers who are not English, such as yourself. Tell me—how can a man swim across a river under water?''

''By using a machine.'' There was no point in silence; the count knew very well what he was asking. With those dark cannon out there there was no point in secrecy about the nature of the enemy. His eyes widened as I said this, and he finished his drink.

''I thought so. And I think you know more about these strange men and their weapons. They are not of the world as we know it, are they? You have knowledge of them, and you are here to fight them?''

''They are from a place of evil and madness, and they have brought their crimes with them. And I am fighting them. I cannot tell you everything about them because I don't know the entire story myself. But I am here to destroy them and everything they have done.''

''I was sure of it! We must join forces, and I will give you whatever help I can.''

''You can begin by teaching me French. I have to get into London, and it appears I will need to speak it.''

''But—is there time?''

''An hour or two will do. Another machine.''

''I am beginning to understand. But I am not sure that I like all these machines.''

''Machines cannot be liked or disliked; they are immune to emotion. We can use them or misuse them, so the problem of machines is a human problem like all others.''

''I bow to your wisdom; you are, of course, right. When do we begin?''

I returned to the Boar and Bustard for my things, then moved into a room in the count's house. A head-splitting evening with the memorygram—headache is a mild word for the side effects of using this memory-cramming machine—taught me conversational French, and to the count's pleasure, we now conversed in that language.

''And the next step?'' he asked. We had dined, and dined well indeed, and were now back to the cognac.

''I need to take a closer look at one of those pseudo Frenchmen who seem to be running things. Do they ever appear alone on this side of the river or, if not alone, in small groups?''

''They do, but their movements follow no set pattern. Therefore I shall obtain the most recent information.'' He rang the silver bell that stood next to the decanter. "Would you like one of these individuals rendered unconscious or dead and brought to you?"

"You are too kind," I said, holding out my glass so that the servant who had soundlessly appeared could refill it. "I'll handle that end of the business myself. Just point him out and I'll take over from there."

The count issued instructions; the servant slipped away; I worked on my drink.

"It will not take long," the count said. "And when you have the information, do you have a plan of action?"

"Roughly. I must enter London. Find He, the top demon in this particular corner of hell, then kill him, I imagine. And demolish certain machinery."

"The upstart Corsican—you will remove him, too?"

"Only if he gets in the way. I am no common murderer and find it difficult to kill at any time. But my actions should change the entire operation. The new weapons will no longer be supplied and will soon run out of ammunition. In fact, the interlopers may vanish altogether."

The count raised one eyebrow but was kind enough not to comment.

"The situation is complex; in fact, I do not really understand it myself. It has to do with the nature of time, about which I know very little. But it seems that this past, the time we are living in now, does not exist in the future. The history books to come tell us that Napoleon was beaten, his empire wiped out, that Britain was never invaded."

"It should only be!"

"It *may* be—if I can get to He. But if history is changed again, brought back to what it should have been, this entire world, as we know it now, may vanish."

"A certain risk must be taken in all hazardous enterprises." The count remained cool and composed, moving one hand in a slight gesture of dismissal as he talked. An admirable man. "If this world disappears, it must mean that a happier one will come into existence?"

"That's roughly it."

"Then we must press on. In that better world some other I will be returning to my estates, my family will live again, there will be flowers in the spring and happiness in the land. Giving up this life here will mean little; it is a miserable existence. Though I would prefer that knowledge of this possibility stay locked in this room. I am not sure that all our assistants will accept such a philosophical viewpoint.''

''I agree heartily. I wish it could be some other way.''

''Do not concern yourself, my dear friend. We will talk of it no longer.''

We didn't. We discussed art and viniculture and the hazards inherent in the manufacture of distilled beverages. Time moved quickly—as did the count's men—and even before we started on a second decanter, he was called out to receive a report.

''Admirable,'' he said upon his return, rubbing his hands together with pleasure. ''A small party of the men we seek are even now disporting themselves in a knocking shop in Mermaid Court. There are guards about, but I presume that offers no barrier to your operation?''

''None,'' I said, rising. ''If you will be kind enough to provide some transportation and a guide, I promise to return within the hour.''

This was done as asked, and I performed as promised. A morose individual with a shaved head and badly scarred face took me in the carriage and pointed out the correct establishment. I entered the building next to it, an office of some kind, now shuttered and locked with a monstrous piece of hardware most difficult to open. Not that the lock mechanisms were beyond me—never!—but they were so big that my lockpick couldn't reach the tumblers! My knife did, though, and I went through and up to the roof and crossed over to the roof of the next building, where I attached the end of my spider web to the most solid of the collection of chimneys. The strand of the web was a fine, almost invisible and practically unbreakable strand made up of a single long-chain molecule. It ran slowly off the reel that was fastened by a harness to my chest, and I dropped down toward the dark windows below. Dark to others. But the dual beams of ultraviolet light from the projectors on my UV sensitive goggles turned all light as day for me wherever I looked. I entered the window silently, caught my man with his pants down, rendered him and his companion unconscious with a dose of gas, and had him dozing in my arms and back up to the roof as quickly as the fiercely whirring spider web reel could lift us. Minutes later my prize was snoring on a table in the count's cellar while I spread out my equipment. The count looked on with interest.

''You wish to obtain information from this species of pig? I do not normally condone torture, but this seems to be an occasion for hot pokers and sharp blades. The crimes these creatures have committed! It is said the New World aborigines can flay a person completely without killing him.''

''Sounds jolly, but there will be no need.'' I lined up the instruments and hooked up the contacts. ''Machines again. I shall keep him unconscious and walk through his mind with spiked boots, even a worse torture in many ways. He will tell us what we need to know without ever knowing he has spoken. Afterward he is yours.''

''Thank you, no.'' The count raised disgusted hands. ''Whenever one of them is killed, the civilians suffer from many reprisals and killings. We will knock this one about a bit, rob him of clothing and everything, then dump him in an alley. It will resemble a crime of robbery, nothing else.''

''The best idea yet. Now I begin.''

It was like swimming in a sewer, going through that mind. Insanity is one thing, and he was certifiably insane like all of them, but outright evil is inexcusable. There was no problem in exacting information, just in sorting it out. He wanted to speak his own language but finally settled for French and English. I plumbed and picked and probed and eventually discovered all that I needed to know. Jules, my companion of the shaved head, was called in for the pleasurable sport of roughing up the subject and dumping him— stripped of his uniform—while the count and I returned gratefully to the unfinished carafe.

''Their headquarters appears to be in a place called St. Paul's. You know of it?''

''Sacrilege, they halt at nothing! The cathedral, the masterpiece of the great Sir Christopher Wren, it is here on the map.''

''The one named He is there, and apparently all the machinery and instruments as well. But to reach it, I must enter London. There is a good possibility that I might be able to pass the wall in his uniform since his body has the same radioactivity count as mine, a test they use to detect strangers. But there may be passwords, other means of identification, perhaps speaking in their own language. What is needed is a diversion. Do you have anyone with a knowledge of gunnery among your followers?''

''Certainly. René Dupont is a former major of artillery, a most knowledgeable soldier. And he is in London.''

''Just the man. I am sure he will enjoy operating one of those high-powered guns. We shall capture a gun ship before dawn. At first light when the gates are opened the bombardment will start. A certain number of shells through the gate, guardhouse and guard should be disconcerting. Then the boat will be abandoned, and the gunners will escape on foot. This will be the responsibility of your men.''

''It will be a pleasurable task that I shall personally supervise. But where will you be?''

''Marching into the city with the troops, as I tried to once before.''

''Most hazardous! If you are too early, you will be apprehended as you appear or perhaps destroyed in the bombardment. Too late and the gate will be sealed against entry.''

''Therefore we must time things exceedingly well.''

''I will send for the finest chronometers obtainable!''

13

MAJOR DUPONT WAS a red-faced and gray-haired man with an impressive rotundity of belly. But he was energetic enough and knew his gunnery and was now consumed with a fierce passion to operate the invaders' incredible weapon. The former crew of the gunboat, including the lookouts, slept a deeper sleep than they had planned belowdecks as I worked out the mechanism of the recoilless cannon and explained it to the major. He grasped it instantly and beamed with fierce joy. After his experience with irregular cannon barrels, muzzle-loaded uneven shot, slow-burning powder, and all the rest of the handicaps of his trade, this was a revelation.

"Charge, fuse, and projectile in the same casing, marvelous! And this lever swings open the breach?" he asked.

"Correct. Keep away from these vents when firing since the exhausted gas from the explosion comes out here, canceling the recoil. Use the open sights, the range is so short. I imagine there will be no need to allow for windage at this distance, and there will also be scarcely any projectile drop. The muzzle velocity is much greater than you are used to."

"Tell me more!" he said, stroking the smooth steel.

Step two. The count would see to it that the ship was moved upstream before dawn and anchored to the embankment below London Bridge. I would see to it that I arrived on the bridge at the agreed-upon time. His nautical chronometer was as big as a cabbage, handmade of brass and steel, and it clacked loudly. But he assured me of its accuracy, and we set it from my atomic watch, as big as my fingernail and accurate to within one second a year. This was the last thing to be done, and as I rose to leave, he put out his hand and I took it.

"We will always be thankful for your aid," he said. "There is new hope now among the men, and I share their enthusiasm."

"It's I who should be thanking you for the help. Considering the fact that my winning might be the worse thing for you."

He dismissed that thought as unimportant: a very brave man. "In dying we win as you have explained. A world without these swine is victory enough. Even if we are not there to witness it. Do your duty.''

I did. Trying to forget that the fate of worlds, civilization, whole peoples rested upon my actions. A slip, an accident, and it would be all over for everyone. There could therefore be no accidents. As mountain climbers do not look down and think about the drop below, I put thoughts of failure from my mind and tried to think of a joke to cheer myself up. None came to mind instantly, so I thought instead about putting paid to He and his operation, and this was cheering indeed. I looked at my watch. It was time to leave, so I went quickly without looking back. The streets were deserted, all honest men were at home in bed, and my footsteps echoed from the buildings along the dark street. Behind me the first gray of approaching dawn touched the sky.

London is full of dark alleys that provide ideal sites for lurking, so I lurked craftily within sight of London Bridge and watched as the first soldiers appeared. Some marched in step, some straggled, all looked tired. I was feeling tired myself, so I sucked on a stimtab and kept an eye on my watch. Ideally I should be on the bridge when the firing began, far enough from the gate not to be hit, yet close enough to get through it during the excitement after the barrage. From my vantage point I timed various groups of soldiers crossing the bridge until I had a good estimate. The digits rolled by on my watch, and at the proper moment I took a military brace with my shoulders and stepped out smartly.

''*Lortytort?*'' a voice called out—and I realized it was calling to me. I had been so concerned with the time I had stupidly ignored the fact that He's future-fiends would be crossing the bridge as well.

I waved, made an evil grimace, and stepped out smartly. The man who had called out looked puzzled, then hurried after me. By my uniform he knew I was one of his gang, but one unfamiliar to him. Probably asking me how things were back in the home asylum. I wanted no conversation with him, particularly since I didn't speak his language. I hurried on—painfully aware of him hurrying after me. Then realized I was going too fast and at my present pace I would reach the gate just in time to be blown up.

There was no time to curse my lack of awareness—just a matter of picking what kind of trouble I wanted. Getting blown up was just a little too much to get involved with now. I could see that the gunboat was in position and that figures were on deck. Wonderful. I could almost hear the explosions already. With me in the middle of them. I would have to stop, here, at the appointed spot. I did. Heavy footsteps hammered up behind me and a hand caught at my shoulder, spinning me about.

"*Lortilypu?*" he cried out; then the expression on his face changed, his eyes widening, his mouth opening. "*Blivit!*" he shouted. He recognized me, perhaps from photographs.

"Blivit is the word," I said and shot him in the neck with the narcotic needle gun I had palmed. But there was another cry of *Blivit!* and one of his teammates pushed through the soldiers, and I had to shoot him, too. This naturally interested everyone nearby, and there were some startled shouts and a certain amount of weapon lifting. I put my back to the bridge parapet and wondered if I would have to shoot the entire French Army.

I did not. The first shell, not too well aimed by the major of horse artillery, hit the bridge not ten meters from where I was standing. The explosion was considerable, and the air was filled with hurtling pieces of masonry and steel. I dropped as did all the others, some of them permanently, and I took the opportunity to put needles into all the nearest soldiers who had witnessed my earlier shootout.

Back on the boat Dupont was learning to master his weapon and the next shell struck the city wall. There was much shouting and running about among the men on the bridge and I shouted and milled with the best of them, looking on with pleasure as the next shell whistled cleanly through the gate and blew up the guardhouse inside. Now most of the motion was away from the gate, as well it should be, so I dropped and wormed my way closer on my belly. Shells were now bursting in and around the gate and causing a satisfying amount of destruction. A quick look at my watch informed me that it was almost time for the barrage to lift. The signal would be a shell hitting the wall far from the bridge. After this a few more shots would be fired for effect at targets of opportunity—but no more at the gate.

The shell struck the wall a good hundred meters downriver, blowing a neat hole in it. I jumped to my feet and ran.

What a fine destructive mess. Wreckage and crumbled masonry everywhere, dust and the reek of high explosive in the air. If there had been any survivors here of the bombardment, they had long since left. I scrambled over the rubble, slid down the other side, and nipped around the first corner. The only witnesses to this unstealthy entrance were a couple watching from a doorway, English by their dress, who turned and ran as soon as they saw me. Despite my little tangle on the bridge, the plan had worked perfectly.

The cannon on the river began firing again.

This was not part of any plan, not at all. Something had gone wrong. After the last shots my accomplices were to have retreated to shore and removed themselves to safety. Then two explosions sounded, almost at the same time. The cannon could not fire that fast.

There was another gun shooting.

The street I was on, Upper Thames Street, ran parallel to the wall. I was far enough from the bridge now so my presence would not be associated with the action there—and a ladder climbed up to the top of the wall to an observation platform there. Now empty. Perhaps prudence should have dictated a single-minded continuation of my plans. But I have spent many years not listening to that particular voice, and I was not prepared to start now. One quick look around—no one in sight—and up the ladder. From the top I had a perfect view of the action.

The major was still manning his gun, busily firing away at another gunboat that was coming upriver under full sail. The newcomer, even though handicapped by a moving platform, was more experienced and accurate with his weapon. A shell had already blown a great hole in the stern of my ally's boat, and even as I watched, another hit amidships, and the gun was silent, its barrel in the air and the gunner gone. A figure ran across the dock and dropped into the now-harmless boat. I dug out my electronic telescope and trained it on the deck, knowing what I would see even before I put it to my eye.

It was the count come to the aid of his troops. But even as he jumped aboard, the major rose, blood running down his face, and manned the gun again. It swung about, aiming at the other boat, and hit it squarely with the next shot.

Well done, right at the waterline below the enemy weapon. The gun was silenced, the ship sinking. When I looked back at the major again, I saw that he had retrained his cannon and was firing at the bridge, at the enemy soldiers there. And the count was loading for him. They both were smiling and seemed to be enjoying themselves. The firing continued faster now, and I let myself back down the ladder.

Neither of them could be blamed; they knew exactly what they were doing. Firing back at last at the enemy they had hated all these years, using a superior and highly destructive weapon. Both would stay there firing until they were cut down. Perhaps they wanted it that way. If this sacrifice were to have any value at all, I had to get on with my own job.

I had studied the count's map well. Along Duck's Foot Lane to Cannon Street and then left. There were people about now, frightened civilians hurrying by, soldiers marching on the double in the opposite direction. No one paid any attention to me at all.

And there, up ahead at the end of the street, the great bulk of the walls and dome rose up, unmistakably St. Paul's.

The end of another road was very near. My final meeting with He.

14

I WAS SCARED. A man is either a liar—or mad—who claims never to have felt fear. I have been touched by it often enough to recognize its smell, but never have I felt the iron hand clamping down as it did now. Ice water in the veins, a hammering in the heart, a rooted feeling in the feet. With a decided effort I grabbed my brain by the throat, no mean feat that, and gave it a good shaking.

Speak, brain, I commanded. Why this sudden case of acute chickenitis? Why the yellow stripe right down the back as far as the heels? Body and brain, we have been in tight spots before, even narrower ones. But we bulled through and came out the other side. Usually victors. What is new here?

The answer came back very quickly. As a rustproof rodent I had penetrated behind the walls of society, doing it on my own and standing or falling on my own. Adventure, rah-rah. But now there was too much riding on the bet, too many people's lives dependent on my actions. Too many! Hopping hafnium, the future survival of the entire galaxy might be at stake. It was almost unbelievable.

"Make it unbelievable," I muttered, digging in my medikit. If I kept dwelling on what was at stake, I would take no risks, probably take no action. I have never resorted to artificial morale before, but there is a first time for everything. I carried the berserker pills as a sort of amulet; I knew they were there if I ever needed them, therefore I never needed them. Until now. I clicked open the case and brushed off the dust off an innocent-looking capsule.

"Get out there and fight, Jim," I said, then swallowed the thing.

They are outlawed everywhere, and for good reason. Not only because they are habit-forming to a great degree, both physically and psychologically, but for social reasons. Inside the gelatin capsule lies a specific form of madness, a compound that dissolves the conscience and morality of civilized man. Superid takes over. No morals, no conscience—and no fear. Nothing but a great chunk of ego and the sure knowledge of might and right, divine permission to do anything and not to feel concern or fear while doing it. Politicians loaded on berserkerite have toppled regimes and controlled worlds.

Athletes have broken all sports records, often destroying themselves or their opponents while accomplishing this. Not nice stuff.

Very nice stuff. I had one fleeting instant of conscience and realization of change as the chemicals took hold of my brain, but it passed even as it began.

"I have come for you, He," I said, smiling with real joy.

This was power unlimited, the most exhilarating sensation I had ever experienced, a cleansing wind blowing out all the dusty corners of my brain. Do what you want, Jim, what you will, because you are the only power in the world that really counts. How blinded I had been for years. Cramped little moralities, puny affections for others, destructive other-orientated love. How crippled I had been. I love myself because I am God. At last I understood the meaning of God that the old religions were always mumbling about.

I am I, the only power in the entire universe. And He is in that building ahead, thinking with mortal foolishness that he can best me, stop me, even kill me. Now we shall see what happens to idiot plans like that.

A stroll around the premises. A solid enough structure, no apparent guards, undoubtedly loaded with detection apparatus. A subtle or secret approach? Not wise. The only advantage I had was surprise, that and the ability to be absolutely ruthless. I was well armed, a walking engine of death, and no one would stop me. Entry would be simple enough, others were going in and out constantly, all in this same uniform, and there was a buzz and a disturbed whine to this beehive at the present. They did not like the attack on the gate. I must strike now while they were disturbed. All devices at the ready and instantly available, I completed my leisurely circuit of the building and started up the white stone steps at its front.

The cathedral was immense, appearing even larger now with all the pews and religious furniture cleared away. I stalked down the length of the long nave as though I owned it, which I did. Weapons ready at my fingertips. The nave was deserted, and all the activity was concentrated at the far end in the apse where the altar usually stood. This was gone, and in its place was an ornate throne.

In which He was sitting. Arrogant with power, his great red body leaning forward to issue orders to his assistants below. A long table reached across the transept here, littered with maps and papers and surrounded by brilliantly uniformed officers. They appeared to be taking their orders from a man in a simple blue uniform coat. He was very short with a black lick of hair across his forehead. From the description this must be the tyrant Napoleon. Passing on instructions from He as I had expected. I knew I was smiling as I shifted my fingertips closer to my weapons.

A familiar crackling of light caught my attention from the secondary apse off to the right—and my smile broadened. The gleaming machinery of a time-helix was stuffed in there with the technicians bent over their tasks. They would be dead soon, like everyone else here. And I would have temporal transportation out of this barbarian era. I would have to leave a small atomic grenade behind when I went. The end was just about in sight.

No one paid the slightest attention to me as I came up to the table. I would have to use sleepgas first since this would work on them all at the same time. Plenty of time to kill the slaves after I had removed their master.

One concussion grenade, two thermite grenades. I triggered them with my thumb and threw them, one—two—three, in high arcs into He's lap. While they were still in the air I rolled handful after handful of gas grenades down the table under the shocked faces of the officers. The grenades were still hissing and banging as I spun about and used my needle gun—I didn't want to injure the controls!—to shoot down the technicians around the time-helix.

It was all over in a matter of seconds. Quiet descended as the last unconscious body fell. Before turning back, I hurled grenades down the length of the nave so that anyone entering would walk into the gas cloud. Then I looked at He.

Lovely. A roaring pillar of fire with something in its core that might have been a man. The throne burned as well and the column of greasy smoke roiled up toward the great dome above.

"You are beaten, He, beaten," I shouted leaning forward across the table to get a better look. He would not be surviving this attack.

Napoleon lifted his head from the table and sat up.

"Don't be foolish," he said.

I wasted no time in thought but tried to kill him. But he was ready and fired before I did with the tubelike weapon concealed in his palm. Fire washed across my face; then it was numb, my body numb, everything, no control. I dropped facedown onto the table. Nor could I feel Napoleon's hands when he rolled me over. He was looking down at me, smiling, roaring with victorious laughter, laughter with more than an echo of madness in it. And he was watching my face as well, my eyes which I could still control, waiting for the widening that meant I understood at last.

"That is right!" he shouted. "I am He. You have lost. You have burned, destroyed that fine android whose only function was to deceive you into that action. It was a trap for you, everything here, even the existence of this world, this loop in time, has no function other than in being a trap for you. Did you forget so quickly that a body is merely a shell for me, the eternal He? My brain has mastered death and lives on. Now in this imitation of a mad emperor. He never knew what real madness was.

"You have lost—and I have won forever!"

15

THIS WAS A temporary setback. I suppose that normally I would have felt defeated, afraid, angry, suffered under some kind of useless emotion. Now I just waited for the opportunity to kill He again. This was getting very boring; after two tries he was still alive. I resolved that the third would be the final one.

He bent and tore at my clothes, searching me with brutal thoroughness. Ripping my clothing into hanging shreds, pulling off devices that adhered to my skin, taking the knife from my ankle, the gun from my wrist, the tiny grenades from my hair. Within seconds every weapon I could reach was gone. The few weapons and devices left were well out of reach. Very thorough. The search over, he discarded me, flinging my limp body face upward onto the table.

"I have prepared everything for this moment, everything!" He bubbled as he talked, and saliva streaked his chin. I heard the rattle of chains as he picked up my wrists and snapped heavy metal fetters about them. They were joined together by a short length of heavy chain. As the cuffs closed, there was a brief flash of light as the ends welded together, and though I could feel nothing, I saw the instant blistered redness of my skin inside the metal. Not important. Only when this was done did he put a needle into my wrist.

Feeling began to return, first to my hands, great pain in my wrists, and then to my arms. There seemed to be a lot of pain associated with the return of sensation. I ignored this although spasms shook my body uncontrollably. In the end I shook myself off the table, falling heavily and uncontrollably to the floor. He bent and picked me up at once, dragging me across the width of the great cathedral. His strength, even in the disguise of this small body, was tremendous.

In the brief instant I had lain on the floor I had grabbed something with my fingers. I did not know what it was, other than small and metallic, and it was now clenched tightly in my fist.

There was a solid metal pillar, waist-high, that stood about five meters from the time-helix controls. This too was waiting for me. He held my wrists apart and laid the chain that joined them into a groove in the top of the pillar. There was another flash of light as the chain was welded to the solid metal. He released me, and I swayed but did not fall. Sensation and control were returning to my body, and I mastered it as he went to the controls and made some adjustments. The vast cathedral was silent; we were alone except for the huddled bodies.

"I have won!" he screamed suddenly, doing a little dance step that sent spittle flying from his chin. He pointed to the coiled form of the time-helix and laughed out loud. "Do you realize that you are now in a loop of time that does not exist, that I called into being to trap you, that will vanish as soon as I leave it?"

"I suspected that. Napoleon lost in our textbooks."

"He won here. I gave him the weapons and aid to conquer the world. Then I killed him when my new body was ready. This loop in time came into being when I did that, and its existence created a barrier in time that will go down as soon as it ceases to exist. When I leave, this will happen, but not instantly; that would be too easy for you. I want to think of you here, alone, knowing that you have lost and that your future will never exist. There is a time-fixator on this building. It will be here after London and the entire world are gone, perhaps longer than you. You might even die of thirst before it shuts off. Then again you may not. I have won."

He screamed this last as he turned to the controls again. I opened my fist to see what weapon I had in my palm that might defeat him at this final moment.

It was a small brass cylinder that weighed no more than a few grams. One end had small holes punched in it, and when I turned it over, fine white sand came out. A sander, used for drying the writing ink on papers. I might have wished for a better weapon, but this would have to do.

"I leave," He said, actuating the mechanism.

"What about the men of yours here?" I asked, needing time to think.

"Mad slaves. They vanish with you, having served my purpose. I have an entire world of them waiting to welcome my return. Soon there will be many worlds; soon it will all be mine."

There was nothing much I could add to that. He sauntered across the flagstones, a monster in the body of that tiny man, and touched his hand to the glowing end of the time-helix and was instantly engulfed by its cold green flame.

"All mine," he said, the same green fire glowing in his eyes.

"I don't think so."

I juggled the sander in my hand, testing its weight, measuring the distance to the controls. I could reach it easily. The settings for the time scale were a bank of keys, not unlike the keys of a musical instrument, and a number of them were depressed now. If I could push one more of them down, the setting would be changed; He would arrive at a different time and place, perhaps not arrive at all. I swung my hand in slow arcs, estimating the distance, the trajectory the little tube must follow to reach the correct place.

He must have seen what I was doing because he began to howl with insane rage, pulling at the time field that neatly held him tight to the end of the helix. Coldly I judged the distance until I was sure I had it right.

"Like this," I said and tossed the sander in a high arc toward the controls.

It rose up, glinting brightly in a shaft of sunlight from a stained glass window, and arced down.

Striking on the bank of keys, then falling off to rattle to the floor.

He's enraged cries cut off as the time-helix released and He vanished from sight. At the same moment this happened the light changed, dimming to dusk. Outside all the windows there was now just gray. I had seen this before during the time attack on the laboratory that had started everything. London, the world outside, everything, no longer existed. Not in this particular part of time and space. Just the cathedral had existence, held briefly by the time-fixator.

Had He won? I felt the first touch of worry; the effects of the drug must be wearing off. I looked hard, but it was almost impossible to see the indicator dials in the dim light. Had one of them moved just before the helix was actuated? I could not be sure. And it didn't really matter, not to me here. Whether the future was hell or a paradise of peace could not affect me. With the return of emotions I felt a desire to know if my world would ever exist. Would there be a Special Corps and would my Angelina someday be born? I would never know. I tugged sharply at the chains, but of course they held fast.

The end. End of everything. The emotions that were returning were only the blackest and most depressed, but I could not help it. End.

16

HAVE YOU EVER been trapped in St. Paul's Cathedral in the year A.D. 1807 with the entire world vanished into nonexistence outside, alone and welded to a steel post and soon to vanish yourself? Not many people can answer yes to that question. I can—but can truthfully add that I do not enjoy this singular distinction.

Without much reluctance I am forced to admit that I felt somewhat depressed. I struggled a bit against the metal cuffs that held my wrists, but my heart wasn't really in it. They were too tight and secure, and I knew this kind of helpless thrashing about would be just the sort of thing that He would enjoy with mad passion.

For the first time in my life I felt utter and absolute defeat. It had a darkening and dulling effect on my thoughts—as though I already had one foot in the grave—that removed any idea of struggle and suggested instead that the easiest thing would be to simply give in and await the final curtain. The sensation of defeat was so strong that it blanketed almost all feelings of rebellion against this untimely fate. I should be fighting, thinking of a way out, yet I just didn't want to try. I was more than a little amazed at my submission.

It was while I was engrossed in this navel-examining introspection that the sound began. A distant whine just on the edge of audibility, so weak that I would never have heard it had it not been for the absolute silence of nonexistence wrapped about my cathedral-sized tomb. The sound grew and grew, as annoying as an insect, making me aware of it although I did not wish to be made aware of anything except my sensation of overwhelming defeat. In the end it was quite loud, coming from empty space somewhere high above beneath the dome. I looked up despite my lack of interest just as there was the loud bang of displaced air.

A figure appeared in the darkness above, someone in a space suit. Wearing a grav-chute because he drifted down slowly before me. I was stunned and ready for almost anything when he opened the dark faceplate of his space suit.

Ready for almost anything other than the fact that he was not a he.

"Get rid of that silly chain," Angelina said. "You always

manage to get into trouble as soon as I leave you alone. You're coming away with me right now, and that is all there is to it.''

There was very little to say even had I been unstunned enough to say it. So I did a fine moronic gaping act and rattled my chains a bit as, light as a falling leaf, she drifted down to the floor. In the end her undoubtedly physical presence jounced my open synapses closed, and I did my best to rise to the occasion.

''Angelina, truly named. You descend from above to save me.''

She opened the faceplate of her space suit wider so she could kiss me through the opening, then took an atomic lance from her belt and began to cut away my chains. ''Now tell me what all this mysterious time-travel nonsense is about. And talk fast, we have only seven minutes; at least that is what Coypu said.''

''What else did he tell you?'' I asked, wondering just how much she knew.

''Now don't you start being mysterious with me, Slippery Jim diGriz! I've had enough of that with Coypu.''

I jumped back hastily as she waved the atomic lance under my chin, then beat out the fire that was smoldering on the front of my garments. An angry Angelina can be quite dangerous.

''My love,'' I said emotionally, attempting to embrace her while keeping an eye on the lance at the same time. ''I conceal nothing from you, nothing! I know better. It is just that my brain is tied in knots from all this time traveling, and I want to know where your knowledge leaves off before I continue with the complete story.''

''You know perfectly well that I talked to you last on the phone. Big rush, you said, top priority, get over fast you shouted—then rang off. So I did, to Coypu's lab, where everyone was running about and playing with the machinery and too busy to tell me anything. Back in time, they shouted, nothing else. And that horrid Inskipp no better. He said you vanished, just vanished out of his office while he was reading the riot act to you. Apparently he found out about that little bit of money you are putting aside for a rainy decade or two. There was a lot of babble about you saving the world or the galaxy or something, but I couldn't understand a word of it. And all of this went on for a *very* long time, until they could send me back here.''

''Well, I did,'' I said modestly. ''Saved you, saved the Corps, saved the whole thing.''

''I was right, you have been drinking.''

''Not in entirely too long a time,'' I muttered petulantly. ''If you want to know the truth, you all vanished, poof, just like that. Coypu

was the last one to go, so he can tell you about it. The Corps, everyone, they were never born, never existed, except in my memory. . . .''

"My memory is slightly different."

"It would be. Since through my efforts He's evil plan was foiled. . . .''

"*His* not *he's*. All that drinking has affected your speech."

"*He* is his name—and I haven't had a drop in hours. Can you possibly listen without interrupting? This story is complicated enough in any case. . . .''

"Complicated and possibly alcoholically inspired."

I groaned. Then kissed her, longer and warmer this time, a distraction we both enjoyed. This softened her a bit, so I rushed on before she remembered that she was supposed to be angry at me.

"A time attack was launched against the Special Corps, so Professor Coypu whisked me back in time to foil the nefarious scheme. I did all right in 1975, but He got away, went back to whenever he came from, then set up an elaborate trap here in 1807 to trap me. Which he did. But his plans didn't work completely because I managed to change the setting on the time-helix so he was sent to a different time from that he had planned. This must have defeated his time-war plans because you appeared to rescue me.''

"Oh, darling, how wonderful of you. I knew you could save the world if you really tried."

Mercurial of mood is the word for my Angelina. She kissed me with what can only be described as true passion, and I, clanking my lengths of chain, got my arms around her in happy response when she squawked and straight-armed me, so I reeled back, choking.

"The time!" She looked at her watch and gasped. "You made me forget. There is less than a minute left. Where is the time-helix?"

"Here!" Hugging my still-painful midriff, I showed her the machine.

"And the controls?"

"These."

"How ugly. Where is the readout?"

"These dials."

"This the setting we must use, down to the thirteenth decimal position Coypu said, most insistent about that."

I played the keys like a mad pianist and sweated. The dials spun and hesitated, then gyrated wildly.

"Thirty seconds," Angelina said sweetly, to encourage me. I sweated harder.

"There!" I gasped as she announced ten seconds. I kicked in the timer and threw the master switch. The time-helix glowed greenly at us as we rushed to its protruding end.

"Stay close and hug me as hard as you can," I said. "The time field has a surface effect, so we must be close." She responded with pleasure.

"I only wish I weren't wearing this silly space suit," she whispered, nibbling my ear. "It would be so much more fun."

"It might be, but it might also be a little embarrassing when we arrived back at the Special Corps in that condition."

"Don't worry about that, we're not going back yet."

There was a sudden stab of anxiety just below my sternum.

"What do you mean? Where are we going?"

"I'm sure I wouldn't know. All Coypu said was that the hop would be about 20,000 years into the future, just before this planet is to be destroyed."

"He and his mad mob again," I wailed. "You've just sent us off to tackle an entire planetary insane asylum—where they're all against us!"

Everything froze as the time-helix actuated and I was whipped into time with that pained expression on my face. That expression lasted 20,000 years, which was exactly how I felt.

17

BLAM! IT WAS like falling into a steam bath—and falling was the right word for it. Hot clouds of vapor rushed past us, and the invisible surface could be ten meters or ten miles below us.

"Switch on your grav-chute," I shouted. "Mine's back in the nonexistent nineteenth century."

Perhaps I shouldn't have shouted because Angelina turned the thing on at full lift and slithered up out of my fond embrace like an oiled eel. I clutched madly and managed to grab one of her feet with both hands—whereupon the boot part of the one-piece space suit promptly came off her foot.

"I wish you wouldn't do that," she called down to me.

"I agree with you completely," I answered incoherently through tight-clamped and grating teeth.

The suit stretched and stretched until the leg was twice its normal length and I bobbed up and on down as though I were on the end of a rubber band. I took a quick look, but there was still only fog visible below. Space suit fabric is tough, but it was never designed to take a strain like this. Something had to be done.

"Cut your lift!" I called out, and Angelina responded instantly.

We were in free fall, and as soon as the tension was relieved, the leg fabric contracted and snapped me back up to Angelina's waiting arms.

"Yum," I said.

She looked down and shrieked and hit the grav-chute power again. This time I wasn't ready and I slipped right down and out of her embrace and was falling toward the solid-looking landscape that had suddenly appeared below.

In the small fraction of a second left to me I did what little I could. Twisting in the air, spreading my arms and legs wide, trying to land square on my back. I had almost succeeded when I hit.

Everything went black, and I was sure I was dead, and darkness overwhelmed my brain as well, and my last thought flashed before me. Not only did I regret anything I had ever done, but there were a few things I wished I had done more often.

I could not have been unconscious more than a few instants. There was foul-tasting mud in my mouth, and I spluttered it out and rubbed even more of it from my eyes and looked around me. I was floating in a half-liquid sea of mud and water from which large bubbles rose and broke with slow plops. They stank. Sickly-looking reeds and water plants grew on all sides.

"Alive!" I shouted. "I am alive." I had struck flat out on the syrupy surface, dividing the blow over the entire back surface of my body. There were some aches and bruises, but nothing seemed to be broken.

"It looks very nasty down there," Angelina said, hovering a few feet above my head.

"It's just as nasty as it looks so, if you don't mind, I would like to get out of it. Can you sort of drop down so I can grab your ankles, which will permit you to drag me out with a wet sucking sound?"

It was a large wet sucking sound as the decaying quagmire fought to hold onto me, parting only reluctantly with a slobbering sigh. I hung from my love's ankles as we drifted over an apparently endless swamp which vanished in the fog in all directions.

"There, over to the right," I called out. "Looks like a channel with running water. I think a wash and brushup are in order."

"Since I am upwind of you, I couldn't agree more."

The current was moving slowly, but still moving as I could tell by a tree trunk that drifted by. In the middle of the sluggish stream was a golden sandbar that seemed made for us. I dropped as Angelina came low, and even before she had settled down herself, I was out of the noisome clothes and scrubbing the muck off in the water. When I bobbed up, spluttering, I saw that she had peeled off the sweltering space suit and was combing out her long hair, which happened to be blond at the present moment. Very lovely and I was thinking the most romantic thoughts when fierce fire pierced my gluteus maximus, and I shot straight up out of the water, yiping like a dog whose tail has been caught in the door. As attractive and feminine as she was, Angelina was still Angelina, and the comb vanished to be replaced by a gun, and almost before I touched the sand, she had fired a single well-aimed shot.

While she was applying a bandage to the double row of tooth-marks in my derriere, I looked at the fish, half blown apart but still twitching, that had mistaken me for lunch. Its gaping mouth had more teeth than a dental supply house, and there was a definitely evil look in its rapidly clouding eye. Grabbing it by the tail to evade its still-gnashing jaws, I threw it far out into the water. This started a tremendous flurry of action under the surface, and from the size of some of the things that leaped out and smacked back down I saw that I had been attacked by one of the smaller ones.

"Twenty thousand years has done no good at all to this planet," I said.

"Finish rinsing off that mud, and I'll stand guard. Then we'll have some lunch." Ever the practical woman.

While I scrubbed, she shot up the pescatorial predators who came after me, including one large fish with fat flanks and rudimentary legs that waddled out of the water in an attempt to have me for lunch. We had it instead; the flanks concealed some fine thick filets that roasted well over a low-set heat projector. Angelina had had the foresight to bring a flask of my favorite wine, which made the meal a memorable one. After which I sighed, eructated, and wiped my lips with satisfaction.

"You have saved my life more than once in the last twenty thousand years," I said. "So I no longer am brimful of anger for being whisked to this steambath world rather than back to the Corps. But can you at least tell me what happened and what Coypu told you?"

"He tends to mumble a good deal, but I got the gist of it. He has been working on his time tracker or whatever he calls it and followed your jumps through time, as well as someone he referred to as the enemy, the one you call He. The enemy did something with time, created a probability loop that lasted about five years, then terminated. Then He left this collapsing loop—and you didn't. That's why Coypu sent me back, to the minutes just before it ended, to bring you out. He gave me the setting for the time-helix that would enable us to follow He to this time. I asked him what we were supposed to do here but he kept muttering, 'Paradox, paradox,' and wouldn't tell me. Do you have any idea of what is supposed to happen?"

"Simple enough. Find He and kill him. That should put paid to the entire operation. I've had two tries at him, shooting once and thermite bombs the second, and haven't succeeded. Maybe this will be lucky three."

"Perhaps you ought to let me take care of him," Angelina said sweetly.

"A fine idea. We'll blast him together. I have had just about enough of this temporal paper chase."

"How do we find him?"

"Simplicity itself, if you have a time energy detector with you."

She did, Coypu's foresight, and passed it over. "A simple flick of this switch and the moving needle points to our man."

The switch flicked but did nothing more than release a little condensed water that ran out into my palm.

"It doesn't seem to be working," Angelina said, smiling sweetly.

"Either that or they are not using the time-helix at this particular moment." I rummaged in my equipment. "I had to leave my space suit and some other things back in 1807, but Slippery Jim is never without his snooper."

I was proud of the gadget and had designed it myself, and it was one of the few things He hadn't taken from me. Rugged, it could resist almost anything except being dropped into molten metal. Compact, no bigger than my hand. And it could detect the weakest of flickerings of radiation across a tremendous range of frequencies. I turned it on and ran my fingers over the familiar controls.

"Most interesting," I said, and tried the radio frequencies.

"If you don't enlighten me quick, I'll never save your life again."

"You have to because you love me with an undying passion. I get two sources, one weak and very distant. The other can't be too far and is putting out on a number of frequencies, including atomic radiation and energy transmission, as well as a lot of radio. And something of more pressing urgency. Get out the sunburn cream—solar ultraviolet radiation is right up at the top of the scale. You can bet I've been well cooked already."

We creamed and, despite the heat, put on enough clothing to shield us from the invisible radiation that was pouring out of the clouded sky.

"Strange things have happened to the Earth," I said. "The radiation, this soggy climate, the wildlife in this river. I wonder—"

"I don't. After completing the mission, you can do your paleogeologic research. Let's kill He first."

"Spoken like a pro. I hope you don't mind if I rig a harness so we can share the benefit of the grav-chute equally this time?"

"Sounds like fun," she said, loosening the straps.

The airborne Siamese twin arrangement lifted and took us low over the sea of gunk in the direction of all the activity. Mud and swamp continued for a boringly long time, and I was beginning to chafe in the straps and worry about the power supply when the higher land finally appeared. First some rocks sticking up out of the water, then sheer cliffs. It took more juice to lift us up the side of these, and the indicator on the power pack dropped quickly.

"We are going to have to walk soon," I said, "which is at least better than swimming."

"Not if the land animals match those in the water."

Ever optimistic my Angelina. As I was phrasing a witty and scathing reply, there was a flash of light from the rampart of rocks ahead, followed instantly by an intense pain in my leg.

"I've been shot!" I shouted, more in surprise than pain, reaching for the grav-chute controls and finding that Angelina had already killed the power.

We dropped toward a wicked jumble of rocks, slowing and stopping only at the last minute. I hopped on one leg to the shelter of an overhanging slab and was thinking of digging out my medikit when Angelina sprayed antiseptic on the wound, tore my pants leg half away, injected instant painkiller in my thigh, and probed the gory opening. She was ahead of me with everything, and I didn't mind in the slightest.

"A neat penetrating wound," she announced, spraying on surgifoam. "Should heal quickly, no problems, keep your weight off it; now I have to kill whoever did it."

All the drugs had slowed me down, and before I could answer, she had her gun in her hand and had faded silently into the rocky landscape. There is nothing like having a loving and tender wife who is a cool and accomplished killer. Maybe I wore the pants in the family—but we both wore guns.

Not too long after this there was the sound of explosions, a great clattering in the rocks above and, soon after that, some hoarse screams that soon ended in silence. It is a tribute to Angelina's prowess that I never for a second was concerned about her safety. In fact, I dozed off under the assault of the drugs coursing through my bloodstream and woke only when I was aware of tugging on the grav-chute harness. I yawned and blinked at her as she buckled in beside me.

"Am I allowed to ask what happened?" I said. She frowned.

"Just one man up there; I couldn't find any others. There is a farm building of sorts, some machinery, crops growing. I must be slipping. I knocked him out, then could not bring myself to shoot him while he was lying there unconscious."

I kissed her as we rose.

"A conscience, my sweet. Some of us are born with them; yours was surgically implanted. The results are the same."

"I'm not really sure I like it. There was a certain freedom in the old days."

"We all have to be civilized some time." She sighed and nodded, then gave me a quick peck on the cheek.

"I suppose that you are right. But it would have been so satisfying to blow him into small pieces."

We were over the last of the tumbled scree now and ascending a small cliff. There was a plateau here on top of which was a low building made of cemented-together stones. The door was open, and I hobbled through it, leaning on Angelina's shoulder. Inside, the dim light through the small windows revealed a large and cluttered room with two bunks against the far wall. On one of them a bound man lay twisting and turning, mumbling and growling into the gag that sealed his mouth.

"You get into the other bed," Angelina said, "while I see if I can get any intelligence out of this awful creature."

I had actually taken the first steps toward the bunk before reason penetrated my soggy thoughts and I stopped dead.

"Beds. Two of them? There must be someone else around the place."

Whatever answer was on her lips was never spoken because a man appeared in the doorway behind us, shouting noisily and firing an even noisier weapon.

18

HE WAS SHOUTING mainly because the weapon was blown from his hands even as he triggered it, and an instant later he was blown back out of the doorway. I saw all this as I dived and rolled and had my gun out just as Angelina was putting hers away.

"Now that is more like it," she said, apparently addressing the silent pair of boots in the doorway. "Civilized conscience or no, I find that shooting in self-defense still comes easily. I saw this one out among the rocks, stalking us as we came in, but I never had a clear shot. Everything should be quieter now. I'll make some nice warm soup and you take a nice nap. . . ."

"No." I doubt if a firmer "no" had ever been spoken. I popped out a pair of stimtabs and chewed them as I continued my monologue in the same tone of voice. "There is a certain retrogressive pleasure in being cared for and treated like an idiot child—but I think I have had enough of it. I have tackled He before this and chased him out of two of his lairs and I intend to finish him off now. I know his ways. I'm in charge of this expedition, so you will follow, not lead, and will obey orders."

"Yes, sir," she answered with lowered eyelids and bowed head. Did this cover a mocking smile? I did not care. Me boss.

"Me boss." It sounded even better said aloud in a firm and declaratory tone.

"Yes, boss," she said and giggled prettily while the man on the bed writhed and chomped and the boots in the doorway were silent.

We went to work. Our prisoner slavered noisily in an unknown tongue when I took out the gag and tried to bite my fingers when I restored it. There was a rough-looking radio on a shelf that produced only grating broadcasts in the same language when I turned it on. Angelina's outdoor investigations were far more productive than mine, and she pulled up by the door in an impossibly ugly conveyance that looked like a scratched, purple, plastic bathtub slung between four sets of wheels. It burbled and hissed at me when I hobbled up to examine it.

"Very simple to operate," Angelina said, showing off her technical skill. "There is only one switch and that turns it on. And two handles, one for the bank of wheels on each side. Forward to speed them up, back to brake them. . . ."

"And neutral in the middle," I said to demonstrate *my* technical skill, as well as the fact that I was a male chauvinist pig and this was my show. "And this lead-covered lump in the rear must be a nuclear generator. Unshield a chunk of radioactive material, heat up the surrounding liquid, a heat exchanger here, secondary liquid to turn this electric generator, motors in each wheel, ugly and crude but practical. Where do we go in it?"

She pointed. "There seems to be a road or trail of sorts going off through that cultivated field there. And unless memory fails—and I *know* you will be quick to correct me—that seems to be the same direction as the radio signals you detected earlier."

A mild blow struck for femlib, and I ignored it. Particularly since she was right as the snooper soon confirmed.

"Off we go then," I said, in command once again.

"Going to kill the prisoner?" she asked hopefully.

"Thank you, no. But I'll take his clothes since mine have reached the old rag stage. If we break up the radio, he'll have a hard job telling anyone we're coming. He'll chew through his gag and ropes in a couple of hours, so we can leave the burial arrangements of his associate to him. We will load our gear and be on our way."

The firmness of authority was dimmed slightly by the *krets krets* of my fingernails inside my tattered shirt scratching at the rapid red-blooming growth of my sunburn. While Angelina stomped the radio, I put on more cream. A few minutes later we were bumping along the well-worn tract that twisted across the high plateau.

There was less fog and haze at this altitude, not that there was anything more to see. The rough landscape was quarried with gullies that carried away the water from the frequent rainstorms, also removing what little topsoil still remained. Tough-looking plants clung to the rocks for protection in the sheltered spots. Occasionally we passed a branching off of the wheel marks, but the direction finder on the snooper kept us on the right track. The hard bucket seats were hideously uncomfortable, and I welcomed the gathering darkness of sunset—though of course I didn't say this aloud—and turned off behind a jumbled hill of great rocks for the night.

In the morning I was stiff but feeling more fit. The growth and healing drugs had whipped my cells into a frenzy of growth that had half healed my various wounds and given me a raging appetite. We dined and drank from the meager supplies that Angelina had brought—eked out by some coarse bread and dried meat liberated from the homicidal farmers. Angelina took the wheel and I rode shotgun, not liking the look of the decomposing landscape at all. The track now wandered down from the hills as the highlands turned into a vertical escarpment of rock. Then there were more swamps and some very nasty-looking jungle into which the road dipped. Creepers hung low enough to brush our heads and the soggy trees touched overhead. The air, which did not seem possible, became even more humid and hotter.

"I don't like this place," Angelina said, steering around a boggy spot that slopped across the track.

"I don't like it even less," I said, gun in hand and a clip of explosive cartridges in the butt. "If the wildlife here is anything like that in the river, we could have some fun and games in store."

Ever alert, I looked ahead, behind, right and left and wished my eyeballs grew on stalks. There were numberless suspicious dark shapes among the trees and occasional heavy crashings could be heard, but nothing appeared to threaten us. That I could see. Of course the one spot I wasn't watching was the surface of the road, and that is where the imminent danger lay.

"That tree has fallen right across the road," Angelina said. "Just bump over it—"

"I wouldn't!" I said, just a little bit too late as our wheels trundled over the green trunk that lay across the track and vanished into the jungle on both sides.

Our center wheels were on it when it shuddered and heaved upward in a great loop. The vehicle turned over, and Angelina and I were hurled clear. But not clear enough. I hit the ground and tucked my head in and rolled and came up with the gun ready. A good thing too. The pseudo tree trunk was writhing nicely, while out of the foliage across the track appeared the front end of the thing.

A snake. With a head as big as a barrel, gaping mouth, flicking tongue, beady eyes, hissing like an exploding boiler. While right under those widespread jaws was Angelina, sitting up and shaking her head dizzily and totally unaware of what was happening. There was time for one shot, and I wanted it to be a good one. As that demonic head came down, I held my wrist with my left hand to steady the gun and squeezed off a round right into the thing's mouth. With a muffled thud its head was blown off in a cloud of smoke.

That should have been the end of it—except for a gigantic spasm that went through the entire length of that muscular body. Before I could get out of the way, a shuddering thrashing loop struck me, bowled me over, and hurled me into the trees. This time there was no fancy roll and dive but a simple crunch splintery bang as I crashed through the branches, and one got me on the side of the head, and with a nice white explosion of pain that was that.

A period of time passed that I was not aware of. It was the ache in my head that drew me reluctantly back to consciousness, plus a new and sharper pain in my leg. I opened one bleary eye and saw something small and brown with a lot of claws and teeth that was tearing an opening in my pants leg in order to make lunch out of my thigh. The first hungry bite was what had woken me, and before it could go on to a second course, I kicked it with my boot. It growled and screeched at this and showed me all its teeth but reluctantly slipped away into the foliage when I attempted another weak kick in its direction.

Weak was the word for everything I felt. It took me some time to do more than lie there and gasp and try to remember what had happened. The road, the snake, the wreck. . . .

"Angelina!" I shouted hoarsely and struggled to my feet, ignoring the waves of pain that washed through me. "Angelina!"

There was no answer. I pushed through the shrubbery to witness a singularly nasty sight. A churning row of brown animals, relatives of the one who had nibbled me, were working on the carcass of the snake and had already reduced great sections of it to neatly polished rib cage. And my gun was gone. I turned back and searched where I had fallen, but it was not there. Something was wrong, very wrong, and the shrill voice of panic was beginning to keen in the back of my head.

As long as I stayed clear of them, the carrion eaters ignored me, so I made a wide circle across the road. The car was gone as well. And so was Angelina.

This required cogent thought which was impossible with the aches and pains that were crippling me. And I had to do something about the insects that were buzzing about the wound in my head. My medikit was still in its pocket and that was next in the order of business. In a few minutes I was soothed, depained, stimulated, and ready for action. But where was the action? Wherever the car was, my clicking thoughts responded. Its tracks were clear enough in the muddy ground—which also revealed the mystery of Angelina's disappearance. There were at least two sets of large, ugly masculine footprints around the churned area where the vehicle had been righted. As well as another set of car tracks. Either we had been followed or a chance bunch of tourists had arrived on the scene after the snake incident. Spatters of mud and bent grass showed that both cars had carried on in the original direction we had been going. I went that way myself, in a ground-eating trot, trying not to think about what might have happened to Angelina.

This trotting didn't last long. The heat and fatigue slowed me to a shambling walk. A stimtab took care of one, and I just sweated out the other. The tracks were clear, and I followed. In less than an hour the road had wound its way up out of the jungle and into the dry hills. Coming around a turn, I had a quick glimpse of one of the cars pulled up ahead and I drew quickly back.

A plan was needed. My gun had vanished, so shooting down the kidnappers was slightly out of the question. The few remaining devices in my clothing were nonlethal, though I did have a wrist holder full of grenades that Angelina had given me. This was the answer. A handful of sleepgas bombs to drop the kidnappers before they could shoot me. And maybe a couple of explosive grenades in the other hand just in case any of the enemy were not near Angelina and needed more dramatic means of disposal.

Thus armed and ready, I crept forward from rock to rock, took a deep breath, and jumped into the clearing where both vehicles waited.

And caught the wooden club in the side of my head, wielded by the guard who had been waiting quietly for someone to pull this kind of stunt.

19

I WAS ONLY out a fraction of a second, long enough for my wrists and ankles to be tied and all my weapons that they could find to be stripped from me. For this disaster I can blame only myself and my inattention. Fatigue and stimulants may have contributed, but my own stupidity had been the cause. I cursed myself under my breath, which did no good at all, as I was dragged across the ground and dumped down by Angelina.

"Are you all right?" I croaked.

"Of course. And in far better shape than you are."

Which was true. Her clothing was torn and there were some bruises where she had been knocked around. Someone was going to pay and pay well for that. I could hear my teeth grating together. And she was tied just as I was.

"They thought you were dead," she said. "And so did I." There was a wealth of unsaid feeling in her words, and I tried a smile which was a little more twisted than I like. "I don't know how long we lay there; I was unconscious, too. When I came to, I was like this, and they had taken the guns and everything and were loading it all into the cars. Then we left. There was nothing I could do to stop them. All they speak is that same horrible language."

They looked as horrible as their language sounded, all scruffy clothing and greasy leather straps, bushels of matted dirty hair and beard. I had an entirely unnecessary closer look at one of them when he came over and twisted my head to one side and the other while he compared my crunched features with a good photograph of myself that he had. I snapped my teeth at the filthy fingers, but he pulled them away in time. These must be He's men; the photo proved that, though I had no idea where he got it from. Taken during one of our tangles in time, no doubt, and treasured in his pocket ever since. At this point I noticed the ugliest and smelliest of the lot ogling Angelina, and I snapped at his ankle and was kicked aside for my pains.

Give Angelina that, she is a very direct-minded girl. When she knows what she wants, she gets it, no matter what. Now she saw the only way we could get out of this mess and she used it. Woman's wiles. With no hint of disgust at the ugly brute she lavished her attentions upon. She could not speak their language, but the language she did speak was as old as mankind. Turning away from me, she smiled at the hairy beast and gave a twist of her head to call him over. Her shoulders were back, her charming figure prominent, her hips tilted coyly.

Of course it worked. There was a bit of lively discussion with the other two, but Hairiest knocked one of them down, and that was that. They looked on with burning jealousy as he stalked over to her. She smiled her warmest and held out her slim, bound wrists.

What man could resist that unspoken appeal? Certainly not this shambling hulk. He cut the thongs on her wrists and put his knife away as she bent to free her ankles. When he hauled her to her feet, she arose eagerly. He locked her in a bearlike embrace, bending his face to hers.

I could have told him that he would be safer off trying to kiss a saber-tooth tiger, but I did not. What happened next only I could see because the jealous watchers were blocked from sight by the bulk of his body. Who would imagine that those delicate fingers could shape themselves into that hard a point, that the thin wrist could propel the hand so deep into bushy's gut? Lovely. He bent to her and, with only a gentle sigh, kept bending. For a moment she supported his weight—then stepped back and screamed as he folded to the ground.

A picture of feminine innocence, hands to cheeks, eyes staring, shrieking at the strange occurrence of a strong man collapsing at her feet. Of course the other two ran over, but there were the beginnings of expressions of cold suspicion on their faces. The first one carried my gun.

Angelina took care of him. As soon as he was close enough and bringing up the gun, she let fly with bushy's knife that she had removed before she dropped him. I did not see where it hit because the third man was passing me and I had drawn my legs back in hopes that he would. He did. I kicked out and got him below the knees, and he went down. Even as he fell I was jackknifing forward, and before he could get up again, I let him have it with both boots in the side of the head. And a second time just because I was feeling nasty.

That was that. Angelina removed the knife from her unmoving target, wiped it on his clothing, then came to free me.

"Will you kill the ones who are still twitching?" she asked demurely.

"I should, but cold-blooded revenge is not for me either. They are what they are, and I suppose that is penalty enough. I think if we took all their supplies and wrecked their wagon, it would be revenge enough. You were wonderful."

"Of course. That's why you married me." She kissed me quickly because she had to turn an instant later to land her heel on the forehead of bushy, who was beginning to twitch. He slept on. We packed and left.

Our goal was not too far away. A few hours later we felt a stirring of the air that grew stronger as we continued down the track through the hills. A sudden turn brought us to the brink of a valley with a sharp drop, and I kicked the vehicle into a swirling spin and darted it back out of sight again.

"Did you see that?" I asked.

"I certainly did," Angelina replied as we slipped forward on our bellies, more cautiously this time, and looked around the turn.

The wind was stronger here, pouring up the wide valley from some invisible source below. The air was cooler, too, and though there were the ever-present clouds above, there was no fog in the valley to obscure the view. Across from us the hill rose, turning to a solid cliff that reared up vertically, glossy black stone. Erosion had carved it into a fantasy of towers and turrets; men had carved these further into a castle city that covered the mountaintop.

There were windows and doorways, flags and pennants, stairs and buttresses. The flags were bright red inscribed with half-seen black characters. Some of the towers had been painted crimson as well, and this, with the mad frenzy of the construction, meant only one thing.

"It's not logical, I know," Angelina said. "But that place sends a definite shiver down my spine. It seems, hard to describe, perhaps insane is the best word."

"The absolute best. Which means that since this is the right world and time, a place that looks like that must be where He is."

"How do we get to him?"

"A very good question," I said in lieu of an intelligent answer. How *did* we get into this kooky castle? I scratched my head and rubbed my jaw, but these infallible aids to thought did not work this time. There was a slight movement at the edge of my vision, and I looked and grabbed for my gun—and froze the motion halfway.

"Don't make any sudden motions, particularly in the direction of your weapon," I told Angelina in a quiet voice. "Turn around slowly."

We both did. Doing nothing that might produce anxiety in the trigger fingers of the dozen or so men who had appeared silently behind us and stood with leveled and firmly aimed weapons.

"Get ready to dive forward when I do," I said and turned back to see another four men who had appeared just as silently in the valley just in front of us. "Belay that last command, and smile sweetly and surrender. We'll chop them up after we get in among them."

This last was meant more as a morale booster than an assurance of action. Unlike the wild-eyed men from whom we had taken our multiwheeled transportation, this lot was much cooler and firmer. They were dressed alike in gray one-piece plastic outfits that turned into hoods to cover their heads. Their weapons were as long as rifles, gape-orificed and lethal-looking. We trotted forward obediently when one of them waved that instruction in our direction. Another member of the closing circle stepped closer and looked us over, but not close enough for anyone who wasn't suicide-prone to attempt to seize his weapon.

"*Stragitzkruml?*" he said, then continued when we remained silent.

"*Fidlykreepi?*"

"*Attentottenpotentaten?*"

When there was no response to these incomprehensible requests, he turned to a bulky man with a red beard who seemed to be in charge.

"*Ili ne parolas konantain lingvojn,*" he said in clearly accented Esperanto.

"Well, that's more like it," I answered in the same tongue. "Might I ask why you gentlemen find it necessary to pull guns on simple travelers like ourselves?"

"Who are you?" Red-beard said, coming forward.

"I might ask the same of you?"

"*I* am pointing the guns," he answered coldly.

"A well-made point and I bow to your logic. We are tourists from the land across the sea. . . ." He interrupted with a short and nasty word.

"That is impossible as we both know since this is the only landmass on this planet. The truth now."

We both hadn't known, though we did now. A single continent? What had happened to Mother Earth during those twenty millennia? Lying had been no good, so perhaps the truth might work. It did upon occasion.

"Would you believe me if I told you we were time travelers?"

This hit the target all right, and he looked startled, while there was a stir of movement among the men close enough to hear what I had said. Red-beard glared them into silence before he spoke again.

"What is your connection with He and those creatures in his city up there?"

A lot depended upon my answer. Truth had worked once, and it might turn the trick again. And he had said "creatures," which was a giveaway. I couldn't believe this calm and disciplined force could be associated with the enemy.

"I have come to kill He and wipe out his operation."

This really did produce the right effect, and some of the men even lowered their guns before being growled back into line. Red-beard muttered a command, and one of the men hurried off. We remained in silence until he returned with a green metal cube about the size of his head that he handed over to the commander. It must have been hollow because he carried it easily. Red-beard held it up.

"We have over a hundred of these. They have been floating down out of the sky for the past month, and all of them are identical. A powerful radio source inside leads us to them—but we cannot cut or dissolve the metal. On the outside, on five faces of the cube, they are covered with lines of writing in what appear to be different languages and scripts. The ones we can translate all read the same way. Bring this to the time travelers. On the bottom of the cube are two lines of writing that we cannot read. Can you?"

He slowly held out the cube toward me, and I took it just as gingerly as every gun was trained on my body with careful precision. The metal looked like collapsium, the incredibly tough stuff used for atomic rocket tube liners. I carefully turned it bottom up and read the lines in a single glance before handing it back.

"I can read them," I said, and they were aware of the new tone in my voice. "The first line says that He and his people will all leave this period exactly 2.37 days after my arrival here."

There was a murmur over that, and Angelina beat Red-beard to the punch with the important question.

"What was in the second line?"

I tried to smile, but it didn't seem much good.

"Oh, that. It says that the planet will be destroyed by atomic explosions as soon as they go."

20

THE TENT WAS made of the same gray fabric as the clothes our captors wore and was a chilled refuge from the steambath atmosphere outside. A squat machine whirred in one corner, dehumidifying and cooling the air. Even cooler drinks had been produced, and I drained and brooded over mine, trying to see a way out of this dilemma before the deadly deadline was reached. Though guns were still in evidence, an unspoken truce was in effect; Redbeard decided to formalize it.

"I drink with you," he said. "I am Diyan."

It seemed very much like a ritual, so I repeated the formula and introduced myself, as did Angelina. After this the weapons vanished, and we were all much more chummy. I sat down where I could benefit from the full breeze of the cooler and decided to ask some questions myself.

"Do you people have any weapons heavier than these handguns?"

"None that are available. The few we brought have been destroyed in battle with He's forces."

"Is this continent so big you can't get more of them here quickly from your country?"

"The size of the continent is of no importance. Our space vessels are very small, and everything must be brought from our home planet."

I blinked rapidly, feeling I was getting out of my depth.

"You are not from Earth?" I asked.

"Our ancestors were, but we are all native-born Martians."

"You wouldn't care to give me a *few* more facts, would you? The sound of confusion I keep hearing appears to be inside my own head."

"I am sorry, I thought you knew. Here, let me fill up your glass. The story really begins many thousands of years ago when a sudden change in solar radiation raised the temperature here on Earth. By sudden I of course mean a matter of years, really centuries. As the climate changed and the ice caps melted, the continued existence of

385

life on the surface of the planet was threatened. Coastlines were altered and immense areas of low-lying land inundated; great cities were drowned. This in itself might have been dealt with had it not been for the seismic disturbances brought about by the shifting weight on the Earth's surface as the poles were freed of their ice burden and the released water covered other areas. Earthquakes and lava flows, sinking lands and the rising of new mountains. All quite terrible, we have seen the recordings many times in our schools. An incredible international effort was launched to terrafy the planet Mars—that is, make it suitable for human habitation. This involved the creation of an atmosphere there with a high carbon dioxide layer to trap the increased radiation of the sun, the transportation of ice mountains from the rings of Saturn, things like this. It was a noble ambition that in the end did succeed, but it bankrupted the nations of Earth who gave their all in this unbelievable effort. Eventually there was dissent and even warfare as weakened governments fell and greedy men fought for more than an equal share of space on the new-made world. Through all this the waters continued to rise on Earth and the first Martian settlers struggled against the harsh rigors of a barely livable world to establish the settlements. In history these are known as the Deadly Years because so many people died; the figures are unbelievable. But in the end we survived, and Mars is a green and comfortable world.

"Earth did not fare as well. Contact was lost between the planets, and the survivors of the once-teeming billions here fought a dreadful battle for survival. There are no written records of that period, thousands of years long, but the results are clear enough. This single large continent remained above the sea, as well as some island chains to mark earlier mountain ranges. And madness rules mankind. When we were able, we rebuilt the ancient spaceships and brought what help we could. Our help was not appreciated. The survivors kill strangers on sight and take great pleasure in it. And all men are strangers. The almost-unshielded solar radiation here produced mutants of all kinds among man, plants and animals. Most mutations died off quickly, but the survivors are deadly to a universal degree. So we helped where we could but really did very little. The earthmen were a continuing danger to each other but not to Mars. That is not until He united them some hundreds of years ago."

"Has he really lived all that time?"

"It appears that he has. His mind is as bent as theirs, but he can communicate with them. They follow him. They actually work together, building that city you have seen, building a society of sorts. He is certainly a genius, albeit a warped one, and they have factories going and a rudimentary technology. The first thing they did was ask for more aid from Mars and would not believe us when we said that they were getting the maximum already. Their mad demands would not have bothered us had they not unearthed rockets armed with atomic bombs that could be directed at our planet. It was after the first of these arrived that this expedition was organized. On Mars we survived by cooperating, there was no other way, so we are not a warlike people. But we have made weapons and will reluctantly use them to ensure our own survival. He is the key to all the troubles, and we must capture or kill him. If we must kill others to accomplish this, we will do that as well. Thousands are dead at home and radioactivity is increasing in the Martian atmosphere.''

"Then our aims are identical," I told him. "He has launched a time attack against our people with equally disastrous results. You have summed up our retaliatory plans quite neatly."

"How do we go about it?" Diyan asked eagerly.

"I'm not sure," I answered gloomily.

"We have a little over ten standards hours left to operate in," Angelina said, precisely. Like all women, she was a true pragmatist. While we wasted time nattering about the past, she faced the fact that the decision would have to be made in the future and tackled that, the real problem. I yearned to demonstrate my affection for her but decided that would have to wait for a more appropriate time, if more time did exist at all.

"An all-out attack," I said. "We have weapons we can add to yours. Attack on all fronts, find a weak spot, concentrate our forces, blast through to victory. Do you have any large weapons left?"

"No."

"Well . . . we can get around that. How about crashlanding one of your spacers inside the castle up there, get a fighting force behind their backs that way?"

"All of them were destroyed by saboteurs, suicidal ones. Others are coming from Mars but will arrive too late. We are not really very good at war and killing while they have always lived with it."

"Not to give up hope yet, ha-ha." I laughed, but it had a very hollow ring to it. The dark gloom was so thick in the air you could have cut chunks of it out.

"The grav-chute," Angelina said quietly so only I heard her.

"We will use the grav-chute," I said loudly so all could hear. A good general depends on able staff-work. The complete plan was now clear, written in letters of fire before my eyes.

"This is a go-for-broke operation. Angelina and I are going to drain the charges from all our unessential equipment to put a full charge into the grav-chute. Then we will rig a multiple harness for this. I'll do the exact computations later, but I would guess that it will lift five or six people up over those walls and inside before it burns out. Angelina and I are two, the rest will be your best people. . . ."

"A woman, no, this is not work for a woman," Diyan protested. I patted his arm understandingly.

"Have no fear. Sweet and demure as she is, she can outfight any ten men in this tent. And everyone is needed. Because the troops outside will be launching a *very* realistic attack that might break through. General at first, then concentrating on one flank. When the noise is at its highest, the commando squad will lift over the opposite wall and bore in. Now let's get things organized."

We got things organized. Or rather Angelina and I did because these peaceful Martian plowboys knew but nothing about scientific slaughter and were only too happy to turn the responsibilities of leadership over to us. Once things were under way I lay down for a quick sleep—I had been awake or clubbed unconscious something like two full days and 20,000 years, so was understandably tired. The three hours I grabbed were certainly not enough, and I awoke chomping and blinking and chewed a stimtab to make up the difference. It was dark outside the tent and still just as hot.

"Are we ready to roll?" I asked.

"Any minute now," Angelina said, cool and relaxed and showing no signs of her labors; she must have been at the stimtabs, too. "We have about four hours to dawn, and we will need most of that to get into position. The attack begins at first light."

"Do the guides know the way?"

"They have been fighting in and around this position for almost a year now, so they should."

This was the showdown. The men were all aware of it. It was there in the set of their faces and the brace of their shoulders. There could be only one winner this day. Perhaps they weren't born fighters, but they were learning fast. If you are going to fight, you fight to win. Diyan came up leading three more of his men who carried the jury-rigged metal harness with the grav-chute built into the center of it.

"We are ready," he said.

"Everyone knows what he is to do?"

"Perfectly. We have already said our good-byes and the first attack units have moved out."

"Then we'll get going, too."

Diyan led the way, though how he found it in that steam-heated darkness I have no idea. We stumbled along behind him, sweating and cursing under the burden of the clumsy harness, and the less said about the following hours, the better. Dawn found us collapsed under the far wall, the highest and apparently the strongest, that was our target. As it appeared out of the haze above us, black and grim, it did not look at all attractive. I squeezed Angelina's hand to show her I was fearless and to cheer her up. She squeezed mine back to show that she knew I was just as frightened as the rest of them.

"We'll do it, Jim," she said. "You know that."

"Oh, we'll do it all right; the continuing existence of our particular hunk of the future proves that. But it doesn't indicate how many are going to die today—or which of us will live on into the foreseeable future."

"We're immortal," she said with such surety that I had to laugh and my morale soared up to its usual egotistical heights, and I kissed her soundly and well for the aid.

Explosions sounded suddenly in the distance, rumbling and rolling like thunder from the rock walls. The attack had begun. The clock was running and everything was timed from here on in. I helped everyone strap in and kept an eye on my watch at the same time. As our scheduled hop-off drew close, I buckled in as well and touched the grav-chute controls.

"Brace yourselves," I said, watching the numbers flutter by. "And be ready to cut free when we hit at the other end."

I hit the button, and with a metallic groan from the harness my little force of six rose into the air to the attack.

21

WE DRIFTED UP the black face of the rock like a slow elevator, sitting ducks for anyone with a good gun and a keen eye. It was uncomfortable to say the least. I had to lift off gradually so our harness wouldn't buckle, but I speeded up as fast as I could until we were on maximum lift. A visible aura of heat began to radiate from the grav-chute as it struggled against all our dead weight. It would be highly uncomfortable if it failed now.

Then deep-cut windows flashed by, happily unoccupied, and the black stone changed to dark wall and the crenellated top of the parapet was ahead. I angled toward it and cut the power completely just before we reached the edge. Our acceleration carried us up and over in a high arc, and after that, things happened at an incredibly rapid pace.

There were two guards on the wall, both surprised, angry, armed, about to fire. But Angelina and I fired first. We were using the needle guns now in order to remain undetected as long as possible. The guards crumpled in silence, their faces and necks suddenly bristly as pincushions, and I hit the power on for the landing.

Landing! There was no courtyard or solid roof below! We were coming down on a domed and transparent cover over a large workship, a canopy made of what appeared to be glass panels held in a tangled web of rusty metal braces. We looked at it, horrified, as we rushed toward it, and I had the power on to the last stop. We groaned at the sudden acceleration, and the harness groaned as well and creaked and bent. The dome was too close, and we were just not going to stop in time.

It was lovely. A silent, secret attack, flitting gray ghosts in the dawn. Six pairs of boots hit at the same instant, and about five thousand square meters of glass were kicked out. The supporting framework twanged and bent, and some of the rusty supports snapped free. For one shuddering instant I thought we were going to follow all the glass that was now crashing and clashing into the chamber below with a hideously loud cacophony. Then the grav-chute gave its all with one shuddering last blaze of energy, halting our forward motion, then burst into flame as well.

"Grab the supports!" I shouted, tearing at the buckles that held the grav-chute to our harness. It resisted, searing my hand, then finally dropped free. Straight down into the hall with its screaming occupants below, where it promptly exploded. I sighed and dropped some smoke and flare bombs as well to add to the confusion.

"Our presence is now known," I said, inching back toward safety. "I suggest we get off this precarious jungle gym and back on the job."

Moving carefully, sending more glass crashing down as our weight bent the frame out of place and the panes slipped free, we crept back to the safety of the parapet.

"Get on the radio," I told Diyan as he climbed up next to me. "Tell your troops to pull back their attack if they haven't broken in but to keep up the firing."

"They have been repulsed on all sides."

"Then tell them to cut their losses. We'll do the blitz from the inside."

We moved out. Angelina and I on the point where we could blast any resistance that appeared, while the others protected our flanks and rear. Forward at a sweaty trot. We had to move fast, sow discord as we went—and find He. The first door opened onto a great circular staircase that seemed to spiral down to infinity. I didn't like the looks of it, so I rolled some concussion grenades down it, and we pressed on across the roof.

"Where to?" Angelina asked.

"That tangle of turrets and buildings up ahead seems to be larger and more functional than most of this place. As good a guess as any." Something exploded on the tiles nearby, and Angelina picked the sniper out of a window above with a single snap shot from the waist. We ran a bit faster, then pressed against the wall above a straight drop to the valley below while I blew out a locked door. Then we were in.

The place had been designed by a madman. I know that is literally true, but you didn't have to know He to get the message. Corridors and stairs, twisted chambers, angled walls, even one spot where we had to crawl on our hands and knees under the low ceiling. This was where we had our first casualty. Five of us were clear of this room before the ceiling silently and swiftly descended and crushed the rear guard before he could even make a sound. We all were sweating harder. The enemy we met were not armed for the most part and either fled or were dropped by our needle guns. It was speed and silence now, and we moved as fast as we could between the bizarrely decorated walls, finding it easy to avoid looking at the incredible paintings that seemed to cover every square meter of available space.

"Just one moment," Angelina panted, pulling me to a stop as we came through a high archway to a staircase that spiraled out of sight below, each stone step being a different height from the others. "Do you know where we are going?"

"Not exactly," I panted in return. "Just penetrating the establishment to get ahead of the fighting, while spreading a bit of confusion."

"I thought we had bigger ambitions. Like finding He."

"Any suggestions how we might go about that?" I am forced to admit that I snapped a bit as I said that. Angelina responded with saccharine sweetness.

"Why, yes. You might try turning on the time energy detector you have slung around your neck. I believe that is the reason we brought it."

"Just what I was going to do anyway," I said, lying to conceal the fact that I had forgotten completely about it in the white heat of the rampaging attack.

The needle swung about and pointed with exact precision to the floor beneath our feet.

"Down and down we go," I ordered. "Where the time-helix coils there will be found the He whom I am about to make into mincemeat." I meant it too since this was the third and last try. I had constructed a special bomb on which I had painted his name. It was a hellish mixture of a curdler—guaranteed to coagulate all protein within five meters—an explosive charge, a load of poisoned shrapnel, and a thermite bomb theoretically to cook the curdled, coagulated, poisoned body of He.

After this the fighting picked up. Some sort of flamethrower below sent a wave of roiling smoke and fire up the stairs toward us that we could not pass. Singed and smoking, we went out through a hole I blasted in the wall and dropped into a laboratory of sorts. Row after row of bubbling retorts stretched away in all directions, hooked to a maze of crystal plumbing. Dark liquids dripped, and valves hissed foul-smelling steam. The workers here weren't armed, and they dropped before us. We were trotting slower now and gasping for breath.

"Uggh!" Angelina said, making a twisted face. "Have you seen just what is in those jars?"

"No, and I don't want to. Press on." Anything that could bother the ice-cool Angelina was something I had no desire to see at all. I was glad when we left this area behind and found another stairwell.

We were getting close. Resistance kept firming up, and we had to battle most of the way now. Only the fact that the defenders were haphazardly armed allowed us to get through at all. Apparently most of the weapons were at use on the walls because these people came at us with knives, axes, lengths of metal, anything and everything. Including their bare hands if that was all they had. Screaming and frothing, they rushed to the attack and slowed us just by the weight of their numbers. We had our next casualty when a man with a metal spike dropped from some cranny above and stabbed one of the Martians before I could shoot him. They died together, and all we could do was leave them and push on. I took a quick look at my watch and broke into a tired trot again. We were running out of time.

"Wait!" Diyan called out hoarsely. "The needle, it no longer points."

I waved everyone to a stop in a wide passage we were traversing, and they dropped, covering the flanks. I looked at the time energy detector that Diyan had been carrying.

"Which way was it pointing when you looked at it last?"

"Straight ahead, down the corridor. And there was no angle to the needle at all, as though this machine it points to were on this level."

"It only works when the time-helix is operating. It must be off now."

"Could He have gone?" Angelina asked, speaking aloud the words I was trying to keep out of my thoughts.

"Probably not," I said with mock sincerity. "In any case we have to push on as long as we can. One last effort now, dead ahead."

We pushed. And had another casualty when we attempted to cross a layer of writhing branches that were covered with thorns. Tipped with poison. I finally had to burn the stuff with our last thermite grenade. Ammunition and grenades were running very short. There was a brisk fire fight at the next corridor junction that emptied my needle gun. I tossed it aside and kicked the heavy door that barred any more progress in this direction. It would have to be blown open, and my grenades were exhausted. I turned to Angelina just as a communication plate next to the door lit up.

"You have lost, the final time," He said, grinning wickedly at me from the screen.

"I'm always willing to talk," I said, then spoke to Angelina in a language I was sure He did not speak. "Any concussion grenades left?"

"I am talking, you will listen," He said.

"One," Angelina told me.

"I'm all ears," I said to him. "Take that door out," I said to her.

"I have dispatched all the people I need to a safe place in the past where we will never be found. I have sent the machines we will need, I have sent everything that will be needed to build a time-helix as well. I am the last to go, and when I leave, the time machinery will be destroyed behind me."

The grenade exploded, but the door was thick and remained stuck in the frame. Angelina sprayed it with explosive bullets. He talked on as though this weren't happening.

"I know who you are, little man from the future, and I know where you come from. Therefore I shall destroy you before you have a chance to be born. I will destroy you, my only enemy; then the past and the future and all eternity will be mine, mine, *mine!*"

He was screaming and slavering before he finished, and the door went down, and I was the first one through.

My bullets were exploding in the delicate machinery of the time-helix as my He-bomb arced through the air.

But he had already actuated the time-helix. Its green glow was gone; He was gone, the machinery left behind no longer needed. My hell-bomb exploded in empty air and was more of a danger to us than to the vanished one it had been intended for. We dropped to the floor as death whizzed overhead, and when we looked next, the machinery was dissolving and smoking.

He spoke again, and the muzzle of my gun looked for him.

"I made this recording in case I had to leave abruptly, so sorry." He chuckled insanely at his own bad humor. "I have gone now; you cannot follow me, but I can follow you through time. And destroy you. But you have other enemies with you, and I wish them to feel my vengeance, too. They will die, you will all die, everything will die; I control worlds, eternity, destroy worlds. I will destroy this Earth. I leave you only enough time to consider and suffer. You cannot escape.

"In one hour every nuclear weapon on this planet will be triggered.

"Earth will be destroyed."

22

THERE WAS VERY little satisfaction to be gained from blowing up the recording machine that had He's hateful voice coiled in its guts, but I did it anyway, one shot. The thing exploded in a cloud of plastic bits and electronic components, and the insane laughter was cut off in mid-cackle. Angelina patted my hand.

"You did your best," she said.

"But just not good enough. I'm sorry I got you involved in this."

"I wouldn't want it any other way. What happens to us happens together."

"This sounds like something very terrible will be done to your people," Diyan said. "I am very sorry."

"Nothing to feel sorry about. We're all in the same boat."

"In one sense, yes. One hour from now. But Mars is saved, and we who die here know that we accomplished at least that much. Our families and our people will live on."

"I wish I could say the same," I said with utmost gloom, borrowing his gun and picking off two of the enemy who tried to rush in through the broken door. "When we lost here, we lost for all time. I'm surprised we are still around at all, should have snuffed out like candles."

"Isn't there anything we can do?" Angelina asked. I shrugged.

"Nothing I can think of. You can't outrun H-bombs. The time-helix equipment is kind of melted, so that is out. What we need is a new time-helix, which we are not going to get unless one appears out of thin air."

In echo to my words there was the sudden crack of displaced air above, and I rolled and ducked, thinking it was a new attack. It wasn't. It was a large green metal case that hung, unsupported in midair. Angelina looked at me in the strangest manner possible.

"If that is a time-helix you must tell me how you did it."

For once in my outspoken life I was silent, even more so when the box began to drift down before us, and just before it grounded, I read the lettering on the side.

"Time-helix—open with care."

I didn't move. It all seemed too unbelievable. The two grav-chutes strapped to the top of the case, the timing device that had caused them to lower the whole thing to the floor, the small record-ing apparatus also fixed to the case with the boldly lettered words "Play me" lettered across it. I boggled and gaped and it was ever-practical Angelina who stepped forward and pressed the starting button. Professor Coypu's rotund voice rolled out to us.

"I suggest you get moving rather quickly. The bombs, you know, go off quite soon. I have been asked to tell you, Jim, that the bomb control apparatus is concealed in a cabinet on the far wall behind the dehydrated rations. It has been disguised to look like a portable radio because it really is a portable radio. With additions. If mishandled, it will set all the bombs off now. Which would be uncomfortable. You are to set the three dials to the numbers six six six, which, I believe, is the number of the beast. Set them in sequence from right to left. When they have been set, press the *off* button. Now turn me off until you have done that. Be quick about it."

"All right, all right," I said, irritated, and switched him off. He had quite a commanding tone for an individual who wouldn't be born for another 10,000 years or so. And how come he knew so much? I complained, but I went and did the job, hurling the dehydrated rations to the floor, where they obviously belonged. They looked like lengths of yellowish-green desiccated octopus tentacles. Suckers and all. The radio was there. I did not attempt to move it but set the dials as instructed and pressed the button. Nothing happened.

"Nothing happened," I said.

"Which is just the way we want it," Angelina said, standing on tiptoe to give me an appreciative kiss on the cheek. "You have saved the world."

Feeling very proud of myself, I swaggered back to the recorder before the admiring gazes of the Martians and switched it on again.

"Don't think you have saved the world," Coypu said. Party pooper. "You have just averted its destruction for approximately twenty-eight days. Once activated, the bombs wait that period, then self-destruct. But your Martian associates can profit from this delay. I believe they have supply ships on the way?"

"Due in fifteen days," Diyan said, hushed awe in his voice at the disembodied oracular powers before him.

"Fifteen days, more than enough time. The Earth will be des-troyed, but when its present condition is considered, this is more of a blessing than a tragedy. It is time to open this case now. On top of the controls is a molecular disrupter. If this is pointed at the outside wall, where the small windows are high up, and angled downward at fifteen degrees, it will cut a tunnel that will exit outside the walls. I suggest this be done as soon as possible. The Martians can get out that way. Now press button A, and the time-helix will form. James, Angelina, strap on the grav-chutes and leave as soon as the ready light comes on.''

Still partially unbelieving I did as instructed. The time-helix crackled into existence and groaned and sparked as it wound itself up. Diyan stepped forward, his hand out to take mine.

"We will never forget you or what you have done for our world. Generations yet unborn will read your name and about your exploits in their schoolbooks.''

"Are you sure you have the spelling right?'' I asked.

"You make light of this because you are a great and humble man.'' First time I have ever been accused of *that*. "A statue will be erected with 'James diGriz, World Saver' inscribed upon it.''

Each Martian shook my hand in turn; it was very embarrassing. There was an admiring gleam in Angelina's eye as well, but women are simple creatures and enjoy basking even in reflected attention. Then the ready light came on, and after a few more good-byes, we put on the grav-chutes as directed and—for the last time I sincerely hoped—were bathed in the cool fire of the time force. Our contact must have triggered the apparatus because before I could make the very apropos remark that was on my lips everything went *zoinng*.

No worse than any other time trip, certainly no better. This was one kind of transportation I would never get adjusted to. Stars like speeding bullets, spiral galaxies whirling around like fireworks, movement that was no movement, time that was no time, all the usual things. The only thing that was good about the trip was its ending, which was in the gymnasium of the Special Corps base, the largest open chamber there. We floated in midair, my Angelina and I, smiling madly at each other and oblivious to the cries of amazement from the sweating athletes below. We held hands in the simple happiness of knowledge that the future still lay ahead of us.

"Welcome home,'' she said, and that was really all there was to say.

We floated down, waving to our friends and ignoring their questions for the moment. Coypu and the time lab first, to report. There was a quick feeling of unhappiness that He had escaped me and the hope that this time, when he was tracked through time, a few very large bombs could be sent in the place of me or any other volunteer.

Coypu looked up and gaped. "What are you doing here?" he said. "You are supposed to be eliminating this He person. Didn't you get my message?"

"Message?" I asked, blinking rapidly.

"Yes. We made ten thousand metal cubes and sent them back to Earth. Sure you would get one of them. Radio direction and such."

"Oh, *that* old message. Received and acted upon, but you are a little out of date. What is that doing here?" I'm afraid my voice rose a bit on this last as I pointed with vibrating finger at the compact machine across the room.

"That? Our Mark One compact folding time-helix? What else should it be doing? We have just finished it."

"You've never used it?"

"Never."

"Well, you are now. You have to strap a couple of grav-chutes to it—here, use these—and a recorder and a molecular disrupter and shoot it right back to save Angelina and me."

"I have a pocket recorder, but why. . . ." He took a familiar-looking machine from his lab coat.

"Do it first, explanations later. Angelina and I are about to be blown up if you don't do this right."

I grabbed some paint and wrote "Play me" on the recorder, then "Time-helix—open with care" on the machine. The exact moment when He had left Earth was determined by the time tracer and the arrival for this cargo set for a few minutes later on the big helix. Coypu dictated the tape under my instruction, and it wasn't until the whole bundle was whisked back into the past that I heaved a grateful sigh of relief.

"We are saved," I said. "Now for that drink you promised me."

"I didn't promise. . . ."

"I'll have it anyway."

Coypu was muttering to himself and scratching on a pad while I prepared some hefty drinks for Angelina and myself. We clunked glasses and were baptizing our throats when he came over, smiling genially.

"I needed that," I said. "It must be *ages* since I last had a drink."

"It is all coming clear at last," Coypu said, tapping his protruding teeth with contained excitement.

"Is it all right if we sit while we listen? It's been a busy couple of hundred thousand years."

"Yes, by all means. Let me retrace the course of events. A time attack was launched upon the Corps by He, a most successful one. Our numbers were quite reduced. . . ."

"Yes, like down to two. You and me."

"Quite right. Though as soon as I had dispatched you to the year 1975, I found that all things were as they had been. Most sudden. All alone one instant, the next the laboratory full of people who never knew they had been gone. We put a lot of work in on improving the time-tracking techniques, took almost four years to get it the way we wanted."

"Did you say *four* years?"

"Nearer five before we got it operational. The trails were distant and hard to follow, most tangled as well."

"Angelina!" I cried with sudden realization. "You never told me you had been here alone for five years."

"I didn't think you liked older women."

"I love them as long as they are you. You were lonely?"

"Hideously. Which is why I volunteered to go after you. Inskipp had another volunteer, but he broke his leg."

"My darling—I'll bet I know how that happened!" She is not the blushing type, but she did lower her eyes at the thought.

"We are getting ahead in sequence," Coypu said. "But that is what happened. We traced you from 1975 to 1807—and traced He and his minions as well. There was a loop in time there, an anomaly of some kind that eventually sealed itself off. We could tell that it was about to collapse with you sealed inside of it and succeeded at last in forcing enough power into the helix to penetrate the sealed time loop just before it went down. That is when Angelina went back with the coordinates for your next skip in time, the long twenty-thousand-year jump after He. You had to go after him because the time paths were there to prove that you had followed him. Though of course history was clear by that point, and we knew how it would all end."

"You *knew?*" I asked, feeling I had missed the point somewhere.

"Of course. The entire nature of the attack was clear, though you all of course had to fulfill your destined roles."

"Could you spell it out again? And slower."

"Of course. You managed to destroy He's operation twice in the remote past and eventually reset his machine and sent him forward to the twilight days of Earth. Here he spent an immense amount of time, almost two hundred years, climbing his way to power and uniting all of the planet's resources. He was a genius, albeit a mad one, and could do this. He also remembered you, Jim, fading memories and half-insane ones after two hundred years, but he remembered enough to know you were the enemy. Therefore he launched a time war to destroy you before you could destroy him, trapping you as he thought on a planet about to be destroyed by atomic explosion. From there he returned to 1975 to attack the Corps. You came after him and he fled to 1807 to lay the time loop trap for you. I don't know where he planned to go from there, but his plans appear to have been altered, and he went instead twenty thousand years ahead.''

''I did that, altered the setting on his machine just before he left.''

''That is all there is to it. We can relax now that it is over, and I do believe I'll join you in that drink.''

''*Relax!*'' The words emerged from my throat with a singularly nasty, grating sound. ''From what you have said it sounds like *I* started the whole attack on the Special Corps by altering the setting on the time-helix that sent He to the world where he launched his campaign to destroy the Corps.''

''That's one way of looking at it.''

''Is there any other? The way I see it He just bounces in a circle in time forever. Running from me, chasing me, running from me. . . . Arrrgh! When was he born? Where does he come from?''

''Those terms are meaningless in this sort of temporal relationship. He exists only within this time loop. If you wish to say it, though it is most imprecise, it would be fair to state that he was never born. The situation exists apart from time as we normally know it. Such as the fact that you returned here with the information to be sent to yourself about the settings on the atomic bombs. Where did this information come from originally? From yourself. So you sent it to yourself in order to send it to yourself to inform yourself about the settings on the bombs in order. . . .''

''Enough!'' I groaned, reaching for the bottle with trembling hand. ''Just mark the mission as being accomplished and put me in for a fat bonus.''

I refilled all the glasses and only when I came to Angelina's did I realize she was no longer present. She had slipped away without a word while I was suffering over having instigated the whole time war, and I was just beginning to miss her and wonder where she had gone when she returned.

"They are fine," she said.

"Who, who?" I said in my best owl imitation. But when I saw the narrowing of Angelina's eyes, I knew I had made a big mistake and I racked my time-trodden brain until understanding burst upon me. "Who indeed! Ho-ho-ho! You must excuse the small joke. Who is fine, you say. Why, our twin, cherubic, gurgling babies are fine. With true maternal instinct you have rushed to their side."

"They are here with me."

"Well, wheel the pram in!"

"The babies," she said as they entered, with what I detected as a strong note of irony.

They were going on six years of age, a little fact that I had neglected to remember. They moved easily, solid chaps with the disconcerting knack of walking in step with each other. Well muscled, their father's firm heritage, I am happy to say, with a tempering of their mother's looks.

"You've been away a long time, Dad," one of them said.

"Not by choice, James. The universe isn't saved in a day."

"I'm James, he's Bolivar. Welcome back."

"Well, thanks." Did I kiss them or what? They settled this by sticking out their hands, and I shook them each quite seriously. Good grips. This family thing was going to take some getting used to. Angelina beamed proudly, and I melted under that look and realized that it was all probably worth it.

"Angelina, I think you have finally convinced me. The joys of married life seem to be worth the price of giving up the happy and carefree occupation of free-lance thief. . . ."

"Thief is the correct word," a nauseously familiar voice cried out. "And crook, con man, blackmailer, briber, and more." Inskipp stood in the doorway waving his florid face and a sheaf of papers in my direction. "Five years I have been waiting for you, diGriz, and this time you are not getting away. No excuses like time wars now. You crook, you steal from your own buddies, *urggh!*"

He said *Urggh!* because Angelina had popped a sleep capsule under his nose, and he folded over while the boys—good reflexes there—stepped forward and eased him gently to the floor. Angelina relieved him of the sheaf of papers while he went by.

"After five years I need you more than this nasty old man does. Let's burn this file and steal a ship before he comes to. It will be months before he can find us, and by that time something else will have happened that will need straightening out badly, and he will have to put us back to work again. Meanwhile, we can have a lovely crooked second honeymoon.''

''Sounds great—but what about the boys? This is not the sort of trip one takes children on.''

''You're not leaving without us,'' Bolivar said. Where had I seen that unshakable scowl before? In the mirror I guess. ''Where you go, we go. If it's a matter of money, we can pay our own way. See.''

I saw indeed as he extended a great bundle of credits that could pay his way right across the galaxy. But I also had a quick glimpse of a familiar golden wallet.

''Inskipp's money! You robbed that poor old man while you should have been helping him.'' I flicked a quick look at James. ''And I suppose you will be able to tell time during the trip with his wristwatch that I see suddenly on your arm?''

''In their father's footsteps,'' Angelina said proudly. ''Of course they come with us. And don't concern yourself with expenses, boys. Daddy can steal enough for all of us.''

It was too much. ''Why not!'' I laughed. ''Here's to crime!'' I raised my glass.

''Here's to time,'' Coypu said, getting in the spirit of the thing.

''Here's to time crime!'' we cried together and drained our glasses and broke them against the wall, and Coypu smiled avuncularly after us as we grabbed the children's hands and leaped lightly over Inskipp's snoring body and were out the door and away.

There's a bright and glorious universe out there, and we are going to enjoy every single bit of it.

EXCITING SCIENCE FICTION BESTSELLERS!